Alan came to a portrait that he realised immediately was of someone who meant a great deal to Vicky. It was almost as if she had written 'I love you!' on the painting. It was of a young man wearing a flying suit, with enough of the heavy jacket unbuttoned to reveal part of a pilot's wings on the left breast, beneath which were a number of medal ribbons.

The subject of the painting had been looking directly at the artist during the sitting and his expression removed any doubt about the uncanny aura of emotion that was so much a part of the painting. Vicky had succeeded in capturing the expression of a young man who was very much in love with the person at whom he was looking.

Alan gazed thoughtfully at the painting for a very long time. He wished he might have had a portrait of Dora that possessed a similar quality. He moved on, wondering about the airman and where he was now . . .

Also by E.V. Thompson

THE MUSIC MAKERS
THE DREAM TRADERS
CRY ONCE ALONE
BECKY
GOD'S HIGHLANDER
CASSIE
WYCHWOOD
BLUE DRESS GIRL
TOLPUDDLE WOMAN
LEWIN'S MEAD
MOONTIDE
CAST NO SHADOWS
SOMEWHERE A BIRD IS SINGING
WINDS OF FORTUNE
SEEK A NEW DAWN
THE LOST YEARS
PATHS OF DESTINY

The Retallick Saga

BEN RETALLICK
CHASE THE WIND
HARVEST OF THE SUN
SINGING SPEARS
THE STRICKEN LAND
LOTTIE TRAGO
RUDDLEMOOR
FIRES OF EVENING

The Jagos of Cornwall

THE RESTLESS SEA
POLRUDDEN
MISTRESS OF POLRUDDEN

As James Munro

HOMELAND

Tomorrow is
For Ever

E. V. Thompson

A *Time Warner* Paperback

First published in Great Britain in 2004 by Time Warner Books
Published by Time Warner Paperbacks in 2005

Copyright © 2004 by E.V. Thompson

The moral right of the author has been asserted.

*All characters in this publication are fictitious and any
resemblance to real persons, living or dead, is purely coincidental.*

A CIP catalogue record for this book
is available from the British Library.

ISBN 0 7515 3151 0

Typeset by Palimpsest Book Production Limited,
Polmont, Stirlingshire
Printed and bound in Great Britain by Clays Ltd, St Ives plc

Time Warner Paperbacks
An imprint of
Time Warner Book Group UK
Brettenham House
Lancaster Place
London WC2E 7EN

www.twbg.co.uk

Tomorrow is For Ever

1

In the wireless office of the fast torpedo boat HMS *Viper*, Telegraphist Alan Carter sat in front of the ship's radio receiver, earphones linked over his head by a flexible metal band. A Morse key was close to his right hand should he need to respond to a message from the wireless station at the torpedo boat's base in Falmouth, but his mind was far from war.

In front of him on the desk was a cardboard-covered exercise book in which he was writing a poem dedicated to Dora, the wife he had not seen since the final day of the week-long honeymoon they had spent at the home of her aunt at Eltham, in Kent. That had been eighteen months ago, early in 1916.

Immediately afterwards, he had been drafted to the *Viper*, based in southern Ireland, carrying out anti-submarine patrols in the western approaches to the ports of Britain. He had remained in Ireland until only a month ago when the *Viper* had been ordered to join a torpedo-boat flotilla based in Falmouth, newly formed to meet the increasing threat posed by German U-boats to Allied shipping in the English Channel.

Although he was once more on the British mainland, naval censorship had prevented Alan from passing information about his whereabouts to Dora, while the seriousness of the U-boat threat meant there was no possibility of obtaining leave to visit her at the home she shared with her parents in the east London borough of Hackney.

Since joining the *Viper* Alan had written a great deal of poetry, together with a number of short stories, mostly composed during the monotonous night hours when the torpedo boat patrolled off the coast of Ireland, ready to speed to the assistance of any merchantman threatened by the German navy's underwater predators.

Glancing out of the porthole, Alan could see the high, rugged cliffs of Cornwall's Lizard peninsula, the most southerly point of Great Britain, only a short distance away. He had been stationed in Cornwall for little more than four weeks, but had already fallen in love with this remote corner of the British Isles. It was certainly conducive to the writing of articles, short stories and poetry, a talent he had developed during his time in Ireland and was now finding increasingly – and unexpectedly – enjoyable. He doubted whether he would have made such a discovery had the war not come along and taken him from the slums of London to more congenial parts of the land.

Other members of the *Viper*'s crew were also thinking of matters that had little to do with the war which had been raging for almost three years.

In the torpedo boat's engine room the muscular stoker 'Gruff' Griffin was hoping there would be work for him at the Arabian Bar in Falmouth's main street that night. Employed to eject the occasional customer who exceeded the bounds of acceptable behaviour, he earned more in one night than the Navy paid him each week.

Eric Fairgrove, the petty officer coxswain at the wheel of the *Viper*, was hoping that Davy Rowe, husband of the receptionist at the Green Lawns hotel, would be on duty at the town's fire station when he called on her at the hotel that night.

Lieutenant Andy Cameron, commanding officer of the *Viper*, was also looking forward to an illicit romantic evening. He was in the habit of spending his off-duty evenings – and occasional nights – with the Honourable Amelia Carew, wife of the heir to Baron Lelant, currently serving in France with the British army.

Suddenly, Alan's muse was interrupted by the staccato sound of Morse code spelling out the *Viper*'s call sign, penetrating the crackling in his earphones. The Falmouth wireless telegraphy station had a message for the torpedo boat. Flicking the switch on his Morse key, he signalled his readiness to receive the message.

The message was coded and brief, but it was prefixed with a letter which indicated it was of the utmost priority. Hurriedly removing a code book from the small safe beneath his desk, Alan set about making sense of the five-letter groups he had written on the signal pad in front of him.

His excitement grew as the message unfolded. Even before it had been completely decoded he was pressing a buzzer that sounded on the bridge, beside the stool where the *Viper's* commanding officer would be seated.

Lieutenant Cameron's voice came down the voice pipe to the wireless office. 'Yes, Sparks, what is it?'

'An "immediate" message from Senior Naval Officer Falmouth, sir. Lizard coastguards have reported a trawler, the *Lady Tamsin*, being attacked by a surfaced U-boat, five miles east-south-east of Lizard Point.'

'Signal back "Am actioning", Sparks.'

With this brief order, the cover of the voice pipe was slammed shut on the bridge and a few moments later the *Viper* performed a tight 180-degree turn. Heading back into the English Channel, bow rising, the torpedo boat shuddered under full power as it surged through the water.

The marauding German submarine was on the other side of the Lizard peninsula, on the edge of Mount's Bay. It was a matter of only minutes before the *Viper*, travelling at full speed, cleared Lizard Point and entered Mount's Bay, about to fulfil the role for which it had been designed and for which it had been patrolling the waters of the English Channel. Finding and destroying enemy submarines.

The U-boat was between the *Viper* and the *Lady Tamsin*, firing from its deck gun at the unarmed trawler, which had already cut its nets free in a bid to escape from the enemy submarine. After desperately steering a zig-zag course to distract the German gunners, the trawler had been struck by a couple of shells and now, without power, was at the mercy of the U-boat.

Concentrating their attention on the unarmed trawler,

4

the crew of the U-boat were not aware of the presence of the *Viper* until it came within range of the submarine and opened fire from its single gun. The first shot fell short, but the second was loaded and fired within seconds. By the time the men on the U-boat became aware of the danger they were in, the *Viper*'s gun crew had ranged upon the German craft.

When the U-boat turned in order that it might bring its main deck gun to bear upon the torpedo boat it presented a broadside target to the Royal Navy gunners.

'Shall we try a torpedo attack, sir?' Midshipman Donald Ferris called up to the bridge from the deck.

'No!' The captain's reply was positive. 'The U-boat's in a direct line with Newlyn. If we miss we'll cause havoc on shore. Chivvy the gun crew into increasing their rate of fire.'

The gun of the torpedo boat was inferior to that of the U-boat, but the *Viper* was maintaining a steady course and rapidly closing upon the enemy submarine. However, once the experienced German gun crew brought their weapon to bear upon the *Viper*, the results were catastrophic for the British torpedo boat.

As Alan was signalling to the Senior Naval Officer Falmouth that the *Viper* was engaging an enemy submarine, the U-boat gun crew scored a direct hit on the *Viper*'s bridge with their very first shot.

The explosion blew a hole in the corner of the wireless office, situated immediately beneath the bridge. Thrown across the office with his chair, Alan crashed heavily against the bulkhead. He felt a severe pain in his upper left arm and shoulder and was temporarily disorientated as the torpedo boat executed a tight change of course. When it resumed an even keel, Alan realised he had been wounded. There was a hole in the deckhead of the wireless office and Alan became aware of a great deal of shouting from the *Viper*'s crew, outside on deck.

When he bent down to pick up his chair from the floor of the office he discovered he was bleeding profusely, the blood streaming down his arm and dripping to the floor from his fingertips. Although not immediately aware of the source of the blood, he had, in fact, been hit by a piece of shrapnel from the shell that had struck the *Viper*'s bridge.

Checking his wireless and discovering it was still operational, Alan shakily resumed transmitting his message as the clatter of feet came from the metal ladder leading from the bridge. A young seaman slipped down the last two rungs and Alan called, 'What's happening?'

'We've had a direct hit on the bridge. The skipper and the coxswain are both dead . . . I'm going to fetch help . . .'

As the seaman hurried away, the torpedo boat juddered beneath the impact of another shell from the submarine. Quite as effective as the previous shot, this one exploded in the boiler room. Although the *Viper* was still under way, its speed dropped dramatically. Nevertheless, its gun was still firing and an excited shout went up from the gun crew as one of their shots struck home low down on the submarine's conning tower.

'The U-boat's running away . . . Keep that gun firing!'

Alan had completed the transmission of his message and the voice which came to him through the bridge voice pipe was that of Midshipman Donald Ferris, barely out of

6

his teens and serving on only his second ship. Alan realised with a start that in spite of his inexperience, Midshipman Ferris was now in command of the *Viper*.

'Sir!' Alan called out urgently to the young midshipman. When he had his attention he said, 'Will you get someone to give me a bearing on the submarine's course? I'll signal and tell the Senior Naval Officer Falmouth what's happened.'

'Yes, of course . . . Are you all right down there, Sparks?'

'I've been hurt but I don't think it's too serious. I'll have it seen to when we've got the signal off. It's urgent, sir. Falmouth will want to send someone after the U-boat, especially if we've hit it hard enough to keep it on the surface.'

While he waited for the information he had requested, Alan hastily scribbled out a signal, trying to ignore the increasing pain in his arm, but it was not easy now.

He had already begun transmitting the message when a seaman came in with the course and estimated speed of the U-boat. While Alan was sending it, and despite his protests, the seaman slit the sleeve of Alan's jumper with his knife, acting on the orders he had been given by Midshipman Ferris. Next it was the turn of the white shirt, which he cut from the square neckline down to the elbow. When it was done the seaman stood back with a worried expression on his face. 'I can't deal with this, Sparks. I'll fetch Doc to have a look at it. He's down in the engine room right now.'

'Doc' was in fact a sick-berth attendant, the only medical staff carried on the *Viper*.

His transmission completed, Alan peered back over his

7

shoulder at the wound and received a shock. It was far worse than he had realised. A deep and jagged gash stretched from behind the shoulder to his upper arm, and it looked extremely ugly. For a few moments he felt a very real fear. He was losing a great deal of blood . . . could it possibly prove fatal? He shook off the thought, but realised the bleeding needed to be stemmed.

Morse code began chattering through his earphones once more and Alan automatically began translating it into words. It was a message from the base victualling officer, complaining of a discrepancy in a requisition form issued by the *Viper* . . . for potatoes.

The sick-berth attendant arrived at the wireless office about ten minutes later. Stained with oil and blood, he was pale and drawn, and close to tears. It was the first time he had been called upon to tend men killed and wounded in action, without a surgeon being present to guide him.

Alan's wound was an awkward one to deal with and he was still struggling with it when Midshipman Donald Ferris appeared in the office doorway.

'How is he, Doc?'

'I'm having trouble stopping the bleeding,' was the tight-lipped reply. 'He needs to get to hospital quickly . . . and so do some of the others.'

The midshipman was showing the unaccustomed strain of command and his next question, to Alan, was almost a plea. 'Will you be able to send another message to Falmouth?'

Alan was in pain and beginning to feel light-headed. Not trusting himself to reply, he nodded his head.

'Good man. Say I'm going alongside the trawler and will take it in to Newlyn. We have thirteen casualties on *Viper* and there are more on the trawler. Request ambulances and urgent medical assistance to meet us at the harbour.'

'Sir.' It gave Alan something to think about and took his mind off his own troubles.

It took great concentration to send the midshipman's message. His hand felt heavy and the delicate touch required to operate the Morse key was missing. Nevertheless, he succeeded in sending the message and, gratefully, leaned back in his chair. Then he saw the exercise book in which he had been writing his love poem when the action started. He had bled over it, obliterating some of the words.

The incongruity of it provoked a weak smile. Love and war . . . the pen and the shell . . . blood and ink. He should work it into a poem . . .

It was the last thought he had before he slumped forward, his head coming to rest on the desk beside the Morse key.

2

When Alan came to, he was lying on his right side in a very large hut that had been fitted out as a hospital ward. He had a vague recollection of regaining temporary consciousness upon a stretcher in a vehicle that seemed to be travelling extremely fast over an indifferent road, but he had no idea how long he had been in the vehicle.

Moving his head, he recognised one or two men in the beds that lined both sides of the hut.

'Hello, Sparks. How you feeling?' The question was called out from the other side of the ward by the heavily bandaged stoker, Gruff Griffin, who was sitting up in a bed. His hand and arm badly scalded, he would never again eject unruly customers from Falmouth's Arabian Bar.

'Where are we?' Alan countered, as memories of all that had happened returned in rapid but disjointed confusion.

'In hospital . . . in Newlyn. The doctor's spent quite some time working on you.'

Alan's left arm felt numb and uncomfortable and as he tried to move he realised the upper arm was bandaged and strapped to his body. Moving was both difficult and uncomfortable. There was also a tube from the lower part of the arm leading to a bottle which looked as though it contained blood.

'Don't move too much, Mr Carter. Dr Scott has worked very hard removing a piece of shrapnel and stitching you up. You don't want to break the stitches.' The voice was that of a nurse who approached the bed from behind Alan. She was accompanied by Midshipman Ferris.

Fussing at his bedclothes, the nurse went on, 'If you want anything, don't try to help yourself, at least not for a while. Call for a nurse.' To Midshipman Ferris she said, 'Don't keep him talking for too long.'

'Hello, Sparks. I'm glad to see you conscious again. I was worried about you. We all were.' The events of the day had left the young midshipman looking strained and tired, but he seemed well pleased with himself and explained why. 'I've just been talking to the Senior Naval Officer Falmouth. He had some splendid news. Thanks to your signal an airship and two destroyers were sent after the U-boat. The destroyers found it first – and sunk it. The captain wants me to submit a full report on our action. What's more, he's coming to Newlyn tomorrow to meet you and the other casualties from *Viper*.'

'Why?' Alan was genuinely puzzled. Compared with the desperate fighting going on in France and the battles that had taken place between the German and British fleets, this had been a very minor action. He expressed his thoughts to Ferris.

'That was my first reaction, Sparks, but it seems that at the moment there's a power struggle going on between

11

the Royal Naval Air Service and the regular Navy about the best way to combat U-boats round the coast. Thanks to *Viper*'s action in crippling the one that attacked the trawler, and your prompt signal, Falmouth was able to divert destroyers to sink it. I've been told I'm to be recommended for a DSO and there should be a DSM for the chief stoker – and for you.'

Alan was momentarily speechless and the midshipman added, 'By the way, I have to notify your next of kin that you've been wounded. I believe you're married now, but your next of kin is still on record as an aunt. Could you give me the name and address of your wife?'

'No!' It was too abrupt and Alan felt the need to explain. 'I don't want to worry her. One of her brothers died at Ypres. My wound isn't life-threatening. I'll tell her about it when I see her. I'll no doubt have some sick leave to come when I get out of here.'

Donald Ferris looked at Alan uncertainly. 'I really should let her know, Sparks. It's procedure.'

'I'll put it in writing that I've insisted she shouldn't be told,' Alan said firmly. He was twenty-four and older than Ferris. Although an officer, the midshipman was still young enough to be influenced by age and experience. Alan added, 'I really don't want her upset. She almost had a breakdown over her brother.'

'Well, as you say, you'll be given convalescent leave when you're well enough,' agreed Ferris uncertainly. 'But perhaps you ought to put your refusal to supply a next of kin in writing. I'll place it in your personal file and see that it's removed when you're fit and well once more. Now I'd better go off and speak to some of the others. I'll see you again tomorrow when Captain Kilpatrick arrives from Falmouth – and thank you, Sparks. If you hadn't remained at your post when you were wounded, and used your initiative, things might have turned out very differently.'

Captain Patrick Kilpatrick, CB, DSO, was a small, busy officer who had been a commander on a battleship at the Battle of Jutland. He would much rather have continued the war in a sea-going appointment. Instead, he had been consigned to an office as Senior Naval Officer Falmouth. However, he was extremely efficient in his post and had a reputation of looking after the men under his command.

He told the wounded sailors of the *Viper* they had done well and assured them that the sacrifices made by the captain and other crew members had not been in vain. Thanks to their courage a German U-boat had been sunk and, as a result, hundreds, possibly thousands, of British lives saved.

Captain Kilpatrick had particular praise for Alan and for the chief stoker, who was suffering from serious burns, caused by the burst boiler. In addition to the recommendation for medals for both men, Midshipman Ferris received immediate promotion to sub-lieutenant and Alan was told that when he returned to duty he would be a *leading* telegraphist, a promotion that carried with it a small but useful increase in pay.

The Senior Naval Officer was a very busy man and did not remain long at the small Newlyn hospital. When he had gone, Donald Ferris returned to speak to Alan. With him he brought the bloodstained exercise book in which

Alan had been writing when the presence of the U-boat was first reported.

He also brought a new exercise book and a handful of pencils, explaining, 'I thought you might like these, Sparks. Your book is so badly stained I asked the woman who drove you here in the ambulance if she could buy another for me, together with a couple of pencils. I told her that you enjoyed writing stories and things. I hope you don't mind. She seemed very interested.'

Embarrassed that the activity he had managed to keep secret from his colleagues for so long should have been discovered, Alan took the presents with no more than a brief 'Thank you', but Donald Ferris pursued the matter.

'I know I had no right to pry, Sparks, but I looked at what you've been writing. The poems are very good. You should do something with them. There are a great many army poets, but few from the Navy – in fact I can think of no one in particular since Rupert Brooke died. I noticed you have made notes for stories too. Have you done anything with them?'

Alan nodded. 'One or two – but they need a bit more work put in on them.' He was not certain whether to be pleased by the midshipman's praise, or indignant that his poems and ideas for stories had been read by someone else.

'I'm serious about the poems, Sparks. Look, I'll write to my father about you and give you his address. He owns a London publishing house and has interests in a great many other publishing ventures. He is always happy to publish poetry and the occasional story – especially if it's about the war. Send something to him.'

14

While Alan was still thinking about his words, the newly promoted sub-lieutenant turned to leave. He had a great many duties to attend to, not least of which was composing letters of condolence to send to the next of kin of those members of the *Viper*'s crew who had died in the action with the U-boat.

Suddenly, he turned back. 'By the way, make a list of the personal belongings you're going to need over the next few weeks. Give it to me when I come in tomorrow. It will probably be the last opportunity I have to visit you. *Viper* is going to Devonport dockyard for an inspection to see whether she's worth repairing. Any kit you don't need right away will be taken to the barracks and stored for you until you return to duty.'

When Ferris had gone, Alan felt a keen sense of loss at the thought of leaving the *Viper*. However, had he given the matter any thought he should not have been surprised. The boat had been badly damaged and was likely to be scrapped. Even were it possible for it to be repaired, the Royal Navy would not keep the surviving members of the crew standing by the craft, doing nothing. They would be accommodated in Devonport barracks until they were drafted to other ships.

3

The Newlyn hospital, built high above the fishing village and overlooking the bay, was a temporary wooden structure with a corrugated iron roof. It was staffed by Red Cross nurses and local volunteers, and among its patients were men from the Royal Naval Air Service airship and seaplane base situated on the waterfront. Professional skill was provided by a doctor who travelled to the hospital daily from the larger, permanent hospital in nearby Penzance.

Alan remained there for a week before it was decided he was well enough to be transferred to the naval hospital at Devonport, the large naval base adjacent to the Devon city of Plymouth. He and two other wounded members of the *Viper*'s crew were to be taken there in the same ambulance that had brought Alan to the hospital from the harbour where the torpedo boat and the crippled trawler had docked.

The three men were seen off by some of the crew of the *Lady Tamsin*. Together with members of their families, they had been regular visitors to the casualties from the *Viper*, bringing them whatever treats they could afford.

Alan had become particularly friendly with the skipper of the rescued trawler, Tom Penhaligon, and his sister Prue. They had exchanged addresses and Tom had extracted a promise from Alan that he would return to Newlyn with Dora and spend a holiday with them one day.

The driver of the ambulance wore the uniform of the First Aid Nursing Yeomanry, known as FANYs, and was the same young woman who had driven Alan to the hospital. Introducing herself as Vicky Hazelton, she greeted Alan warmly, saying, 'You were unconscious when I delivered you here. I'm happy to see you up and about.'

Alan's bandaged arm was supported by a sling and, holding it up, he said, 'It's wonderful what a good doctor and a few pints of blood can do. They say it's better than Guinness.'

With a faint smile, Vicky said, 'I wouldn't know about that, but you have some of my blood flowing in your veins. They put out a call for donors soon after you arrived and it seems you and I have the same blood group.'

'Then I have to thank you for helping me on the road to recovery,' Alan said gratefully. 'I'll always be in your debt . . . but where do I go? There are only two stretcher beds in the ambulance.'

'You're well enough to ride in the front with me,' Vicky replied, 'but we'll put a cushion behind your shoulder. The road between here and Penzance isn't the best I have driven on.'

Inside the cab a number of large, flat parcels were piled upon the passenger seat. Apologising, Vicky stowed them

17

carefully in a rack built into the roof space above their heads. As she did so, she explained they were paintings she was taking to a gallery on the Barbican, in Plymouth.

'Are they yours?' Alan asked.

'Some are. The others were done by artists who live here in Newlyn. There are a surprising number of us.'

'You're an artist?' Alan was impressed. 'Do you sell your work?'

'If I'm lucky,' Vicky replied. 'But make yourself comfortable before we set off. It's a lengthy journey.'

Talk was difficult until the ambulance reached Penzance and the road improved. Then, still curious about Vicky, Alan asked, 'Have you been an ambulance driver for very long?'

Without shifting her gaze from the road, Vicky replied, 'Long enough. But I've only been in Cornwall for a few months.'

'Where were you before?' It was a purely conversational question and the reply took him by surprise.

'In France for much of the time. Taking wounded soldiers from the front to hospitals in Paris.'

Looking at Vicky in a new light, Alan asked, 'Wasn't that very dangerous?'

Giving him a brief glance, Vicky said, 'It had its moments, but I doubt if it was any more dangerous than exchanging shots with a German U-boat.'

They travelled in silence for a short while before Alan asked, 'What did you do before the war? It couldn't have been anything to prepare you for what you must have seen in France.'

Her glance this time carried open amusement, but she

did not reply until she was giving her full attention to the road once more. 'I spent much of my time locked up in prison.'

'In *prison*! What for? What did you do?' Alan was genuinely astonished. Vicky quite obviously came from a background far superior to his own East End London upbringing. He could not imagine what crimes she might have committed that would warrant a prison sentence.

'I spoke at one or two illegal rallies; broke a few windows; caused trouble at political meetings – and hit one or two policemen.'

It took a few moments for the import of her words to sink in. When it had, he queried, 'You mean . . . you were a campaigner for women's rights? You were a suffragette?'

'That's right.' Vicky slowed down to overtake a horse-bus, accelerating once more when it was well behind the ambulance.

'But . . . where? Surely not here, in Cornwall.'

'Don't sound so surprised. There were plenty of suffra-gettes in Cornwall – and still are – but I was in London, in Dalston. Unless I'm very much mistaken it's an area you might know well.' Vicky had lived and worked in London for long enough to recognise an East End accent. 'But I've always wanted to come to Cornwall to meet some of the Newlyn artists and was happy to be sent here.'

'I know Dalston very well. I was brought up there and my wife is living with her parents not far away, in Scawfell Street. Where exactly did you live?'

'In a flat above a Chinese laundry, next door but one to Sylvia Pankhurst's old office in Dalston Lane. The suffragette movement printed a magazine there. I used to

19

do some of the illustrations as well as making posters for putting up around London. I still go up there to visit Sylvia whenever I have the opportunity. I know where Scawfell Street is, too. I once went to a meeting held in the school there. I expect you'll be returning for a while after you've enjoyed a week or two of convalescence.'

'I hope so. I haven't been home for about eighteen months.'

'Do you have any children?' It was another question Vicky asked without shifting her gaze from the road.

'No. I was only married for a week before I had to join *Viper* in Ireland.'

Vicky's expression showed immediate sympathy. 'Then your wife will be delighted to see you again. What's her name?'

'Dora. Yes, I'm sure she'll be pleased, although I haven't heard from her for more than a month now. She's working all hours as an orderly in a hospital in Edmonton and she's never been much of a writer.'

'Didn't she write when she learned you'd been wounded?' Vicky voiced incredulity.

'She doesn't know. I asked Sub-Lieutenant Ferris not to notify her. I'll tell her when I get home on leave . . .' Alan told Vicky about the death in action of Dora's favourite brother. The family had been notified that he had suffered a minor wound in France, only to be informed two days later that he had died.

'That isn't all you'll have to tell her, is it? I've heard you're to be decorated for your part in the sinking of the U-boat.'

Alan was surprised that she should know about the

20

award before he had received any official notification. 'So Sub-Lieutenant Ferris said. I'll believe it when it happens.'

'Oh, it will happen right enough,' Vicky said. 'The Newlyn fishermen are already talking about it. I know from my experience here, in Cornwall, that they have an uncanny knack of getting news before anyone else – and they're seldom wrong.'

'Do you like being in Cornwall?' Alan felt surprisingly at ease chatting to Vicky.

'Yes. There are places to go where I can be alone, to think and to sketch.'

'That must be a great luxury after your experiences in France.'

'It is, but I learned how to cope with doing things I don't enjoy during the time I spent in prison.'

Alan looked at her. She was small, slim, lively – and very attractive. He found it difficult to think of her behaving violently. Assaulting policemen. For some reason the thought made him smile.

Vicky caught the fleeting expression and said, 'Do you think it funny that I should have been sent to prison?'

'No!' he said hurriedly. 'It's just . . . I find it difficult to imagine you doing some of the things for which you went to prison. Picking a fight with a policeman, for instance.'

'It surprised him too,' Vicky said, with a certain amount of satisfaction. 'Even the magistrate treated it as some sort of joke. He said that if I could leap far enough into the air to give a policeman a black eye, perhaps I should think of taking up high jumping. He was very pleased with his own joke – but it didn't stop him sending me to prison for a month.'

'Were you able to do any sketching in prison?'

'I shouldn't have done – it wasn't allowed – but one of the wardresses learned I was an artist and got me to sketch her. Soon I was doing portraits of many of the wardresses. As a result I was able to get hold of paper and pencils, and I made some unofficial sketches of conditions in the prison. They were smuggled out and published in our suffragette magazine. It caused an awful row.'

Alan realised that despite her small stature and quiet, somewhat refined manner, Vicky was a very resourceful and determined young woman. 'Will you go back to being a suffragette when the war's over?' he asked.

'Some of us have never stopped campaigning,' Vicky replied. 'Sylvia Pankhurst still operates from the East End of London, but now she works from her home in Old Ford Road, in Bow.'

It was not far from Dalston Lane and Alan knew it well – but Vicky was still talking.

'She's doing a great deal for the women in the East End. Many were suffering enough before the war, but they are a lot worse off now. How about you? Will you remain in the Navy?'

Alan shook his head. 'I don't know what I'll do. After seeing what it's like in the country, away from London, I feel I'd like to come to somewhere like Cornwall, but I don't know what I'd do to earn a living.'

'You could always try your hand at writing. Donald Ferris told me you're rather good.'

Alan felt a brief moment of resentment that the young officer had not only read what was in his notebook, but discussed it with Vicky. However, the feeling quickly

22

passed. 'Calling my scribbling rather good is probably over-generous. It's certainly not good enough for me to think of earning a living with the pen.'

This was not strictly true. He enjoyed writing more than anything he had ever done and had thought about making money from it many times. However, he could not see how it could ever earn him enough to keep a wife and a home.

For the remainder of the journey, they continued to chat easily, learning about each other's lives. As Alan had guessed, Vicky came from a good background. Her father owned a small estate in Oxfordshire and she had studied at the Kensington School of Art, in London, where she had first met Sylvia Pankhurst and become deeply involved with the suffragette movement. For a time her shocked parents had disowned her, but there had been a reconciliation when the war began and she became an ambulance driver.

For his part, Alan told her of his early years in London. They had been happy times even though his father was in the merchant navy and came home only infrequently. Then, when Alan was ten, his mother died after a short illness and he went to live with an aunt who was already coping with a sick husband and five children of her own.

His father did not give up the sea. In fact, he returned home even more infrequently and Alan remained with the aunt. He had not seen his father for some years now. Nevertheless, despite all the family difficulties, he won a scholarship to the local grammar school, only to be forced to leave when he was fourteen in order to bring money into the household. Then his uncle died and his aunt married again, and soon after Alan joined the Navy she and her new husband moved to another part of London. He had not seen her since.

Listening to him, Vicky formed the opinion that it had come as a relief to the aunt when war came and Alan joined the Royal Navy.

By the time the ambulance arrived at the naval hospital in Devonport, both felt they had become friends. Alan left her with a promise that if he took Tom Penhaligon up on the offer of a Cornish holiday, and Vicky was still in Newlyn, he would bring Dora to meet her.

4

Alan was kept in the Devonport hospital for two weeks before being transferred to a convalescent hospital on the outskirts of nearby Plymouth. There was a much more relaxed atmosphere here. Recuperating sailors were allowed to go into the city, where their convalescent uniform ensured they received the sympathy and generosity of residents and shopkeepers alike.

There was also time for Alan to write long letters to Dora. He still did not tell her he had been in hospital, but sent her a number of his poems and said that he hoped to be home for a fortnight's leave in the very near future.

It was the latter information which prompted an immediate response in the form of the first letter Alan had received from Dora for many weeks, but there was none of the excitement he had expected at the prospect of an imminent reunion.

Dora explained that she would not be in London while he was on leave. Her hospital work was in a ward given over entirely to wounded American soldiers. Their numbers were increasing so rapidly it had become necessary to take over a whole hospital, in addition to the ward in the Edmonton. The new American hospital was somewhere in the north of England. She was not quite certain exactly where and was not likely to know in advance, but she had been told she would be required to go there with them, and to remain for a few months until they were well settled in. She might have been able to find someone else to take her place had she known earlier that Alan was likely to be home, but was now far too involved in the move to back out.

This was not the only bad news in her letter. Her parents, with whom she was living, were about to move house. She pointed out that her mother would not be happy to have him under her feet during such a fraught time.

Not staying with her parents would be no hardship for Alan. He had never got on well with either of them. Her mother had a sharp and occasionally vicious tongue and her father was drunk for much of the time, the two facts being closely connected. The only member of the family he liked was Dora's younger sister Mabel. He had also got on well with Micky, the brother who had been killed in France.

Nevertheless, the thought of not being able to spend his leave with Dora left him stunned. Until now their marriage had existed in little more than name. He was longing for an opportunity for them to share life together as a married couple – even though it might be for only a brief while, and in the same house as her mother and father.

However, he realised that many married couples were suffering similar problems, brought about by the war. He could only hope that, now the support of the United States

26

was being increasingly felt by the Allies, the war would soon be over and allow some normality to return to everyday life.

For the present, though, Alan was faced with the problem of finding somewhere to spend his convalescent leave. His aunt, with whom he had lived before joining the Navy, had moved away. Even if she was still in London, he had been out of touch with her for so long that he could not consider asking if he might stay at her home.

He contemplated telling Dora he had been hurt, in an attempt to persuade her to change her mind, but he reluctantly decided this would not be fair on her. She had work to do. Work that was probably every bit as important as his own.

Nevertheless, one thing was certain. If she was not going to be in London he had no reason to go there at all. Having seen a great many other places during his naval service he had come to realise that he preferred the countryside to the city – and he particularly liked Cornwall. And therein lay a possible solution to his problem. He had an invitation to stay with Tom Penhaligon and his family whenever an opportunity arose and believed it was a genuine invitation. Alan decided to write to Tom and explain the situation he now found himself in.

Alan travelled to Newlyn with mixed feelings. Tom had replied to his letter by return post, and with great enthusiasm. The family would be delighted to have Alan to stay with them. They were only sorry his wife would not be accompanying him.

Despite this reassurance, Alan stepped down from the train at Penzance station – the most westerly point of

27

the Great Western Railway line – slightly apprehensive of the welcome he would receive. His misgivings disappeared immediately. Tom hurried to greet him with a warm handshake and there was a kiss from Prue, the fisherman's sister.

'I see they've given you your medal.' Tom pointed delightedly at the blue and white ribbon of the Distinguished Service Medal, sewn on the left breast of Alan's uniform. The medal had been presented to him by the Flag Officer Plymouth at a ceremony held in the Devonport naval base while Alan was convalescing. 'Once the Newlyn fishermen see that, you'll not be allowed to buy a beer for yourself in the Fisherman's Arms. By the way, the *Lady Tamsin* will be ready for sea again in a few days' time. You must come out with us for a day's fishing – and I promise to try to steer clear of U-boats.'

Taking Alan's arm, Tom guided him from the station. 'We've a small pony-cart waiting outside. It belongs to Eli Roskilly. His son was one of those on the *Lady Tamsin* who was injured when the U-boat opened fire on us. He firmly believes that if it wasn't for the *Viper* his son would have died. I wouldn't argue the point, especially when he offered to provide his transport to pick you up and bring you to Newlyn, free of charge.'

It was a pleasant ride along the sea front to Newlyn. Eli and Tom included Alan in their chat about recent catches in the area and Prue told him about a concert that was being put on by the village women to raise money for the local hospital. With a warm sun adding a sparkle to the near-calm sea, war seemed a long way away. Alan wished Dora might have been with him to enjoy the day.

Emily and George Penhaligon welcomed Alan as warmly as had their son and daughter. Emily was a plump and busy wife and mother and her husband was a fisherman who had been forced to retire early when he injured a leg in a fishing accident. In spite of this he still enjoyed going to sea with his son whenever the weather was calm enough for him to keep his balance.

Alan had been in the house for no more than half an hour before a meal was put in front of him that was the equal of anything he had ever tasted before. He told Emily so when he placed knife and fork down on an empty plate and leaned back in his chair. Red-faced and beaming, Emily said, 'I thought you deserved something special. It must have come as a great disappointment not being able to spend your leave with your wife.'

For the duration of the meal the lively conversation had helped Alan to forget the bitter disappointment he felt at not sharing his leave with Dora. Emily's words brought it flooding back. 'Yes . . . yes, it did.'

Aware by his expression that he was upset, Emily said sympathetically, 'This war has affected the lives of so many folk, but there'll be another time. She'll be just as welcome here, whenever it is. Now, why don't you and our Tom take yourselves off to the Fisherman's Arms and enjoy a drink or two while me and Prue do the washing up? You can take Tom's pa with you, too. We'll get on much faster with all of you out of the way.'

The Fisherman's Arms was well frequented by fishermen, and immediately the trio entered the bar word went round that Alan was one of the men responsible for saving the

Lady Tamsin from the U-boat. The first drink arrived 'with the compliments of the landlord' and the fishermen in the bar ensured his glass was never empty.

Unaccustomed as he was to drinking so much beer, it was not long before Alan felt the need to pay a visit to the outside toilet. Making his way back he passed the snug, a small room that offered more privacy than the busy saloon bar. The door was open and inside was a group of perhaps a dozen men and women. Vicky Hazelton was among them and she saw Alan at the same moment he saw her.

Breaking into a delighted smile, she rose to her feet and hurried to greet him. 'Alan! What a lovely surprise. What are you doing here?'

'I'm on convalescence leave, staying with Tom Penhaligon, the skipper of the *Lady Tamsin*. I only arrived in Newlyn today.'

'How nice. Is your wife here with you?'

The pleasure disappeared from his expression. 'No, it wasn't possible for us to meet up. I came here on my own.'

Aware he was unhappy but not wishing to press him for details, Vicky asked, 'How long will you be in Newlyn?'

'If Tom and his family don't get fed up with me I'll spend the whole of my fourteen days' leave with them.'

'That means you'll have plenty of time to call on me. I'm renting a studio from Fiona and Rupert Graham, who have another home in the village. The Penhaligon family will know where it is. My driving duties are usually over by six o'clock and I have something I'd like to show you. There are also one or two of my friends I'd like you to meet. I think you'll find them interesting. They might prove useful to you and your writing.'

After a few more minutes of conversation, Alan made his way back to Tom Penhaligon and his friends in the saloon bar and Vicky returned to the table in the snug. As she took her seat, one of her companions said mockingly, 'I didn't think *you* were one to be attracted by a uniform, Vicky, but perhaps it's his body you're interested in – as a model, of course?' The speaker was Cecil Gormley, a somewhat fragile-looking artist, poet and writer. An extremely talented young man, he had been rejected by the armed services on health grounds.

'Neither,' Vicky retorted. 'He was the telegraphist on the *Viper* and was badly hurt in the battle with the U-boat. I drove him to the hospital here, on the hill, and then to Devonport after he'd been operated on. He's on convalescent leave, staying with the owner of the trawler that was saved.'

One of the older artists who had been drinking in the snug for much of the evening joined in the conversation. 'I watched the fight from the cliffs. I consider it my patriotic duty to send a drink to the young man . . . landlord, a drink for the sailor in the saloon bar . . .'

Vicky was not listening. Instead she was wondering why she had felt so angrily defensive when Cecil made his comments about Alan – and why she had felt a sudden thrill at seeing him once more.

She was also curious about the reason why he had come to Newlyn instead of spending his leave in London, with his wife. Vicky believed that if she were married and her husband had an opportunity to come home on leave,

31

nothing in the world would have prevented her from spending all the time possible with him.

She wondered what sort of woman Dora Carter could be.

5

Alan paid Vicky a visit in her studio a couple of evenings after they had met in the Fisherman's Arms. He was at a loose end because Tom Penhaligon had taken the *Lady Tamsin* to sea for the first time since the action involving the *Viper* and the U-boat. It was felt the sea was just a little too rough for Alan to risk going with him. His wound was healing well, but a fall, or a heavy collision with an object on the boat, might still cause it damage.

A small flotilla of Royal Navy torpedo boats was patrolling just off the coast, awaiting the arrival of a convoy which they would escort through the dangerous waters of the English Channel. Because of their presence, no U-boat would dare to surface in order to attack a fishing boat and the submarine's commander would not waste a torpedo on such a small craft. As a result the Newlyn fishermen had left port and would remain at sea for as long as the torpedo boats were present to offer them protection.

Prue was working on a nearby farm, helping to bring

in the harvest, and Alan had felt the older Penhaligons might welcome an opportunity of having their cottage to themselves for a few hours.

Vicky's studio was in the upper storey of a rambling building on a steep hill overlooking the harbour. It had a spectacular view across Mount's Bay, including the part-time island of St Michael's Mount. Climbing the exterior wooden stairs to the studio, Alan thought this must be a near-perfect place for an artist to work. He was keen to see what inspiration it had provided for Vicky.

When Vicky came to the door in response to his knock, she was not the smart, uniformed young woman he was used to seeing. She wore a paint-smeared smock and her hair, usually coiled in a tight bun beneath her uniform cap, was drawn back behind her neck, a brightly coloured comb preventing it from falling forward about her face. She seemed slightly annoyed at being disturbed, but her frown disappeared as soon as she saw him. 'Alan! What a lovely surprise! Come in.'

Entering the studio he passed an open door to a bedroom. Vicky's uniform was dangling from a hanger on the front of the wardrobe, the bed was unmade, and a variety of items of female apparel were strewn about the room.

Aware that he had glanced into the bedroom, Vicky apologised. 'I'm sorry, I wasn't expecting visitors. I was late getting up this morning and when I came home I wanted to finish a painting before the light failed. I've been trying to complete it for much of the week.'

She walked towards an easel standing beside a French window which opened out on a tiny balcony. From here

34

there was a breathtaking view over the rooftops of the fishermen's cottages to the bay, where Alan could see the Newlyn fishing fleet working in the distance. Turning back to Alan, she asked, 'Can I make you a cup of tea, or coffee?'

'No, please carry on with your painting. If you don't mind me being here I'm very happy just to wander round the studio and look at your work while you take advantage of the light.'

'Are you quite sure? It's just . . . I've promised to have the painting ready for a local exhibition which opens on Monday.' It was now Friday.

Alan realised that Vicky must be an accomplished artist if her work was to be placed on view in an exhibition. 'I'm sorry, I really shouldn't have called without any notice. Would you rather I left?'

'Of course not!' It was a very positive response. 'And should you happen to find yourself in the kitchen and the kettle is boiling you can make a cup of tea for both of us. I didn't stop for one when I came in – and I'm gasping!'

Alan quickly found the kitchen and after making tea for both of them wandered, cup in hand, round the studio. There was much to see, with many paintings and sketches in various stages of completion. They hung on the walls, were scattered on table and chairs and stood on the bareboard floor, leaning against the walls. All showed a degree of skill which Alan found very impressive.

Suddenly, a near-completed painting lying on the table caught his attention. It was of a damaged torpedo boat – the *Viper* – edging in to the Newlyn harbourside with the *Lady Tamsin* secured alongside by ropes at bow and stern. Sailors carrying hatchets stood by the ropes, ready to cut them should the fishing boat sink and risk capsizing the *Viper*.

It was so realistic that Alan felt his stomach contract as memories that had been pushed to the darker recesses of his mind flooded back.

Vicky was aware he was looking at the painting and she said, 'Have I got it right? I made some quick sketches as the *Viper* came in and was able to check the details when another torpedo boat docked here, a couple of weeks ago.'

'It's so realistic it's awesome!' Alan said, unable to hide the emotion he felt. 'Just looking at it took me back immediately.'

With a brush in her hand, Vicky left her easel and walked across the room to stand beside him looking down at the painting. 'Do you really think it's that good?'

'Yes . . . yes, I really do.'

'Then you'd better have it. Take it with you when you go.'

Alan looked at her in disbelief. 'I can't do that, Vicky. You sell your paintings – and you'll have no trouble finding a customer for this one. It's worth money to you.'

'Perhaps, but it cost me nothing except my time. I'd *like* you to have it. It will mean far more to you than it possibly could to anyone else.'

She was certainly right, as Alan was well aware. If he accepted the painting from her he would never be able to look at it without feeling both pride and sorrow – and a degree of fear he had not been fully aware of at the time.

'I wouldn't argue with that, Vicky. It would be very special indeed – always.'

'Then it's yours, but it needs to be completed. I'll have it ready for you by the time you go back off leave.'

'It's not a good idea for me to take it back to the barracks with me. It wouldn't be safe and I don't know where the Navy are likely to send me next. Could you keep it for me until I'm able to send for it, or, better still, come and collect it at some time in the future?'

'Of course. I'll hang it on the wall in there.' She pointed to a large alcove beside her bedroom. 'It's where I put paintings that are not for sale. But I really must get on and complete the one I'm working on. I shouldn't be more than half an hour or so.'

Vicky resumed painting and Alan made his way to look at the paintings in the alcove. Many were of places she obviously found particularly beautiful. There were also one or two paintings of small dogs and portraits of a man and woman he took to be her parents. He was surprised there were few of Cornwall's very picturesque coast, but imagined, correctly as it turned out, that such paintings were probably forbidden during wartime.

Then Alan came to a portrait that he realised immediately was of someone who meant a great deal to Vicky. It was almost as if she had written 'I love you!' on the painting. It was of a young man wearing a flying suit, with enough of the heavy jacket unbuttoned to reveal part of a pilot's wings on the left breast, beneath which were a number of medal ribbons.

The subject of the painting had been looking directly at the artist during the sitting and his expression removed any doubt about the uncanny aura of emotion that was so much a part of the painting. Vicky had succeeded in capturing the expression of a young man who was very much in love with the person at whom he was looking.

Alan gazed thoughtfully at the painting for a very long time. He wished he might have had a portrait of Dora that possessed a similar quality. He moved on, wondering about the airman and where he was now.

6

The fourteen days' leave went all too quickly for Alan. The *Lady Tamsin* was fully operational once more and Tom took the boat to sea every day, trying to make up for the fishing he had lost during the time the trawler was undergoing repairs, yet Alan never felt at a loss for something to do. The weather was fine enough on two days for him to go to sea with Tom, but for the remainder of the time he wandered along the coast, finding small coves and other places where he could sit in the warm sunshine and write.

He wrote numerous poems, some he was happy with, others not. He also wrote a number of stories and felt confident enough about one to ask Vicky to make a couple of drawings to illustrate it. After reading the story she agreed – but only on condition that he submitted it to Sub-Lieutenant Ferris's father when the drawings were done.

As Tom was spending so much time at sea, Alan whiled away many of his evenings with Vicky and her artist friends. They were very good company, particularly Cecil Gormley, the man who had made a sarcastic remark to

Vicky when she and Alan had met in the Fisherman's Arms on the first evening of his leave.

Cecil had been at King's College, Cambridge, with Rupert Brooke and the two had become friends. When Brooke joined the Royal Navy at the beginning of the war, Cecil tried to join too, but failed the medical. He tried to hide his deep disappointment by writing a great deal of anti-war poetry, much of which had been published. As a result he was mistakenly thought by many to be a conscientious objector and derided as such. Yet those who came to know him soon realised that he was opposed only to the horrific waste of life brought about by the conflict, not to the need for war.

Cecil persuaded Alan to let him see some of his poetry and gave him both encouragement and constructive criticism. As a result, Alan decided to send a couple of his poems to magazines recommended by the other man. The main difficulty was going to be giving a return address to which the magazine editor could reply. When his leave was over he had orders to report to Devonport naval barracks. From there he might be sent anywhere in the world.

The problem was solved by Vicky. She suggested he should give her address when he sent out his work. If he kept her informed of his movements she would act as intermediary between Alan and prospective publishers, opening any mail coming in for him. Should there be an offer of publication requiring swift action she would seek the advice of the more experienced Cecil to ensure that the terms were satisfactory.

Alan found the arrangement very exciting. On board

the torpedo boat he had felt it necessary to keep his writing a closely guarded secret. It was something that would have set him apart from his shipmates, and being part of the crew of a small warship called for close teamwork. Individuality among lower-deck sailors was not encouraged. Besides, writing poetry was hardly a pastime that would go down well among a crowd of hard-drinking, hard-working and hard-living men.

Here, among the artists of Newlyn, it was all quite different. The artistic fraternity were every bit as hard-drinking and hard-working as sailors, but many of them, like Cecil, were also writers and poets who enjoyed discussing their own writing and the works of others. Alan joined in their discussions and felt he learned a lot during his fortnight in Cornwall.

On the morning of the day his leave ended, Tom was already at sea and Prue had set off to work on her bicycle by the time Alan had finished packing for his return to the barracks in Devonport. Saying an emotional farewell to the older Penhaligons, Alan hoisted the bag containing his belongings to his shoulder and set off up the hill to the hospital, where he had arranged to meet Vicky. She was making a journey to the larger hospital in Penzance to pick up medical stores and had offered to give him a lift to the railway station.

Their relationship had become an easy one now they had mutual friends and he greatly enjoyed her company. She was very easy to talk to. They would have remained in touch even had his poems and stories not given them an excuse and he had promised to send his new address to her as soon as it was known to him.

He had written to Dora, care of her mother, using the old address in Scawfell Street, but was not surprised when he received no reply. With Dora away and her parents moving – if they had not already moved – communication would be difficult for the family.

He had told Vicky of his problems, but she made no comment, preferring to keep her opinions to herself. Dora was not behaving as *she* would behave, but Vicky had accepted long ago that she marched to a different drumbeat from most other women.

Soon after they left Newlyn hospital behind, Vicky said, 'We're all going to miss having you around, Alan. You've become part of our group.'

'I've enjoyed being with you all,' Alan admitted. 'In fact, I don't think I've ever felt quite as at home anywhere else. I've certainly never met such a crowd of talented people. Your paintings in particular are very, very good.' Believing this was a good opportunity to satisfy the curiosity that had been with him since his first visit to her studio, he added, 'There is one of them I especially like.'

Throwing him a brief smile, she said, 'You mean the one of the *Viper* with Tom Penhaligon's boat? Yes, it's not bad, even though I say so myself.'

Alan shook his head. 'No. That one's very good, of course, but there's another that I think is probably special to you too. It's a portrait you have in the alcove in your studio. The pilot.'

Vicky's hands gripped the ambulance's steering wheel more tightly, but she said nothing, her gaze not shifting from the road ahead.

Aware he might have touched on a raw nerve, he said,

'I'm sorry, Vicky. I'm not being nosy, it's just . . . the paint-ing seemed so real. So *alive*. The sort of painting that brings you to a halt and makes you keep looking at it.'

'Thank you.'

That was all. There followed a silence that lasted for a long time and Alan was regretting mentioning the portrait when Vicky said suddenly, 'I met Paul – the pilot in the painting – in the same way I met you. I picked him up close to the front line in France where one of our aero-planes had been shot up and forced to make a crash-landing. Paul was the pilot. He was in hospital for some weeks and I visited him there. We got to know each other well. So well that he asked me to marry him.'

'And you said yes?' Alan remembered the depth of feel-ing he had detected in the portrait.

'Not immediately. I told him he'd only asked me to marry him because of the circumstances in which we'd met and the fact there were so few women around . . . it was wartime . . . Oh, so many things that would cause an active and brave young man to think he was in love. When he left hospital I started the portrait you saw. He was going on leave to his parents in England. I told him if he still felt the same way when he returned to France I'd give him an answer.'

She fell silent again. Aware that they would soon reach the Penzance railway station, Alan prompted her. 'Did he? I mean . . . did he still feel the same way when he came back?'

She nodded, but it was not the happy nod of someone who was to marry the man she so obviously loved. Slowing down on the approach to the station, she said,

'Yes, he still felt the same way. He'd even told his parents about me and that he'd asked me to marry him. He brought me a wonderful letter from his mother, who said how happy she was that Paul had met someone special in the midst of such an horrific war.'

She brought the ambulance to a halt in the station yard. 'He was shot down and killed a week after he returned to France. At the time I felt it was a punishment for both of us. For being so happy in the midst of so much tragedy and pain. I hadn't even completed his portrait then. I did that later.'

Vicky was close to tears, but when she turned to him she managed a forced smile. 'You must be a particularly sympathetic listener, Alan. That's the first time I've ever told anyone about Paul.'

'I'm sorry, Vicky, truly I am. I wouldn't have even mentioned the painting had I thought . . .'

'You'd better go, Alan. You don't want to miss your train.'

'No, but thank you for telling me about Paul, Vicky – and thank you for helping me to enjoy a leave I shall always remember.'

He climbed out of the ambulance, expecting her to do the same. Instead, she remained in the driving seat and spoke to him through the open window of the driver's door.

'Take care of yourself, Alan . . . and let me know what you're doing as soon as you can.'

Feeling strangely empty, he lifted his bag and walked to the station entrance. Turning, he waved to her before disappearing inside.

In the ambulance, Vicky drove away, her eyes burning and very close to tears.

She told herself it was because Alan had brought up the subject of Paul.

7

Alan was in Devonport barracks for less than a week before being drafted to Gibraltar. Writing to Vicky to tell her he was about to leave England, he was unable to say where he was going, but gave her the address of the fleet mail office from which correspondence would reach him.

In his letter he reiterated how much he had enjoyed the time he had spent in Newlyn, but his main theme was one of concern. He had still not heard from Dora, and the letters he had sent to her since returning from leave had been returned marked 'Gone away, new address unknown'.

The fact that Dora's family had moved without leaving a forwarding address did not unduly alarm him. In that particular part of London it was an established practice to run up as many debts as possible before moving home, then to disappear, leaving no forwarding address. It was highly probable that Dora's family had done the same thing before.

Alan's concern was that Dora had not given *him* the family's new address.

Vicky replied on the day she received his letter. She told him she would be travelling to London in a few days' time to exchange her present ambulance for a newer model. Whilst there she intended taking a few days' leave and spending it with Sylvia Pankhurst and other suffragette friends in the East End. In order to allay his fears she promised Alan she would make time to visit Scawfell Street and enquire after Dora and her family.

Vicky took two days to reach London, where she handed over her ambulance. She was then left with four days at her disposal before taking delivery of the new vehicle.

London was busy, noisy and grubby after Cornwall, but there were a great many men and a few women in uniform and the city had an air of bustle about it that she found exciting.

At Old Ford Road, where Sylvia Pankhurst now lived, Vicky learned there had been many changes since the pre-war days of the suffragette movement, when most of the suffragettes' activities had been illegal. Now, although Sylvia Pankhurst and her mother and sister no longer agreed on suffragette policy, all were engaged in far more law-abiding pursuits. Indeed, Emmeline and her elder daughter Christabel Pankhurst were actively encouraging women to support the government and the war effort.

Sylvia, on the other hand, disagreed with her mother and sister and preached pacifism and socialism. She had thrown herself wholeheartedly into social work in the East End, where the departure of so many men to war and the subsequent very heavy casualties suffered in France and Belgium had left many women and children destitute.

Sylvia and her followers opened welfare clinics, cost-price eating houses and even small factories to provide work for such women and their children.

Although overwhelmed with work, Sylvia gave Vicky a warm welcome, and that evening, in the company of a number of other suffragettes with whom Vicky had shared incarceration in Holloway prison, they sat down to a meal together.

As they ate, Vicky mentioned Alan and his concern about Dora.

'Scawfell Street?' Sylvia frowned. 'That's one of our least salubrious areas, but Molly Shields should be able to tell you something about it. She works in the Bethnal Green office. Go and see her tomorrow. If she can't help you I doubt whether anyone can.'

The following day Vicky made her way to Bethnal Green, through streets where the front doors of the houses opened directly on to narrow pavements. Many doorsteps were occupied by old men smoking pipes, or young children dressed in threadbare, handed-down clothes, their grubby faces staring at her in solemn curiosity as she passed by.

Here and there a woman stood on a chair on the pavement, cleaning a downstairs window. Others were on their knees, scrubbing a stone doorstep, at the same time carrying on a shouted conversation with a near neighbour who was similarly occupied. They were among the poorest of the East End residents, yet they possessed a fierce pride, coupled with a determination to 'keep up appearances'.

These were the families to whom Sylvia Pankhurst had devoted herself and the resources of the Workers' Suffrage

Federation, as the East London suffragettes now called themselves.

Vicky had worked in this area before the war began, but she was seeing it through different eyes now. She thought it must be because she had become a different person, having seen other lands and other people. Lives blighted by more than poverty. And then she realised with a sudden start that there was another reason why she was viewing the East End of London anew. This was where Alan had lived his life and would return when the war was over.

This was where his wife lived.

When Vicky met Molly Shields they both realised they had met before – in Holloway prison. Molly had been within a few days of completing her sentence when Vicky was admitted to begin hers. They had been able to speak only fleetingly and furtively. Conversations between prisoners were forbidden and it was a rule that was rigidly enforced among the suffragette inmates by the women warders.

After the two women had recalled their earlier meeting, Vicky told Molly the purpose behind her visit to Bethnal Green.

At first, Molly declared she knew no Dora Carter, adding that she found this puzzling as she spent a great deal of time among the women and children of Scawfell Street and had believed she knew the names of most of the families there.

'That's something I really should have thought about,' Vicky confessed. 'Dora was living with her family, and I didn't think of asking Alan for her maiden name.'

'Can you tell me anything else about her, or the family?' Molly asked. 'Something might just jog my memory.'

'Well, she was married to Alan – a sailor – a little more than eighteen months ago and she had a soldier brother who was killed in France earlier in the war.'

Molly grimaced. 'There are very few families in this part of London who *haven't* lost someone in France, although not too many have a sailor in the family. Is there anything else you can tell me?'

'Only that in a letter to her husband about a month or six weeks ago she told him she was going away to work in an American military hospital in the north of England. While she was there her family would be moving from Scawfell Street to a house in Bethnal Green.'

'Ah! That should narrow it down a lot,' Molly said. 'Let's go along to Scawfell Street and see what we can learn.'

The walk from the suffragette office was depressingly similar to the one Vicky had made from Old Ford Road, but Scawfell Street was possibly the worst of all the streets in the district. However, it soon became apparent that Molly was well known here. She was greeted warmly by women and children in the street and, returning their greetings, Molly asked questions about children, husbands and parents.

After the last exchange of information, she said to Vicky, 'We'll pay a call on old Mother Hennessey. She knows all that goes on in the street. If she doesn't know the family personally she'll be able to find out for us, even if it means reading the tea leaves.'

Vicky looked at Molly, expecting to see a smile on her

face, but there was no discernible humour in her expression. 'You surely don't believe in such mumbo-jumbo?' she asked incredulously.

'I *didn't*,' Molly replied. 'Mother Hennessey may well be a charlatan, and probably is, but she's been uncannily accurate in some of the things she's predicted in the past. The women who live round here swear by her.' Aware of Vicky's continuing scepticism, she added, 'Anyway, we're here to make use of her knowledge of the neighbours, not her psychic powers.'

The house occupied by Mother Hennessey was no different from any other in Scawfell Street, except that the doorstep was not scrubbed and the front door and window frames were in dire need of a fresh coat of paint.

Molly knocked twice before the door was opened by a small, plump woman with grey hair tied back at the neck. She had a chubby, red-cheeked face and one of her eyes was permanently closed. She was wearing a faded and grubby pinafore, wrinkled stockings and threadbare felt slippers.

Looking up at Molly, she said, 'Oh, it's you. I don't suppose you've come calling just to stand on the doorstep looking at me. You'll be wanting something, so you'd better come in and bring your friend with you.'

There was just enough accent in her voice for Vicky to realise that, however long the old woman might have lived in Scawfell Street, her roots were in the west of Ireland.

Leading them along a dark, narrow passageway that had a mixture of patterned and curling linoleum on the floor, Mother Hennessey opened the door leading to the front room of the house. The curtains in here were only partly drawn, making the room almost as gloomy as the passageway, and there was a strong smell of cats.

'Sit yourself down and tell me what you've come to see me about.' Mother Hennessey waved her hand in the direction of an ancient two-seater sofa.

Vicky seated herself gingerly, but Molly seemed quite at home. Leaning back, she said, 'This is my friend Vicky Hazelton. She's looking for a woman named Dora Carter who apparently lived in Scawfell Street until very recently. The name didn't mean anything to me, but I said that if she's ever lived here then you'd know her.'

'Dora Carter? There's no family of that name here . . . and there hasn't been since Harriet Carter moved away from number seventy about ten years since.'

'Carter is her married name,' Vicky explained. 'She would have been living with her own family. Unfortunately, I don't know what they are called.'

'Why do you want to find her?' queried the old woman, fixing Vicky with a penetrating look from her single, dark eye. 'Is she in trouble?'

'No, nothing like that . . .' Vicky gave Mother Hennessey an outline of Alan's concern about his wife, adding, 'He's very worried about her, and as I was coming to London, I said I would make some enquiries about her on his behalf.'

'If he's so concerned, why hasn't he come here himself?' Mother Hennessey was still suspicious.

Vicky explained that Dora had written to tell him *not* to come to London as she would be working in an American hospital in the north of England and her parents were moving house. She added, 'His leave has expired now, but he still hasn't heard anything from her.'

'Then it'll be Dora Platt, as was, you'll be talking about – daughter of Winnie,' Mother Hennessey said. 'The family did a moonlight flit about a month ago – but they won't be missed round here. They left owing more money than most, so there are others just as keen as yourself to know where they've gone. Mind you, I hadn't seen Dora here for a while before the family left, not since soon after she came to me for her palm to be read. I thought she might have been upset by what I told her. But if she's all legally married there's no reason why she should be. She never struck me as being so keen on working that she wouldn't welcome an excuse to give it up.'

'Why would she be giving it up?' Vicky asked curiously. 'I thought she was doing worthwhile work in a hospital, helping to look after wounded American soldiers.'

'And so she might be,' Mother Hennessey retorted. 'But no matter how important the work, you can't do it while you're having a baby – and you can't take the baby to work with you once it's arrived.'

'A baby!' Vicky looked at the other woman in consternation. 'We can't be talking about the same woman. Alan hasn't seen her since they were married – and that was more than eighteen months ago. Unless . . . Did she tell you she was expecting, or is it something you thought you saw in her palm?'

'Well, she wasn't showing that she was expecting, but it was certainly there in her hand, dearie, there was no doubt about that.'

'Is there anyone in the street she was particularly friendly with? Someone who might know where the family have gone?' Molly asked hurriedly, aware that Vicky's scepticism might upset Mother Hennessey.

'Only Mary Powell, the Welsh woman at number seventy-eight. She and Winnie Platt were thick as thieves. Mind you, they weren't quite so friendly after Mary's husband had a fight with Dora's father because he'd got a bit too friendly with Mary's step-daughter, but I think they made it up again. You'll remember that, Molly. You spoke up for Mary's husband in court.'

'I remember . . . Not that it did him any good,' Molly added ruefully. 'The judge still gave him two years.'

'That was because he used a hammer on Dora's father. But what happened to him doesn't matter. Mary was glad enough to get rid of him, but you put her in your debt for speaking up for him, and she'll be eager to pay it off. Go and see her. She knows more about the Platt family than anyone and she'll speak to you.'

Turning to Vicky, Mother Hennessey went on, 'Mary's a very suspicious and violent-tempered woman. She won't say anything in front of a stranger, especially one wearing a uniform. She's got one son who ought to be in the army and another who's a deserter. You'd better stay here with me until Molly comes back.'

Vicky would have preferred to go with Molly rather than remain in this claustrophobic and smelly house, but Molly was in agreement with Mother Hennessey.

'She's right, Vicky. It's very easy to get on the wrong side of Mary Powell. You stay here while I go and see if I can find out where Dora and the Platt family have gone.'

8

Vicky's fears that during Molly's absence she and Mother Hennessey would sit in the gloomy front room in an awkward silence were swiftly dispelled. Having seen Molly out of the house the one-eyed woman put her head round the door of the front room to say, 'You stay here and I'll go and make us a cup of tea.'

As she spoke, a large, overweight tabby cat ran in through the open door with tail held high. With no hesitation it leapt upon Vicky's lap. 'That's right, dear, you sit and make a fuss of Kitchener while I'm gone.'

Kitchener had a purr that resembled the noise made by the engines of the tanks Vicky used to see rumbling towards the battlefront, in France. Despite the cat's friendliness, the irregular outline of his ears indicated that he had probably been involved in as many battles as his human namesake.

Before long, she discovered that Kitchener was moulting and put him on the floor, only to have him return to her lap immediately. She thought to fool him by standing to brush the hairs from her skirt, but Kitchener immediately jumped on the sofa and occupied the spot she had just vacated.

In the end, Vicky gave in. Occasionally extending his claws in painful happiness, the cat was still on her lap when Mother Hennessey returned carrying two cups on a small tray.

Beaming, she said, 'I see the two of you have become friends. He's named after Lord Kitchener, you know. His lordship was born close to my own home at Ballylongford, in Kerry. Many's the time I would see him when he was a boy, but no one then ever dreamed he would one day become such a great man as he did. It was sad that he should be lost just when his country needed him most.'

Vicky had respect for very few of the senior British army officers involved in the war in France and she said only, 'I arrived back in London from France on the day he was reported lost at sea last year. Everyone was very upset at the news.'

Her statement provided Mother Hennessey with an opportunity to talk about the apparent lack of progress being made in the war. The conversation continued until Vicky finished drinking her tea, trying not to pull a wry face at the quantity of tea leaves present in the bottom of her cup.

'You finished, dear? Would you like another cup?'

When Vicky declined, Mother Hennessey said, 'Well, if you're quite sure you've finished, I'll read your tea leaves for you.'

Vicky shook her head, but Mother Hennessey ignored the gesture. 'I know you don't believe in what I do, so I won't be offended if you laugh at what I tell you – but I don't think you will. Now, swill what little tea's left in your cup around three times . . . that's it. Now turn the cup upside down in the saucer and pass the cup and saucer to me.'

Deciding it would be easier to humour the eccentric old Irish woman, Vicky did as she was told and passed cup and saucer to her.

Mother Hennessey lifted the cup and peered inside. Then she carried it to the window to take advantage of the light entering between the curtains. Turning the cup this way and that, she said nothing for so long that Vicky began to feel vaguely uncomfortable.

Eventually, Mother Hennessey looked up and said, 'You've had an interesting life, dearie. But one that's not always met with the approval of those in authority. It might be your parents – or it could be the police.'

Vicky was unimpressed. She had come to the house with Molly and Molly was a well-known suffragette. Suffragettes were not universally popular and most had fallen foul of the law. She was similarly unimpressed when told she had lived 'close to danger' while others were dying about her. She had already told the older woman of returning from France.

Then Mother Hennessey said, 'But that isn't all your life is about, is it, dear? You see more in people's faces than most and are able to show others what it is you see. You're interested in photography – or painting, perhaps? You certainly have an eye for beauty.'

For a moment Vicky was startled. She thought Molly might have let something slip about her painting, then realised the suffragette was not aware of that aspect of her life . . . but there was more to come.

'You've also suffered a great unhappiness and lost someone very dear to you. I see something flying . . . a bird? It isn't too clear. I see a man in your life too . . . but it isn't very easy to see at the moment. There's happiness here for you – but there's more sorrow too . . . and much uncertainty. Yet I can see success in what you do best. Yes, great success.'

Somewhat shaken, but determined to reassert her disbelief, Vicky said flippantly, 'I don't suppose the tea leaves say whether or not we're going to find Dora Carter?'

'No,' Mother Hennessey said, unperturbed. 'But I see a woman here who is going to play a prominent part in your life – and she's not good news. So if it *is* Dora Carter it might be as well if you don't find her. You could save yourself a whole lot of grief.'

On the way back to the Bethnal Green office, Vicky told Molly what Mother Hennessey had 'read' in her tea leaves, adding jokingly, 'A cup of tea is never going to be the same for me again.'

'I agree that one's first reaction is to scoff and dismiss what Mother Hennessey says,' Molly said seriously, 'but don't dismiss it all out of hand, Vicky. She is a legend in this part of London. If there were such people as witches, she'd be one. She's told me things that have come true, even though I thought them highly unlikely at the time.'

Molly's visit to Mary Powell had not been particularly successful, but it had not been a complete waste of time, either. The Welsh woman was able to tell her that the Platts *were* Dora's family and confirm that she had another brother in the army, in addition to the one who had been killed. There was also a younger sister, Mabel, who was still living with her parents.

However, Mary had said that Dora had not been home for at least a week before the family moved. She believed Dora had gone away because of the rumours that were beginning to circulate that she was pregnant. Mary was unable to either confirm or refute the rumours, adding that it was possible Dora had gone to live with an aunt in order to be closer to the hospital where she worked.

Nevertheless, Mary made it clear that she would not be surprised if the rumours proved to be true. Dora was in the habit of bringing home some of the American men with whom she worked. Men who had far more money to spend on having a good time than their British counterparts.

She also said that another woman in the street claimed to have seen Dora's mother shopping in Bethnal Green only a few days before, so it seemed the family had not moved very far away.

'Dora told Alan in her last letter that the family was only moving as far as Bethnal Green,' Vicky said, 'but I'm not happy about the Americans she's said to have brought home. I shan't mention that to Alan.'

Molly made a sympathetic sound. 'It's an all too familiar story, Vicky. A lot of young girls have been attracted by a uniform and married the man without giving very much thought to what they were doing, only to have him go off to war and leave them behind, sometimes for years. It'll be no easier for some of them when their husbands return.

They'll find they are married to strangers, with whom they have absolutely nothing in common.' She cast a speculative glance at her companion. 'Is this Alan someone special to you, Vicky?'

Vicky's first reaction was one of anger at being asked such a personal and impertinent question, but the feeling passed as quickly as it had come. 'He's a good friend – and a very brave man . . .' She told Molly how she had first met Alan, of his subsequent leave spent in Newlyn and about his budding talent as a poet and writer.

'He doesn't sound the type who should be mixed up with the Platt family,' Molly commented. 'I'll see what I can find out about them for you. In the meantime go off and enjoy your few days' leave. If I learn anything more I'll bring it to you at Old Ford Road.'

Vicky enjoyed the time she spent with Sylvia, even though she was kept busy helping with the tasks the suffragettes carried out. The work pleased her almost as much as it did her friend. Before the war the suffragette movement in London had consisted in the main of middle-class volunteers with whom Sylvia had fallen out because of her sympathy for the women who lived in the East End slums, and it was a real pleasure to her to spend time with someone who shared her concerns.

Vicky thought her friend was doing a magnificent job and produced some illustrations for Sylvia's weekly newspaper, the *Workers' Dreadnought*, using the East End women and children as models. Despite their abject poverty, they possessed an inexplicable air of cheerfulness and Vicky enjoyed working with them.

The night before she left Old Ford Road to collect the new ambulance and return to Cornwall, Vicky received a visit from Molly.

After they exchanged greetings Molly told Vicky why she had called. 'I've learned more about your friend's wife, Vicky, but if you care for him I must tell you straight away that what I have to say will put an unhappy responsibility on you. He'll not want to hear it and you'll need to decide whether or not you really want to tell him.'

'Until I know what it is I won't be able to make a decision,' Vicky replied. 'I think you'd better tell me, Molly.'

'I wish it was happier news,' Molly began. 'It would seem Mother Hennessey and the rumour-mongers are probably right. Our Hackney Road welfare office has a file on a Dora Platt. She came in to see them about three months ago, claiming it was on behalf of a friend – a single girl – who'd got herself pregnant. She wanted to know how she could keep the birth quiet and have the baby adopted right away. She was told the friend could be helped with the birth, but that having the baby adopted would be more difficult. The woman who interviewed Dora told her either to bring her friend along, or come to the office on her behalf closer to the time of the birth, when arrangements would be made to find a place where she could have the baby, somewhere away from her home area. The woman Dora spoke to is a trained nurse, Vicky. She said that in her opinion there was no friend and that Dora showed all the signs of a mid-term pregnancy.'

'So what has happened? Has Dora been in to see her again?'

'Yes, but only very recently. She called in just to say her

61

'friend' wouldn't need any help after all, she'd had a miscarriage – and the woman who spoke to her said that Dora was a whole lot slimmer than when she had last called.'

'Is that all?'

'Not quite. I visited the hospital in Edmonton where Dora worked and it wasn't too hard to find someone there who'd once been a suffragette. She told me that Dora reported sick about six weeks ago, producing a sick note from a Dr Kumali. He's someone our Hackney Road office have had a file on for a very long time. He's known to have carried out abortions for anyone who can afford to pay him.'

'If you know this, why has no one done anything about him?' Vicky asked angrily, the anger fuelled by the news Molly had just given her.

Molly shrugged. 'There have always been abortions, Vicky. Most are carried out in some back street room by a woman with no medical training who has probably fortified her nerves with a plentiful supply of gin. At least Dr Kumali knows what he's doing.'

'Did you find out how long Dora was off "sick"?'

Molly nodded. 'A fortnight.'

'And she was never sent to an American hospital in the north?'

'No, and isn't likely to be. She's a ward orderly, not a skilled nurse.'

Vicky had been standing but now she sat down suddenly, her hands clasped in her lap. 'You're right, Molly, this does put an appalling responsibility on me. If I tell Alan, he'll be devastated. He might not even believe me. He'll certainly not thank me . . . and I treasure his friendship. He's a good man and doesn't deserve this.'

'You're very fond of him, aren't you?' Molly said sympathetically.

'As I said, he's a very good friend.'

'Well, if you ever decide to take the relationship beyond the bounds of friendship you need not feel guilty. Dora Carter – or whatever she wants to call herself – is *not* good. She's a tart. This Alan of yours would be better off without her.'

9

On her return to Newlyn, Vicky was much relieved to be able to defer a decision on whether or not to tell Alan what she had learned in London. There was a letter from him. He had heard from Dora shortly before he left Devonport.

Dora's letter informed him she was back in London and gave him the family's new address in Bethnal Green. Alan thanked Vicky for offering to help him find her, but was happy it was no longer necessary.

Vicky grappled with her conscience for more than a week about whether or not she should disclose what she had learned. In the end she decided to say nothing. Perhaps Dora had learned a lesson – a very traumatic lesson. As a result she might settle down to become the sort of wife Alan believed her to be. There was something else, too, that made the decision easier for Vicky. Two of Alan's poems had been accepted by a magazine recommended by Cecil Gormley and they were offering him a generous price for the right to publish them.

After she had forwarded the letter of acceptance to

Alan, Vicky learned that Cecil had also received a letter from the editor, thanking him for introducing Alan's work to them and hoping there would be more from him in the future. It was felt he had the potential to make a name for himself in the coming years.

Vicky wrote to Alan telling him what the editor had said, knowing how delighted he would be. This was not the time to inform him he was married to an unfaithful wife.

Besides, it seemed that temptation would soon be removed from Dora's life. The war in France was turning in favour of the Allies. When it ended, the Americans would return to their own country, Alan would leave the Navy, and he and Dora could make a new beginning to married life.

Fully fit for duty once more, Alan took passage from Devonport in a destroyer, HMS *Undine*, bound for Gibraltar and the Royal Navy's signal station on the famous rock. It was a posting that was eagerly sought after by all naval telegraphists. Life at sea was both dangerous and uncomfortable. In Gibraltar he would work and live in congenial surroundings, enjoying a much warmer climate than in England. Because of the proximity of neutral Spain he would also be able to enjoy luxuries that were no longer obtainable in wartime Britain. Many of the sailors stationed on 'the Rock' also obtained passports, in order that they might spend an occasional weekend in Spain.

Alan was not able to tell Dora exactly where he was going, only that he would be somewhere safe and, thanks to the pay rise that came with his recent promotion, in a position to send her the occasional present.

Situated on one side of the narrow strait where the Mediterranean met the Atlantic, and catering for the needs of the Royal Navy's Home and Mediterranean Fleets in addition to merchantmen, Gibraltar had always been a very busy international port. It still was, despite the absence of the merchant vessels of Germany and her allies. Because of this, and the increased wartime garrison of soldiers, Gibraltar boasted an astounding number of bars and restaurants, providing entertainment to suit all tastes.

Alan had never visited the busy colony before, but as a leading telegraphist he was now in charge of others and there was no shortage of juniors to show him what Gibraltar nightlife had to offer.

He had been in Gibraltar for a week when he was taken on an evening tour of the bars. After visiting a couple of somewhat seedy establishments, the party of seven telegraphists settled down at a table in the Trocadero, where there was a floorshow composed of Flamenco dancers and Spanish singers. The bar was owned by Maria Rapello, a Spanish woman in her forties, who owned several other properties in the colony in addition to the Trocadero, even though she resided in Algeciras, a Spanish town a short distance to the west of Gibraltar.

Many of the telegraphists with Alan had been stationed on the Rock for some time and, as regular customers in the Trocadero, were greeted personally by the proprietress. When they introduced Alan to her, she ordered that the first round of drinks should be on the house, in his honour. A shrewd businesswoman, she knew that Alan was likely to be stationed on Gibraltar for the foreseeable future, and would be inclined to spend his off-duty hours in an establishment where he was made to feel welcome.

At ten o'clock that evening, when the bar was crowded, a party of some nine or ten merchant seamen came in through the door while Alan was speaking to one of the telegraphists. As the newcomers stood gazing round the room in search of a table that would accommodate the whole party, Alan glanced up and broke off in mid-sentence. He had recognised one of the merchant seamen, even though they had not met for almost five years.

It was his father!

'Pa!'

Alan's shout rang out across the crowded bar, audible even above the sound of Flamenco music.

John Carter heard the call. His glance fell upon Alan, fell away, then suddenly returned in growing disbelief.

'Alan!'

Both men pushed through the crowds between them and met in the middle of the bar room. There was a moment's hesitation, and then they clasped each other in an embrace that provoked a variety of ribald shouts from those about them.

Maria Rapello, always on hand when anything untoward occurred in her bar, was on the scene within seconds. Aware of her concern, John Carter said, 'Maria, this is my son. We haven't seen each other for many years!'

Before Alan had time to recover from his surprise that his father had greeted the proprietress by name, Maria said, 'Your son? You have never said anything to me about a son, but I thought his face seemed familiar as soon as I saw him. This calls for a celebration . . . Champagne!'

Tables were hastily cleared and pushed together and soon telegraphists and merchant seamen were raising glasses to toast the reunion of father and son. The celebrations went on until the early hours of the morning, while Alan and his father caught up with the details of each other's life during the years they had lost touch with one another.

John Carter was a seaman on the *Baluchistan*, a cargo ship trading between Liverpool and the Persian Gulf. He had been with the ship for three years. Prior to that he had spent two years on a coaster in the Pacific Ocean, during which time Alan's aunt had moved home and Alan had joined the Royal Navy.

Before signing on with the shipping line that owned the *Baluchistan* John Carter claimed to have gone to London in an attempt to find his son, only to learn that war had changed the places and the people he had never known well, even in the brief periods when he had been home from the sea. Friends of Alan's mother were no longer around and the aunt with whom he had lived had also moved, without informing him of her new address.

Alan felt that his father had not tried as hard as he might have to find him, but there was no doubting his delight at being with his son now. With the telegraphists of Alan's watch, and the crew members of the *Baluchistan*, they made it a night that would long be remembered at the Trocadero.

They parted company vowing never to lose touch with each other again. Alan and his friends made their way unsteadily to the naval quarters, leaving the merchant navy crewmen to conclude other arrangements for the remainder of the night with the girls who worked in the Trocadero.

Alan and his father had said they would meet again in two days' time, when Alan would once more be off duty, but it was not to be. Twenty-four hours after their brief reunion, the *Baluchistan* together with seventeen other merchant vessels slipped out of Gibraltar harbour in convoy, with an escort of Royal Navy warships, bound for Liverpool.

Disappointed, Alan sat at a table in the Trocadero, and was joined by Maria.

'Your father's ship has sailed,' she said.

'Yes, but it was good to see him again.'

'You have really not seen each other since the war began?'

'It's even longer than that. But he's been on the same ship for a long time. You must have seen him in here quite often.'

'He always comes to see me when his ship calls at Gibraltar. We are very good friends.'

Alan thought that his father and Maria were probably more than just 'good friends', but he made no comment and Maria continued her questioning.

'You have other brothers and sisters? Has he seen them?'

Alan shook his head. 'There's no one else. I'm an only child.'

'That is sad for you. It is good to have brothers and sisters around. What of your mother? Have you lost touch with her too?'

Alan felt the question was more than just idle conversation and he said, 'My mother died when I was a boy. Didn't my father tell you?'

'Yes, he told me, but almost every man who comes to

the Trocadero tells my girls he is not married. I sometimes think there can be no more marriages in England.'

Alan smiled. 'Well, before you ask, I'm a married man.'

'Would your wife not mind if she knew you were drinking with me, in the Trocadero?'

He smiled again. 'Why should she? I'd tell her I was drinking with a friend of my father.'

'Of course – and you will find that talking to me is cheaper than talking to my girls. They are paid a small percentage of the price of the drinks that are bought for them – and most are very thirsty. You are a telegraphist, so you'll be watch-keeping, with time off during the day. I know you're a married man, but even married men get lonely. Come here in the daytime, when it's quiet, and you'll find my girls are not so greedy. I'll introduce you to a nice girl who'll be happy to sit and play cards and talk with you and expect nothing more. It is not an offer I would make to anyone. You must thank your father. He and I have known each other for a long time.'

Suddenly brisk, she stood up. 'But now I must work. I have a bar to run. Enjoy your evening, Alan.'

Alan put Maria's offer to the test a week later and spent a pleasant afternoon playing cards with Maria and two of the bar girls. It was something he did on a number of occasions afterwards, although he preferred to spend most of his off-duty hours either writing, or exploring the tiny colony. He also acquired a passport, intending to venture into nearby Spain when an opportunity arose.

Although Alan wrote regularly to both Dora and Vicky, he received far more letters in reply from the latter. He was gaining more success with his poems and stories now, greatly encouraged by Vicky. Sub-Lieutenant Ferris's father was keen to publish his work, as was an editor friend of Cecil Gormley.

John Carter's ship called at Gibraltar on three occasions before the autumn of 1918 and the merchant seaman always spent part of his time ashore with Alan – and with Maria. By now, it was evident that it was only a matter of time before Germany surrendered and the war came to end. Aware of this, Alan wrote to Dora, saying that he hoped he would soon be home with her again and urging her to write.

He had not heard from her for three months. Although he told himself she must be exceptionally busy as a result of the appalling number of casualties being suffered by Britain and her allies in their final bid to bring the war to a rapid close, he was unhappy at not receiving news from her.

He did not often mention Dora in his letters to Vicky, but one evening, when he wrote to thank her for a cheque she had sent on for an amount equal to two months' naval pay, he found himself pouring out his misgivings about not having heard from his wife for so long.

The following day he regretted saying anything about it, but it was too late. The letter had been posted.

Vicky read Alan's letter with increasing concern. A few weeks earlier she had heard again from Molly, who had been visiting a distressed family in Bethnal Green's Quilter Street when she had learned, quite by chance, that the Platt family were living next door. She did not know whether Vicky was still interested in the family, but she gave her their address.

Molly also wrote that the Platt family were no more popular in their new surroundings than they had been in Scawfell Street. The neighbours complained about Henry Platt's rowdy drunkenness, the noise of argument from the house, and the presence of the police who regularly visited the house for various reasons.

They were also scathing about Dora. Although no one in the street had ever met Alan, they were aware that Dora was married to a man who was away at war, in the Navy. They were scandalised by the fact that she was constantly bringing American servicemen home with her.

Finally, Molly passed on the news that with the end of the war in sight, the American ward in the Edmonton hospital would be closing when patients had recovered sufficiently to be sent home.

Having read the letter, Vicky had once more to decide whether she should pass on any of the information she possessed to Alan. As before, she thought a great deal about it, but eventually decided, somewhat reluctantly, that she would say nothing. She believed it was something he *should* know about, but did not want to be the one to tell him.

Vicky tried to tell herself that the neighbours of the Platt family might – just might – be wrong. Dora's friendship with the American soldiers could be no more than compassion for wounded men who were far from home, casualties in a war that should not have involved their country.

Unfortunately, no matter how charitable she *wanted* to be, she was unable to convince herself.

10

The armistice of 11 November 1918, bringing the fighting with Germany to an end, was celebrated throughout Britain with great jubilation. Fireworks exploded in the sombre grey sky, church bells rang out, factory owners gave a holiday to their workers and it seemed that the whole population of London was out on the streets, cheering, singing and waving flags. Soldiers, sailors and airmen were kissed and hugged by girls and carried shoulder high through the streets by men, and there were unprecedented scenes of public rejoicing everywhere.

Nevertheless, the armistice was not celebrated with unequivocal joy by everyone. Dora received the news with very mixed emotions and did not return to the family home in Quilter Street that night, but her family were not concerned. It seemed the whole city was out, celebrating. Besides, Dora had recently spent many nights away from home. There had been a huge influx of American casualties to the hospital in the last few months of war and Dora had either worked double shifts or remained at the hospital so late that transport home was not available.

However, when Dora failed to return home for a second night, Winnie Platt began to worry. Voicing her concern to her younger daughter, Mabel, she added, 'Mind you, knowing the amount of money them she's working with have to throw around they're probably still having a knees-up, but if she's not home this evening you can go to the hospital and find out what's going on.'

Pouting rebelliously, the young girl complained, 'Our Dora's old enough to look after herself. Besides, I've promised Joe I'll let him take me out dancing tonight.'

Mabel was eighteen years old and worked in a factory, making cardboard boxes. Joe was a delivery driver for the same company, having been rejected for military service because he was asthmatic.

'You can go dancing – but not until you've been to find out what Dora's up to.'

Mabel flounced out of the room, slamming the door noisily behind her, but the extent of her rebelliousness was never put to the test. Dora returned home that evening looking tired and dishevelled.

Winnie's greeting to her elder daughter was hardly that of a concerned mother. 'And where do you think you've been these last two nights? You can count yourself lucky you didn't come home and find all your stuff outside on the pavement!'

'In case you haven't heard, the war's ended,' Dora retorted. 'Everyone's out celebrating – even them as are in hospital wounded and with little to be thankful for. Some of us have had to stay on to make sure the celebrations didn't get too out of hand and that the soldiers didn't hurt themselves.'

'Do you think I was born yesterday, girl?' Winnie asked scornfully. 'Look at you! I know very well what you've been up to and if you end up in trouble as a result you can sort yourself out this time. We're not uprooting ourselves again for you. Me and your pa are getting too old for all that sort of thing now.'

'You don't have to do anything for me. I may be living in your house but I'm paying my way – more than my way – and I'm a grown woman. I'll do what I want.' Dora was angry, but so too was her mother.

'That's right, you're a grown woman. You're also a *married* woman – or have you forgotten?'

'I've not forgotten anything, but I hardly know Alan. How much married life have we had – a week more than two years ago? Sometimes I can't even remember what he *looks* like.' The belligerence had disappeared as quickly as it had shown itself. Dora was now an uncertain and unhappy daughter, appealing to her mother.

Winnie Platt had known Dora for far too long to be taken in by her. 'Well, you'll soon get the chance to remind yourself. Alan only signed on in the Navy for the duration of the war. Now it's over he'll be home again – and your American friends will be thousands of miles away, never to be seen or heard of again. Think about it.'

'I don't have to,' Dora said defiantly. 'Delroy says that if I want to I can go over there to where he lives. He'll see I'm all right.'

Delroy was an army sergeant in charge of the stores in the American wing of the Edmonton hospital, but not one of those who had been frequent visitors to the Platts' Quilter Street home. Such visitors never came empty-handed. The family's cupboards contained huge tins of ham, tinned fruit and a host of other delicacies not seen before by the Platt family, even in the pre-war days when such items were available to those with money to purchase them. Dora's friends had also introduced Henry Platt to the pleasures of American bourbon.

'Is Alan included in Delroy's invitation?' Winnie Platt viewed her daughter scornfully. 'What's the matter with you, Dora? Have you gone simple, or something? Delroy – and all the others you've met since you started working at that hospital – would promise the earth in order to get what they want from you. Especially when they know that by the time you realise you're in trouble they'll be thousands of miles away and you'll never hear from 'em again.'

'Delroy's not like that,' Dora declared defensively. 'He's . . . well, he's *different*.'

Winnie made a contemptuous sound deep in her throat. 'I seem to remember saying a similar thing to my mother about your father – and look how *he's* turned out! Anyway, before you get all carried away with any so-called "plans" you might have made with Delroy, you'd better read the two letters that came yesterday for you from Alan. He might have other ideas for you. They're on the mantelpiece, behind the clock.'

Dora lifted down the envelopes, casually checked the date stamps on them and opened the earlier. It contained a poem, which she threw on the kitchen fire, unread. After she had taken no more than a cursory glance at the letter which had also been in the envelope, it went the way of the poem.

Opening the second letter, she was about to throw it after the first when she suddenly stopped and read it more carefully. Then, her expression one of alarm, she looked up at her mother and said, 'Alan's coming home! He's in Gibraltar, wherever that is, and has been there for much of the year. He's only waiting for a damaged torpedo boat to be repaired in the dockyard there and then he'll be bringing it back to Portsmouth. From there he expects to go to Chatham to get his release from the Navy.'

Looking at the date stamp on the envelope, she looked up in dismay, 'This was posted ten days ago. He could be almost here by now! What if he's home before Christmas? I've made plans . . .'

'Then you'll have to unmake 'em. He's your husband. Like I said, it's about time you remembered that you're a married woman. You'd better make yourself ready to give your husband the welcome he's expecting from you, then prepare to settle down, my girl. You've had more fun than most wives ever get to know, but it's time to put all that behind you and buckle down to finding out what married life is about.'

11

The torpedo boat took longer to repair than had been anticipated and Alan and the crew put together to bring it back to England became increasingly frustrated at the lack of progress. They had all been hoping to be home for Christmas, but as time went on it was clear they were likely to still be in Gibraltar. However, when the dockyard workers declared the boat ready just in time to enable its crew to reach England and share the festivities with their families, they wasted no time in going on board and readying the craft for sea.

They left Gibraltar in high spirits. Many of them, and Alan was one, were looking forward to spending their first Christmas at home for a number of years. Then, less than eight hours after setting out from Gibraltar, the engines failed. Despite the desperate efforts of the chief stoker and his engine-room crew, it was not possible to start them again and Alan was obliged to send out an urgent message requesting help.

Early the following morning a tug reached them and,

less than two days after setting out, the torpedo boat was once more tied up alongside a jetty in Gibraltar harbour. The dejected crew had to accept that they would not reach England until early in the New Year.

The weather too turned against them. The torpedo boat was only a small vessel and storms were particularly fierce in the Bay of Biscay, through which it would need to pass en route to Portsmouth. The admiral in charge of the naval base decided the craft should remain in Gibraltar harbour until there was a significant improvement in conditions.

Resigning themselves to the situation the crew agreed that Gibraltar was a better place to be than on the high seas during the holiday period – especially when they accompanied Alan to the Trocadero. Maria greeted Alan like a returning relative and, in a customary generous gesture, the first drinks for the crew were 'on the house'.

Ever since the meeting with his father, Alan had spent much of his off-duty time at the Trocadero and he was there, seated at a table talking to Maria, on Christmas Eve. Maria had just received a letter from John Carter. Telling Alan the news, she said, 'Your father expects to be here in a week or two. It will be nice for you to be together again. It is only a pity you cannot be together for Christmas.'

'It would have made it a special time,' Alan agreed, trying to put aside the thought that Christmas would have been even more enjoyable had he been spending it in London with Dora. 'How is he? Does he say he's keeping well?'

'He is very well. Now the war is over I will be able to take him to my home in Algeciras once more. It will be

79

good for him to leave his ship behind and enjoy a few hours of home life. He says it has been a long time.'

'Yes, I suppose it has.'

Reaching out a hand to rest it on his arm, Maria said sympathetically, 'It has been a long time for you too – you and your wife who is still no more than a bride. How long do you expect to be in Gibraltar?'

'Only until the engines are fixed and the weather improves. Possibly a week or ten days, or so.'

'Then I will take *you* to see my home. Now the war is over the border is open for everyone once more – and you will not be working for the next two days. Tomorrow is Christmas and there will be many things for you in the naval barracks. I will take you the next day. My brother has a motor-cab; he takes officers to Algeciras where they have their parties. He will take us.'

'That sounds great, Maria . . . I will have to look out my passport.'

'You will not need a passport with my brother driving you. He also drives the chiefs of police – on both sides of the border. You come here as early in the morning as you can. But tonight is going to be busy, so I must leave you for now . . .'

It was the first peace-time Christmas since 1913 and it seemed everyone was in an extremely relaxed mood. There were no checks at the border between Spain and the British colony and, with Maria's brother driving as though he wanted to impress his English passenger, Alan and Maria were in Algeciras early enough for Maria to say she would cook breakfast for him.

Maria owned a pleasant, small house close enough to the coast to see the impressive heights of Gibraltar, across the bay. When he commented on the view, Maria said, 'Yes, your father likes it too. He particularly enjoys sitting out on the patio on a summer's evening, drinking wine and listening to the music of the orchestra on the terrace of Hotel Reina Cristina.'

'You are fond of him, Maria.' It was a statement, not a question.

'Yes.' She did not amplify her reply. Instead, she poured him more coffee, then excused herself and went to the kitchen to begin washing up the pots in which she had cooked his breakfast.

After breakfast, Maria took him into the town where she did some shopping, then helped him buy presents to take home to England, saving him a great deal of money by persuading the shopkeepers to reduce their prices by far more than they would have had he been alone.

Alan bought a number of presents for Dora, and small gifts for her mother and sister. He also bought mementos for the women of the Penhaligon family in Newlyn. Then, passing another shop, he saw a large gypsy shawl that was similar to a smaller one he had seen adorning a chair back in Vicky's studio. This one was large enough to throw over an armchair.

Vicky had been very helpful as an intermediary between Alan and the various editors and publishers to whom he had sent his poems and stories. He thought the shawl would be an acceptable 'thank you' gift for her. When Maria obtained it at a price he would have been embarrassed to offer the shopkeeper, he was doubly delighted with his purchase.

After taking the packages back to her house, Maria took him to a restaurant on the sea front for lunch. Although she had been so helpful with his purchases, he had felt she was quieter than usual and as they settled down with a jug of wine to await the meal they had ordered he asked hesitantly, 'Maria . . . I hope I didn't offend you by asking whether you were fond of my pa.'

Maria looked at him for so long before replying that Alan was convinced he *had* offended her. Then, as though arriving at a decision, she said, 'No, you didn't offend me, but I was not sure whether *you* would be offended if I told you the truth. Whether it is not something your father should tell you.'

Playing with the cutlery on the table in front of her, Maria looked up at him suddenly and said, 'I am more than *fond* of your father, Alan, and he of me. He has asked me to marry him.'

'Have you said you will?'

'I have promised to give him an answer when he next comes to Gibraltar. It is a very big step for both of us, even though I love him very much and believe he really does love me.'

'Where would you live if you married? Would he give up the sea and take you to England?'

Maria shook her head. 'No, I have too much here. Once I too worked in the Trocadero as a bar girl. I was no better and no worse than any of the girls who work there now. But then I married the owner, a man very much older than myself. When he died he left me the bar, a shop here in

Algeciras, this house and two others, and interests in a number of other businesses. John knows of my past life but he said he too has things in his past of which he is not proud. He says he loves me for what I am now and would be happy to give up his life at sea and settle down here with me. Yet I am not sure. I think he might one day be unhappy to have given up such a carefree life as he has now, for me.'

'What would he do here, Maria? I think he might settle if he was doing something useful with his time.'

'He would manage the Trocadero while I built up my business interests on this side of the border. There are a great many things that could be improved in both places. We would discuss them together, as we do now, when he is here.'

'Then I don't think you have anything to worry about. In Gibraltar he'll be close enough to the good things of his old life, without having to put up with the things a sailor doesn't enjoy. Besides, he'll have you – and, although I never saw very much of him when I was younger, I don't ever remember him being as happy as he is when he's with you.'

'Thank you.' She looked at him searchingly before adding, 'But how would you feel about his marrying me?'

The question should not have taken Alan by surprise, but it did. 'Me? Why . . . I'd be delighted for him . . . for both of you. More than that, I think he's a very lucky man, Maria – but I shall refuse to call you Mother. You'll still be Maria to me.'

It took a moment for Maria to realise he had made a joke, albeit a weak one. Then, beaming, she said, 'Thank you, Alan. When John comes to Gibraltar this time I shall tell him yes – and you and your wife must come to Spain for the wedding. I shall send the money for you to buy tickets to travel here on a ship. Now, a special drink to celebrate . . . Juan!' She called to a waiter, before saying to Alan, 'You may not call me Mother, but you shall be the son I used to dream would one day be mine.'

12

The gales in the Bay of Biscay did not abate until the last day of December and Alan welcomed in 1919 on the torpedo boat as it encountered seas that were still far from calm, in the area where Admiral Lord Nelson had fought his last great battle against the French and Spanish fleets, off Cape Trafalgar.

Alan had been hoping he would be able to celebrate the New Year at the Trocadero, with Maria and the friends he had made while working at the Gibraltar naval wireless station – and perhaps his father too. Unfortunately, the admiral in charge of the naval base had decided the torpedo boat should take advantage of what might prove to be only a temporary lull in the long spell of bad weather in the Atlantic.

Although the conditions had improved there was a heavy swell and a strong side wind, which made the torpedo boat's progress uncomfortable for the crew. In addition, it was not long before it was discovered that the Gibraltar dockyard engineers had not succeeded in eliminating all the faults in the small craft's engines. The chief stoker and his men were called upon to work many more hours than the remainder of the crew, trying to keep at least one of the two engines going.

Eventually, when the torpedo boat was still two hundred miles from the Isles of Scilly, both engines broke down. Once again the crew found themselves on a helpless ship wallowing uncomfortably in a heavy swell while Alan sent out an SOS signal calling for assistance. They spent seven uncomfortable hours on the crippled vessel before two destroyers arrived on the scene, by which time the chief stoker had succeeded in getting one engine started again. Escorted by the destroyers, the torpedo boat made slow but steady progress and eventually limped into the naval dockyard at Devonport, on the Devon side of the River Tamar.

An inspection by dockyard engineers concluded that work on the engines would take at least a week. Because of the degree of uncertainty, the crew would remain with the vessel during that time, resuming the voyage to Portsmouth when repairs were completed. The crew members, most of whom, like Alan, had not seen their families for a couple of years, were disappointed that they were not being allowed to go home, but with censorship no longer in force some were able to contact their wives and have them come to Devonport to meet them.

Alan wrote to Dora, as soon as they docked, suggesting she do the same. The letter would have reached her the following day, but a week went by and he received no reply. When the dockyard engineers said the torpedo boat would be ready for sea in two days' time, and in the absence of news from Dora, Alan decided he would pay a visit to Newlyn. It was only a couple of hours' rail journey away and he had no difficulty obtaining permission to be absent from the boat for a day. He intended delivering the present he had bought for Vicky, together with the small items he had bought in Gibraltar and Algeciras for the Penhaligon family.

It was midwinter and the weather was cold, but it was dry and Alan enjoyed the train ride through the Cornish countryside, especially when the railway line followed the south Cornish coast. As the train neared Penzance he began to feel a sense of excitement at meeting all those in Newlyn he regarded as friends.

He was given a lift from Penzance to Newlyn by the pilot of one of the seaplanes based at the naval air base there. The two had met on the train from Plymouth and during their conversation discovered that both had been involved in the action against the U-boat for which Alan had won his DSM. The pilot told him that the base at Newlyn was shortly to be closed down and dismantled. He also knew Vicky and said that she too would become redundant when the naval flyers moved away.

Vicky's studio was Alan's first call when he reached Newlyn. To his great disappointment, she was not at home. He wondered whether she might already have left the FANYs and returned to her family home in Oxfordshire. He thought Tom Penhaligon would know, but here too he was disappointed. Tom was at sea on the *Lady Tamsin* and had taken his father with him. His sister Prue was also away from the house, washing and cleaning for an elderly aunt who lived in a nearby village.

Only Emily Penhaligon was at home, but when Alan would have handed over his presents and left, she would not hear of it. 'No, m'dear,' she said. 'You've come all this way and been disappointed by not finding the family at home. It's nigh on one o'clock and you're not leaving before I've put some food inside you! The family would never let me hear the last of it if I was to let you walk away like that. Sit yourself down by the fire while I make a pot of tea. You can tell me all about what you've been doing in those foreign countries you've been to.'

Fussing over him, she tried to persuade him to stay and have lunch with her. When he declined, politely but firmly, she insisted that he at least have tea and cake and wait until the pasties she was cooking were ready in order that he might take a couple with him, adding, 'I don't know what they feed you in the Navy, but it won't be like a bit of home cooking. You stay there by the fire while I get things ready.'

As they sat and drank tea, waiting for the pasties to be done, Emily examined the presents he had bought for the family and expressed delight. She also gave him all the local gossip, much of it about people he never knew, or had met only briefly. She knew a little about what went on in the artist community in Newlyn, but was unable to tell him anything about Vicky.

Alan remained in the Penhaligon cottage for more than an hour and left clutching two hot wrapped pasties in one hand and Vicky's present in the other. He intended calling at the house of one of her artist friends to find out whether she was still in the village.

On the way he passed the building where Vicky had her studio. Looking up, he noticed that one of the transom windows was open. He was certain it had not been when he called earlier. Hopefully, he climbed the outside stairs and knocked at the door. He felt an unexpected thrill of anticipation when he heard a sound inside the studio, then the door opened and Vicky was standing there. Her initial frown swiftly turned to delight. 'Alan! What a wonderful surprise!'

Opening her arms wide she embraced him and gave him a kiss. Then she stepped back, her arms dropped to her sides, and both stood awkwardly, looking at each other, taken by surprise by the warmth of her greeting.

Vicky recovered first. 'I'm sorry if I embarrassed you,' she apologised. 'It . . . it's just . . . it's such a lovely surprise to see you.'

'There's no need to apologise,' he replied. 'It's been a long time since anyone kissed me.' Even as he said the words, Alan realised they were not true. Maria had kissed him when she bade him a tearful farewell in Gibraltar, but that had been very different.

'Come in, Alan. What are you doing in Newlyn? When did you return to England – and how long can you stay?'

'I can only stay for a few hours . . .' He told her about bringing the torpedo boat from the Mediterranean, and the problems they had encountered.

'How dreadful! Wasn't it very dangerous to have the engines break down so far from land?'

'It was pretty uncomfortable for a while,' he admitted. Then, changing the subject and handing her the parcel containing her present, he said, 'I bought this for you in Spain. It's a thank you for all the help you've given me with my poems and stories.'

'I've been very happy to do anything I can, Alan,' she said. 'It's always exciting to be able to help someone who has a very real talent.' As she was talking she had unwrapped the Spanish gypsy shawl and now she shook it out and said delightedly, 'It's *beautiful*, Alan. Thank you very, very much.'

Pleased with her reaction, he said, 'I thought you could perhaps throw it over an armchair, or something.'

'It's far too nice to have people come in here and sit on it. No, I will have it in my bedroom, as a bedcover. Oh, I *do* like it, Alan – but can I get you something to eat? Have you eaten today?'

He explained that he had called at the Penhaligon house. 'Emily Penhaligon gave me tea and cake. She also insisted that I take a couple of pasties back to the ship with me. They're still warm. Would you like them? To be honest, I don't fancy carrying them all the way back to Devonport.'

'Why don't I heat them up again and we can have one each? We can wash them down with some cider that was given to me by a grateful farmer. He waved my ambulance down to say his wife was in labour. There wasn't time to get her to hospital, so I delivered the baby myself – it was quite an experience, I can tell you!'

'I'm sure it was. Yes, I think pasty and cider would go very well together.'

13

While Vicky was busy in the small kitchen, Alan looked round the studio. There were lots of new pictures and he was reminded anew of how skilful and talented Vicky was. Remembering the painting of the Royal Flying Corps pilot, he thought he would like to look at it again and went to the alcove where it had been hanging.

The portrait was still there, but it was not this that attracted his attention. On the floor, leaning against the alcove wall, was another portrait. It was not completed, but the subject was unmistakable. It was a portrait of himself!

At that moment Vicky put her head out of the kitchen doorway and saw him looking at the half-finished painting. 'I see you've found it. I was about to tell you it was there. I started painting it from some photographs that were taken by Percy one evening in the Fisherman's Arms, do you remember? I'm not particularly happy with it yet. If you have an hour to spare this afternoon I'd like to make some sketches of you to help me finish it.'

Percy Fordham was a painter-turned-photographer

91

who lived in Newlyn and took many photographs of artists and their friends. He had taken a photograph of Alan to send to Dora.

'My train leaves from Penzance at six. I have nothing else to do until then.'

'Splendid! I should be able to sketch enough detail to paint a passable portrait, at least.' Vicky retreated into the kitchen once more and it was not long before they were sitting down to pasties and cider.

It was a pleasantly cosy meal and, as they ate, Alan told Vicky about meeting his father in Gibraltar and of the forthcoming marriage to Maria. Vicky was delighted that Alan had been reunited with his father and found the story of the Gibraltarian romance very touching. Alan was so easy to talk to it was as though he had never been away, and Vicky found herself broaching a subject she had been carefully avoiding, about which she had still not made up her mind how much she should tell him. 'What does your wife think about your father getting married to Maria?'

'Dora?' His expression lost much of its animation. 'I haven't told her yet . . . I told her about meeting him, of course, but until Maria took me to her home on Boxing Day I didn't know about their plans. I've sent Dora a letter since we reached Devonport, but I forgot to mention it. I'll break the news to her when I get home, which should be some time next week. I hope to be given a bit of leave before reporting to the naval barracks at Chatham to be demobbed.'

'Have you heard from Dora lately?'

'No.' Alan looked unhappy. 'I haven't heard from her for some months. I had hoped there would be some mail for me before I left Gibraltar but the mail office here might have been holding it for me, expecting me to be back in this country at any time. Hopefully there will be some letters waiting for me when we reach Portsmouth.'

Her heart beating faster, Vicky realised this would be the moment to tell Alan what she had learned of his wife, but her courage failed at the last moment. Instead, she asked, 'What will you do when you leave the Navy?'

'I don't know,' he confessed. 'I suppose I'll find work in London, though that might not be easy with so many others coming home from the war. I'd like to try to earn a living by my writing, but it would be a very uncertain way of life. I would give it a go if I only had myself to think about, but Dora will want to give up work and we'll need to find a place of our own and buy furniture and things.'

Vicky was aware she was behaving cravenly by not telling Alan what she knew about Dora, but she realised how terribly hurt he would be. Even worse, he might not believe her. Either way, if she told him, their friendship would be at an end – and she did not want that to happen.

To tell or not to tell was a decision that had troubled her ever since Molly had written with the further revelations about Dora. Now the opportunity to speak to Alan about it had come and gone. Vicky had been unable to summon up the courage to tell him.

She tried to excuse her cowardice by telling herself that Dora might, after all, settle down as the wife Alan believed her to be. If not . . . then he would have need of friends.

'I put a cheque for fifty pounds in the bank for you last week,' she said. 'It should tide you over while you reach a decision about working. It seems that Donald Ferris's father sent some of the stories from his paper to an American magazine. Yours were among those they accepted.'

Vicky had set up a bank account in Alan's name when he first went to Gibraltar, and had paid in a number of cheques on his behalf. Telling him this, she added, 'I'll give you a copy of all the accounts before you return to Devonport. Now, let's get down to the sketches I want to make of you, before the light goes.'

Vicky sat Alan close to the studio window and began to draw, occasionally making him change his position so she could see him from a different angle. She had been working for perhaps an hour when there came a knock at the outer door. Scowling, Vicky answered the summons reluctantly. When she opened the door a young, frothy-haired woman entered the studio.

The newcomer's name was Fiona Graham, and when she was introduced to Alan she gave him a cursory nod before returning her attention to Vicky. 'I do hope I'm not disturbing you, but I've come to invite you to dinner tonight. The son of one of Rupert's friends is visiting – he's a pilot. Rupert and I told him about you and he's dying to be introduced to you, so we thought it would be splendid for you to meet over dinner. You'll like him, Vicky, I just *know* you will.'

'Thank you, Fiona, it's very kind of you to think of me, but I'm very busy with Alan's portrait right now. After I have finished I am taking him to the station to catch a late train. Perhaps some other time.'

Alan looked at Vicky in surprise. He had already told

her he needed to leave Newlyn early enough to catch the six o'clock train from Penzance. She would have plenty of time to go to dinner afterwards.

Pouting, Fiona said, 'That's very disappointing, Vicky. Couldn't Alan come back and sit for you another day?'

'No, this is all the time either of us has to spare. Now, I'm sorry to have to throw you out, Fiona, but I really do need to have the sketching done while there's still enough light.'

'But . . . I've told Rupert's friend so much about you. Perhaps you could pop up to the house for a drink or two when you come back?'

'Another time, Fiona. Now, I really do need to get on . . .' So saying, Vicky withdrew her attention from her uninvited visitor and resumed her sketching.

Looking at Vicky uncertainly, Fiona appeared to be about to speak. Instead, she glanced from the artist to Alan before turning away and leaving the studio, the door closing noisily behind her.

As Fiona could be heard clattering down the wooden steps outside, Alan said, 'You could have gone to dinner with her, Vicky. My train leaves early enough for you to get back here in time. Anyway, I wasn't expecting you to take me to the station.'

'I know, but I didn't want to go to dinner at Fiona's house. I don't like people organising my life for me. Fiona is very generous and well-meaning, but she and her husband are the most awful snobs and they make me cross sometimes. They came to Newlyn only a few months ago when they bought a number of properties, including this studio. Rupert has made a lot of money manufacturing munitions in one of the factories he owns and they thought they would like a place in the country. They live in a big house just inland from here and Fiona decided to take up painting to impress her friends. She and her husband, Rupert, throw huge parties for which she dresses outrageously and thinks she's being terribly daring.'

Vicky frowned and for a couple of minutes concentrated on the sketch she was making before resuming her conversation about Fiona and her husband.

'Fiona also enjoys organising people, in much the way she behaved just now, arranging dinner parties and pairing off her guests – especially particularly obnoxious male guests – with artists like myself. Those who aren't obnoxious are usually pompous or boring. Some possess all those qualities. No, Alan, I would have had a thoroughly miserable evening in such company.' She grimaced ruefully. 'Mind you, Rupert does buy my paintings and he pays well, but that doesn't mean that he and Fiona have bought my soul – or my body – along with them.'

Taken aback, Alan said, 'It can't be quite as bad as that, surely?'

Vicky smiled at him. 'That's one of the things I particularly liked about you when you came on leave to Newlyn, Alan. You arrived here with no preconceived ideas about artists. You took us as you found us – as we did you. Others, like the Grahams, think we all live Bohemian lifestyles, hold regular orgies and are devoid of all morals. They like their friends to think so too. The trouble is, many of their friends believe them. One or two women artists have had to fight off their attentions.'

'Have you?' Alan asked bluntly.

'No, and I have no intention of putting myself in a situation where it might become necessary. If it were not for the fact that times are particularly hard for artists, the Grahams would probably have been run out of Newlyn by now.'

14

The torpedo boat made a fast voyage from Devonport to Portsmouth. The work carried out by the dockyard engineers had succeeded in restoring the engines to their full power and the lieutenant in command of the craft was as impressed by the vessel's performance as was Alan.

As they roared along the English Channel, creating an impressive wash in their wake, the commanding officer said to Alan, 'A pity we didn't have a few boats like this during the war, eh, Sparks?'

'I think we were very lucky the Germans didn't have any of them,' Alan replied. 'We would have been hard pressed to keep up with them, that's for sure. But the Devonport dockyard mateys have done a good job. Had they got their hands on the engines in Gibraltar we might have been home for Christmas.'

'True. Never mind, we'll hand over the boat and move into barracks as soon as we arrive in Portsmouth. With any luck you could be on your way home by noon tomorrow. How long is it since you were last there?'

'Almost three years. I'd only been married a week when I left.'

The lieutenant looked at Alan sympathetically. 'Never mind, Sparks, you'll be a civilian again within the month, and you and your wife have a lifetime ahead of you.'

The naval officer's prediction of the crew's timetable proved accurate. At six o'clock in the evening of the day after the torpedo boat berthed in Portsmouth dockyard, Alan emerged from Bethnal Green underground station, in London. Shouldering his kitbag, he made his way along Bethnal Green Road, heading for Quilter Street – and Dora.

His overwhelming emotion was one of great excitement, yet he was nervous too. He had been hoping there would be a letter from Dora awaiting him at Portsmouth, telling him that she was equally excited at the thought of having him home with her at last. There had been no letter, and the uncertainty of what to expect when he reached the Platt home added to his nervousness.

The war had ended only a couple of months before and those who lived in this part of London were used to seeing men in uniform, but it did not prevent several elderly women from touching Alan's light blue square sailor's collar 'for luck'. It was a custom he remembered from his boyhood days. It gave a degree of familiarity to surroundings where he no longer felt entirely at home. When he turned off the main road the houses seemed smaller and dirtier and the streets narrower than he remembered. Women and children too showed more obvious signs of poverty than he recalled.

Once in Quilter Street he began searching the door

numbers, his excitement increasing until his heart was beating faster than when he had gone into action on board ship, his lungs incapable of drawing in all the air they needed.

Arriving at the door of the Platt family's home, he hesitated for a moment before reaching out for the knocker. It was stiff and the sound it made hardly audible. Trying once more, he used more force, and this time brought it down harder than he had intended. There were sounds from the passageway inside the house, then the door was opened and he was face to face with a scowling Winnie.

'Hello, Ma. I'm home at last.' It was not what he had intended saying, but his homecoming was already an anticlimax.

'So I can see. I thought someone was trying to bang the door down. Dora's not in. Was she expecting you?'

There was no warmth in her voice and for a moment Alan wondered whether he was about to be turned away from the house. 'I wrote to tell her I was coming, but I couldn't say exactly when because I didn't know myself. What time will she be home?'

'Who knows? They're busy getting the last of them American soldiers ready to go back to their own country. If our Dora's needed she could be at the hospital all night long.'

Alan could not hide his dismay and belatedly Winnie said, 'I suppose you'd better come indoors.'

Lowering the kitbag from his shoulder and holding it awkwardly in front of him, Alan asked, 'Can I put this somewhere? It's got all my things in it.'

'I don't know where I'm going to find room for it. Our

100

Charlie's home from the army with one of his mates. They've taken Mabel's room and she's moved in with Dora.'

Alan had difficulty hiding his dismay. Charlie was Dora's soldier brother and he and Alan had never got along with each other.

'But . . . where am I going to sleep? Me and Dora?'

Winnie shrugged. 'I dunno. If you'd let us know you were coming we might have been able to sort something out. As it is . . .' She held out her hands, palms upwards, in a gesture of resignation.

Suddenly angry, Alan said, 'I thought Dora and me paid rent for a room in the house. I've certainly been adding rent to the allowance the Navy have been paying her.'

'So you might have, but we're not living in normal times. The war's not long over. We all have to make sacrifices.'

'I think I've made quite enough sacrifices to the war,' Alan said, still angry. 'If there's nowhere else I'll leave my kitbag here in the passage while I go to the hospital and find Dora. I'll see if we can't take a room for the night somewhere. Tomorrow we can start looking for a place of our own.'

Winnie was taken aback by Alan's forceful manner. She was also alarmed at the thought of Dora's leaving so soon. She relied upon the money given to her by her elder daughter each week. With Mabel's contribution it was all the income that came into the house on a regular basis.

She had never tried to like Alan and there was no reason why he should feel affection for her, but he had always been anxious to avoid a confrontation with her. This was a harder, more self-assured man than the young sailor who

101

had married her daughter. She felt she needed to re-assess him before she pushed him too hard.

'Put your kitbag under the stairs and I'll make a cup of tea. You won't do any good by going to the hospital; our Dora's helping the nurses to move out the Americans who are still there. She could be anywhere between Edmonton and Tilbury docks. That's where the American hospital ship is.'

Tilbury was a large port at the mouth of the River Thames and a considerable distance from London. Winnie had heard Dora mention that wounded Americans were being taken there. Whether Dora had ever gone there with them was doubtful, but Winnie did not think it would be a good idea for Alan to go to the Edmonton hospital making enquiries about her.

There was no one else in the kitchen and Alan asked after Henry, Dora's father.

'He's where he usually is,' Winnie said, 'in the pub round the corner. You won't see him till closing time. Our Mabel will be home before then.'

'What time does Dora usually get back from the hospital?' Alan asked.

'There ain't no "usual" time,' Winnie replied. 'Could be any time between six o'clock tonight and eight in the morning. Depends what there is to be done.'

Her words did not make Alan any happier, but his spirits received a boost when Mabel came home from work. The youngest member of the family, Mabel was fond of her brother-in-law. Squeaking with delight, she gave him a warm hug and a kiss. 'What a lovely surprise. No one told me you'd be home.'

'No one knew.' Her mother sniffed her disapproval. 'I answered a knock on the door and there he was, large as life – and you needn't look so pleased to see him. You'll probably end up sleeping in the front room on an armchair.'

'No I won't!' Mabel declared promptly. 'I'll go round to Rene's house and sleep there. Her mum will understand.' Smiling at Alan, she explained, 'Rene's my best friend. We were at school together. Does our Dora know you're home?'

Alan shook his head. 'I wrote from Devonport to say I was back in England, but didn't know exactly when I'd be coming home.'

'Well, after I've had a cup of tea I'll call on Rene and me and her will go up to Edmonton and leave word for Dora that you're here.'

Looking from Mabel to her mother, Alan caught a strange look that passed between them. Winnie said quickly, 'Alan wanted to go to the hospital himself, but I told him that Dora's likely to be helping some of her patients to Tilbury, to the hospital ship. It would be a wasted journey for him. Besides, he might well have missed her if she'd come home while he was out. But the hospital's not far from Rene's place, so it won't hurt for you to call in there.'

'I'll come with you, if you like,' Alan said to Mabel, but Winnie shook her head vigorously.

'You stay here and I'll make something for you to eat. Our Dora would be very upset if she was to come home and find you'd gone out looking for her.'

15

At nine o'clock that night, Alan heard the front door of the Platt house open and he started up eagerly, but it was not Dora. It was her brother Charlie, and his friend, Alfie. Between them they were supporting the head of the household. Henry Platt was too drunk to even notice Alan – but Charlie was not.

'Well, look who it is,' he said scornfully. 'It's Alan, the bleedin' poet.'

Alan flushed angrily. Dora must have mentioned his poetry to her family. It was something he had not considered. The poems he had sent to her were of a very personal nature . . . but Winnie was talking to Charlie about his father. '. . . Just look at the state of him! Where did you find him?'

'In the pub round the corner,' Charlie replied. 'Me and Alfie called in there for a drink on our way home from the pictures and the landlord asked us to bring him home. He said that if we hadn't come in when we did he'd have had the old man thrown out in the gutter.'

'Where'd he get the money to get himself into a state like this? Have you given anything to him?'

'I gave him a couple of quid,' Charlie said defensively. 'After all, he is my dad.'

'And I'm your mother, so you can give some to me too, before you eat me out of house and home. Now you've brought him home you can get him upstairs – but don't put him on the bed. I'm not sleeping with him in that state. You can make up a bed for him on the floor, in the corner, by the washstand – and put the bowl on the floor beside him.'

When the two soldiers left the room, half carrying Henry between them, Alan said placatingly, 'I expect he was out celebrating Charlie's safe return home. It's something a great many fathers will be doing, all over the country.'

'He doesn't need an excuse to get himself in that state,' Winnie retorted, 'only enough money.'

It was ten minutes before Charlie and his friend returned to the kitchen, and it was immediately apparent that Charlie had not finished with goading Alan. Turning to his companion, he said, 'I didn't introduce you, did I? Alfie, this is my brother-in-law, Alan.'

'Pleased to meet you,' Alfie said, extending his hand. 'Have you just come back from sea?'

'Back from sea?' Charlie sneered. 'He's spent the war years tucked up somewhere nice and quiet, writing poetry to our Dora.'

'Not on your life,' Alfie said. 'A bloke don't get the medal he's wearing by writing poetry.'

'What are you talking about?' Charlie asked. 'They give medals just for wearing a uniform.'

'Not that one,' Alfie declared. 'It's a DSM, ain't it – a Distinguished Service Medal? I once travelled on a train with a matelot who got one at Jutland. Where did you get yours, Alan?'

'On a torpedo boat. We crippled a U-boat.' He did not feel like amplifying his explanation in the presence of Dora's sneering brother, but Alfie persisted.

'Only crippled it? Did it get away?'

'No, we'd damaged it and it couldn't dive, but the U-boat had damaged us too, so we couldn't chase it and finish what we'd started. A destroyer was called in to finish the job.'

'A torpedo boat isn't very big, is it? Were any of your lot hurt?'

'The captain and some of the crew were killed . . .'

Aware that Winnie was listening intently to the conversation, Alan hoped the inquisitive soldier had completed his questioning, but he had one more to ask. 'How about you? Were you hurt?'

'I spent a while in hospital,' Alan admitted, and Winnie seized upon his words immediately.

'You were in hospital? Dora said nothing about it.' In fact, Dora had always been very dismissive about her husband, declaring he lacked the gumption and drive shown by the American soldiers she had met in the hospital and wishing he was a little more like them.

'I never told her,' Alan admitted. 'I thought she would worry . . . after what happened to your Micky.'

'Dora said you'd been given some medal or other, but she didn't say anything about it being for anything special.' For the second time that day she looked at Alan

106

speculatively, as though seeing him for the first time. Then she said, 'There's more to you than meets the eye, young man.'

Secretly, Winnie believed that Dora might have greatly underestimated Alan. Her daughter had always been dismissive of him, boasting that she could wrap him round her little finger. Winnie now realised the whole family had been deceived by Alan's quiet manner, mistaking it for weakness. Unless Dora changed her ways, Winnie felt she was likely to be taught a very sharp lesson.

Alfie's recognition of Alan as a hero effectively silenced Charlie for the moment. Avoiding Alan's amused glance, he suggested to Alfie that they should return to the public house where Henry Platt had interrupted their plans and enjoy a few drinks before closing time.

'A good idea,' Alfie agreed. 'Why don't you join us, Alan? It will only need someone to recognise your medal for what it is and we won't need to pay for a drink all night!'

'Thanks for the invitation,' Alan said, 'but Dora should be home any time now. We've a whole lot of catching up to do.'

'Of course,' Alfie said. 'It's going to be like a second honeymoon for you both. I envy you, Alan. I was engaged to a girl when I joined the army, but by the time I came home on my first leave she was married to a fireman and expecting her second. Some girls just can't resist a uniform – no matter who's inside it!'

Winnie heard his words and said nothing, but she was thinking a great deal!

16

Dora arrived home at ten-thirty that night. When she saw Alan standing in the kitchen, waiting to greet her, the blood drained from her face and for a moment Alan feared she would faint.

Instead, reaching out for the support of a chair back, she gasped, 'Alan . . . Why didn't you let me know you were coming home today?'

It was not the welcome about which he had fantasised for so long, and he felt deeply hurt. 'By the time I knew for sure, it was too late to write. I would have beaten the letter home – but does it matter? I'm home after nearly three years away. Don't I even get a kiss?'

She kissed him then and gave him a hug, but it lacked the passion he had anticipated. He told himself he was being unreasonable in expecting more. She could not be expected to throw all her reserve to the wind and show her feelings in front of her mother – or even to him, right away. After all, they had been married for only a week before he went away, and he had been gone for a very long time.

Hoping to break the awkward silence that followed Dora's belated and muted greeting, he said, 'Didn't you see Mabel? She was coming to the hospital to tell you I was here.'

Dora was momentarily taken aback. Recovering quickly, she said, 'I spent the last few hours working in the annexe, away from the main hospital. Matron sent me there to gather all the soldiers' belongings together, and label and list them. It isn't something I usually do, so the sister in charge of my ward probably thought I'd come home. Talking of Mabel . . . she's sharing my room. Where are you going to sleep, Alan? Our Charlie and a friend of his have taken over Mabel's room.'

'Don't worry, that's all sorted out.' Winnie spoke with just a hint of malice in her voice. Although it was lost on Alan, Dora recognised it for what it was. 'Mabel's staying with her friend Rene. You and Alan have your room to yourselves.'

Dora's expression was one of dismay and Alan asked, 'What's the matter, Dora? Aren't you happy to have me home? It's something I've been dreaming about ever since our honeymoon. I felt certain you'd feel the same.'

Gathering her wits together, Dora stood in the centre of the kitchen, breathing heavily before saying, 'It's not that, Alan, truly it isn't. It's just . . . well, it's been such a long time I feel we need to get to know each other all over again.'

'You're quite right, girl.' Winnie broke in on the conversation. 'And there's nowhere better for a married couple to get to know each other than in bed, so off you go – and don't hurry yourself getting up in the morning. You've put in enough hours at that hospital to please *them*; now you can go into work to suit yourself. Go on, the pair of you, off you go, upstairs . . .'

Alan's first night home with his wife was not the night of passion he had wanted it to be. True, she allowed him to make love to her during the course of the night, but it was not the abandonment of a woman who had been longing for her husband for nearly three years, and when he was about to make love to her for a second time he tasted salt tears on her cheeks and stopped.

He cuddled her close to him for the remainder of the night, but felt a tension in her body that was quite unlike the soft and loving pliancy he remembered from the brief week of married life they had shared on their honeymoon.

Alan felt he must somehow be to blame. That he was expecting too much from her, too quickly. He told himself it would be only a matter of time before things improved between them and she would once more be the warm and loving woman he had married.

However, as the days passed there was no improvement. Alan tried hard to be patient with her but their relationship became increasingly strained. He believed it would have been better had she not been working and they had more time together, doing things they both enjoyed. He suggested she should ask for a few days off work to be with him, but Dora insisted it would not be possible.

She made the excuse that many orderlies had already been laid off at the hospital, leaving the remaining staff to cope with the decision to repatriate all the remaining wounded soldiers, not to mention a huge quantity of stores and equipment that remained the property of the United States government and which needed to be checked and recorded.

As a result, Dora was working more and not fewer hours each day and she pleaded extreme tiredness as an excuse not to go out with Alan during the time she was at home. She used the same excuse for not responding to him when they were in bed.

Charlie and his friend returned to their unit four days after Alan came home, leaving Mabel free to return to her room once more, but she was reluctant to do so. She found Rene's home more to her taste than the house in Quilter Street, because she was allowed far more freedom there. As the youngest member of the Platt family, Mabel was constantly complaining that she was treated as a child and not as a young woman. It was an argument she had put forward again and again and the disagreement between mother and daughter came to a head two days after Charlie had left the house.

It was ten o'clock at night and Dora had just returned from work and gone straight upstairs to bed, pleading a severe headache.

Alan would have followed her, but Winnie asked him to go out to the public house in nearby Columbia Road to find Dora's father and bring him home. She knew from years of experience that if he had not come in by this time it meant that he had somehow acquired money and would be too drunk to make his way back to Quilter Street without assistance.

At the street door, Alan met Mabel coming into the

house and quietly warned her that her mother was angry with her for not returning home as soon as Charlie left. 'I suggest you go straight up to your room and stay quiet for a while. Once I get home with your dad, your mum will be so busy sorting him out she might forget to have a go at you.'

Alan had always got on well with Mabel and she smiled at him gratefully. 'Thanks, Alan. You go off and fetch the old man, then hurry back to Dora. I'll be all right.'

Ignoring Alan's warning, Mabel went straight through the house. When her mother would have taken her to task, Mabel declared she needed to go to the toilet, which was outside in the back yard. She would speak to her mother when she returned.

However, when Mabel came back into the house, Dora was in the kitchen, having heard Alan leave. She and Winnie were having a fierce argument. They broke it off when Mabel entered. Turning on her younger daughter, Winnie said, 'So you've finally decided to come home, have you? And just where do you think you've been? I sent word to Rene's house days ago that Charlie was going and you should come home.'

'I know.' There was no hint of an apology in Mabel's voice. 'I wasn't ready.'

'Not ready! You're eighteen . . . who are you to say you're not ready? Don't you think I've had enough trouble with your sister? I'm not having you play me up just when I look like getting her off me hands!'

'You'll have neither of us off your hands if Dora doesn't start bucking her ideas up,' Mabel retorted. 'It beats me why Alan stays around here with her playing him up the

112

way she is. She's the one you should be having a go at, not me.'

'I was putting Dora to rights when you came in – and having one in the family like her is quite enough. I can't take it from both of you.'

'Well, you won't have to take it from me for much longer.'

Dora spoke defiantly and Winnie said, 'Oh? Are you and Alan planning to move out to a place of your own? It's not before time. Can I start looking round for a paying lodger now?'

'Alan has nothing to do with it,' Dora said. 'When I go I'll be leaving him too. I'm going to America.'

Winnie and Mabel both looked at her in disbelief. Winnie was the first to recover.

'Going to America? What sort of nonsense are you talking now?'

'It's not nonsense. Delroy says if I go there he'll look after me.'

'What are you talking about?' Winnie asked scornfully. 'Doesn't this *Delroy* know you're a married woman?' She put all the contempt she could muster into the name of the unknown American.

'He says it's easy to get a divorce in America,' Dora declared.

'*Divorce*, is it? What's the matter with you, girl? Poor people like us don't get divorces. We marry for better or worse, and though it's usually for worse, we stay married. Divorce, indeed! Some men will tell a woman anything to get what they want, but no sensible woman will believe 'em, even though she might let him think she does.'

'What about Alan?' Mabel spoke for the first time since Dora had disclosed her plans to them. 'What's he going to do?'

'Much the same as he's done these last couple of years,' Dora replied callously. 'Get on with his life without me.'

'And when are you going to tell him?' Mabel persisted.

'She's not,' Winnie declared firmly. Glaring at Dora, she added, 'You'll remember who you're married to, my girl, and you're going to keep him sweet. If this Delroy really means what he's put into your head then he'll find some way of getting you to America. If he doesn't – and I'd bet my life on you never hearing from him again – if he doesn't, you'll still have someone here to keep you. So, whatever you may feel, do nothing to sacrifice your marriage. One day you'll be glad you've got Alan to fall back on.'

'That's not fair on Alan,' Mabel protested. 'He deserves better than that.'

'He might, and then again he might not,' Winnie replied. 'We don't know what he's been getting up to while he's been away, but at least he's come back to his wife – and she's going to stay with *him*.' She returned her attention to Dora once more. 'You think about what I've said to you, my girl, and think very, very carefully. I've bailed you out once, I'll not do it again. You get rid of Alan and find yourself in trouble, then you're out on the streets – and I've no doubt at all that's where you'll stay.'

17

For a while it seemed that Dora might be heeding her mother's advice. However, any hopes the family entertained that the marriage could be retrieved were dashed two days before Alan was due to report to the naval barracks in Chatham to be demobilised.

In an uncharacteristic moment of sensitivity and understanding, Winnie had suggested that Mabel spend the night at the home of her friend Rene, while she and Henry would pay a visit to his ageing mother who lived with a daughter in Romford. She let it be known they would not be returning to Quilter Street until well after midnight.

It was an opportunity for the young married couple to be on their own in the house for a few hours for the first time since Alan had come home on leave. Unfortunately, Winnie's efforts were wasted.

Dora did not return from the Edmonton hospital until 11.30 p.m., and Alan was not happy. There had been no opportunity for them to talk privately all the while he had been home. The only time they were alone was in bed, when Dora was invariably so tired that she wanted only to sleep. They had managed to recapture nothing of the magic of the week that had followed their wedding.

Pointing this out to Dora, Alan suggested she should take the next day off work, so they might at least go out somewhere on their own and talk of their future together.

When Dora demurred, saying she could not be spared from her work at the hospital, Alan said he would go there and explain the situation to the matron and plead for Dora to be given the day off.

Rounding on him fiercely, Dora accused him of behaving like a husband from the Victorian era. 'I'm doing something worthwhile,' she said. 'Just as important as anything you did during the war, and I'm not having you tell me what I *ought* to be doing. Your war might have ended, but the men I'm helping are still suffering. They deserve all that can be done for 'em.'

'I probably realise that more than most,' Alan said patiently, 'but I don't think it's asking too much to have you to myself for just one day – one day in almost three years. Surely you must feel the same?'

'I feel nothing of the sort,' Dora snapped. 'All I feel is that you've returned home after leaving me to cope with things on my own and now expect me to jump whenever you want something.'

It was such an unfair remark that Alan had to protest, but this served only to make Dora angrier. 'I'm right – and I don't intend to put up with any of it. When we were going out together I was young and had little knowledge of life. I'm older and wiser now and I think getting married was a mistake . . . No, I *know* it was a mistake. I've changed,

116

Alan, and so have you. You're not the man I knew then, and I'm certainly not the wife you expect to be at your beck and call for twenty-four hours of the day. I've tried to make allowances for the time we've spent apart, but it makes no difference. We need to face up to the fact that we're neither of us the same as we were when we married. We're practically strangers. To put it bluntly, I don't love you any more. Knowing what I know now I'm not at all certain I ever did. I certainly can't face the thought of a future living with you for ever when you leave the Navy.'

Utterly dismayed by her outburst, Alan said, 'You don't mean that, Dora. We've been apart for a long time, but so have millions of other couples. We'll sort things out when we're together all the time . . .'

'No!' Dora brought his pleas to a halt. She was more assured now she had brought matters into the open. 'I've told you, I don't love you. What more is there to say?'

'But . . . we've lived as a married couple since I came home . . . we've made love.'

'That was something you wanted to do – I didn't. But the time for talking is over. I want you to move out of the house . . . tonight! If you don't, I will.'

'I don't believe this, Dora. Lots of other couples are facing the same problems. We'll be able to sort it out . . .'

'You're not listening to me, are you?' Dora's anger flared up once again. 'I've said it's *over*. Our marriage is at an end. I don't want anything more to do with you. Now, are you going, or shall I?'

'What about your mum? What is she going to say?' Alan was clutching at straws and he was aware of it. 'Let's speak to her before we do anything we might regret.'

'What she has to say will change nothing. If she feels very strongly about it I'll leave her house and go off on my own. I probably ought to have done it before this.'

Recognising Alan's very real distress, Dora felt a prick of conscience and relented – but only a little. 'Perhaps I'm being unrealistic by expecting you to go out into the night with nowhere to stay, but I don't want to see you again, Alan. I shall spend the night in Mabel's room – and the door will be locked behind me. You can stay in our room – for tonight. I shall get up in the morning and go straight out to work. If you're still here when I come home I shall go out again and stay somewhere else. That's all I have to say.'

With that, Dora turned and hurried from the room. Alan started after her, but came to a halt before he even reached the door. He realised that pleading with her would be of no avail and would only add to the contempt which she so obviously felt for him.

He sat down in the kitchen and tried to gather his thoughts. Half an hour later he went upstairs to the bedroom he had shared with Dora and gathered all his belongings together. Leaving the house, he shouldered his kitbag and set off down the street. He would go to Victoria station and catch the first available train to Chatham. He was officially still on leave, but they would accommodate him there.

Upstairs, in Mabel's bedroom, Dora heard the sound of the front door closing and peered from behind the curtain to see Alan walking away from the house along the gaslit street. She felt a brief twinge of guilt, but it passed quickly. Leaving her sister's bedroom, she went downstairs to make herself a cup of tea.

118

Winnie and Henry returned to Quilter Street in the early hours of the morning and found Dora seated in the kitchen, a cup of tea on the table before her. She was pale-faced but calm.

'Where's Alan? In bed?'

Winnie put the question to her daughter while Henry went off to find a quart of ale he had hidden in the cupboard under the stairs. He had complained all the way home because his sister kept no alcoholic drink in her house and he had been offered nothing more than tea during his visit.

'Alan's gone,' was Dora's short reply.

'Gone? Gone where?' Winnie demanded.

'I dunno – to wherever sailors go when they return from leave, I suppose.'

'But he's not due back yet.' Winnie looked at Dora suspiciously. 'What's been going on between the two of you?'

'I told him the marriage is over and that I don't want to see him again,' Dora said, matter-of-factly.

'You said *what*? Are you absolutely stupid, girl? Alan might not be the greatest prize a girl could have, but he thinks the world of you – and he married you, didn't he? He's your insurance for the future.'

'He wouldn't be for very long . . . Oh, you might as well know now as later. I'm pregnant. I knew it before Alan came home.'

Winnie looked at her daughter in angry disbelief. 'How long gone are you?'

'Two months,' Dora replied flatly.

'I don't need to ask about its father; he'll be one of your precious Americans. Where is *he* now?'

'He's gone back to America – and before you ask, he doesn't know about the baby yet. When he does, he'll send for me to go there so he can look after me. That's what he wanted to do anyway.'

Hands on hips, Winnie stood in the centre of the kitchen, looking down at her daughter in disbelief. 'I can't believe I brought up a girl to be so stupid. Thousands of miles separate you from the bloke who's got you pregnant and if I know anything about men it's likely to stay that way. You need someone here – and Alan is that someone. All right, so you're two months pregnant and Alan's only been home a week. We could have got over that easy enough, but what's going to happen when the baby's real father decides he's not going to do the right thing by you? What do you do then? I told you once before that you'll not stay here expecting me to take care of you. There's an old saying that a bird in the hand is worth two in the bush. You're going to have cause to remember that, my girl!'

18

Although he was still officially on leave, Alan felt he should report to his divisional office to let them know he had returned to barracks. His hope was that he might be allowed to begin his demobilisation routine right away. Much to his surprise, he was told he was required to report to the drafting office, from which men were given postings outside the barracks.

Explaining that he was due to leave the Royal Navy, Alan suggested there must be some mistake. The clerk in the divisional office merely shrugged, saying, 'There might very well be a mistake, mate, but I've got your name on a list here and written alongside it is "To report to drafting office immediately upon return". That's what it says, so I suggest you go along there and find out what it's all about.'

Still convinced there had been an error, Alan made his way to the drafting office, which was situated in the vast drill hall where occupants of the barracks would be assembled on special occasions.

When he reported to the petty officer on duty, Alan was

more convinced than ever that he should not be here. Thumbing through the huge ledger on the desk in front of him, the petty officer said, 'Leading Telegraphist Carter? No, I can't find anything here. You've been on leave, you say? When did you come back?'

'I arrived back overnight . . . but I'm not actually due back until the day after tomorrow.'

Exhaling his breath in a resigned sigh, the petty officer turned a couple of ledger pages and ran his finger down the list of names. It came to a sudden halt and the petty officer looked up at Alan with an interest that had been lacking before. 'Yes, I've got you now. You're to report to a Lieutenant Ferris over at the officers' mess, right away.'

More mystified than ever, Alan made his way to the tall, red-brick accommodation block which housed naval officers, wondering whether 'Lieutenant Ferris' might be Donald Ferris, the midshipman with whom he had served on HMS *Viper*, and who had been so helpful by introducing his writing to his publisher father. If it was, it meant he had gained rapid promotion, something that was in itself unusual in the Royal Navy.

It *was* the same Donald Ferris, and his rapid rise in rank was explained by the fact that he was, in fact, an acting lieutenant. After asking about Alan's writing successes and saying how much he had enjoyed the work that had been published, he said, 'No doubt you are wondering why you have been told to report to me?'

Alan confessed that he was, adding that with demobilisation imminent he did not feel there would be time for him to undertake any new task, no matter how minor it might be.

'That's what I wanted to talk to you about, Sparks. I know you have been away from home for a long time, and signed on to serve only as long as hostilities with Germany lasted, but I was hoping I might be able to persuade you to stay on in the Navy for a while longer, probably no more than a few months. During that time you would be under my direct command. Of course, I have no idea of your present circumstances, or what you might have planned in civilian life, but as an incentive to remain in the Navy I could offer you promotion to petty officer for the final six months of your service.'

Had everything been well with his marriage, Alan told himself, he would never have considered subjecting himself to the strict discipline of the Royal Navy for any longer than was necessary, but he felt he owed a debt to Donald Ferris, and without a wife to consider it did not particularly matter when he parted company with the service. Besides, as a petty officer, he would become a member of the petty officers' mess both on board ship and in barracks, enjoying far more privileges than in his present rank.

'What would we be doing?' he asked.

Delighted that Alan had not immediately turned down his offer, Donald Ferris said, 'I can't give you any details immediately, except to say that it is important and I think you will find it quite interesting.'

Alan realised that common sense ought to tell him he would not be offered promotion without having to earn it. He was also aware of the lower-deck dictum which ruled out volunteering for anything. If he was honest with himself, what he wanted to do was write and one day become sufficiently proficient to earn a living by writing. Without a wife to support it would not matter if he occasionally went hungry, and with a petty officer's pay for a few months he would be buying extra time to try to achieve his ambition.

'Should you decide to accept, I am afraid you will not be able to tell your wife anything of what you will be doing,' Ferris said.

'That will be no problem,' Alan said ruefully. 'My marriage is at an end. To be perfectly honest, it never really even began.'

'So that's why you returned early from your leave! I am sorry about that, Sparks. Very sorry.' Ferris's expression belied the words, and he continued, 'But it might make it easier for you to reach a decision – and I really would like to have you with me. I am being entrusted with something that is somewhat unusual and I want a team with me I can trust, and who know what they're doing.'

In spite of his misgivings, Alan was intrigued. 'All right, sir, I'll sign on and come with you.'

'Splendid! You've made my day, Sparks. Now you have agreed I can go back to the admiral and tell him my team is complete. We can make a start immediately.'

The British cruiser HMS *Clarissa* arrived at Copenhagen in the second week of February, 1919. There were a great many comings and goings between the cruiser and other ships of the British Navy anchored here. Officials from the British embassy also visited HMS *Clarissa*, and a considerable quantity of stores were loaded on board. Then, shortly before the cruiser sailed, a number of Royal Marines came on board, gathered from other ships stationed in the Baltic Sea and the Gulf of Finland.

They made HMS *Clarissa* uncomfortably overcrowded. In addition to its full war-time complement, the British cruiser already carried the forty-five additional sailors who were the responsibility of Lieutenant Donald Ferris.

The sailor passengers, like Alan, were volunteers, but none knew any more than he did what their future duties were likely to be, although Alan had quickly realised that every man on board had spent at least part of his service life serving on torpedo boats.

Not until HMS *Clarissa* sailed from Copenhagen was Lieutenant Ferris's team told why they were on board the cruiser, and where they were going.

Information had been received that the prototype of a revolutionary new torpedo boat had not been declared by the Germans when they signed the Armistice. Instead, it had been secreted in a small harbour on the German Baltic coast, not far from the major port of Rostock.

Lieutenant Ferris explained that the situation in the Baltic and the adjacent Gulf of Finland was both confusing and volatile. Although an armistice had been signed between the warring nations, the terms of a treaty which would bring a lasting peace had yet to be agreed. Meanwhile, in this part of the world German influence was still strong and that country had considerable support among the Baltic states. There were also moves in some of the states to gain full independence for themselves.

To add to this confusion, bitter fighting was taking place in Russia between the Bolsheviks, who had executed the Tsar and his family, and supporters of the old regime.

The British supported the old regime – the 'White' Russians – and the Royal Navy had been deployed to keep the Bolshevik navy contained within its ports. However, as Britain was not officially at war with the Bolsheviks, the role of Admiral Cowan, commander of the British Baltic fleet, was almost impossible. It was made even more difficult by deliberate German provocation.

There were fears in the Admiralty that the advanced German torpedo boat might be put into the hands of those ill-disposed to Britain. If so, it was capable of creating havoc among the British Baltic fleet.

The marines on board the *Clarissa* were to land and secure the small harbour where the German boat was hidden. As soon as this was done, Lieutenant Ferris and his crew were to commandeer the boat and take it to Copenhagen for the Admiral to decide its future.

The operation succeeded without a shot being fired. The cruiser reached the area before dawn and lay off the coast, its guns trained on the harbour as the boats carrying the marines went ashore. Following their instructions to the letter, they took possession of the jetty alongside which the torpedo boat was moored. Minutes later, Lieutenant Ferris and his crew followed.

The surprise was complete. When dawn broke, news of what had happened was carried to a tiny garrison of German troops billeted on the edge of the village. They turned out hastily but, faced with an overwhelming number of Royal Marines, obediently laid down their arms and spent an hour in cold discomfort seated on the jetty while the British sailors carried out a cursory survey of the torpedo boat before starting the engines and putting to sea, escorted by the marines. A small tanker had accompanied the cruiser and it refuelled the torpedo boat before the tiny convoy set sail for the harbour of the Danish capital, no more than five hours distant.

The torpedo boat's radio, like the rest of the equipment on board, was superb and Alan was in touch with the cruiser's wireless office almost immediately. The engines too were impressive and the engine-room sailors found they needed to keep them throttled back to less than half-speed to allow the *Clarissa* to stay with them.

When the Admiral came on board the torpedo boat at Copenhagen, the crew expected it to be no more than a brief, congratulatory visit before they took the boat back to a British dockyard to allow naval engineers to assess its capabilities. Ordered to take the senior naval officer out into the Baltic Sea to test the speed and handling of the torpedo boat, they were delighted to put the craft through its paces for him.

The crew were less pleased when, back in harbour once more, the Admiral announced that he was so impressed with the torpedo boat's performance he intended to keep it in the Baltic for a month or two before sending it to Britain. He believed that with its shallow draught and impressive turn of speed, he would be able to find a use for it when the ice broke up in the shallow waters of the Gulf of Finland, at the eastern end of the Baltic.

However, Alan did not mind. He had been given two telegraphists to man the wireless office and was quite happy to remain on the torpedo boat until it was sent back to Britain.

19

When the need for Vicky to drive an ambulance as a member of the First Aid Nursing Yeomanry came to an end, she handed her ambulance back to the Red Cross with only a modicum of regret. She had served the organisation with both dedication and considerable courage, but was now happy to return full-time to her first love in life. Painting.

Her output of pictures increased dramatically, and when the outstanding Newlyn artist Stanhope Forbes invited her to assist him at the school of painting he had founded in the small town many years before, she felt her career had taken a significant step forward.

She accepted the invitation and, enjoying teaching her art to others, realised that her own techniques were being greatly improved by the advice given to her by the head of the school, who was recognised as the doyen of the Newlyn painters.

With the ending of the war, the colony of artists centred upon Newlyn and the nearby town of St Ives greatly increased in size. Many had been in Cornwall before serving in the forces during the war. Others had been drawn to the area by its increasing reputation within the painting world. Experts in other fields of the arts also found their way here, potters, copper-workers, sculptors and silk-workers among them.

John Appleton, an innovative and talented designer in this latter field, had been in Newlyn before the war, but was called up for the army and spent the war years serving in the Middle East. When he returned, his marriage had broken up and he decided to teach his art to others, at the same time building up a market for his own completed work.

Appleton hailed from the same part of the country as Vicky and she came to know him quite well. Among his pupils was Prue Penhaligon, sister of the skipper of the trawler *Lady Tamsin*. Freed from the restraint imposed upon her and other young women by the wartime employment regulations, Prue had taken a job in the Appleton silk works, where raw silk was dyed and printed to the owners' own designs. She became particularly friendly with Appleton and it was not long before they were close enough for whispers to begin circulating in the close-knit fishing community.

The rumours of their relationship reached the ears of Emily and George Penhaligon through the medium of a strongly disapproving Methodist minister. As a result, Prue was told by her parents that she must give up working for John Appleton. When she protested that she had done nothing wrong, Emily told her daughter that there was seldom smoke without fire. She could either obey her

129

parents' wishes, or move out of the Penhaligon house and accept the fact that they would have nothing more to do with her. Tom Penhaligon took his sister's side in the argument, but his mother, in particular, felt so strongly about her becoming involved with a married man that he did not pursue the matter as forcefully as Prue would have liked.

Vicky was alone in her studio one evening when there was a timid knocking on the door. Had she not been watering a potted plant on the table just inside the door it is doubtful whether she would have heard the knock. When Vicky opened the door she found Prue Penhaligon standing uncertainly outside.

Startled that her knock had resulted in such a prompt response, the fisherman's sister was momentarily lost for words.

'Do you wish to speak to me?' Vicky was the first to break the silence between them.

'Yes . . . I'm sorry, I wasn't certain you'd be in.'

Recognising the younger girl's nervousness, Vicky said, 'Well, as you can see, I am, so why don't you come inside and tell me what it is you want?'

Prue entered the studio timidly, almost as though she felt she had no right to be there. One of the first paintings to catch her eye was that of HMS *Viper* entering Newlyn harbour with the *Lady Tamsin* secured alongside.

'That's Tom's boat,' she said excitedly, her nervousness temporarily forgotten. 'Does he know you've painted it?'

'I don't know,' Vicky replied, 'but Alan does and he might have told him. I gave the picture to him. It's only here until he comes back to collect it.'

'You're a wonderful artist,' Prue said admiringly. 'John says that those who know are saying you're one of the best painters Newlyn has ever seen.'

Aware that she was referring to John Appleton, Vicky said, 'That is very kind of John, but I don't think you have come here just to tell me what a wonderful artist I am!'

The animation left Prue's face immediately. 'No . . . I've come to ask your advice – and for any help you can give me.' Plaintively, she said, 'You know John and what a good man he is. A decent and honest man.'

'I would not argue with that,' Vicky agreed. 'I don't think anyone who knows him could, but what are you trying to say, Prue – and how can I help you?'

Unhappily, Prue said, 'You know all about John being a married man and his wife going off and leaving him while he was away at war? Yes, of course you do. Well, there's been gossip about John and me and Ma got to hear of it. We've had a big row and she's forbidden me to go back to work with him.'

'Are you upset because you've been told not to see John, or because you enjoy the work you're doing with him?' Vicky asked.

'Both,' Prue admitted. 'But I'd be most unhappy if I wasn't able to see him again.'

Vicky realised that the true answer to her question had been contained in the other girl's reply, even though Prue felt unable to admit outright that she was in love with John Appleton.

'How old are you, Prue?'

'Just turned twenty.'

'Well, it won't be long before you are old enough to go

your own way, regardless of whether or not your parents approve.'

'A lot could happen in that time,' Prue pointed out. 'John will be a free man soon, when his divorce comes through, and if I'm not seeing him . . .' Unhappily, she added, 'Besides, I don't want to cause a breach in the family. Ma and Pa are good people too and we've always been very close. It's just that . . . well, they are old-fashioned. They don't realise that times have changed and that if marriages don't work out then people don't have to stay tied to each other no matter what happens.'

'Why are you telling me all this, Prue? What makes you think I can help you?' Vicky was genuinely puzzled. 'I have never said more than a passing hello to either of your parents, so they are not likely to listen to me.'

'No . . . I suppose you're right, really. It's just . . . well, you know John, you know what he's really like . . . and you were a suffragette, fighting against the unjust prejudices that older people have. Ma, in particular, respects you for all the things you did when you were driving your ambulance. She says you're an asset to the village and hopes you'll stay on . . .'

Vicky might have told Prue that she had no intention of becoming involved in the affairs of the Penhaligon family. However, on her bedside table was the latest letter she had received from Alan. It told of the problems of his marriage to Dora, his uncertainty about everything, and his decision to remain in the Navy for a few more months, during which time he said he intended to arrive at a decision about the future.

Vicky had read and re-read the letter when she went

to bed the previous evening. Afterwards, she had lain awake in the darkness, composing a reply in her mind. A reply that had faded into fantasy in the cold light of dawn.

'All right, Prue. I can't promise I will be able to change anything, but I will try to think of something.'

20

It was more than a week after Prue's visit to the studio when Vicky called at the Penhaligon cottage. Guessing that the decisions in the household were made by Emily, Vicky chose a fine day. She trusted the two men of the family would be at sea fishing in the *Lady Tamsin*, and knew that Prue was helping out at the home of one of her elderly relatives.

As she had hoped, Emily was alone in the house, but when she opened the door to Vicky's knock she did not immediately recognise the caller.

'Hello, Mrs Penhaligon.' Vicky greeted her with a smile. 'I am Vicky Hazelton. Is Prue at home?'

'No, she's gone to Mousehole for the day, doing a bit of tidying for an elderly aunt of mine. I'm not expecting her back until shortly before dark. I'm sorry I didn't recognise you right away – it's you not being in uniform! I don't think I've ever seen you when you weren't wearing it . . . but, there, with the war over, uniforms will be a rare sight in these parts now.'

'That's right, Mrs Penhaligon. The war came along and changed everything. It's over now, but there are a great many things that will never go back to being the way they were.'

'More's the pity, I say,' Emily remarked. 'I sometimes despair of what I see going on around me. I'm told I'm old-fashioned, and I suppose I am – but where are my manners? Don't stand here on the doorstep, come in and have a cup of tea and a piece of cake. It was fresh out of the oven this morning.'

Vicky followed the older woman through the house to the kitchen, where the warm aroma of baking still hung on the air. As Emily pushed the kettle from the hob to the hot coals, she said, 'Was there something special you wanted to see our Prue about?'

'Yes,' Vicky replied. 'I have something here for her – it's from John Appleton.'

Emily stiffened perceptibly and, without turning round, said, tight-lipped, 'I don't think we want anything in this house from that man.'

'It's not exactly *from* John,' Vicky said, choosing to ignore Emily's overt disapproval. 'It's money for a few of the things she designed and made while she was at John's craft workshop. He had a customer in who was very taken with Prue's work. I think he is from Liberty's, the famous shop in London. He paid forty pounds for what she had there for sale and said he would take everything she made in the future.'

Emily looked at Vicky in astonishment. 'Someone paid forty pounds for things our Prue made? Why, that's nigh on a year's wages for a man – and more than our

Tom makes most months, even though he has a crew to pay!'

Vicky had been aware that Emily would be impressed by the sum of money paid for her daughter's work. It was not that Emily was greedy, but she was the wife and mother of fishermen. Her life, like theirs, had been hard and, more often than not, precarious. Every pound was hard-earned. For a *girl* to earn forty pounds for making patterns on silk was beyond her comprehension.

'Your Prue is a very clever girl,' Vicky said. 'And John Appleton is an excellent teacher, with a very good business sense. He's going to go far.'

The tight expression of disapproval returned to Emily's face. 'That's as may be, but he'll do it without our Prue to help him. I'm not having her pointed out and talked about whenever she goes out in the village.'

Pretending to be surprised, Vicky said, 'Why should anyone do that, Mrs Penhaligon? I have not heard anyone say a bad word about her, and John is very fond of her.'

'He has no right to be fond of her – or of any other girl,' Emily snapped. 'He's a married man and should keep his fondness for his wife.'

'I don't think his wife wants that – or anything else – from him,' Vicky said. 'Besides, she won't be his wife for very much longer. John is getting a divorce from her. You know that during the war she ran off to Scotland with one of the officers from the Royal Naval Air Service base, here in Newlyn, while John was away in the army?'

'No, I didn't know,' Emily admitted, 'but that doesn't make any difference. He married his wife, and marriage isn't just for as long as it suits either of you. It's for life.'

'I am inclined to agree with you, Mrs Penhaligon,' Vicky said. 'We are both probably a little old-fashioned in that respect, although I never thought I would hear myself say so – certainly not where marriage is concerned.' Taking the cup of tea which Emily had made and poured while they were talking, Vicky continued, 'I was a suffragette before the war, fighting for the rights of women. It's still something I feel very strongly about, but it doesn't mean I am anti-men, and I know that during the war a great many very nice men have been let down by the women who married them and made the same vows as their husbands. John is one of them – and I believe the Newlyn man who recently threw himself over a cliff when he returned from the war and found his wife had been unfaithful was another. I admire the way John Appleton took the news. He was hurt very badly, but after a while he pulled himself together and built up a business that is going from strength to strength . . . Oh, that reminds me. John sent these silk scarves that Prue designed and made. He is very, very sorry to be losing her because he said she showed such great promise that she would probably have made both of them quite rich. Never mind; he'll no doubt find someone else to work with him. There are designers all over the country who would jump at an opportunity to work for John Appleton.'

Emily was taking in all that Vicky was saying, at the same time opening out the gaily coloured silk squares. Looking at them in amazement, she said, 'Did our Prue make these?'

'She not only made them, but designed them too,' Vicky replied. 'As I said, she is a very clever girl.'

137

'But . . . where did she learn to do such things?'

'John taught her the skills,' Vicky said, 'but most of the ideas are her own. She has a very real talent and is an artist in her chosen field. I put my ideas on canvas; she makes beautiful things of silk.'

Emily was silent for a very long time. Then she said, sorrowfully, 'If only he wasn't a married man . . .'

'Mrs Penhaligon, we've both admitted we are old-fashioned about such things – and so, unfortunately, are many older people who still think that things should be the way they were in Victorian days. The trouble is, they are not, and never will be again. The world is moving forward and a great many people are going to be left behind. John Appleton is not one of those – and I am glad. The reason his marriage failed is not his fault. He was away fighting a war and could do nothing about it. I, for one, think he has suffered enough. He deserves to find some happiness again. I believe Prue thinks so too – and she is a very sensible young woman.'

Vicky felt she had made her point. Not wishing to pursue the issue of the relationship between Prue and John Appleton too far, she said, 'Oh, by the way, I had a letter from Alan Carter this morning. He said that if I were to see you or any of your family, I should give you his regards.'

Speaking sharply once more, Emily said, 'You've heard from Alan? What's he doing writing to you? He's a married man too.'

'I am afraid his marriage is another casualty of the war,' Vicky said sorrowfully. 'I thought things might be going wrong when he came to stay at Newlyn because his wife

138

said she couldn't see him when he had leave. While he was here he met a friend of mine who gave him the names of some publishers – did you know that Alan is a very promising writer? No? Well, he is, and as he had no address for his wife at that time I said he could use mine and I would forward his letters on to wherever he happened to be until he was able to give the senders a new address.'

'You say that Alan's marriage has broken up too?' Shocked, Emily spread her hands wide in a gesture of despair. 'Whatever is the world coming to? He is such a nice young man.'

'Yes, and so too is John Appleton,' Vicky said. 'He's also an honest and caring man. You would like him if you got to know him, I'm certain of that.'

Vicky left the Penhaligon cottage with high hopes that she might have sown sufficient seed for Emily to relax her decision and allow Prue to go back to work with John Appleton. She sincerely hoped so. She liked them both.

Opening the door to her studio, Vicky realised that someone was inside. For a moment she felt unreasonably excited, thinking it might be Alan. Instead, it was Cecil. He had let himself in through the unlocked door and was now sprawled in her armchair, puffing contentedly at his pipe.

Cecil was always a welcome visitor and Vicky greeted him with real pleasure, saying, 'Have you come to take me out for a drink at the snug, Cecil, or is it just because you feel like company?'

'Neither,' Cecil replied. 'I come bearing exciting news – and to inform you that you have extra work to carry out on one of your favourite paintings.'

Vicky frowned. 'You are talking in riddles, Cecil. What news, which painting – and what work?'

Rising from the armchair, Cecil crossed to the alcove and took down Alan's portrait. 'This one, darling, the portrait of your favourite man. My publisher, as you know, is aware I am a friend of Alan and he has sent me a copy of the latest edition of the *London Gazette*. It seems that Alan has been playing the hero once again. He has just been awarded a Conspicuous Gallantry Medal – oh yes, and has also been Mentioned in Dispatches.'

'But . . . what for? The war is over now. How can he have been awarded medals? Are we fighting anyone anywhere?' Vicky was bewildered.

'Quite a few people, I would think. We usually are. At the moment the Bolsheviks seem to be attracting a great deal of our attention, so I should imagine it has something to do with them, although the *London Gazette* is unusually short on detail. It merely says that he and another sailor have both been awarded medals in the same action, without giving any further details. But, whatever the circumstances, you'll need to get painting again, old thing, and bring his medal ribbons up to date. Unless you prefer to wait, just in case he picks up any more?'

21

Alan received his Mention in Dispatches when the ex-German torpedo boat on which he was serving under Lieutenant Donald Ferris made a reconnaissance sortie in a river estuary and came under heavy fire from a Bolshevik artillery battery. Alan called up assistance from a heavy cruiser providing back-up beyond the estuary and continued relaying details of their fall of shot until the Bolshevik battery was destroyed.

This incident excepted, the crew of the torpedo boat found little to do during the first month they spent in the Baltic Sea, but as the ice began to break up their patrol area gradually moved closer to Bolshevik strongholds in and around the Gulf of Finland, where the Russian fleet had a heavily defended base at Kronstadt, on Kotlin Island, which guarded the approaches to Petrograd, Russia's capital city until the recent Communist revolution.

Then, when there was little ice left, the torpedo boat was ordered to return to Copenhagen for 'special instructions'.

When the boat arrived in Copenhagen harbour Lieutenant Ferris went ashore and remained there for some hours. On the bridge, Alan was examining the Danish capital through the telescope kept there when he saw the torpedo boat's launch returning. Focusing on the small boat, Alan saw that the launch contained Lieutenant Ferris, accompanied by a civilian.

At first, Alan thought the civilian might be the British ambassador to Copenhagen, paying a courtesy visit to the captured German vessel, but as the launch drew nearer he realised that he was too young to hold such an important post in the diplomatic service.

Alan warned the petty officer on duty of the approach of the boat, and when it came alongside Lieutenant Ferris was piped on board. After no more than a perfunctory salute, he hurried the civilian off in the direction of the commanding officer's cabin as a number of trunks and cases were lifted on board. Half an hour later the boatswain's mate toured the torpedo boat, shouting instructions for the crew to muster and prepare to get under way.

When the boat weighed anchor, rumours were rife below decks about the reason for their sudden departure, but it was more than an hour before the vessel hove to and the crew were mustered on deck to be told why they had set sail from Copenhagen at such short notice.

Ignoring a brief flurry of snow, and flanked by the sub-lieutenant who was his second-in-command and the civilian who had come on board, Donald Ferris gave the sailors their first indication of what they would be doing.

Introducing the civilian to the surprised crew as

Commander Marcus Buchanan, 'a Foreign Office official', the lieutenant began his address by apologising to the assembled men for the secrecy that surrounded their mission. He said they had been chosen to carry out a clandestine operation of a most sensitive nature, using the ex-German craft.

There was some muttering among the assembled British sailors and Donald Ferris said, apologetically, 'I regret that I cannot give you full details at the moment, but I would like you to hear what Commander Buchanan has to say.'

Stepping forward, Marcus Buchanan looked round the semicircle of men, his glance missing none of them. Then, speaking quietly, he said, 'I am able to go into little more detail than Lieutenant Ferris about the specific task we are to carry out, except to say we will not be undertaking a belligerent role. That means we should not be involved in any fighting – unless, of course, we ourselves are attacked. If we are, we will defend ourselves – and those who might be on board with us – to the last man. I realise this is frustratingly vague, but if I tell you that His Majesty King George wishes to be advised immediately of the outcome of our operation, it will give you some idea of its importance. Now, having told you very little – and being unable to enlighten you to any greater extent at this stage – does anyone have a question that I might possibly be able to answer?'

'Yes, sir.' The voice was that of the chief petty officer who was the coxswain of the torpedo boat. 'Will you be coming with us when we do – whatever it is we'll be doing?'

'Not exactly,' Buchanan replied ambiguously, 'but I won't be far away and will do my best to ensure you all

143

stay out of trouble.' Grinning, he added, 'Does that fill you with confidence, Chief?'

Answering in the same vein, the chief petty officer said, 'I'll reserve judgement on that until it's all over, sir, but I think you've convinced us that we will be engaged on a very important mission. You can be sure you have our full support.'

'Thank you, Chief. I never doubted that for one moment.' Transferring his attention to Lieutenant Ferris, he said, 'I think that is all from me for the moment, Lieutenant.'

'Thank you, sir.' Ferris turned to the assembled sailors. 'Thank you for your attention. I will tell you more when the time is right to do so. In the meantime, try not to speculate on what is likely to happen. You will all be given full details in due course.'

As the crew of the torpedo boat turned away, Lieutenant Ferris called to Alan. 'Will you stay here for a few minutes, Sparks? Commander Buchanan would like to have a chat to you.'

Wondering why he should have been singled out for special attention, Alan returned to where the civilian stood with the two officers. After shaking hands, Buchanan said, 'I see you have a DSM, Sparks. Where did you earn that?'

'On the *Viper*, sir, a torpedo boat – at the same time Lieutenant Ferris was awarded his DSO.'

'Ah! That explains why he speaks so highly of you. Good! On an operation such as the one we will be engaged on it helps if two of the most important participants know each other well enough to anticipate how the other is likely to react in difficult circumstances.'

Startled to learn that he was to be an 'important participant', Alan wondered what was coming next.

'I asked to meet you today so that you and I could get to know each other . . . Alan is your name, I believe? Well, Alan, you and I are to be principal players in what will take place when we go into action, so I am going to tell you more about what is planned – but first I need your word that you will not breathe a word to anyone.'

'You have that, sir,' Alan said, aware that he could hardly say anything else.

Buchanan seemed satisfied and said, 'Before I go any further, there is something I must ask you. If you were told to put together a wireless receiver and transmitter, of the type used in an aeroplane, do you think you could do it?'

The question took Alan by surprise. 'It's not something I've done, sir, but when I was in Newlyn recently I visited the Royal Naval Air Service base there and was shown over one of their seaplanes. I was particularly interested in the wireless it carried and had it explained to me. I think I could put one together if I needed to.'

'Splendid!' Commander Buchanan beamed. 'Hopefully there will be someone to take you through the details before we arrive at our destination, but when the need arises you'll be on your own. It's important – *very* important – that it works.'

'Are you telling me I'm going to need to fit a wireless set in an aeroplane?' Alan was incredulous.

'No, Alan,' Buchanan reassured him, 'but we'll be using a wireless set of the type used in an aeroplane. It will be delivered to us before we reach our destination. The present plan is that we take it on board and later take it ashore on what we hope will prove to be a quiet spot on the Russian coast. We will there set up a wireless telegraphy station to keep in constant contact with the torpedo boat. You will be the operator.'

'That will need a great many batteries,' Alan said. 'Are we going to be able to keep them charged?'

'That is a very good question,' Buchanan said. 'The short answer is . . . probably not, so we will need to think about ways of conserving them, although I am hoping you will not need to maintain the station for more than a couple of days.'

Suddenly professional, Alan said, 'You've told me what's expected of me, but if whatever we will be doing is to succeed, I think you should tell me everything, sir. What exactly are we going to do, and what is your part in this?'

Buchanan was silent for a few moments. Then he looked at Lieutenant Ferris, who gave him an almost imperceptible nod.

'Very well, Alan. You certainly have a right to know. We will be attempting to rescue members of the Romanov clan whose lives are threatened by the Bolsheviks who murdered the Tsar and his family – to whom the Romanovs are related. They are also distantly related to His Majesty King George. At present the British Navy has no boats in the Baltic Sea capable of operating in the shallow waters off the Russian coast where we hope to find the Romanovs. Finding the German torpedo boat, with its high speed and shallow draught, was a godsend for us. We hope it will play a significant part in the rescue. For myself . . . well, I had a Russian mother and worked in the Russian embassy in Petrograd for some years. I know the area and speak the language, so I will go ashore and, hopefully, find out where the Romanovs are being kept. I hope to receive this information from a family loyal to the late Tsar. I also hope they will permit us to set up a wireless telegraphy station in their home. When the Romanovs are located and ready to be taken on board the torpedo boat, you will inform Lieutenant Ferris when and where by means of a code I shall give you.' Commander Buchanan shrugged nonchalantly. 'Basically, that is all there is to it.' Grinning cheerfully at Alan, he added, 'If all goes well there should be absolutely nothing to worry about. If it doesn't . . . well, you'll be wearing a naval uniform and can expect to receive the consideration given to a prisoner of war.'

Alan was aware that Buchanan would not be wearing a uniform and could not expect the same consideration were *he* to be caught. At the same time, he did not fully share Buchanan's confidence in the success of the operation. It certainly sounded easy the way the other man told it, but Alan had a nasty suspicion that it was not going to be quite as simple an operation as he made it out to be.

22

A rendezvous was made with a seaplane the following day and, as it circled the torpedo boat, the launch went out to ensure that none of the winter ice floating on the surface of the sea was of a sufficient size to damage the frail aircraft's floats. The whole of the torpedo boat's crew was on deck to watch the seaplane make a safe landing and a spontaneous cheer went up as it taxied alongside the warship.

The wireless equipment needed for the clandestine operation was quickly taken on board, after which a Royal Naval Air Service mechanic spent almost two hours on the ship with Alan, teaching him how to put everything together. This done, the torpedo boat's launch once more cleared a passage through the floating ice and the seaplane took to the air again, quickly disappearing over the horizon.

On board the torpedo boat, Alan went over the process of assembling and testing the wireless equipment time and time again, taking care to conserve the batteries that would be essential to the proposed operation.

The next day, confirmation was received from the Foreign Office in London that the operation had been approved. Commander Buchanan called the crew together once more, but this time gave them full details of the mission they would be performing and of the parts to be played by Alan and himself.

There were many glances cast in Alan's direction as Buchanan spoke, and when he finished talking it was once again the coxswain who asked a question. This time it was about the role of the torpedo boat while the two men were ashore on Russian territory.

'You will remain close to the Russian coast,' Buchanan replied, 'but try to stay out of trouble – and that may not be as easy as it sounds. The ice is breaking up rapidly in the Gulf of Finland, which means we might have not only the Bolsheviks to contend with, but also the Germans. Under the terms of the Armistice they have been allowed to keep troops and ships stationed in those Baltic states which were under their control when hostilities came to an end. They have no love for us and will cause trouble if they can – but it is vital for the success of our mission that we provoke no one. If trouble seems imminent you will run and leave any fighting to ships under the command of Admiral Cowan. He will be close enough to come to your help if needed. Always bear in mind that the lives of myself, Petty Officer Carter, and members of the Romanov family will depend upon your actions.'

After his talk to the crew, Buchanan called Alan to the cabin he was sharing with Donald Ferris and the three went over the code they would use for their signals. It was a simple one-time code, which would change each day. In addition, copies of a map of the particular area of the coast where they would land had been marked with a grid. When it was time for the torpedo boat to send the launch to take them off, a coded message would be telegraphed to Lieutenant Ferris, giving only the grid reference and the time at which they required to be picked up.

Buchanan intended going ashore that night. It would be bitterly cold, but in this part of the world at this time of year the long hours of darkness would favour their planned operation. He would take a torch with him and the following night would signal to the torpedo boat, which would have returned to the scene. His signal would be a single letter, flashed in Morse code: Y for Alan to land, N to remain on board for another twenty-four hours – and H for help if things had gone wrong and Buchanan needed to be taken back on board

As the three men left Lieutenant Ferris's cabin, Buchanan said, 'Are you feeling nervous, Alan?'

'No,' Alan replied, 'I think terrified might be a better word.'

Buchanan looked at Alan sharply, then relaxed and patted him on the shoulder. 'That makes two of us, but just look forward to meeting Alyona Romanov. She is the most beautiful woman I have ever met. I am told her daughters take after her – and there are four of them. The knowledge that you have helped them to escape from certain death will live with you for ever.'

Commander Buchanan was rowed ashore in the darkness in a pinnace that had been put on board the torpedo boat especially for this operation. The area was probably remote enough for the motor launch to have been utilised, but sound would carry a great distance on such a still night and it would have been foolish to take even the slightest risk of being discovered.

Having landed him, the pinnace returned to the torpedo boat, which then crept away from the coast with muted engines, to patrol some distance from the coast until the following night.

Buchanan's mission was a perilous one. The whole area was under Bolshevik control and the revolutionaries were in the habit of executing anyone who aroused their suspicions and was unable to give satisfactory replies to their questions. Once ashore he would need to rely entirely upon his own initiative. His first task was to make contact with a retired married couple, Georgi and Yulia Zhukovsky, who had once been retainers in the court of the Tsar. They were known to have been intensely loyal to their late employer, but times had changed dramatically, and they might have changed with them. Even had they not, it was by no means certain they would be willing to take part in a mission to save other members of the royal family when it was so fraught with danger.

On board the torpedo boat, Alan resisted the temptation to check the wireless equipment all over again. Instead, he tried to get some sleep, knowing there would be little rest during the coming night. It was not easy. Quite apart from the everyday, routine noises of shipboard life, his mind was active, trying to anticipate everything that might possibly be encountered if – and when – he went ashore.

The next night the torpedo boat returned to the coast.

Coming as close inshore as possible, it dropped anchor opposite the spot where Buchanan had landed. The pinnace, loaded with wireless equipment, was slung outboard, ready to be lowered into the water as soon as a favourable signal was received from the shore.

Alan, dressed in warm clothing, ready to go ashore, kept a vigil on the bridge with Ferris, the midshipman and a signalman, all eager to be the first to spot Buchanan's signal. At 2.30 a.m., when Alan had come to the conclusion that there would be no message that night, the signalman said suddenly, 'Look! Over there, slightly to the right. Someone is signalling with a torch . . . it's a Y! He's saying it's all right to go ashore!'

The next few moments were hectic as the pinnace's crew lowered the boat and took their places at the oars. After a whispered 'Good luck!' from Donald Ferris, Alan took his place in the boat and was rowed ashore, heading for the still winking light.

When the boat grounded on a tiny shingle beach, Buchanan and another man were there to pull it further in. Gripping Alan's shoulder, the Englishman's voice whispered, 'Do you have everything?'

'It's all here and in good order,' Alan replied, in a voice as quiet as the other man's, 'but I was getting worried. I thought something might have happened to you.'

'I was worried too!' Buchanan replied. 'There had been no noticeable Bolshevik movement around here – until yesterday. A small group of about a dozen revolutionaries came to a village close to the Zhukovsky home and demanded a list of everyone who lives in the area, together with details of how long they have lived here and what

152

they do for a living. It frightened everyone – especially the Zhukovskys. They are fearful they might have been looking for them!'

Alarmed, Alan asked, 'So where are we going?'

'It's all right. The Zhukovskys' love of the Tsar and his family is greater than their fear of the Bolsheviks and I have told them I will take them out of Russia with the Romanovs if that's what they want when the time comes. But let's hurry and get everything off the boat. Georgi has a pony and a small cart, but we need to be hidden in the house before dawn. Not everyone in the area is anti-Bolshevik.'

The sailors from the torpedo boat helped to load the wireless equipment on the cart and then silently rowed away from the shore.

On the way to the Zhukovskys' home, Buchanan told Alan that the set-up there far exceeded anything he could have hoped for. When the revolution began in Russia, someone in the royal household with more foresight than most had arranged for a number of houses to be adapted as secure hideaways for the Tsar and his family. The Zhukovskys' home was one of these.

Unfortunately, the Tsar and his family were taken and brutally murdered before they could make use of any of them, but the attic of the house to which Buchanan was taking Alan had been fitted out as a self-contained flat, with access via a retractable ladder that could be lowered from a trapdoor hidden in the ceiling of a high built-in cupboard in one of the bedrooms.

'It's really very, very ingenious,' Buchanan declared, 'but we're going to need all our muscle to get the wireless equipment up there.'

The problem was solved by using a sheet and a rope and it proved easier than Buchanan had forecast. Once ensconced in the hideout, Alan realised it was a luxurious, if somewhat cramped, suite of rooms.

His first task was to set up the wireless in a corner of the sloping-ceilinged lounge, the aerial following the ridge of the roof. It was light outside by the time Alan had finished putting everything together and there were brief moments of concern when he called up the torpedo boat and anxiously awaited a reply.

Then, suddenly, the Morse characters chattered through Alan's earphones and his expression of delight told the relieved Buchanan that this part of the operation, at least, was in place.

Now all that remained was for the commander to locate the Romanov family and lead them to safety.

23

Alan and Buchanan slept for most of the day following the installation of the wireless equipment and in the evening made contact with the torpedo boat once more, leaving the set switched on only long enough for their own brief signal of 'OK' to be acknowledged. Then, after a meal and a few games of cards in their attic quarters, they slept again.

The next morning, before Buchanan set off from the house, he gave Alan a loaded revolver and a pouch of ammunition, 'just in case it's needed'. Alan hoped it never would be, but he took the unfamiliar weapon and listened carefully to the other man's instructions about its use.

Buchanan was on his way to a suburb of Petrograd, about fifty kilometres away, where the Romanov family were last known to be in hiding. Not only did he have the problem of locating them, but Georgi Zhukovsky had told him that the Bolsheviks in the city were preparing for an expected attack by the White Russian army, which was rumoured to be advancing on them. As a result, the city's defences were being strengthened and there was a great deal of Bolshevik troop movement throughout the whole area.

With Buchanan gone, Alan found the lantern-lit attic increasingly claustrophobic, but he tried to tell himself his problem was a small one when compared with the very real danger Buchanan would be facing on his journey. He would need to bluff his way through any checkpoints he could not avoid; locate the Romanov family – and bring them back to the Zhukovsky house. Alan did not want to think about the odds against his succeeding.

That night, he sent a brief 'OK' signal to the torpedo boat, but he did not sleep well. The home of the Zhukovskys was close to a forest and, with only a thin layer of slates between the attic and the world outside, the sounds of woodland beasts and birds seemed uncomfortably close. Such noises were quite alien to him and his imagination ran riot in the darkness.

The following morning, despite the language barrier between Alan and the Zhukovskys, Yulia managed to convey to him from the bottom of the high cupboard that she wanted him to come down and join her and Georgi for breakfast.

Alan tried to explain that his orders were to remain in the attic until Buchanan's return, but the Russian woman insisted and Alan eventually gave in to her demands.

Emerging from the attic for all the world like a mole forsaking its underground tunnel, Alan was led from window to window in both the kitchen and the adjacent lounge as Yulia made it clear that it was possible to see the two paths that led to the house from the forest. On the seaward side, one quick glance from the dining area would be sufficient to spot any boat long before it came close to the house.

Satisfied, Alan enjoyed a good breakfast with the ageing couple, although communication was well-nigh impossible. After they had eaten he was proudly shown a collection of photographs of the Zhukovskys with a number of members of the late Tsar's family, and Yulia wept openly over pictures of the son and young daughters of the Russian royal family.

Despite the language difficulties, Alan was able to learn that Yulia had been nursemaid to the children, and her husband, Georgi, head gardener at the palace.

Alan spent the remainder of the day in the secret attic, declining an invitation to come down and share dinner with Georgi and Yulia. It was one thing to leave the attic when it was possible to keep the approaches to the house in view, but quite another to sit eating a meal in the kitchen when he was unable to see anything that might be going on outside.

The night passed without incident, and the second day on his own followed the monotonous pattern of the first. By the third day Alan had become concerned for Buchanan and by the fourth he was seriously worried. The arrangement was that if Buchanan had not returned to the Zhukovskys' house by the seventh day Alan was to telegraph the torpedo boat and ask to be taken back on board. The assumption would be that Buchanan had either lost his life, or been captured.

It was an arrangement that Alan had already decided he would ignore. He would wait for Buchanan for at least two weeks, in the hope that he might still succeed in his mission. However, his long absence was causing Alan great concern. He believed it would be having the same effect on Lieutenant Ferris and, consequently, on Admiral Cowan.

Then, on the sixth day after Buchanan had left, Alan was awoken sometime before dawn by a great deal of commotion in the house below him. Prepared for the worst, he found his revolver and waited.

The trapdoor in the ceiling of the cupboard was opened from below and the telescopic ladder lowered. Alan stood by the gaping hole, gun in hand, ready to shoot the first Bolshevik who reached the attic.

He was about to lever back the hammer of the revolver when a head of red hair rose above the rim of the trapdoor. The next moment he was looking into the face of a startled girl who appeared to be more indignant than frightened when he moved forward in the dim light from below to show himself – and the revolver.

Climbing into the attic from the ladder, she declared belligerently, in Russian-accented English, 'I do not like to have guns pointed at me.'

Flustered, Alan said, 'I'm sorry. I didn't know who it might be.'

Her face maintained its expression of stern disapproval for a moment. Then she smiled – and suddenly she was a very beautiful girl. 'I am sorry. You are very brave to be here. You must be Alan. I am Anoushka . . . Anoushka Romanov.'

As Alan lit a lamp to allow the girl to take stock of her surroundings, another head came into view above the trapdoor. This too was a woman with red hair. Older than Anoushka, she was still beautiful, and Alan knew he was looking at Alyona Romanov, the woman whom Buchanan considered to be the most attractive he had ever known.

Alan helped her from the ladder to the attic and, almost immediately, Buchanan followed.

'Hello, Alan. Is everything all right here?'

'So quiet it's been boring,' Alan replied. 'But where are the rest of the family? I thought there were a husband and wife and four daughters.'

'And so there are,' Buchanan agreed. 'But Alyona and Anoushka are very tired. We'll settle them in their sleeping quarters, and then I will tell you all about it.'

Half an hour later, when the two women were already sleeping, Commander Buchanan shared breakfast with Alan in the kitchen and told him how he had brought them out of Petrograd, and what he had planned for the others.

'I am going to have to make a couple more trips. Unfortunately, the only way I could get Alyona and Anoushka out of Petrograd was in a hearse, complete with a pauper's body in a coffin, heading for a cemetery outside the city. The hearse has a false floor, and it's a marvellous subterfuge, really. Unfortunately, there is room for only two between the floors. I ride on the hearse as a funeral assistant with the undertaker, who is a White Russian sympathiser. When we reached the cemetery, Alyona, Anoushka and I hid in a small church until nightfall, when we walked to the home of another sympathiser, halfway between Petrograd and here. After resting through the daylight hours, we completed our journey during this last night. It means the women are very tired by the end of the journey, but I don't think we could succeed any other way. As it was we were obliged to hide off the road on more than one occasion in order not to be seen. Unfortunately, I fear things can only get worse. The Bolsheviks seem very active in this region at the moment.'

Aware that each journey Buchanan made put him in great danger, Alan said, 'Making three trips will increase the risk for you – and extend the time of the whole operation. Will you send the women to the torpedo boat two at a time?'

Buchanan shook his head vigorously. 'No. It would increase the risk still further if we asked Lieutenant Ferris to bring the torpedo boat back here so many times. We will wait until everyone is gathered in the house, and take them all off together.' Giving Alan a wry smile which only served to emphasise his tiredness, he added, 'I know it's going to get dreadfully crowded up there, Alan, and ensuring they don't make too much noise, especially at night, will be quite a responsibility for you, but I could name many men who would envy you. The Romanov mother and girls really are renowned international beauties.'

'I had noticed,' Alan said drily. 'Do you think I should code a very brief message to Lieutenant Ferris, saying merely, "All well but completion not expected for twelve days"? It sounds as though it will take at least that length of time and he'll be getting worried. Besides, he'll need to contact the Admiral and arrange for more food and fuel to be brought to him. He won't want to go out of radio range in order to collect it for himself.'

'That's a very good idea, Alan. Even if the Bolsheviks

intercept the message and succeed in decoding it – which is extremely unlikely – it gives nothing away. Yes, send it off. In the meantime, I am going to follow the example of the two women and catch up on my sleep.'

24

Anoushka was the first of the sleeping trio in the attic to wake. She came into the space where the wireless set was installed just as Alan was switching it on to let those on the torpedo boat know all was well with him and Buchanan.

Although she was still not fully awake and her clothes were dishevelled, Alan thought she was a very lovely girl and put her age at about nineteen or twenty. Unselfconsciously, she said, 'I feel as though I have been asleep for a week. What time is it?'

Alan looked at the clock standing on top of the wireless receiver. 'Eight o'clock.'

'Eight o'clock morning, or evening?'

'Evening,' Alan replied. 'You've slept for about twelve hours.'

'Is that all? I feel as though I have slept for days and my legs ache so much I must have walked at least a hundred miles.'

Alan smiled. 'I doubt if it was quite that far, but you certainly walked a very long way.'

'I would like to go downstairs,' Anoushka said. 'How do I get down?'

'You don't,' Alan said firmly. 'We are only able to go downstairs when it is daylight and we can see anyone approaching the house. Even then we need to keep away from the windows and are not allowed outside.'

'Who says we must not go outside?' Anoushka demanded imperiously.

'It's common sense,' Alan replied, taken aback by her sudden show of arrogance. 'The Zhukovskys are known to live alone. If anyone else was seen here we might have Bolsheviks coming to find out who was visiting the house. They would be very interested to learn it was a Romanov family.'

For a moment Alan thought Anoushka was about to argue with him. Instead, the arrogance left her as suddenly as it had appeared. 'Of course, you are quite right. We are very lucky to be alive. These are terrible times. What is more, you, Marcus and the Zhukovskys are risking your lives for us. You are all very brave.'

'Commander Buchanan is the brave one.' Looking at the clock again, Alan said, 'I must call the boat and tell them all is well with us.' He put on the earphones and called the torpedo boat. When he did not receive an immediate reply, he called them again.

'Please . . . can I listen?' Anoushka pointed to the head-phones he was wearing.

After a moment's hesitation, he removed the headset. Holding one earphone, he motioned for her to take the other.

As she put it to her ear, the torpedo boat replied and the sound made her jump.

Alan sent the agreed signal to say all was well and the telegraphist on the torpedo boat acknowledged receipt, adding an unauthorised 'Good luck'.

The whole procedure took less than twenty seconds. When it was over Alan switched off the wireless and Anoushka looked mystified. 'Is that all? It was no more than a few funny noises.'

'It was Morse code,' Alan explained. 'I told them we were well, they acknowledged receipt and wished us good luck.'

'All that from a few funny sounds? It is very clever.'

'What is very clever?' The question came from Marcus Buchanan, as he emerged from the cramped bed space which he and Alan would share now the women were also accommodated in the attic.

'I let Anoushka listen to the Morse being transmitted from the torpedo boat,' Alan said. 'She thought it was no more than a few funny noises.'

'And so it is to all of us except Alan,' Buchanan said. 'You are right, Anoushka, he is very clever – but then so are you. Anoushka is an excellent artist,' he explained to Alan. 'She insisted that we bring her sketch pad with her things. Choosing it in preference to clothes. In fact, I don't think she would have come with us otherwise! I am sure she will show it to you and you will be as impressed with her work as I am . . . But I must call down and see if Mrs Zhukovsky can make something for me to eat before I set out again.'

Alyona Romanov woke while Buchanan was eating his meal in the attic and they conversed in a mixture of Russian and English until it was time for him to leave the house and set off once more for Petrograd.

Alyona was genuinely concerned for his safety and she and Anoushka kissed him warmly before he shook hands with Alan, saying, 'Take care of them while I am away.'

When he had gone, Alyona said, 'It makes me feel so . . . so . . . *humble*, that Marcus should risk his life in this way for me, and for my family. Why? Why should he do it?'

Alan doubted whether Alyona or any of her family knew what it was to feel humble, but he said, 'He believes in what he is doing – and it is much easier to be chivalrous when you are helping to save the life of beautiful women.'

For a moment he thought he might have been too familiar, but after looking at him without saying anything for some moments, Alyona said, 'I think he would do the same for any woman who found herself in my situation. Now, what are the arrangements for eating tonight?'

The supper cooked by Yulia was carried to the attic with difficulty by the ageing Georgi and the meal was a quiet affair. Both women were still tired from their exertions of the past few days, and soon after eating they returned to their beds.

They felt better the following morning and were happy to be allowed to leave the loft and go down into the main house, although Alan felt that Alyona resented it when he gave her the same instructions as he had given to Anoushka about not leaving the house, and keeping away from windows. However, backing him up, Yulia pointed out the dangers to them all if such precautions were not taken, and they accepted that they were still not safe, even in such a remote house as this.

Later that day, Alan discovered Anoushka sitting well back from an upstairs window sketching a scene which

165

included forest and sea. It was a very competent piece of work, and she handed him the pad in order that he could look through her drawings. As he turned the first page, she asked suddenly, 'Are you married, Alan?'

It was an unexpected question, and he thought about it for a moment before saying, 'The answer to that is both yes and no.'

Puzzled, she said, 'How can you be married yet not married?'

'I was married during the war, but went away before my wife and I had time to get to know each other. When I returned home after almost three years we found we were virtual strangers and she said she didn't want to be married to me.'

'I am so sorry.' Her sympathy sounded genuine. 'The war has changed so many things, for people of many countries. When we go from here I do not think I will ever see Russia again unless the Bolsheviks are defeated, and my father thinks that very unlikely. In the meantime they are murdering everyone who was in a position of any power under the poor Tsar. They are animals!'

Anoushka shuddered violently and Alan decided he should change the subject. Turning the pages of the sketch pad, he said, 'You have a real artistic talent, Anoushka. Will you take it further when you are settled once more? Where do you think you will be living?'

'Thank you. I have studied art for some years and would like to be able to study further in Paris, or perhaps London.'

'Have you ever heard of the artist colony in Newlyn, in my country? It is called the Newlyn School? There is another very close by, at St Ives.'

'Yes, of course, many famous artists have visited there. One was James Whistler, who lived in Russia for some years. I have also heard much of a Stanhope Forbes. Do you know Newlyn?'

'Yes – and I met Stanhope Forbes while I was there. It is a place you really should visit if you have the opportunity. There is one artist in particular I think you would like. Her name is Vicky Hazelton. She will be famous one day.'

Something in the way he spoke made Anoushka ask, 'This Vicky Hazelton . . . you know her very well?'

'Yes . . .' He explained about their meeting, when he was wounded on the *Viper*, discovering she was an artist, and meeting up with her again when he stayed in the village.

Anoushka seized on the fact that he had been wounded and, concerned, asked, 'Were you hurt very badly?'

'I spent some time in hospital, but I'm quite all right now.'

Alan thought of the dangers that threatened Anoushka and her family, the loss of what must have been a very comfortable way of life – and the very real danger that they could lose life itself. The fact that she could still express concern for him raised his opinion of her considerably. He decided that, despite her natural arrogance, Anoushka Romanov was a remarkable young woman.

25

On the fifth morning after the women's arrival, Anoushka was sketching from a rear upstairs window while her mother was stitching a small piece of embroidery in the living room, where Alan sat in a corner, composing a poem. Suddenly Georgi Zhukovsky rushed into the house in a state of alarm, calling out something in Russian.

It was Alyona who translated for Alan's benefit. 'He says there are armed men coming along a path from the forest towards the house. We must go to the attic immediately.'

'You go – now,' Alan said. 'I'll fetch Anoushka. Hurry – and take the embroidery with you.'

Running upstairs, he quickly located Anoushka and sent her after her mother. After a hurried inspection to check they had left nothing incriminating behind them, he too climbed the ladder to the attic, pulling it up after him before easing the hidden trapdoor carefully into place.

Whispering for the two women to remain still and silent, Alan found the revolver and ammunition left for him by Commander Buchanan, then nervously settled himself close to the trapdoor. It was not long before they heard heavy footsteps tramping the stairs between the two floors of the house and the sound of loud voices as men called to each other.

'They are searching the house,' Alan hissed. 'Remain absolutely still.'

Close to him, Anoushka whispered in return, 'What shall we do if they find us?'

'They won't,' he replied, with more confidence than he felt. The trapdoor was cunningly disguised, but the attic was large and if the men searching the house were acting on specific information they might turn their attention to the roof space. He believed he would be able to hold them at bay for a while, but the outcome was inevitable . . . And what if they did not leave, but decided to occupy the house? It was not something he wanted to think about.

For more than three hours the occupants of the secret attic flat dared not move and spoke only in low whispers, each of them aware that the slightest sound could attract the notice of the armed men.

Then, when Alan was becoming increasingly concerned about what might be happening in the house below them, there was a double tap on the trapdoor, the pre-arranged signal from the Zhukovskys. Still, Alan whispered for the two women to remain quiet, fearful that the men who had come to the house might have managed to extract information about their presence from the aged couple.

When the trapdoor began to open, Alan, lying on his stomach, wriggled towards it, revolver in hand. When the trapdoor was fully open, he peered over the edge of the gap and to his relief saw Georgi standing below him in the cupboard.

The old man called out something in Russian and Alyona translated. 'He says all is well, the Bolsheviks have gone.'

'How many were there? And where have they gone?'

Alyona passed the question on to Georgi, who was visibly shaken by his recent experience. He replied that there had been fourteen of them and they spoke of meeting with other Bolsheviks in a forest village about four or five kilometres away.

Alan and the two women descended gratefully from the attic. The nervous Georgi said he would go and work in the garden in order to keep watch in case the Bolsheviks returned, while Alyona and Yulia began an animated conversation, listened to with considerable interest by Anoushka.

When Alan asked the young woman what they were talking about, she said, 'It is not good. The men who came here are part of a larger party searching the countryside for Tsarist sympathisers. Someone had told them that Georgi once worked for the Tsar and they came here to arrest him. It would have meant certain death, but he was able to persuade them he had been no more than a lowly gardener tending a vegetable garden at the palace and had never even seen the Tsar.'

'It was fortunate they believed him,' Alan said, with great relief. 'I don't fancy anyone's chances had they not.'

'None of us is safe just yet,' Anoushka said grimly. 'Not all the men did believe him. They wanted to take him with them, but the leader of the party said if they learned he was lying they could always return for him. Yulia is saying that Georgi has always been so proud of having worked for the Tsar that he would boast to anyone who would listen of what an important man he was in the royal household. Fortunately, Yulia said, she doesn't like people to know her business and she forbade Georgi to say anything to anyone about her years in the royal nursery. Had she not, both she and Georgi would have been executed on the spot today.'

Anoushka shuddered. 'I no longer feel safe here. What if they return?'

'Try not to think about it,' Alan said. 'I had hoped Commander Buchanan would have been back by now. When I signal the torpedo boat this evening I'll ask them to come in close. If Buchanan doesn't return tonight I will call them again and tell them to send a boat to take you off before morning.'

'But what of my father and sisters?' she asked. 'What will happen to them?'

'They are in safe hands with Buchanan,' Alan said, with far more confidence than he felt. 'He won't let anything happen to them.'

It came as a tremendous relief to Alan when Marcus Buchanan returned to the house shortly before midnight that night. There was great joy too from Alyona and Anoushka when they discovered that the rest of their family was with him.

It seemed that Bolshevik activity was intensifying in Petrograd as well as in the rural areas and Buchanan had felt the city was no longer safe for them. He had hit upon an ingenious, if somewhat macabre, method of getting them out of Petrograd together. The hearse was used once again, but this time not only were there two Romanov girls hidden in the space beneath the false floor, but the third girl was screwed down in the coffin carried in the horse-drawn vehicle. Meanwhile, the head of the family, disguised as a second undertaker's assistant, rode with Buchanan on the outside of the hearse.

Making a joke of the escape, Commander Buchanan said, 'We did have an anxious moment when we were stopped by a Bolshevik patrol and they wanted to look inside the coffin. Fortunately, the undertaker was a resourceful man. He said it contained the body of a vagrant who had been dead for some time and was particularly unwholesome. He said he was quite happy for the Bolsheviks to open the coffin, but that we would move well away and not return until the coffin had been screwed down again and the stench blown away by the wind. The Bolsheviks decided we should proceed on our way without further investigation.'

'What if they hadn't changed their minds?' Alan asked.

'I would have been forced to shoot them,' Buchanan replied matter-of-factly. 'I was holding a revolver inside my pocket the whole time we were talking. But enough of our experiences. What is this Georgi told me when I arrived, about a Bolshevik search party coming to the house?'

Alan gave him the details and Buchanan looked concerned. 'I believe it to be more than coincidental, Alan. Let's move over by the transmitter, away from the others. We need to have a serious talk about what is going on.'

When they were out of hearing of the Romanovs,

Buchanan said in a low voice, 'I believe the Bolsheviks' visit was more than a random search. I didn't say anything earlier about what is going on in Petrograd because I didn't want to frighten the women, but I think that those who are helping the Romanovs escape from Russia have a traitor in their midst. When I reached the city I found that the family had been moved to another house only hours before the place where they had been hiding was raided and the owners taken away. That was really why I decided they must all leave with me right away.'

The rescued family were still talking excitedly among themselves nearby and Buchanan continued, 'When we reached the house where I had broken the journey with Anoushka and her mother I left everyone hidden off the road and went ahead to ensure all was well. It was not. The house was being watched. As a result, we gave it a wide berth and spent a very uncomfortable day in a tumbledown cattle shed, disputing occupancy with some rather aggressive cows. Tonight we skirted the village where the Bolsheviks who came here said they were going and there was a great deal of activity happening there. I think someone has been informing them of what we are doing. If I am right they will be back here to search every inch of the house.'

'Tonight?' Alan asked, startled.

'They might leave it until dawn, but we daren't risk remaining here. We will have to go – and Georgi and Yulia will have to come with us. The problem will be how quickly the torpedo boat can reach us.'

Alan told Buchanan of the signal he had sent to Ferris and Buchanan said, 'Good man! That makes everything very much easier. I'll tell the Romanovs, and the Zhukovskys too. Call up the torpedo boat and tell them to send the pinnace ashore to the place where they landed us – wherever that happens to be on the grid – and be prepared to take off ten passengers. The crew are to be heavily armed and ready to use their weapons if necessary. Tell Ferris the pick-up is to take place at three o'clock. That will give the Zhukovskys time to gather any valuables they have, and hopefully we will still be ahead of the Bolsheviks.'

26

Yulia was dismayed at the suggestion that she and her husband should leave their home. It had been bought for them as a farewell gift by Tsar Nicholas II when they retired from the royal household, and they were very happy there.

Marcus Buchanan's reply was that had he known the house had been purchased for them by the Tsar he would never have risked the lives of the surviving Romanovs by bringing them here. The purchase would be on record and, sooner or later, the details were bound to be passed on to the Bolsheviks. If, as he suspected, they had been told that moves were afoot to get the family out of the country, they would come to the house in force and take it apart in a search for them. When they found the secret accommodation provided in the attic they would know exactly why it was there.

Fortunately, he believed that such information had not yet come into their possession, although they were undoubtedly aware that this area was tied in with the family's escape plans. He told Yulia she had the choice of leaving the house with Georgi, or dying at the hands of the Bolsheviks. After a tearful exchange with Alyona, Yulia finally agreed to go, and Buchanan told Alan that Alyona had promised Yulia that the Romanovs would buy her and Georgi another home of their choosing, somewhere in Europe.

Now the decision to leave had been made, there was great excitement among the escaping family. After many months in hiding they were within a couple of hours of safety and a new life in another country. Alexander Romanov was a very successful businessman with money and interests in many countries. Their lives might be threatened in their homeland, but the lifestyle they had enjoyed before the Revolution would be resumed in the country of their choice.

When all was ready for their departure, Alan sent a last coded message to the torpedo boat, checking that it was in position and ready to collect them from the shore and take them on board. The reply came back 'Affirmative', and Alan signalled that there would be no further transmissions from him. He then proceeded to remove valves from the receiver and transmitter and spun the tuning dial so the Bolsheviks would not discover the frequency he had used.

Before leaving the house, Marcus Buchanan surprised Alan by appearing wearing the rather creased uniform of a naval commander, explaining that he had brought it with him in order to demand that he be treated as a prisoner of war in the event of capture by the Bolsheviks.

'Unfortunately, in view of what we are doing I doubt whether it will make any difference to them,' he said grimly. 'They will be so angry that if I am captured I will be killed, uniform or not.'

Aware that he faced the same fate, Alan asked, 'Do you think they are likely to be out there?'

'I hope not, Alan, but I have a very nasty feeling that if we get out of here safely it will be by the very skin of our teeth, so be sure you have your revolver with you and don't hesitate to use it if the need arises. Remember, our task is to get the Romanovs safely on board the torpedo boat. *Nothing else matters.* The horror of what will happen to the women if they are caught doesn't bear thinking about. Now, I'll go down and have the lights put out while you muster everyone in the kitchen with whatever baggage they have to take. Then I'll go outside and check that all is well.'

After waiting nervously in the darkened kitchen for what seemed like hours, Anoushka whispered to Alan, 'He has been gone a very long time.'

'Commander Buchanan is a very thorough man,' Alan replied. 'He will want to make absolutely certain there are no Bolsheviks out there before leading us to the boat.'

At that moment, the kitchen door opened and Marcus Buchanan slipped inside, closing the door quickly behind him.

Breathlessly, he said, 'They *are* out there. I almost walked into a couple of them on the path to the sea. I know there are more because they were discussing going to find their leader, to discuss the significance of the house lights going out.'

There was a gasp of fear from the girls of the Romanov family, all of whom understood English, and their father said, 'What do we do? Can we still reach the boat?'

'Not unless I create some kind of diversion on the other side of the house . . .' Turning to Georgi, he spoke to him in rapid Russian. Then, to Alan, he said, 'I am going to make my way towards the forest. When I come up against whoever is there I'll open fire. Hopefully it will draw everyone away from the seaward side of the house. Use your initiative on this one, Alan. When you think everyone is likely to have gone to see what the shooting is about, take the Romanovs and Zhukovskys down to the beach – Georgi will lead you there and the boat should be waiting. I'll give you time to get away before trying to make my own way to the shore. I have a torch with me. Tell Lieutenant Ferris to post look-outs to watch for my signal, but he's to wait for no longer than half an hour after everyone is on board. If he hasn't received a signal from me by then, he is to leave and take the family to the admiral, on his flagship.'

'But—'

Buchanan cut Alan's protest short. 'No buts, Alan. For all we know the Bolsheviks on shore may be in touch with their navy. They have a couple of coastal motor boats that could turn our success to failure if they are close at hand. Our mission – yours and mine – has been to find the Romanovs and get them safely out of Russia. We are on the verge of succeeding, and I am not going to allow our chances to be ruined now. Good luck . . . Good luck to all of you.'

The door to the outside world opened and closed again . . . and Commander Marcus Buchanan had gone.

Behind him, each of the nine people inside the house was left with thoughts they could not express. For the

Zhukovskys it was a confused numbness. They were getting on in years and the events of the day had happened with frightening speed. They were being uprooted from a home they loved and taken to . . . they knew not where. Wherever it was, it would be in a land where a different language was spoken, and they would be foreigners.

Alexander Romanov was an intelligent and courageous man, and he felt guilt that others should be risking their lives for him and his family. But he was also fearful for the safety of that family, and the horror of what had happened to his blood relatives was uppermost in his mind. He asked Alan if there was anything he might do to help.

'Yes,' Alan replied. 'When we leave the house, bring up the rear and make certain that no one gets lost on the way to the beach.'

Alan too was feeling guilty. He felt he should be outside with Commander Buchanan, seeking out the Bolsheviks who lay in wait for the fugitive party. Although keenly aware of the responsibility he had been given for their safety and ultimate escape, he was nevertheless deeply concerned for Commander Buchanan. He had come to both like and admire the man during the time he had known him. He was undoubtedly the bravest person Alan had ever met.

His thoughts were interrupted by the sound of two shots, somewhere at the back of the house, towards the forest. It was followed by a great deal of shouting and shooting from other heavier weapons, probably rifles.

Soon afterwards there were shouts from a path that ran some distance away to the side of the house. Realising that they probably came from Bolsheviks who had been guarding the way from the house to the sea, and were now hurrying to the aid of their comrades, Alan told the party in the kitchen it was time to go.

His words were translated by Alyona, and as they went out through the door Alan said to her, 'Tell Georgi to go quietly – but he must hurry. If the Bolsheviks realise Commander Buchanan is on his own, they will guess what is happening and come after us.'

Georgi was frightened, and fear added speed to his legs, but Marcus Buchanan's ploy proved a hundred per cent successful. Encountering a couple of Bolshevik guards on the path leading from the house to the forest, he had opened fire, wounding one of the men, and they had immediately assumed it was the party from the house trying to make good their escape. All the Bolsheviks who had been moving into position, waiting for dawn, had hastened to the scene of the shooting, and the Romanovs and Zhukovskys met with no resistance on their way to the shore.

Everything here went according to plan. The pinnace was waiting for them and the Romanovs and Zhukovskys were hurriedly lifted on board. But when it was time for Alan to join them, he pulled back.

'I'm going back to see what's happening to Commander Buchanan,' he said to the coxswain of the boat. 'Tell Lieutenant Ferris that the commander is trying to create a diversion. Ask him to come as close to the shore as possible and send up a couple of star-shells between the house and the forest. If he sees anything, then use the searchlights. If you can pick out the Bolsheviks from the torpedo boat open fire on them with Lewis guns and send the motor launch inshore with as many armed men as can be spared – but tell them to stay with the launch. I'll try to help Commander Buchanan to make it back and we'll no doubt need to get away in a hurry. Right now I need a rifle – quick, someone, give one to me – and ammunition to go with it.'

One of the seamen vaulted over the side of the pinnace. He carried two rifles, one of which he handed to Alan. 'Here, take this. I've got a couple of pouches of ammo. I'm coming with you . . . but by the sound of things we'll need to hurry.'

As he was speaking, the sound of increased gunfire could be heard. Knowing the area, Alan realised it was closer to the Zhukovsky house now.

This was not the time to argue with the volunteer who had provided him with the rifle. Alan began running towards the house, aware that the sailor was close behind him.

As they neared the house, they were fired upon by someone who was a short distance off the path and Alan fired back. There was no return fire and, guided by the shots, which were now just beyond the Zhukovsky house, Alan headed in that direction, followed closely by the sailor from the torpedo boat. They were not far past the house when they heard the firing of a revolver nearby.

Stopping, Alan called, 'Sir . . . Commander Buchanan, are you there?'

'Alan! What the hell are you doing here?'

Heading in the direction of the voice, Alan called, 'I've come back to help you reach the shore. A sailor from the torpedo boat is with me. Are you all right?'

'No. I've been shot in the thigh. Go back to the shore. I have enough ammunition left to hold the Russians off . . .'

There was the sound of a shot and a bullet passed close to Alan's cheek. Both he and the sailor from the torpedo boat fired back at the same time and there were no further shots from that direction. They were still moving forward and a few moments later reached Commander Buchanan. He was in obvious pain and was squatting awkwardly in a slight depression in the ground, but his first question was not about himself.

'What have you done with the Romanovs?'

'They should be safely on board now. They were picked up by the pinnace. Now we need to get you back to the beach. How badly are you hurt?'

'I can move, with a little help – but you shouldn't have come back, Alan. Your first duty was to the Romanovs . . .'

'I've told you, they're safe . . .'

Just then there was the sound of a shell exploding and a moment later the area was illuminated by a star-shell, fired from the torpedo boat. By its glare it was possible to see the Bolsheviks, startled by the sudden unexpected light.

Alan fired at them and so too did the crew member from the torpedo boat. Their shots had an effect, but far more effective was the fire that opened up from the torpedo boat's Lewis guns. There were some forty Bolsheviks in two main groups and the initial burst from the torpedo boat's automatic weapons mowed down at least a third of them.

Commander Buchanan could not walk without help, so Alan and the seaman supported him on either side.

They headed for the shore as fast as was possible, dragging the naval officer between them and ignoring his occasional stifled cry of pain. The Bolsheviks mounted sporadic rifle fire at them, but the continuing bombardment from the Lewis guns forced them to keep their heads down and their shots were not well aimed.

Long before Alan and his companion reached the shore with the wounded officer, the star-shell burned itself out. It was immediately replaced by another, and as that one died they tumbled down a slight bank to the shore. Here they found the launch from the torpedo boat waiting for them. Commander Buchanan was lifted aboard, Alan and the seaman quickly followed, and a few minutes later they were skimming over the water towards the torpedo boat, which Lieutenant Ferris had brought as close to the shore as the depth of water would allow.

Once on board, Buchanan was swiftly committed to the care of the boat's sick-berth attendant, but before he was carried below he grasped Alan's hand, saying, 'Thank you, Alan. I had three rounds of ammunition left and had already reserved the last for myself. My report will be going in to the Admiral as soon as we reach the flagship. I owe you my life.'

'Thank you, sir – but don't forget Able Seaman Dickson. His support made all the difference. I couldn't have carried you back on my own.'

'I'm grateful to you both. Thank you.'

27

Alan's demobilisation was deferred by some months. Many of the Royal Navy's ships were being taken out of commission, to be laid up ready to be used again should the need arise in the uncertain years following the Great War. Specialist staff, like Alan, were needed to ensure that each ship's equipment was in such a condition that it could be brought into almost immediate use should the ship be recommissioned.

Alan had agreed to stay on after his return from the Baltic because he had nothing definite planned for civilian life and the work in the Reserve Fleet gave him adequate free time to pursue his writing. But eventually the need for his services came to an end and it was time for him to leave the Royal Navy.

Before he did so, Alan tried once more for a reconciliation with Dora. He wrote to suggest they should get together to talk over their problems. When this prompted no reply, he wrote again, this time saying he would come to Quilter Street to speak to her.

There was a letter from her by return of post, stating bluntly that she did not want to see him ever again. Their marriage was over and there was nothing more to be said about it. Alan was forced to concede that there was no further point in pursuing the matter with her. She had not changed her mind during the time since he had walked out of the Quilter Street house. He would need to make a new life for himself without her.

Alan emerged through the high iron gates of the Chatham naval base wearing an ill-fitting civilian suit and carrying a suitcase which contained all of his belongings. The suit was all that could be had in the Medway towns, so great had been the numbers of sailors from the naval base and soldiers from the nearby Royal Engineers barracks who had been demobilised in the months since the end of the war.

From force of habit he avoided meeting the eyes of the white-gaitered naval patrolmen on duty at the gate, lest he be singled out for a search of his person and belongings, but such caution proved unnecessary. The feared patrolmen had nothing but smiles for men who were no longer subject to the strict naval discipline. The Royal Navy was returning to the role with which it was most comfortable. A meticulously trained body of professional sailors who had no equal in the world.

Alan turned his back on his naval service with few regrets, even though he had no home to go to and faced an uncertain future. He had toyed with the idea of returning to Quilter Street and Dora, to plead with her yet again in an attempt to make their marriage work, but he realised it was the worst thing he could do. She would despise him for not accepting the fact that he meant nothing to her.

On the bus to the railway station he took from his pocket a letter that had arrived from Vicky as he was about to leave the barracks for the last time. It was little more than a brief note in which she told him that an editor friend of Cecil Gormley at a London publishing house would like to speak to him with a view to having him compile a book about the wartime exploits of torpedo boats against German U-boats. If successful it could be followed by others, drawing upon his personal experiences. Re-reading the letter on the train to Victoria station, Alan decided he would call on the editor straight away and discuss exactly what was wanted.

The publishing house was close to the Strand and the editor, Julian Gimblett, was a fussy, bespectacled little man who greeted Alan enthusiastically. 'My dear boy, I am delighted to meet you at last. May I first of all thank you for the *wonderful* stories and articles that Cecil sent to me. I do hope you will agree to write about torpedo boats for us. You would be the perfect choice.'

After discussing the project in more detail, Alan said he would be delighted to write the book and the exuberant editor clapped his hands together in an expression of delight. 'Wonderful . . . just *wonderful*. Cecil will be so pleased. He's passing through London on his way to spend a holiday in Italy. We were talking about you only last evening. While he's here, Cecil will be attending the private view of an exhibition of the work of one of his artist friends from Newlyn. I'm taking him to lunch today, so why don't you join us? In fact, I *insist*. It's not often I am able to entertain two writers at the same time.'

Alan was self-conscious about his clothes and reluctant to accept, but Julian was determined and Alan eventually capitulated.

'*Splendid!*' Julian beamed benevolently. 'I'll make a telephone call to change the booking to three. We'll have a drink here, then go and meet Cecil.'

The restaurant was situated in a basement close to Covent Garden, and the moment he entered the establishment, Alan realised that the cheap suit he was wearing was quite out of place here. However, it was too late to change his mind now.

Cecil was waiting in the restaurant lounge and he was both surprised and delighted to see Alan. After greeting him and congratulating him on his most recent award for bravery, he asked what Alan planned to do now he had left the Navy.

'Before he does anything else he is going to have a drink,' Julian said. 'We are celebrating the fact that Alan has agreed to write the book you and I discussed, the one about torpedo boats. What are we all drinking?'

The talk over aperitifs was of writing, Julian's publishing list – and the menu, which was written in French. Cecil translated, Julian claiming to have no more knowledge of the language than Alan.

Afterwards, inside the amazingly high-ceilinged dining room, Alan felt even more ill at ease than before. The room was not particularly crowded, but seated at a nearby table was a man Alan recognised immediately as being a senior member of the wartime cabinet. Among others at the same table was someone wearing the uniform of a full admiral.

Alan's nervousness increased when he was faced with an alarming array of gleaming silver cutlery. However, Cecil, like Julian, was aware of Alan's lack of familiarity with such surroundings. Seated opposite Alan, he made a great show of picking up the correct cutlery for each course, in order that Alan might follow his lead.

Halfway through the main course, Cecil reminded Alan that he had not replied to his question about his plans now he had left the Navy.

'I don't know,' Alan replied evasively. 'I haven't had time to give it a great deal of thought. I haven't even decided where I'm going to live.'

'Do you have any family?' Julian asked.

Alan hesitated before saying, 'No . . . only my dad, and he's at sea, in the merchant navy.'

Cecil looked at him sharply and Alan recalled a conversation in the Fisherman's Arms in Newlyn, when he had mentioned being married to Dora. Cecil obviously remembered it too, but he said nothing until the meal was over and they had left the restaurant.

Julian was hurrying away, heading for a meeting with another author who was due at the publishing house. As they watched his hurried, but somewhat unsteady, progress along the Strand, Cecil commented that he hoped the author was not a teetotaller. Then he said, 'I thought you had a wife here in London, Alan?'

'So did I,' Alan replied bitterly. 'But she's changed – we've both changed during the time I've been away.'

'Oh, I'm sorry.' Cecil's sympathy was genuine. 'Will you be remaining in London?'

'I suppose so, but as I said earlier, I haven't had a great deal of time to think things over. I was only demobbed this morning. I've left my kit at Victoria station.'

'What about the book you're to write for Julian? Will it give you enough to live on for a while?'

'I suppose so – once I've written it. Until then money is going to be a bit tight.'

'Are you saying that you haven't been given an advance on the book?' Cecil came to a halt.

'No. Is there any reason why I should have received one?'

'But of course! My dear boy, you're a writer now, not a sailor – or even a painter. You can expect to be given an advance of anything up to a half of what they're paying you to write the book when you sign the contract. You *have* signed a contract?'

'Not yet. Julian said I'm to write to him when I have an address.'

'We'll go and see him in the morning,' Cecil said firmly. 'The trouble with Julian is that he comes from a very wealthy family and doesn't always understand the needs of mere mortals. Now, let's deal with more immediate matters. Where are you staying tonight?'

'Probably at the Union Jack Club, close to Waterloo Station. I'm no longer a matelot, but I think they'll let me stay there for a couple of nights while I sort myself out.'

Cecil looked at Alan sympathetically. 'We can do better than that, dear boy. I am staying with my sister Clarice in Knightsbridge. She and her husband have a house that's far too large for just the two of them. Besides, hubby's away in Germany on some government commission at the moment. I am quite certain Clarice will be delighted to put you up for a while.'

'But . . . she doesn't know anything about me,' Alan protested. 'Come to that, you don't know much yourself.'

'I know your writing, and you're a friend of Vicky; that is quite enough for me. It will be enough for Clarice, too. She knows Vicky and is very fond of her. I'll telephone to her right away and tell her you are coming to stay. Then we will take a taxi and collect your belongings. Tonight we can all go along to the private view of Vicky's exhibition together.'

'Vicky has an exhibition here, in London?'

'Yes, I thought you knew. Vicky will be there. She's staying with one of her suffragette friends. I brought her up from Cornwall in my motor car. She'll be delighted to see you.'

28

Alan was excited at the thought of meeting Vicky again and by the end of that afternoon he was wearing clothes more suitable for the company they were likely to be mingling with at the Piccadilly gallery where her paintings were on display.

He had expressed his misgivings about the cheap suit to Cecil, explaining that he did not want to be an embarrassment to Vicky, but had been unable to find anything better in Chatham. In any case, he could not afford to spend too much money until his future was settled.

A kindly man, Cecil would not agree that Alan's suit was cheap and ill-fitting, but did suggest it was not in keeping with Alan's new status in society as a poet and writer. When Alan protested that he had not yet earned the right to such a status, Cecil said, 'Of course you have! How many artists have sold anything when they first refer to themselves as "artists"? You are selling your stories and articles – yes, and poems too. As far as anyone else is concerned you *are* a writer. As such you are allowed a certain latitude in your mode of dress, but I know you will feel far more comfortable if you are suitably attired for tonight's preview.'

On a more practical level, Cecil took Alan along to his own tailors. As well as advising on his choice of clothes, he had them charged to his own account, telling Alan he could settle up with him after an advance from Julian's publishing company was safely deposited in the bank. He added, in a low voice that did not carry to the sales assistant, that however long that might take, it would be even longer before it reached the tailor.

Alan's confidence was boosted greatly when Clarice, Cecil's sister, told him he looked so handsome that he was her choice of escort for the private view. Her friendliness and easy manner swiftly removed any doubts he had entertained about staying in her house for a few days.

That evening Clarice, Cecil and Alan took a motor taxi-cab from Knightsbridge to the exhibition, which was in a gallery behind the Burlington Arcade. At Clarice's request, they alighted from the vehicle in busy Piccadilly because she wanted to walk through the arcade to look at the shops.

Unfamiliar with this part of London, Alan was amazed at the quantity of luxurious goods on offer – and the prices being asked for them. It was not long before he began to feel nervous at the prospect of meeting Vicky in such surroundings. He felt she must be far more important than he had realised when they had been together, in uniform, in Cornwall.

His apprehension increased when they arrived at the gallery and he saw the number of people already there.

Aware of his nervousness, Clarice understood the reason for it. Before they entered the gallery she took his arm, saying, 'Stay close to me, Alan. I love these exhibitions and am very excited at the thought of seeing so much of Vicky's work, but I find one or two of the people who attend such functions somewhat awesome.'

Inside the gallery, Alan was glad he had expressed misgivings about his only suit to Cecil. It would have been glaringly out of place here. Some of the men, artists in particular, were dressed in a casual fashion – but it was *expensively* casual. Others were dressed as though they had called in at the gallery en route to an evening at the theatre, as were many of the women.

It was a few moments before Alan spotted Vicky. She was at the centre of a crowd of viewers and he recognised her immediately – but this was not the Vicky he had known in Newlyn.

The khaki uniform had, of course, gone. In its place was a pale blue, off-the-shoulder gown. Her long blonde hair, which had either been coiled up in a tight bun beneath her uniform hat or tied back casually when she was paint-ing, was now swept back into a long chignon decorated with a bow of ribbon to match her dress.

Alan thought she was without doubt the most elegant woman in the room and his heart sank. He should not have come here tonight. He was out of place among these people; in these surroundings.

'Come on, let's go and say hello to Vicky.' Aware of his sudden uncertainty, Clarice squeezed his arm.

At that moment, Vicky's glance fell upon the new arrivals. There was a delighted smile for Cecil, a nod of acknowledgement for Clarice, and then her glance just touched on Alan before moving away again.

His confidence sank to a new low, but suddenly Vicky's glance flicked back to him and her expression registered an astonishment that was as quickly replaced by sheer delight. Abruptly breaking away from the startled circle of art-lovers and sycophants, she hurried to greet the newcomers. Clarice had seen Vicky's reaction to seeing Alan and she released her grip on his arm as Vicky hurried towards them.

'Alan, what a wonderful surprise . . . and look at you! I never recognised you in civilian clothes.'

As Vicky kissed him warmly, Alan was aware of the interest shown by others in the gallery and he felt the colour rising in his cheeks as he said, 'You look very different in these surroundings too, Vicky.'

'Well . . . I'm the belle of the ball this evening,' she replied happily. Belatedly acknowledging the presence of Cecil and Clarice, she added, 'It's lovely to see you both here, too. Thank you for bringing Alan along . . . but where did you find him?'

'Alan called in at the publishers as Julian was about to go out for lunch with Cecil,' Clarice replied. 'Afterwards Cecil brought him home. He'll be staying with us for a while.'

Vicky's interest shifted back to Alan immediately. 'You're staying at Clarice's house? What of Dora? Have you been home?'

'It's a long story,' Alan replied unhappily, 'and not one for tonight. This is a very special occasion for you.'

'It certainly is now . . . Come with me.'

Taking Alan firmly by the hand, she led him across the gallery floor and guests moved aside to let them pass. Eventually, she came to a halt and, turning, called out, 'Ladies and gentlemen, I have a very special and quite unexpected treat for you this evening. I know from your comments that you have all been very taken with the two portraits I have put together under the single heading of "Heroes". Well, I am delighted to say that here with us this evening is one of those heroes. May I introduce to you Alan Carter, CGM, DSM, late of His Majesty's Royal Navy.'

Having attracted the attention of the guests in the gallery, she moved aside to reveal the portrait of the RFC pilot Alan had last seen hanging in her Newlyn studio. Beside it was another he had seen only in its unfinished state. It was the portrait of himself.

There was a buzz of interest and applause from the guests in the gallery and a surge of movement towards the portraits. Alan suddenly found himself the centre of much attention. Vicky spent as much time as possible with him, but for the remainder of the evening it seemed there were always men and women, both young and old, eager to talk to him. He was beginning to feel the strain of his unexpected celebrity status before those attending the private view began to leave and Vicky, Clarice and Cecil were able to join up with him once more.

A great many of the cards alongside each painting were adorned with a small red sticker indicating it had been sold, and Cecil commented, 'This is one of the most successful private views I have ever attended, Vicky. You must be very pleased indeed.'

'It has been an absolutely magical evening in every

way,' Vicky replied. 'And having Alan here is the icing on the cake. I have spent much of the time listening to ladies saying how charming he is – and so appealingly shy. What's more, Lady Bellingham offered me two hundred and fifty guineas for his portrait! She said he reminded her of a young nephew who was lost at sea during the war. The offer quite took my breath away, but I told her it was not mine to sell, but yours, Alan. I promised I would put her offer to you.'

Alan stared at her in disbelief. 'You can't give something to me that's worth so much money!'

'It didn't have a value on it when I told you it was yours,' Vicky pointed out happily, 'and I would never have dared to put such a price on *any* of my paintings. It was because you were here that the offer was made. Your presence also helped to sell many of the others.' Bubbling with happiness, she went on, 'Now, why don't we all go out and celebrate a wonderful and successful evening? I know a delightful little restaurant just round the corner . . .'

29

Dinner, like the private view of Vicky's exhibition, was a very happy occasion. The restaurant served excellent food and wine even though it was not in the grand style of the restaurant where Alan and Cecil had eaten lunch. Instead, it was small and intimate and Alan felt quite relaxed and comfortable.

Dora was not mentioned once in the animated conversation at the table, but she was never far from the thoughts of either Alan or Vicky. Alan could not help comparing the vivacious and open chatter of the two women at the table with the surly and secretive manner of Dora, while for her part, Vicky wondered how much Alan had learned of his wife's conduct while he was away and how serious was the rift between them.

Clarice was an intelligent and observant woman and it had become apparent to her at the gallery that Vicky and Alan were more than mere acquaintances. Yet she was equally certain they were not, and had never been, lovers. Gradually during the course of the meal she learned how they had first met and of the part Vicky had played in furthering Alan's writing ambitions.

There was another question that intrigued Clarice and she broached the subject over coffee, asking Vicky, 'Tell me, when did you paint that wonderful portrait of Alan?'

'It took me most of nineteen eighteen,' Vicky replied, and explained the reason why it had taken so long.

'The result is well worth the wait,' Clarice commented. 'I am also convinced it is worth the sum Lady Bellingham offered you. There may well have been sentimental reasons for her wanting it, but she is also a very shrewd collector. Tell me, who is the other "hero" you painted, the Royal Flying Corps pilot?'

In a sudden change of mood, Vicky said, 'That was Paul. I met him much earlier in the war. We were to be married, but he was shot down and killed.'

'I'm terribly sorry, Vicky. I really shouldn't have been so inquisitive. It is unforgivable of me.' Clarice was genuinely upset.

'You weren't to know,' Vicky replied. Smiling wanly at Clarice, she added, 'It all seems such a long time ago now. A great many things have happened since then.' Suddenly looking around her, she changed the subject abruptly. 'Do you realise we are the last customers left in the restaurant?'

'I'm not surprised,' Cecil said. 'It's after one o'clock.'

'Is it really?' Vicky was startled. 'It has been such a lovely evening, the time has simply flown by. Fortunately I need not fear waking Sylvia when I get back to the flat. She is attending a meeting somewhere in the west country and won't be home until tomorrow evening – I mean *this* evening, of course.'

'You are not considering returning to the East End at this time of night?' Clarice was horrified. 'How will you get there?'

'On the Underground,' Vicky replied. 'It runs all through the night.'

'I don't care *when* it runs,' Clarice declared. 'No, Vicky, I won't hear of such a thing. You'll come home to Knightsbridge with the rest of us . . . and I will accept no argument. It has been such a lovely evening, I have no intention of spoiling it by lying awake worrying about you for the remainder of the night. Cecil will settle the bill and then we will call for a taxi.'

Within minutes of returning to Clarice's Knightsbridge house and showing Vicky the room she would occupy for the night, Cecil and Clarice announced their intention of going to bed. Before leaving the room, Clarice insisted on pouring drinks for Alan and Vicky, commenting that she was quite certain Vicky would not be able to sleep right away after such an exciting evening, and suggesting that Alan remain to keep her company for a while.

It was so blatantly obvious that Clarice and Cecil had conspired to leave the two in each other's company that, when they had left the room, an embarrassed Alan apologised to Vicky and offered to leave her alone to think about the events of the day.

'Why on earth should you do that?' she replied. 'It would be churlish after all the trouble our hostess has taken to bring us both under the same roof and leave us together like this.'

Vicky had drunk more than she was used to that evening and the success of the private view had added to her heady sense of well-being. Had it not been so she might have hesitated before asking, 'Have things gone totally wrong between you and Dora, Alan?'

'Yes, very wrong.'

When he failed to amplify his brief statement, Vicky prompted, 'Do you want to tell me about it?'

'There's very little to tell, really. We're both three years older than we were when we married and we've changed. Dora certainly has – or it could be that I never really knew her when we married. Perhaps she somehow felt it was glamorous to be married to a man in uniform during wartime, but the glamour has disappeared now the war is over. Whatever the cause, I don't think either of us is the person the other thought we were.'

Vicky wondered whether she ought to reveal what she had learned about Dora, but although drink had made her light-headed, it had not turned her reckless. As she had on an earlier occasion when such an opportunity had arisen, she deemed it wiser to remain silent.

'What will you do – about your marriage to Dora and your life too, now you have left the Navy?'

'Cecil asked me the same question. The truth is I just don't know, Vicky. I need time to think things out. But don't let's talk about me. You've had a wonderful day. When I saw you in the gallery looking absolutely stunning and the centre of attention, I felt very proud just knowing you. What will *you* do now? Are you going to remain in Newlyn, or will you move to London?'

'I certainly won't move back to London. Life would be far too stifling to do what I enjoy most – painting. No, I will stay in Cornwall, although I might decide to move just a little way along the coast, to Lamorna. I particularly like it there.'

As she talked, she stifled a yawn, and Alan said, 'You must be tired after such an exciting day. I mustn't keep you up any longer.'

Vicky protested, but when Alan said he was going to bed, she admitted, 'Yes, I suppose I ought to go too. I need to call at Sylvia's flat to change before returning to the gallery to face whatever tomorrow will bring. You go on upstairs. I'll stay here and relax for a few minutes more.'

When Alan had left the room, Vicky wondered why she had not told him of the way Dora had behaved while he was away. She decided it was because she had sensed the pain in him over what had happened between them and she did not want to hurt him any more.

The next morning at breakfast everyone was decidedly jaded, although they all agreed it had been a memorable evening. When the meal was over, and Vicky announced her intention of hurrying away to the underground railway station at Sloane Square, Alan said he would walk to the station with her. He explained that he would have gone all the way to Old Ford Road with her, but Cecil was taking him to see the publisher.

On the way to Sloane Square, Vicky asked, 'Have you thought any more about Lady Bellingham's offer for your painting?'

'I wouldn't sell it, Vicky. I doubt whether anyone will ever want to paint me again, and . . . well, it's special.'

'I could always paint your portrait again, if you wanted me to – and you could do a great deal with two hundred and fifty guineas.'

'I realise that. If Lady Bellingham comes into the gallery again, tell her that if ever I do decide to sell, it will be to her.'

'I am not yet an expert, but I feel that with an offer like that you need to strike while she is in the mood to buy.'

'Had you not given the painting to me, would you have sold it to her?'

The question was not one Vicky had been expecting. 'I'm an artist, Alan. I paint pictures to sell them to people. It's how an artist earns a living.'

'That's not an answer, Vicky.'

'No . . . no, it isn't,' she agreed, after a few moments' hesitation.

'Well, would you have sold it?'

Vicky shook her head. 'No, I wouldn't have sold it to her.' Looking at him, she added, 'Your portrait and the one I painted of Paul are probably the best works I have ever produced. I would not be happy parting with them on a purely commercial basis.'

It was the truth, but not the whole truth. Both portraits had an emotional value for her. She would never sell them.

'What you are saying is that both portraits are special?'

'Yes.'

'That's the way I feel too. Quite apart from that, one day you are going to be very famous, so I will know that I am leaving something valuable to my son or daughter.'

Vicky could not immediately think of an appropriate reply. When she remained silent, Alan asked, 'Can I see you this evening?'

'When?'

'When the gallery closes. I'd like to take you for a quiet

meal somewhere. The place where we ate last night, perhaps?'

Vicky shook her head. 'It was a very enjoyable evening to celebrate my success and your demobilisation from the Navy, but I think I would prefer somewhere a little quieter tonight. There is a very small restaurant in Jermyn Street that I have often passed and thought I would like to eat there someday.' She looked at him questioningly. 'How about the expense? London restaurants are notorious. Will you allow me to pay half towards it?'

'No. If Cecil can persuade Julian to give me an advance it will be no problem. If he can't . . . well, I can always take you back to the East End. I know some very good pie shops there.'

Vicky laughed, 'If you did, you would probably discover that I know the owners. Sylvia and I have often eaten in pie shops. In fact, in pre-war days their best customers were probably suffragettes.'

30

Accompanied by Cecil, Alan left the publishing house happy in the knowledge that he would not be reduced to treating Vicky to a meal in an East End pie shop. Julian had parted with an advance of fifty per cent of the sum he had agreed to pay Alan for writing the torpedo boat book.

Even after settling the debt he owed to Cecil, Alan was richer than he had ever been at any time in his life, and that evening he arrived at the Piccadilly art gallery filled with a rare confidence in himself.

Vicky's welcome was just as warm as it had been on the previous day. She was happy, and eager to show him the reviews her exhibition had received in the daily papers.

'They have been wonderful,' she said delightedly, 'and they all mention your portrait and the fact that you were here. As a result I have sold almost all my paintings – and I could have sold yours a dozen times over, for even more than Lady Bellingham was offering!'

'Then we have both had another happy day.' Alan told Vicky of Julian's advance, adding, 'It's all thanks to Cecil. I feel I should buy him a present of some sort as a thank you. I would never have been given the advance had he not spoken for me.'

'Cecil will not be expecting anything,' Vicky said, 'but he *is* so kind to everyone, it would be wonderful for him to be given something in return. Yes, it's a lovely idea – and I know something he has seen that he said he would really like. It would be useful, too, when he's on his travels. It's a Waterman fountain pen. There was one in a shop in the Burlington Arcade that particularly caught his eye – and it's not too expensive. Would you like me to show it to you? I can leave the gallery for a few minutes.'

The fountain pen that had attracted Cecil's attention was still in the window of the shop in the Burlington Arcade and Vicky came into the shop with Alan to purchase it. The price was higher than Alan would have dreamed of paying for anything before today, but he felt proud of the fact that he was now able to comfortably afford to do so. Later that evening, he and Vicky enjoyed a meal together in the small, intimate restaurant she had mentioned to him and they left feeling very happy and slightly intoxicated.

In his present state of unaccustomed affluence, Alan would have hailed a taxicab to take Vicky back to Sylvia Pankhurst's flat, but Vicky refused point-blank to use such an expensive form of transport. She would travel, as she usually did, by the underground railway. Unable to persuade her to change her mind, Alan said he would accompany her, in order to satisfy himself of her safe arrival at her destination.

On the train they chose a compartment that had no other passengers inside, but at the next stop along the line the door opened just as the train was about to depart and three noisy youths tumbled inside. They too had been drinking, but drink had not mellowed them. It was not long before they began remarking on the other two occupants of their compartment.

Alan paid little attention to them until they began making comments about Vicky, using language that became increasingly offensive. Then he rose to his feet, moved to where the loudest of the three was seated and sat down beside him. The youth started up as though anticipating the need to defend himself. However, with a disarming smile, Alan said, 'It's all right. I just want to whisper something in your ear.'

The youth sat warily on the edge of his seat as Alan put his mouth close to his ear and spoke in a voice that was too soft to carry as far as Vicky. Colour rose in the young man's cheeks and, when Alan finished talking and straightened up, he said indignantly, 'There was no call for that!'

'No? Well, I seem to have made myself perfectly clear,' Alan replied, with the same enigmatic smile.

The train was slowing to enter a station. When it stopped, the youth to whom he had been speaking stood up and said to his companions, 'Come on, let's find another compartment. This one's too crowded.'

The three young men left the carriage without a backward glance and, as the train jolted into motion once more, Vicky said, 'That was most impressive! What did you say to him?'

'You really don't want to know!' Alan grinned. 'I combined a little naval jargon with some East End talk. Something I thought they might understand. It seems to have done the trick.'

At their destination, Alan fielded the attentions of a belligerent drunk before handing a coin to a small and extremely grubby boy who wore outsize boots on his feet, but no socks, and whose ragged coat was secured by a single button, pushed through the wrong buttonhole.

Vicky walked beside him thoughtfully for a while before saying, 'You are very much at home in this part of London, Alan. Do you think you will ever leave it to live somewhere else?'

'I don't *feel* at home here, Vicky. Not any more. The small boy begging, the drunk . . . yes, and the youngsters on the train, too, are the same as others I've met up with all over the world in the Navy. It has nothing to do with being at home in any one particular place. To tell you the truth, I don't really know where home is right now.'

Later that evening, after Alan had left to return to Clarice's house, Vicky was undressing in her room in Sylvia Pankhurst's flat. She thought of what Alan had said about having no place he could look upon as home. She felt he deserved far more from life than that.

Alan was a regular visitor to the gallery during the next few days, but Vicky was kept busy with promotional dinners and functions in the evenings. It was not until some days later that she was able to come to Knightsbridge for dinner.

It was to be her final evening in London. The exhibition had been such a huge success that all the paintings offered for sale had been purchased. They would remain on exhibition for a few days more, but there was no need for Vicky to be in attendance. The gallery owner had already made a provisional booking for her to have another exhibition in twelve months' time, and Vicky was anxious to return to Cornwall as quickly as possible and begin work on more paintings.

Cecil too was due to leave London in a couple of days, heading for his holiday in Italy. Alan was aware he should leave the house before then.

Clarice had invited half a dozen close friends to join them for dinner and Alan's portrait was displayed in the dining room for the occasion. Vicky's success had attracted a great deal of publicity and, as Clarice had intended, having the artist, sitter and portrait in the same room provoked a great deal of interest, especially as Cecil had insisted upon introducing Alan as 'a very promising author and poet'.

During the course of the meal, one of the guests asked Vicky what she intended doing now she had made such an impact upon the London art scene.

'I shall return to Cornwall and paint with renewed confidence,' she replied. 'Cecil has insisted that I drive his car back there for him. I mean to leave early tomorrow morning.' To Alan she explained, 'Cecil is very, very proud of his motor car. He says he will be happier knowing it is safely garaged in Newlyn until his return.'

Alan was seated next to Vicky at the table. He had been unaware that she would be leaving London so soon. Upset at the thought of losing her company, he said quietly, 'I shall miss you, Vicky, but I can understand your eagerness to be back in Cornwall. Although much of my time there was spent in hospital I have very fond memories of the place – of Newlyn in particular.'

'Then why not come back with me?'

Vicky's suggestion took him by surprise. 'Come to Cornwall? What would I do there – and where could I stay? I couldn't impose upon the Penhaligons again.'

'You wouldn't need to impose upon anyone. There would be no difficulty in finding a place for you to stay – and can you think of anywhere better to work as an author? The book you've been commissioned to write is about the sea and it would be right there, on your doorstep.'

Listening to their conversation from across the table, Cecil said, 'Vicky's quite right, you know, Alan. Cornwall is as good for authors as it is for artists. I have found more inspiration there than anywhere else. I would offer you my place while I am away, but I have let it out to a couple who are acting as resident housekeepers until my return. However, I agree with Vicky: you will have no trouble at all finding somewhere to stay.'

For a few minutes, Alan picked at his food distractedly as he thought over what Vicky and Cecil had suggested. He had never really contemplated going away from London to live and work but, thinking about it now, he realised it made a great deal of sense. There was nothing to keep him in London now his marriage to Dora had broken up. Indeed, it would be an opportunity to make a new start, to set out on a new career with no need to feel guilty should his writing fail to sell sufficiently to earn a living. He had no one to consider but himself and he could fit in very easily with the artist community. Most had lifestyles very similar to the one he would be adopting.

Suddenly aware that Vicky was talking to him, he remembered where he was. 'I'm sorry, Vicky, I was deep in thought. What did you say?'

'It was nothing of any importance. Were you thinking about Newlyn?'

'Yes.'

'And have you reached a decision?'

Alan nodded and a forkful of food halted halfway to Vicky's mouth as she awaited his reply. 'If you're happy about driving me to Cornwall tomorrow, I'll come with you.'

Vicky's uninhibited squeal of delight brought conversation at the table to a temporary halt and she waited until it resumed and she was no longer the centre of attention before excitedly turning to Clarice, who was seated on the other side of her. 'Alan has decided to come to Newlyn to write. I shall be taking him with me tomorrow.'

'I can think of nowhere better to pursue such a way of life,' Clarice commented approvingly. 'I am very pleased – for both of you.'

31

Vicky stayed the night in Knightsbridge after telephoning Sylvia Pankhurst to say she would be at Old Ford Road with Cecil's car early the next morning to collect her things. Unfortunately, Clarice's friends remained at the house until much later than had been anticipated, with the result that Vicky and Alan left the house rather later than intended the following morning and both were feeling tired.

On the drive across London Vicky complained bitterly about the amount of traffic on the roads. Since the war years motor traffic in the city had increased enormously, but there were still a great many horse-drawn vehicles in use and it was these which reduced traffic to a crawl for a great deal of the time.

Once they reached Sylvia's flat it took no more than fifteen minutes for Vicky to gather her belongings, and then it was time to negotiate the heavy traffic once more.

In a bid to avoid the congestion of the main East End roads, Vicky decided it would be quicker to drive through some of the back streets of Bethnal Green. All went well until they turned into a narrow slum street and found a horse-drawn coal cart blocking the road.

Annoyed, Vicky sounded the horn of the Hotchkiss, startling the horse. Fortunately, the brake had been applied to a wheel of the cart, but the noise brought the coalman from a nearby house, grumbling, 'All right, all right! There's no need for all that bleeding noise and frightening the horse. It won't hurt you to wait for half a minute.' Releasing the brake, he moved horse and cart close enough to the pavement to allow the motor car to pass.

At that moment a second coalman came from the house on the side of the road closest to the car and he gave a start of surprise when he saw Alan. Recognition was mutual and, when they were clear of the coal cart, Vicky said, 'One of the coalmen seemed to recognise you, Alan. Is he someone you know?'

'Yes,' Alan said in a strained voice. 'It was Charlie Platt. Dora's brother.'

'It *was* him, I tell you. There's no doubt about it. He was sitting in this car as large as life, being driven by some posh-looking woman.' Charlie Platt was sitting in the kitchen of the Quilter Street house, noisily sipping tea as he related details of his encounter with Alan to his parents and a disbelieving Dora.

'Who would he know who has a car?' Dora asked scornfully. 'You was seeing things.'

'I tell you it *was* him. I was as close to him as I am to you – and he recognised me too. You should have seen the expression on his face. Mind you, he was wearing clothes that were a sight more expensive than that uniform he used to wear. I wish I had some like 'em to take down to Uncle Solly's when I'm a bit skint.'

'Uncle' was the East End term for a pawnbroker and 'Uncle' Solomon Percival was a well-known money-lender, with a shop in nearby Hackney Road.

'He'd loan me enough on 'em to keep me and Pa in drink for a week or two. If that's what writing poetry gets you I might start writing some meself.'

'It's as much as you can do to write your own name,' Winnie retorted scornfully, 'but it certainly sounds as though Alan has fallen on his feet. I always thought he would.' It was a blatant lie, but she turned to Dora nevertheless. 'I told you so when you and he fell out. You never have known which side your bread's buttered, me girl.'

'He wouldn't have stayed long with me like this,' Dora retorted, resting a hand on her bulging stomach.

'That's where you're wrong,' Winnie snapped at her. 'It would have kept him here like nothing else ever would have. He hung on your every word and you wouldn't have had to work very hard to convince him it was his, had you wanted to. All right, the timing of it would have been a bit out, but so what? There's any number of babies who don't go their full time. You're a fool, Dora. I told you so at the time and I'm telling you again now. You'd have had someone to look after you for the rest of your life and be a sight better off than you are now.'

'It's all right for you to talk,' Dora said sulkily. 'You're not the one who would have had to live with him – to live a lie. I don't love him and I don't think I ever have.'

'What's love got to do with anything?' Winnie asked

213

angrily. 'You told me you loved this American and that he loved you! Where has that got you, I'd like to know? I'll tell you, it's got you a bun in the oven and the cook's disappeared. You want to forget all about this love nonsense. Find out where Alan is and tell him the baby's his. Swallow your pride and say you want to try again to make a go of things. If you don't you've got hard times ahead of you – far harder than any you've known up until now. Like I've told you before, you'll pay your way in this house, or you're out on the street. Think about it.'

The weather for the first half of the journey to Cornwall was fine and, with Vicky driving, she and Alan made good time. Then the skies became overcast and it began to drizzle, then to pour. Vicky brought the tourer to a halt and she and Alan raised the hood to protect them from the rain, but the bad weather reduced their speed considerably. They had hoped to arrive in Newlyn before nightfall, but they were still a hundred miles from their destination when the weather brought on a premature dusk. And then one of the rear tyres punctured.

The sudden emergency tested Vicky's driving skill to the full and when the Hotchkiss finally came to a halt she sat leaning her forehead on the wheel and saying nothing for several seconds.

'Are you all right?' Alan asked anxiously.

Expelling her breath noisily in an expression of relief, Vicky raised her head from the wheel. 'Yes, I'm fine. It's not the first time I have had a puncture, but never in such weather and driving at speed.'

'You did wonderfully well to avoid an accident,' Alan

214

said admiringly. 'No one could possibly have done better – but what do we do now?'

'We change the wheel,' Vicky replied. 'Fortunately, the Hotchkiss carries a couple of spares . . . but it's not going to be much fun in this rain.'

'There's no need for both of us to get wet,' Alan said. 'I'll get out and change it. You stay in the dry and tell me what to do.'

'No, we'll have it done far more quickly if we both do it. Besides, I have changed wheels many times. Have you?'

Alan had to admit it was something of which he had no experience.

'Then it's settled,' Vicky declared. 'We do it together. Now, I wonder where the jack is kept?'

While Vicky searched for the jack, Alan unfastened one of the two spare wheels carried on the Hotchkiss's running boards. The jack located, Alan went down on hands and knees to place it in position beneath the car. Then, working the handle, he raised the side of the car sufficiently for Vicky to remove the wheel with the punctured tyre and replace it with the spare he had in readiness.

Carrying out the work swiftly and efficiently, Vicky informed Alan that she had driven a Hotchkiss in France, during the war. Then, soaking wet but triumphant, they both climbed back inside the car and resumed their drive along the darkened road.

The second puncture occurred when they were no more than twenty miles from their destination, and it was raining harder than ever. Fortunately, it happened when they were driving comparatively slowly, but changing the wheel was no more comfortable than before. Alan commented that if they had to get out of the car again there would soon be as much water inside as out.

The weather and their two mishaps threw their timetable into chaos and it was midnight before they drew up outside Vicky's studio flat and she gave a relieved cheer.

'Well, that's you home safely,' Alan said despondently, 'but I don't know what I'm going to do. The Fisherman's Arms will have closed long ago and I can't think of anywhere else I can try at this time of night.'

'Don't even consider it!' Vicky said positively. 'Just look at yourself! Even if there was somewhere open, do you think they would give you a room in the state you are in? No, come into the studio. We'll light a fire to get warm and both change into some dry clothes. Then I'll make up a bed for you.'

Alan realised there was no sense in arguing with her. Vicky was right. Even if somewhere was open they were hardly likely to welcome him in his present state.

'Thanks, Vicky. You're quite right, I feel like a drowned rat. You open up and I'll bring our things inside.'

Vicky hurried up the outside staircase and Alan unloaded the luggage from the back of the Hotchkiss. After securing the vehicle, he struggled up the wet steps with his load. Pushing his way inside the studio, he saw a welcoming fire burning in the studio grate and Vicky, wrapped in a warm dressing-gown, thumbing the cork from a champagne bottle.

When he expressed surprise, Vicky said, 'Isn't it great? I left a key to the studio with Fiona and sent a postcard to say I would be home tonight. This is the result. She has also built up the kitchen fire and left a basket of goodies in there, together with another bottle of champagne. I will be able to cook something for us. Fiona is an awful pain at times, but she can also be very kind. Go into the bedroom and change those wet clothes – and take this with you.'

Vicky handed him a glass of champagne and, carrying this and the bag containing a change of clothes, Alan disappeared into the bedroom.

When he returned to the studio wearing dry clothes, with his hair combed and feeling a whole lot tidier, there was a mouth-watering smell drifting from the kitchen. He put his head inside the small room, and Vicky said, 'There was some steak in the basket. I'm cooking it now – we can have it with some bread. In the meantime, pour yourself more champagne.'

'I feel I should be doing something. After all, you've driven the car all the way from London.'

Vicky gave him a smile. 'It *was* a pretty horrific journey and with some people I know it would have been utterly miserable, but despite everything it was somehow . . . *fun*! But, to tell you the truth, I'm so happy just to be home, nothing else seems to matter.'

Alan grimaced. 'I know what you mean. Had I made the journey with anyone else we would have ended up hating each other . . . but let's not have *too* many such "fun" days, eh?'

They both laughed, and there was suddenly such a tangible feeling of closeness between them that they were both momentarily embarrassed.

Vicky broke the silence by saying, 'I think this champagne is going to my head. We had better start on the steak right away.'

When Alan lifted the bottle to top up Vicky's glass while she served up the meal, he realised she had not been holding back while he changed into dry clothes. Smiling, he poured himself a hefty refill to catch up.

The second bottle was opened before they had finished eating and afterwards they sat in front of the studio fire, Alan occupying the only armchair and Vicky seated on a rug on the floor, just in front of him.

Suddenly she said, 'I have a bottle of armagnac in the kitchen. Cecil brought it back for me from Paris when he made a trip there just after the war ended. Have you ever had a champagne cocktail?'

'No, but we've drunk a bottle and a half of champagne . . .'

'Then we have just enough left to mix with the armagnac to make the cocktail. We're celebrating, Alan. I'm celebrating a successful exhibition, you the beginning of a new career – and we're both celebrating reaching Newlyn after overcoming two punctures and some atrocious weather.'

She scrambled to her feet and made her way, only slightly unsteadily, to the kitchen. She returned with two glasses filled with a mixture of armagnac and champagne and handed one to Alan before resuming her seat on the floor at his feet.

Tasting his drink, Alan realised there was a great deal of armagnac mixed in the cocktail and for a moment he hesitated. They had started drinking before they had eaten, and it was the only food they had taken since breakfast. They had forgone a midday meal in the hope of beating the weather and reaching Newlyn before nightfall.

However, the cocktail tasted good, the fire was warm and it felt even cosier when Vicky leaned her head against his leg. Then the glass she was holding almost slipped from her hand, spilling what little alcohol remained on the floor.

'Are you all right, Vicky?' he asked.

'I'm not terribly sure,' she replied ambiguously. 'I think it might be time I went to bed.'

Alan smiled. 'I think that's a good idea. Before you go, do you have a couple of spare blankets and a pillow? I'll make up a bed on the studio couch.' The couch was an ancient, heavy chaise-longue at the far end of the studio, on which Vicky sometimes posed her models.

'I don't think I do have any spare blankets. The only ones I possess are on my bed. You're welcome to share those, if you want to.'

Her words took Alan aback. After a moment, he said, 'Let's not do anything you're likely to regret in the morning, Vicky.'

Vicky turned her head to look at him and for a moment he forgot they had both drunk too much.

'I've recently been through a war, Alan – we both have. I've seen many men – pitifully young men – die before they discovered what life had to offer them. I made a decision – a *sober* decision – that when *I* die I am going to regret nothing I have done, only the things I have failed to do.'

Lost for words, Alan said nothing.

Recognising his uncertainty, Vicky said, 'This isn't a spur-of-the-moment decision, Alan. It's something I have thought about a lot, for a very long time. Almost from the day when I took you from Newlyn hospital to Devonport, probably. It could not have happened then, but the only barrier now is the disapproval of others, and I realised just how little *that* means when I became a suffragette.'

Looking at him as though hoping to read his thoughts, she said, 'Have I shocked you, Alan? Perhaps I have misread your feelings for me. If I have, I'm sorry – but I still have no spare blankets.'

She struggled to rise to her feet, but Alan's hand on her shoulder held her back. Looking down at her upturned face he surprised her – and himself – by kissing her.

When he eventually drew back, he said, 'You're like no other woman I've ever known, Vicky. I've realised that for a very long time too, but have never dared say so. You and I come from very different worlds and I've always been aware of the difficulties that poses.'

Rubbing her cheek against his hand, Vicky said, 'That is open to discussion, Alan – but not tonight. We'll talk about it in the morning – if you still feel you must. For now, think about what I have said. Don't regret anything you do, only the things you leave undone . . .'

32

It was late when Alan woke the next morning, but Vicky was still asleep beside him, lying on his left arm, her breath whispering softly against his neck.

The events of the previous night had moved with a speed he found difficult to comprehend, yet the outcome had not come as a complete surprise. He had always been aware that he was attracted to Vicky, but had never allowed himself to dwell on the direction their relationship could take. Had he done so, his marriage to Dora, coupled with a background so far removed from Vicky's, would have seemed an insurmountable barrier.

Now Vicky had shown such barriers to be illusory – for one night, at least – and during that night had shared with him the passion that had been so hurtfully lacking from Dora on his return home to her.

He wondered where they would go from here. Whether Vicky would wake and regret what had happened between them . . .

'Will you accept a penny for them, or will I need to

increase my offer?' Vicky's sleepy voice broke into his thoughts.

'Pardon?' Her question startled him; he had not been aware she had woken.

'Your thoughts . . . I'm making a bid for them.' She made no attempt to move and seemed very snug lying cradled in his arms.

'I was worrying about how you would feel when you woke. Whether you might be appalled at finding yourself in bed with me and think I took advantage of you. I mean, we did have quite a lot to drink.'

'Yes, we did,' Vicky admitted, 'but it hasn't erased my memory. I seem to recall that we are sharing a bed at my invitation – and I have no regrets at all.' Shifting her position, she supported her weight on one elbow and looked down at him. 'Do you, Alan? Are you wishing it had never happened?'

'What sort of question is that?' Reaching up, he pulled her down to him once more. 'It's how I've always imagined making love should be, but . . . where do we go from here, Vicky?'

'Where do you want us to go?' she countered. 'Would you like to forget it happened and go back to being the way we were? I don't think I could do that.'

'Neither could I,' Alan admitted, 'and it certainly isn't what I want. Nothing is ever going to be the same again for me. But I'm still a married man – and we come from very different family backgrounds, Vicky.'

'We're not talking of a relationship with each other's family, Alan. Besides, we've both been closely involved in a war – a horrific war, but if any good *did* come out of it,

222

.t was that it has been a great melting-pot for social inequalities. There could be no barriers between two men when they cowered together in a muddy shell-hole. If either of them showed himself, a German would not take his social standing into consideration before shooting him As for your marriage . . . I thought it was over.'

'It is,' Alan said hurriedly.

'So, who have we hurt?' Vicky asked. Raising herself on one elbow once more, she said, 'I wanted you last night, Alan, and I still do. As I told you last night, I think I have felt that way since those very early days, right here in Newlyn – but I believed you to be happily married then. You've asked me what happens now . . . well, that's very much up to you.'

Alan looked up at her for a long time before replying. 'I've never met a woman like you, Vicky. Never!'

'If that means I don't play silly games, then you are quite right,' Vicky said. 'At least, not when something really matters. It was one of the first things I learned as a suffragette, although it was always one of the most misunderstood things about us. We were not playing games. We all believed passionately in what we were doing. It was important – and this is important too, Alan. At least, it is to me.'

'It's important to me too, Vicky, believe me. I've known for a long time how I feel about you, but, like you, I realised I had no right to feel that way. Then, when I saw you at the gallery in London, surrounded by your admirers, I believed you to be further away from me than ever. You belong among such people. When I heard and read what was being said about your work, it only confirmed what

223

I felt. Now, here we are in bed together and I'm very confused . . . you're already a great success, while I'm just an unemployed ex-sailor.'

'Don't talk yourself down, Alan. You are far more than that. One day you will be a successful and well-thought-of author and poet. You must remember that only a week ago I was a struggling artist whom nobody had heard of – and who could just as quickly be forgotten again.'

Vicky lapsed into silence for a while. Then she said, quietly, 'If I ask you a question, will you give me an honest reply – *truly* honest, whether or not you think it might hurt me? If you don't, I am going to be hurt far more in the future.'

Alan nodded, wondering what she was going to ask him.

When she spoke again, Vicky said, 'Have you been honest with me about the reasons why you are concerned about our relationship – or is there something more?'

When he did not reply immediately, Vicky said, 'Please, Alan, tell me – and be truthful. What I'm asking is, am I just a one-night stand for you? Don't deny it because you think I might be upset and offended. That isn't important. In fact I would admire your honesty. What I could never forgive is for you to say it's more than that when you know in your heart it is not. It's the truth I want, Alan . . . please!'

When Alan still remained silent, Vicky felt he was trying to pluck up the courage to say her fears were well founded, but when he did speak his reply was serious and considered.

'When I joined the Navy at the beginning of the war I was in training with an Irishman and we became good friends – very good friends. Like me, he'd lost his mother and his father wasn't around. He too remembered the days when he'd been part of a happy family and we'd often speak of one day marrying and having such a family of our own.'

Vicky was once more lying in the crook of his arm, and Alan spoke without looking at her. 'When I met Dora I took Seamus – that was his name – to meet her and asked him to be my best man. The night before the wedding he and I went out for a few drinks and Seamus drank enough to tell me what he really thought. He believed I wasn't marrying a wife but a dream. He felt it wasn't going to work. As a result of what he said, we fell out with each other. He still acted as my best man, but our friendship ended, even though we were both telegraphists in the same torpedo boat flotilla. I've thought a lot about him recently. He was right. I didn't marry for love, but for a way of life. If he was still alive I'd find him and tell him, but he died when his torpedo boat was sunk by a U-boat.'

Turning to look at Vicky, he said, 'It isn't the same with you, Vicky. The first time you and I spoke, I realised you had something I'd never found in anyone else. I enjoyed *being* with you and was unhappy if something prevented me from seeing you. I tried to fight against it because I thought I loved Dora, but I've come to realise that I never did. Breaking up with her upset me, but only because it shattered the dream I had – a foolish dream – that marriage itself was more important than the person to whom I was married . . . does that make sense?'

When Vicky nodded, he continued. 'The thought of not seeing you again, of not being able to talk to you, to touch you, and now to make love to you . . . the thought of that's unbearable. I *am* concerned when I think about our different backgrounds and what you've already achieved, but I don't want to stop being with you, Vicky – ever. Maybe one day you'll tire of me. If that happens I'll be very, very unhappy, but I'll be a better man for having known you.'

Suddenly embarrassed, he said, 'I feel as though I've made a speech, yet I probably still haven't said what I wanted to say – or what you wanted to hear. But I've tried to tell you how I feel about you, Vicky, and I meant every word.'

Putting a finger on his lips, Vicky said emotionally, 'Don't say any more, Alan. You have told me what I wanted to hear. Now I wouldn't care if you were married to fifty wives. You want me, and I want you. As long as that never changes I don't care what anyone else in the world thinks about us. Now, don't let's talk any more. I can think of so many things I would rather we were doing . . .'

33

Vicky and Alan awoke for the second time that morning when the front door of the studio was opened. Then the voice of Fiona called, 'Vicky? I hope I'm not disturbing you. Are you awake, dear? I know you must have arrived home very late. I waited here for you until after eleven. It was such shocking weather I was extremely concerned for you . . .'

Leaping from the bed, Vicky grabbed her dressing-gown and donned it hurriedly before opening the bedroom door and entering the studio.

Beaming at her, Fiona said, 'Hello, you clever girl. Your reviews were wonderful. Rupert and I read *every* one. I've brought you some milk. I forgot last night and there was none here, of course.'

'Thank you, Fiona – and thank you for having everything so welcoming. It was just what was needed. I drove Cecil's car home and managed to pick up a couple of punctures along the way.'

'How dreadful, and in such awful weather! I knew

something must have happened, but now you're here I have some exciting news for you. Desmond is staying with us again – you know, dear, the pilot to whom I wanted to introduce you, when he was here before? And guess what?' Without waiting for a reply, she said excitedly, 'There is going to be a by-election, here in this constituency. Desmond expects to be chosen as the Conservative candidate. Isn't that wonderful? You must come to dinner and meet him and this time I positively refuse to take no for an answer. He too has read all your reviews and is so excited about meeting you . . . Oh!'

Her expression of surprise was the result of Alan's emerging from the bedroom. He had slipped on shirt and trousers, but it was quite obvious from his dishevelled appearance that he too had just woken – and Fiona was aware there was only one bed in the room.

Offering no explanation, Vicky said, 'You remember Alan, Fiona? You came here when I was painting his portrait. We met again in London. He had been to see his publisher and was staying with Clarice, Cecil's sister. I brought him back to Newlyn with me – thank goodness. Changing wheels in that rain was hard enough as it was. I doubt if I would have succeeded on my own.'

Vicky realised Fiona had written Alan off after their first meeting as being 'NOCD' – 'Not Our Class, Darling' – one of her favourite expressions. Vicky knew she would be impressed that Alan had been staying with Clarice, who was, in fact, *the Honourable* Clarice, not only because her husband was the son of a titled diplomat, but also in her own right, she and Cecil being the children of a viscount.

'I see . . . Good morning!' Fiona's greeting to Alan was subdued and embarrassed, but Vicky continued as though she had noticed nothing amiss.

'As you know from the reviews, Alan's portrait was one of the great successes of my exhibition. Lady Bellingham offered to buy it for two hundred and fifty guineas, but I had already given the portrait to Alan and he refused to part with it.'

'Refused two hundred and fifty guineas?' Fiona was impressed, despite her reservations about Alan. She felt she might have to revise some of her opinions of him. She was also quite flustered about the compromising situation in which she had found Vicky.

'You must tell me all about it some time, dear, over dinner.' As an afterthought she added hastily, 'Alan must come too, of course – if he is still in Newlyn. But I really must rush away now. I just popped in to satisfy myself that you had arrived back safely.'

'Thank you, Fiona, it was very kind and thoughtful of you. I see from the mail waiting for me that Ella and Frieda are having a party tonight to celebrate their fifth anniversary together. I hope you will be there. Perhaps we will have an opportunity to chat for longer then.'

'Of course, Rupert and I have already accepted – but I really must dash.' After a quick nod to Alan, Fiona made her exit and they heard her clattering down the wooden stairs.

'Poor Fiona,' Vicky said, shaking her head. 'It's a great pity she is such a frightful snob. She can be a really kind and considerate person when she puts her mind to it.'

'I'm afraid I embarrassed her,' Alan said. 'Perhaps I

should have stayed in the bedroom. I hope I haven't caused the break-up of a beautiful friendship, or ruined your reputation.'

Vicky laughed. 'You have probably enhanced it. I am an artist and an ex-suffragette and was beginning to get funny looks from people because there wasn't a man in my life. Now I have you everyone will be happy . . . but especially me.'

On their way to the home of Ella and Frieda, Alan felt unsure about going to the two artists' party, pointing out to Vicky that their invitation did not include him.

'How could it?' she asked. 'They didn't know you would be here, but they will both be delighted to meet you. However, I might need to protect you from Ella. She may have lived with Frieda for five years, but she still has an eye for men and will certainly make a play for you.'

'It sounds as though it will be quite a bash,' Alan commented, not entirely sure it would be one he was going to enjoy.

Sensing his uncertainty, Vicky squeezed his arm affectionately. 'You *will* have a good time, Alan, I promise you.'

Vicky was happier than Alan had ever seen her. So happy that he knew he was going to have to enjoy the party for her sake, however ill at ease he might feel.

He need not have been concerned. He liked both hostesses immediately. Frieda was outrageously masculine, wearing a suit complete with collar and tie and a panama hat, and smoking a long, thin cheroot. Ella was as Vicky had described her, delicately feminine, utterly charming – and extremely flirtatious. She also knew immediately who he was, explaining that she had admired his portrait when it was hanging in Vicky's studio.

'I have *always* wanted to meet a real hero in the flesh,' she prattled, retaining a firm hold on his hand after they were introduced. 'I do *adore* men who have actually done something. We must find a quiet corner and you can tell me *all* about the things you have done.'

The party was being held in the garden of a large house overlooking the harbour, the rains of the previous night having been followed by a hot, sunny day that heralded a heat wave. Alan felt that the whole of the artist community must be here. As Ella began leading him towards the house, he turned his head to look back and was relieved to see that Vicky was following. She smiled at him reassuringly.

At the door, they were prevented from entering by a large and noisy group of young artists and Vicky caught up with them. 'I have already warned Alan about allowing you to get him alone somewhere,' she said good-naturedly to Ella, 'and I think you have more guests to greet right now. Frieda is signalling to you.'

Releasing his hand with exaggerated reluctance, and promising to catch up with him again later, Ella left to join Frieda in greeting the new arrivals.

Vicky rescued Alan again a short time later when he was cornered by a large and loud-voiced man who was describing a cavalry charge against the Zulus he had taken part in as a young subaltern, some forty years before.

Leading him away, Vicky explained, 'That was old Colonel Trecarrow. He can become rather boring when he has had too much to drink, but he is a staunch and very important supporter of the Newlyn artists. He can be relied upon to buy paintings when times are hard. As a result, he is invited to most parties. He is also landlord to many of them and is very understanding if they are unable to pay their rent on time.'

'Then I'm glad I was polite to him,' Alan said. 'There can't be too many like him around.'

There were a small number of artists at the party whom Alan had met on his earlier visit to Newlyn and most seemed delighted to see him again. He and Vicky were talking to a group of these when Alan glanced up and saw Fiona arriving accompanied by two men, one much older than herself. When he pointed them out to Vicky she said, 'The older one with the very well-kept beard is Rupert, Fiona's husband. The other must be Desmond, the future MP.'

Fiona saw Vicky almost immediately and hurried to greet her, with Rupert and Desmond following in her wake. Reaching her target, she said, 'I am so glad you are here. Rupert and I have brought Desmond along with us. As I told you, he is simply dying to meet you.'

It was as though the embarrassing meeting of the morning had not taken place. Fiona's failure to greet Alan did not go unnoticed by Vicky, but she decided to say nothing for the moment.

Rupert greeted Vicky with a kiss on the cheek, and then Fiona introduced their companion. 'Darling, this is Desmond . . . Desmond Stileman. I have told him so much about you he feels he knows you already.'

'It is always exciting to meet a celebrity,' Desmond said, smiling and showing very white and even teeth while retaining his grip on Vicky's hand. When she eventually succeeded in pulling it away, he added, 'I was delighted to read the reviews of your exhibition. It is rare for there to be such unanimity among the critics.'

Declining to acknowledge his praise, Vicky said, 'Having read the reviews you will remember that the highest praise was for my portraits of two heroes. I would like you to meet one of them. Alan, this is Desmond. Fiona you have already met and this is Rupert, her husband.'

Desmond greeted Alan somewhat guardedly, but when Rupert shook his hand it was evident that Fiona had said nothing to him about Alan's relationship with Vicky.

The introductions over, Rupert said to Alan, 'The reviews mentioned that one of the heroes was a pilot . . . is that you?'

Alan shook his head. 'No, I was Navy. Sadly, the pilot did not survive the war.'

'I believe the casualty rate among fliers was frighteningly high,' Rupert said. 'Desmond would know far more about that, of course. He was a Royal Flying Corps pilot, you know.'

'So Fiona told me,' Vicky said. Speaking to Desmond, she asked, 'Were you flying in France?'

'Yes, I arrived there in nineteen seventeen,' Desmond replied, pleased that Vicky was speaking to him. 'They were hectic days, but we were doing what we had joined the Royal Flying Corps for.'

'Where were you stationed?' It was apparently no more than a polite, conversational question.

'A place that is no more than a dot on the map,' Desmond replied. 'A small village named Henneville.'

233

'Desmond was very well thought of.' Fiona had been listening to the conversation and felt that her guest was not impressing Vicky quite as much as she had hoped. 'He was brought back from France to train pilots in combat tactics and when the war ended they offered him promotion to remain in the service. They don't do that for everyone.'

'Quite true,' Vicky agreed. 'Have you accepted their offer, Desmond?'

'No,' Desmond replied with an exaggerated expression of regret. 'I am expected to follow in my father's footsteps and enter politics. He is Member of Parliament for a constituency not very far from your home, I believe?'

Failing to gratify his obvious desire to draw her into conversation, Vicky said enigmatically, 'I have no doubt at all that you will make as fine an MP as your father, Desmond. Now, if you will excuse us, I think I see Crosbie Garstin arriving. He is a writer I would like Alan to meet . . .'

Dawn had broken when Vicky and Alan walked back to the studio from the party and Vicky was very content. Alan had got on well with Crosbie Garstin, who was the son of an established Newlyn painter. The two had promised they would meet up again soon.

In fact, with the possible exception of Fiona and her house-guest, Alan had been made to feel welcome by most of the artistic community at the party and Vicky was happy for him. Resting her head against his shoulder as they walked along holding hands, she shared her thoughts with him, adding, 'It was a lovely evening, but now I am looking forward to getting home and going to bed with you.'

'Shouldn't *I* be the one saying that? . . . No, I forgot, you were a suffragette. You fought for the right to say such things.'

When she did not reply immediately, he said, 'I'm sorry. It was meant to be a joke, but it was a very poor one. It must have taken a great deal of courage to do what you did – but you've never been lacking in courage, have you?'

Thinking of their present situation, he added, 'I wish I had met you years ago, Vicky. It would have made life so much simpler . . . although I have to admit that almost no one at the party so much as raised an eyebrow at the fact that I'm staying with you.'

'Of course not. Artists are not judgemental. They accept people as they accept everything they paint . . . as they are. But you said *almost* everyone accepts us. Who do you think does not?'

'Fiona, for one . . . Desmond for another – but I must admit to taking an instant dislike to him and I have no doubt he was aware of it. Mind you, I was probably prejudiced from the moment I saw the way he looked at you.'

'Yet I don't think *he* realises that we are sleeping together. Fiona certainly would not have told him. Mind you, I quite like you being just a *little* bit jealous of other men who look at me. But you have nothing to worry about – especially with Desmond. He's a poseur.'

'Oh? In what way?'

'All his talk of hectic days and doing what he had to do is a load of poppycock,' Vicky declared. 'I know the French airfield where he was stationed. It's where the Royal Flying Corps took crashed and damaged aeroplanes in order to build new ones out of the parts they were able to salvage. A pilot stationed there would be testing the rebuilt aeroplanes before handing them back to front-line squadrons. I visited Henneville once or twice.'

'But Fiona said he trained pilots,' Alan pointed out. 'He must have had a great deal of experience in order to do that.'

236

Vicky gave a short laugh. 'One would think so, but it was not often the case. Skilful pilots were worth their weight in gold to front-line squadrons. Paul used to say that many pilots were appointed as instructors when they failed to make the grade in combat.'

It was the first time Vicky had mentioned Paul in conversation with Alan and he felt this was significant, but she had more to say.

'There's another reason why *I* am not terribly fond of Desmond, although it's hardly his fault. One of my prison sentences was for throwing eggs at one of the MPs most opposed to giving women the vote. His name was Sir Randolph Stileman. I had not associated the two until Desmond mentioned following his father into politics.'

Smiling at Alan and squeezing his arm happily, she added, 'It might be highly amusing to become friendly enough to have him take me home to meet his parents! Fortunately, I am far too happy here with you to want to go off and embarrass him, however much fun it might be.'

Later that day, Alan paid a visit to the Newlyn post office to arrange to have his mail delivered there to await his collection. That settled, he called on the Penhaligons to tell them he was back in Newlyn, and let them know where he was staying.

The Penhaligons were a Methodist family and he expected them to disapprove of his new lifestyle. Instead, he found Tom, at least, surprisingly understanding, and it was not long before he learned the reason.

Prue Penhaligon was working with John Appleton once

more, practising the art of printing designs on silk. As Vicky had predicted, Emily Penhaligon had reluctantly agreed that, although still married, he was a very likeable young man, and after a difficult family conference they had decided they must accept the situation if the family was not to be torn asunder. As a result, they were far more understanding of Alan's position.

When Alan left the Penhaligon cottage later that afternoon, Tom walked with him through the village and made the comment that the war had produced many casualties far from the battle front. 'Vicky Hazelton drew Ma's attention to that fact when she came to speak to her on behalf of our Prue. She mentioned poor young Jimmy Williams. He was one of my crew before he went off to war as a submariner. His submarine was sunk and Jimmy was one of only three survivors taken prisoner by the Germans. It was three years before he came home. As if all he'd been through wasn't enough, when he got home his wife told him she was carrying someone else's baby. Three days later his body was washed up on a beach on the Lizard. They say he jumped off a cliff, down the coast a way. After serving his country in the way he did he deserved more than that. So do you, Alan – and so does John, our Prue's man. The war may be over, but the suffering hasn't ended by a long way. I hope you and Vicky will be very happy together. I, for one, am glad you'll be settling down with us in Newlyn.'

More moved than he cared to reveal, Alan said, 'You're a good friend, Tom, and I'm very glad you understand. Vicky will be too.'

'She's a fine maid,' Tom said. 'We're all thrilled that

she's become so famous. She endeared herself to folk here-abouts when she was driving that ambulance of hers. She acted as midwife to Sam Coombe's wife, then when Rosie Ladner up at the farm had a bad time with her first, and the midwife thought the baby would be lost, Vicky took her to Penzance hospital in her ambulance, even though it was supposed to be only for wounded soldiers and sailors. Young Harry Ladner's coming on for two now and as lively as they come.'

The two men walked on in silence for a few minutes before Tom said, 'Years ago all the goings-on between married folks would have mattered far more, but the war has changed a great many things. Lots of 'em for the worse, I know, but I reckon that one or two are for the better. Only time will tell.'

A few days after the party, Alan returned from a trip to the village post office to find Desmond Stileman in the studio, studying the paintings hanging on the walls. His surprise when Alan walked in matched Alan's own at finding him there.

Casually, Desmond commented, 'You seem to be very popular today, Vicky. If any more visitors arrive you might be forced to abandon work and throw a party.'

Desmond's words made it clear to Vicky that Fiona had said nothing to him about her relationship with Alan, but his light-hearted remarks were in marked contrast to the annoyed frown that had crossed his face when Alan had walked into the studio.

'Desmond was passing by and thought he would call in and view my work,' Vicky explained to Alan. He could tell she was relieved he had returned so quickly from the post office and the reason made him angry. He had sensed at the party that the ex-pilot had designs upon Vicky and that they had been fuelled by what Fiona had no doubt told him about her and the artist colony in general.

Determined not to allow his feelings to show, Alan said, 'As you can see, there aren't a great many paintings here at the moment. You should have come to the exhibition in London. Vicky had some wonderful paintings on show there.'

'*You* were at the exhibition?' Desmond expressed surprise.

'Alan was not only there, but quite stole the evening when he showed up,' Vicky said. 'It lifted the exhibition out of the ordinary.'

'I saw his portrait just now,' Desmond said, and immediately changed the subject. 'Fiona mentioned something about another painting, of a Royal Flying Corps pilot. I can't see it here.'

'I haven't unpacked it yet,' Vicky said. 'It will go back on the wall in due course.'

'Is it of anyone I might know?' Desmond asked.

'I doubt it. He was a highly decorated pilot who was unfortunately killed in action,' Vicky explained briefly. Looking in Alan's direction, she added, 'Fortunately, my other hero is alive and well.'

Still determined not to include Alan in the conversation, Desmond said, 'I would very much like to see it, Vicky. As an ex-pilot myself I might consider purchasing it.'

'It's not for sale.'

'Why? Did he mean something special to you?'

It was an over-familiar question, but if Desmond expected Vicky to be evasive in the presence of Alan, he was disappointed. 'Paul and I were to be married, but he was shot down. However, I have been very lucky. It is not every woman who can say she has had two heroes in her life. Were you given any awards, Desmond?'

It was a question that amply repaid Desmond for his own bad manners and for a few moments he struggled for a reply. Then, with a shrug, he said, 'Unfortunately, I never seemed to be in the right place at the right time.' He looked at his wristwatch. 'I must be off. I am leaving early tomorrow morning, but hope to return to Newlyn in a week or two. I will be passing quite close to your home, Vicky. Would you like me to pay a call on your parents and tell them how you are? No doubt they would like to have news of you – and of the many interesting friends you have made, here in Newlyn.'

Vicky declined his offer, informing Desmond that she was in regular contact with her parents, whereupon he left the studio with only a perfunctory nod of his head to Alan.

When he had gone, Alan said, 'I don't think he was very pleased to see me. What's more, I think he had more than pictures on his mind.'

'I don't doubt it,' Vicky agreed. 'His father is one of the most unscrupulous men I have ever known. He would stop at nothing to get his own way. I have no doubt that Desmond is exactly the same.'

During the next few weeks, Alan's visits to the Newlyn post office became more frequent. The reason was that he had been told to expect a cheque from the Royal Navy in

241

respect of a shortfall of pay due to him for his extended service after the war's end, together with extra allowances he should have received for the time he had spent in the Baltic, before bringing the ex-German torpedo boat back to a British naval dockyard.

He had informed the Royal Navy pay office at Chatham of his change of address from London to Newlyn, but when the cheque failed to arrive he contacted them once more.

The reply he received was disturbing. There was an apology for not sending the cheque to Newlyn post office, as instructed. Instead, the cheque had gone to Alan's last notified address – Quilter Street, in Bethnal Green. Furthermore, the cheque had been cashed in the area, endorsed on the back with what purported to be Alan's own signature, in favour of a name he knew well.

The cheque had been for thirty-three pounds and a few shillings. It was not a huge amount, but neither was it a sum he felt he could afford to lose. Of more concern was that it seemed any letters still being sent to him at the Quilter Street address were being opened.

There were unlikely to be more containing cheques, but there were still a few people who would send correspondence there – including his father and Maria. He had not written to inform them of the failure of his marriage, something about which he felt guilty. He promised himself he would send them a postcard to tell them his Newlyn postal address.

When he mentioned the missing cheque to Vicky, and his concern about any other letters that might have been addressed to him at Quilter Street, she went straight to the heart of the problem. 'The cheque must have been taken and cashed by someone at the house. Do you suspect anyone in particular?'

'It could be Dora's mother, or her brother. I doubt if it would be her father; I don't think he can read or write. I don't think it would be Dora, either.'

Vicky did not share his confidence in Dora's honesty, but she kept her thoughts to herself. 'Does it really matter? I know you don't like losing such an amount, but it is not a serious problem for us. The exhibition solved our money problems for quite a while.'

'I have no intention of living off you, Vicky, and if I knew the money had gone to Dora I might shrug it off, but I wouldn't want her brother Charlie to get away with it.'

'Forget it, Alan. Think of the difference between our life here and the life they are leading in the East End of London. Who are winners, them or us?'

Alan tried to do as Vicky suggested, but the loss of the cheque rankled with him. He disliked Dora's brother intensely and was unhappy at the thought that he might have stolen the money. He wrote a brief note to Dora in which he said he believed there might be some mail for him at Quilter Street and giving her the address of the Newlyn post office to which she could reply.

It proved to be a disastrous error of judgement.

A few days later, just when he was beginning to accept the loss of the missing money, a letter arrived for him at the Newlyn post office that changed everything for him and Vicky.

He recognised the handwriting immediately. He had looked in vain for it during much of his service in the Royal Navy.

It was from Dora.

Wondering why she should choose to write to him now, he opened the letter as he walked back to the studio. He had read no more than a few lines when he came to a sudden halt, hardly able to believe what he was reading.

Dora was expecting a baby. His baby!

The letter assured him that it changed nothing as far as their relationship was concerned. She did not want to see him and he would not be expected to play any part in the upbringing of the child. All she asked was that he should provide sufficient money to help it enjoy a reasonable life as it grew up.

Dora informed Alan that she knew he would be able to afford it. Charlie had seen him in a car, dressed in expensive clothes – and with another woman. Dora stated that although she accepted she was no longer a part of his life and that he had doubtless found someone else to take her place, she would like to bring up their child wanting for little.

The letter left Alan feeling numb and finding it difficult to think straight. He hurried back to the studio – and to Vicky.

One look at his expression was sufficient to cause her to stop painting immediately. 'What is it, Alan? What's the matter?'

'This was waiting for me at the post office.' He handed her the letter to her and stood in silence as she read.

When she had finished, she gave the letter back to him. Her face was expressionless when she asked, 'How did she know where to write?'

When he explained, she asked, 'What are you going to do about it?'

'I don't think I have any choice in the matter, Vicky. I must go to London to see her.'

'But she says in the letter she doesn't want you . . . only your money.'

'That's what she *says* – but she's having a baby, Vicky . . . my baby. This changes things.'

Feeling as though a bottomless chasm was opening in front of her, Vicky nevertheless knew there was one more step she had to take. One more question to ask.

'What about us, Alan? You and me?'

Confused and increasingly desolate, Alan said, 'I'm happier with you than I have ever been, Vicky – than I ever could be with anyone else. You know that. It's something I don't want to lose, but I must go to London and find out for myself what's going on.'

'What if Dora wants you to return to her?' Even asking the question left Vicky feeling almost physically sick.

'She doesn't want me back, she made that very clear when I left – and she says the same in her letter.'

'But there's nothing to say that she won't change her mind once the baby arrives – if there really is a baby. Has it occurred to you that she might be lying, just to get money from you?'

'So many things have crossed my mind. It was Charlie who saw us in the car when we were leaving London. That would have immediately spelled "money" to him.

He'd have mentioned it to Winnie and between them they could have put Dora up to this.'

'There's also the possibility that even if she is having a baby, it might not be yours. Have you thought of that too?'

Alan looked at Vicky as though she had suggested Dora might have committed a murder. He shook his head vigorously. 'No! Dora might have realised she didn't love me and regretted marrying me, but she wouldn't have done anything like that.'

Vicky controlled an overwhelming urge to tell Alan what she knew of Dora. She should have said something about it when the opportunity occurred, a long time before. If she told him now he would believe it was no more than a desperate attempt to turn him against Dora and keep him here with her.

Suddenly calm, Vicky knew she would just have to hope this *was* no more than a clumsy ploy to obtain money from him. That – and pray very hard.

35

Alan left Newlyn for London early the next morning, a Wednesday, leaving a pale and unhappy but dry-eyed Vicky behind in the studio.

It had been a difficult and largely sleepless night. Knowing far more about Dora than did Alan, Vicky argued that he should do as she wished and send her money without becoming involved in her life again. She even offered to contribute to the amount he would send her.

Alan pointed out that if he did so the Platt family would look upon it as an easy source of income and he might find himself supporting the whole family. He wanted to go to London, discuss the situation and have everything put on a legal footing so that only the baby would benefit.

There was also the future of the baby – his child – to be decided. Even if he and Dora were living apart he felt the child should be aware he was its father and grow up knowing him.

He and Vicky had talked far into the night and it was this last point that was of most concern to her. No matter how much Alan tried to assure her he no longer loved Dora – and probably never had – she feared his love for the child he believed to be his might prove greater than his love for herself.

Vicky was not convinced he was the father of the baby Dora was carrying. She wished fervently that she had been courageous enough to tell him, long ago, what she knew of Dora's behaviour while he was at sea.

She could not tell him now. He would be convinced she was doing it out of spite against Dora, whether or not he accepted the truth – and she doubted whether he would believe that the woman he had married could have behaved in such a manner.

She watched from the window of the studio with a heavy heart as Alan walked away, heading for Penzance and a London-bound train. She wondered whether she would ever see him walking back to her.

Alan was very aware of the deep hurt felt by Vicky and wished fervently that he had been able to assure her of their future together. He had no doubt about the strength of his love for her, but the revelation that Dora was carrying his baby had left him confused, unable to gather his thoughts together.

Had his marriage to Dora not failed, he would have been overjoyed at such news. He had often imagined himself as a father, bringing up a son or daughter to enjoy the sort of safe and happy home life he had never known. Alan knew this would not be the lot of the child Dora was having. It would face the same difficulties and uncertainties he had known during his own childhood.

Worse, it would be brought up in the home of the Platt family.

He would love to be able to bring the child to Cornwall, to be brought up by him and Vicky, but he realised this was unlikely to be acceptable to anyone except himself.

Alan wrestled with the problem for the whole of the journey to London. He had still not reached a satisfactory solution by the time the train pulled in to Paddington station. The only thing beyond any argument was that his life was in a mess.

He found a small but respectable boarding-house not far from the station and booked in for two nights, with the option of extending his stay if it should prove necessary. After an indifferent meal in a nearby restaurant, he returned to the boarding-house with the intention of having an early night, in order to be fresh when he faced whatever the next day would bring, but sleep did not come easily. He was missing Vicky. More than anything else, he wished he might share his thoughts with her.

Although he still believed he was duty-bound to speak to Dora and discuss the future of the baby she was expecting, he was aware that Vicky had become the most important person in his life. Whatever was decided would have to take this into account.

In the early hours of the morning he fell asleep with only one clear thought in his head. He loved Vicky and wished he had put off coming to London until they had discussed the situation in more detail, so that he could have left her confident in the knowledge of how he felt about her.

* * *

The day of Alan's departure to London was a miserable one for Vicky. She had hoped to put the reason for his absence behind her by painting, but found it impossible to concentrate on anything she did. Soon after mid-morning she gave up trying to work and set off on a gentle walk a few miles westward along the coast to the Lamorna valley. This was one of her favourite spots and where she had painted many of her coastal scenes.

The valley was becoming increasingly popular with artists, a number of whom had moved here from Newlyn, including one of the best-known members of the Cornish artist community. 'Lamorna' Birch lived with his wife and young daughters in a cottage on the hill overlooking the cove at the seaward end of the valley.

After sitting for more than an hour contemplating the sea, Vicky decided to pay a call on the Birch family, who had been very kind to her when she first came to Newlyn, but whom she had not seen for some time.

She was halfway along the long track that led to the cottage when she saw a group of two men and a woman walking towards her, coming from the direction of the Birch cottage.

As they drew closer she recognised them as Fiona and Rupert Graham, with their frequent house-guest Desmond Stileman. Vicky would have preferred not to meet up with any of them today, but it was impossible to avoid them now.

Waving a greeting, as soon as they came within hearing Fiona called, 'Darling, what a lovely surprise! What are you doing all this way from home?'

'I was unable to settle to my painting today, so, as it

was such glorious weather, I thought I would come out for a walk.'

'You have *walked* all the way from Newlyn – and alone? Darling, how terribly brave of you.'

Vicky was aware that the 'alone' part of the question was Fiona's way of asking why Alan was not with her. She did not enlighten her. 'I'm on my way to visit Lamorna Birch,' she said. 'I haven't seen him for a long while.'

'We can prevent you from wasting your time, darling,' Fiona said. 'We have just come from there and no one is at home. Desmond is returning to his family in a few days' time and wanted to take a painting for them. His father met Lamorna in London some years ago, so we thought one of his paintings would have been rather nice.'

'I have just thought of something that would be even nicer,' Desmond said. 'Why don't I take them one of Vicky's paintings?'

His suggestion took Vicky by surprise, but, addressing her, he said, 'You have been much in the news recently. I can tell them I have met you and that one day you are likely to be even more famous than Lamorna Birch. It will make the painting really special for them.'

Despite the misery she felt deep inside, Vicky found it difficult to conceal a smile. If Desmond's father remembered her, the painting might have a significance quite different from the one intended.

'I think that's a very nice idea, Desmond. I would be delighted to sell you a painting to take home for your father. When would you like to come to my studio and choose one?'

Delighted that Vicky was at last behaving with a degree

of friendliness towards Desmond, Fiona said hurriedly, 'Why don't we go there now?' For Vicky's benefit, she added, 'We came here in our car. Rupert has left it a little way along the valley.'

'Why not?' Vicky agreed. 'I haven't too many completed paintings at the moment, but I am sure we can find something suitable.'

There were perhaps twenty-five paintings on display around the walls of the studio. Many were recent; others were those she had not considered to be quite of the standard required by the London gallery where she had held her exhibition.

As they walked round the studio, Vicky's glance fell upon Alan's portrait and she realised that he would soon be arriving in London. The next day he would be with Dora. The thought hurt.

Fiona saw Vicky's sudden change of expression and voiced her concern.

Forcing a smile, Vicky said, 'I'm fine, Fiona. Just a muscle twinge from all the walking I have done today.'

Fiona's gaze went from Vicky to the portrait on the wall before her and, uncomfortably perceptive, she asked, 'Where is Alan? Is he likely to be here soon?'

'He has had to go to London,' Vicky replied. 'He left this morning.'

'Oh, poor Vicky. You must come to dinner with us tonight.' Fiona was never one to waste an opportunity such as the one offered by Alan's absence from the scene.

'I am afraid I have a great deal of work to catch up on,' Vicky said firmly. 'Thank you all the same. Now, I will go and make us some tea while you help Desmond to choose a painting.'

When tea was made, Vicky took four cups to the studio on a tray and found her three visitors discussing the portrait of Paul which had been replaced on the wall of the alcove. 'Have you found anything you particularly like?' she asked.

'I like them all,' Desmond replied enthusiastically, 'but this portrait is the one I particularly like.'

'As I told you once before, Paul's portrait is not for sale.' Vicky placed the tea tray on a small table. 'I intend to give it to his parents. He was their only son and I feel they should have it.'

'That is a very kind and thoughtful gesture,' Fiona said. 'But you are particularly skilful at portrait painting. Why not have Desmond sit for you? You could paint it as though he was wearing air force uniform. His parents would absolutely love to have such a portrait of their only son.'

'I really am committed to a great deal of work,' Vicky replied. She had no wish to be alone in her studio with Desmond for the hours it would take to complete such a portrait.

'I would pay you well, of course,' Desmond said, eager to pursue Fiona's suggestion.

'There you are, Vicky. Surely you won't refuse the offer of such a commission. What do you charge for a portrait? You told me how much you were offered for Alan's, but I have forgotten. How much was it?'

'Two hundred and fifty guineas.' Vicky hoped the sum was high enough to put Desmond off, but Fiona and Rupert also bought her paintings and she did not want to deter them from buying by setting the price at an unacceptable level. 'Of course, that was for a portrait that had received a great deal of publicity because it is the portrait of a hero. I could not possibly ask such a sum for one of Desmond, especially as he is a friend of yours. However, I could not sell at a price that would devalue my work. I don't think I could take such a commission for less than a hundred and twenty-five guineas.'

It was still a considerable sum of money and, as Vicky had anticipated, was far more than Desmond had considered paying for a painting for his parents. However, he was aware he either had to agree, or be humiliated.

'I really feel I should pay at least as much as was offered for Alan's portrait,' he said, 'but since you are happy to paint me at a special rate for the sake of friendship, it would be churlish to refuse. When shall I come for my first sitting?'

'When do you plan to leave?' Vicky queried.

'There is a show jumping event this Sunday that I particularly want to attend,' Desmond replied. 'I will have to leave on Saturday.'

It was now Wednesday and Vicky shook her head. 'If we began the portrait immediately I would only have the outline completed by then. I am sorry, Desmond; I could not possibly have it completed in time for you to take it with you on Saturday, or for many weeks after that. Even when the paint had dried it would need to be varnished and that would take weeks rather than days to dry.'

'Then we will have a change of plan,' Desmond said, suddenly enthusiastic. 'You make a start on the portrait right away, we'll have it completed as far as we can by

Friday and you can put the finishing touches to it when I next come to Newlyn, which shouldn't be too long because I am hoping my selection as a parliamentary candidate will be confirmed very soon. I am not committed to giving my parents a present this weekend. In fact, it would be something extra special to give them for their wedding anniversary, which is in a couple of months' time. Yes, I think that would be an excellent idea.'

'Oh! Well, perhaps Rupert and I should leave you and Desmond to get on with the painting . . .' Fiona felt slightly hurt that she had not been consulted about the arrangements, which would cut across her own plans for the remaining days of Desmond's visit.

'Oh no you don't,' Vicky said. 'You can stay with us for now and I insist that you come with Desmond for his sittings, to keep us liberally supplied with tea and the occasional sandwich. I am going to have to work very hard to complete as much as I can before the weekend.' Vicky knew she would feel happier if she were not left alone in the studio with Desmond.

Slightly mollified, Fiona said, 'Of course, darling. I will be delighted to help in any way I can. I can't wait to see the finished portrait. Desmond's parents are going to be absolutely thrilled. They will have a portrait of their son that will become a family heirloom. I am so pleased.'

36

The morning after his arrival in London, Alan turned the corner into Quilter Street just as Mabel, Dora's younger sister, closed the door of the Platt house and walked along the street towards him. Seemingly deep in thought, she had her head down, gazing at the pavement, and was not aware of his presence until they met and he spoke to her.

'Hello, Mabel. How are you?'

Mabel looked up, startled. When she saw Alan, the blood drained from her cheeks. 'Alan! What are you doing here? We all thought you were living in Cornwall.'

'I am,' Alan replied, 'but then I had Dora's letter telling me about the baby and I felt I should come up to London and have a chat with her about the future. Is she in the house?'

'No.' As she spoke, Mabel was looking about her in something like desperation and Alan was given the impression that she would rather be anywhere than here, talking to him in the street. 'Dora's in hospital. The baby was born yesterday . . . it's a boy.'

'She's had it *already*?' Alan expressed disbelief. 'It can't be due yet.'

'It was born early and surprised us all,' Mabel said, desperately ill at ease. 'Dora was rushed into hospital and had the baby hardly an hour later.'

'Which hospital is she in?' Alan asked. 'I'll go along there now.'

'She's in the Salvation Army hospital, in Lower Clapton Road,' Mabel replied, 'but I don't know whether she's allowed to have visitors. Besides, she said you wouldn't be coming to see her because she'd written to you and told you not to. That you'd just be sending money to help her out.'

'That is what she wanted,' Alan agreed. 'But in view of all that's happened I felt there was a need for us to talk about the future.'

Mabel seemed to have gathered her wits together somewhat. 'I was very unhappy when you and Dora broke up, Alan,' she said. 'I wish I had been able to help.'

'Thanks. You and I have always got on well, Mabel. But I'll go along to the hospital now and find out when I can see Dora. Afterwards I'll come back to the house and check whether there are any letters for me. Perhaps I'll see you then?'

'There *was* a letter – from Gibraltar. It came for you yesterday afternoon when Mum was taking Dora into hospital, but I posted it on to you last night. That's all there was – and I think it might be better if you don't come to the house. Our Charlie's lost his job again and he's blaming everyone but himself for his troubles. You'd just be someone new to take his anger out on.'

257

'I'll risk that,' Alan said. Thinking of the missing cheque, he added, 'There's something I need to sort out with the family. But thanks for the warning. Now I'll make my way to the hospital. Are you going in that direction?'

'No, I'm meeting Rene, and we're going to see if we can get jobs in the new tea-packing factory over by the canal. If you do go to the house I'd rather you didn't mention that I was the one who told you where Dora is.'

'Don't worry, I won't say a word. Good luck with the job – and thanks again, Mabel. I hope to see you again before I go back to Cornwall.'

Turning back the way he had come, Alan headed off in the direction of Bethnal Green Road, from where he would catch a bus to the hospital in Lower Clapton Road.

Mabel watched him walking away and half turned, as though she would go back home. She hesitated uncertainly before changing her mind and continuing on her way to meet her friend. Whatever happened between Alan and Dora and the rest of her family there would be trouble. Big trouble. She wanted to keep out of it. If she was lucky enough to be taken on at the tea-packing factory, she and Rene would take a room somewhere together and she would free herself of the family's problems.

At the hospital, a near-hysterical young woman in an advanced state of labour was being admitted and a harassed Salvation Army receptionist informed Alan that visiting hours were between two and three and six and seven, with no exceptions made.

It was now almost midday. Deciding it would be counterproductive to argue the point when the attention of the

258

nursing staff was so obviously required elsewhere, Alan decided to find somewhere to have something to eat before coming back during the two to three o'clock visiting hour.

There was a pie shop not very far from the hospital. Remembering a conversation he had once had with Vicky about East End pie shops, he decided he would eat here in order to tell her about it when they met again.

When they met again . . .

Simply thinking about Vicky was sufficient to make him wish things could return to the way they were only a couple of days before. He wanted to be with Vicky more than he had ever wished for anything, but life was no longer as simple as it had seemed then. There was now a baby to think of . . .

A clock somewhere near at hand was striking the hour of two as Alan made his way to the front door of the hospital. The same uniformed receptionist was on duty, but there was no emergency now and surprisingly few visitors. The reason for the latter was made clear to him a few minutes afterwards.

The receptionist frowned when Alan said he wished to see Dora and, in answer to her question, replied that he was her husband.

'Most of our ladies have no husbands,' she said suspiciously. 'If they had I doubt whether they would be in here.'

'We're not living together at the moment,' Alan admitted, 'but I've just heard about the baby and am here to see what can be worked out between us.'

The reply appeared to satisfy the receptionist, and Alan looked respectable. A few minutes later he was being escorted to an extension at the back of the building. Here, in a room with five other women, was Dora.

She was lying back in bed with her eyes closed, but as he looked at her she put up a hand to scratch her forehead and he realised she was not asleep. Nodding at Alan, the Salvation Army nurse who had brought him turned and left the room without speaking.

Approaching Dora, Alan reached the bedside and said, 'Hello, Dora. How are you feeling?'

Dora opened her eyes. When she saw him, her expression registered disbelief, but changed almost immediately to something that might have been fear.

'What . . . ? What are you doing here? I wrote to you and said I didn't want to see you. Who told you where I was?'

'That doesn't matter, and I know what you wrote in your letter,' Alan said, 'but this is something that can't be decided by post. I'm here because we need to *talk* about the future.'

'We have no future, not together, we ain't . . . and there's nothing to talk about. All I need is money for me and the baby.'

'We'll get to that in a minute,' Alan replied. 'Where's the baby now? I'd like to see him.'

'You can't,' Dora said hastily. 'He's premature, and not very well. Nobody's allowed to see him.'

'Is he going to be all right?' Alan was genuinely concerned. 'How premature is he?'

'You can work that out for yourself,' Dora replied belligerently. 'When was it you came home on leave? He's almost a couple of months too early.'

'Was there anything that caused him to be so premature?' Alan asked.

Irritably, Dora replied, 'How should I know? I'm not a bleedin' doctor. All I know is I've had your baby and I thought I was going to die giving birth to him. I've never known such pain in all my life.'

'I'm sorry,' Alan said, 'but I don't think any woman finds giving birth particularly easy.'

'Never mind about that,' Dora snapped at him, her confidence returning. 'You've had your fun; now it's time to talk about paying for it.'

'I'm sure we can sort something out,' Alan agreed. 'But since we're on the subject of money, there was a cheque for thirty-odd pounds that the Navy sent to Quilter Street for me. I never got it.'

'I don't know anything about any cheque,' Dora declared angrily, 'and don't think you're getting out of paying me by saying I've had some of your money already. It won't work.'

'All right, we'll leave that for now.' Alan did not want to upset Dora unduly; she had been through a bad time. 'I've come all the way from Cornwall to see exactly what it is you expect from me, so why don't you tell me.'

'I don't know . . . it's all happened so quick, what with the baby coming early. I haven't had time to think about it,' Dora lied. 'But looking at the clothes you're wearing now, and the motor car Charlie saw you in, you must be doing all right for yourself. I don't reckon as how three or four quid a week is too much to ask for.'

'Three or four pounds? For how long? And what do I get in return? It's you who decided our marriage was at an end. You who say you want my money but not me. All right, I'll give you money – not as much as you want, but

261

enough to keep you and the baby. In return I want my freedom. Freedom to live my life without being at your beck and call whenever you feel like it. In return for giving you money I want a divorce.'

Dora, in truth, knew very little about divorce, although she had discussed it with her American lover. In her present circumstances it meant that she would no longer be married to Alan – and if she was not his wife she would have no claim on his money. Nine months before, she had looked forward to going to America and divorcing him there, but that was when she believed there was another husband in the offing.

Vigorously shaking her head on the pillow, she said, 'No. You can go your own way, but we'll stay married.'

'That's a stupid attitude to take, Dora. You wouldn't lose from it. I'd see a solicitor and have a proper agreement drawn up, once we've decided how much I should give you. But I want a divorce first.'

'I've said no!' Dora repeated. 'I've already told you you can do whatever you like. I don't care – but we stay married. Now go away. I don't want to see you again. You can write and tell me how much you're going to give me. If it's not enough I'll get the Salvation Army to help me claim money from you. Go on, leave me. Talking to you has tired me out. I need to sleep.'

Alan wanted to continue the discussion, but Dora did look tired and he thought it best not to stay. However, he intended to come back to see her again. Dora had closed her eyes and turned her head away from him, so he did not even say goodbye before leaving the room.

He was walking along the corridor towards the

entrance hall when a nurse came out of a side room carrying a baby wrapped in a shawl. Through the open door behind her he could see a number of cots and he heard the sound of more than one baby crying.

Acting on a sudden impulse, Alan spoke to the nurse. 'Excuse me, is this where premature babies would be looked after?'

The nurse seemed surprised at his question, but she replied, 'It depends very much how premature the baby is. We have no special facilities here, so if it was very early mother and baby would be sent to one of the larger city hospitals. Is there a particular baby you have in mind?'

'Yes, the baby boy born to Dora Carter yesterday. I'm Alan Carter, her husband. The baby's father.'

The nurse gave him a strange look. 'You are Mr Carter? The baby's father?'

'That's right. I've come up from Cornwall to see Dora and the baby.'

The nurse seemed momentarily flustered. 'Will you wait here for a few minutes, Mr Carter? I have to take this baby to its mother, then I'll have a word with Matron and bring her to speak to you.' Pointing to a number of chairs lined up against the wall outside the room, she said, 'Take a seat. I'll try not to be too long.'

Alan had been seated for some three or four minutes, pondering what the nurse had told him about premature babies, when a young girl he presumed to be a trainee nurse came along the corridor to the door of the nursery room. Seeing Alan seated outside, she said, 'Is someone attending to you?'

263

'I'm waiting to be taken in to see my son . . . he was born yesterday.'

Giving Alan a warm smile, the young nurse said, 'What's the baby's name?'

'Carter . . . my wife is Dora Carter.'

'I haven't seen the baby myself,' admitted the nurse, 'but then I have only just come on duty and I wasn't working yesterday. Come in with me and I'll find him for you.'

There were perhaps a dozen babies in the room, each in a small plain wooden cot. At the foot of each cot was a clipboard to which was attached a sheet of paper with the baby's name, weight and other details.

Looking along the cots, the young nurse came to a halt. 'Here we are. Delroy, born to Dora Carter at three o'clock yesterday afternoon. A fine healthy boy he is too, weighing in at nine pounds and ten ounces.'

Alan knew nothing about the weight of babies, but peering excitedly inside the cot he caught his breath in sudden shock and drew back, startled. 'Are you sure this is my . . . is Dora's baby?'

'Only two babies have arrived since I went off duty and the other poor little soul was stillborn. Why . . . ?'

As she was speaking, the young nurse had moved to the cot side. Gazing down at the baby, she too drew back in sudden surprise. Looking at Alan, she asked, hesitantly, 'Mrs Carter . . . is she from Africa?'

Shaking his head, it was some moments before Alan trusted himself to speak. Dora's baby had black curly hair and skin that was only marginally lighter in colour. 'No. Dora is London born and bred – and as white as you and me . . .'

37

The matron in charge of the Salvation Army hospital, accompanied by the nurse Alan had first seen carrying a baby from the nursery, intercepted him before he reached the room where Dora was lying. One look at his face was sufficient to tell the matron what he knew.

'You've seen the baby, Mr Carter.' It was a statement rather than a question.

'That's right, and now I'm going to see his mother.'

'I don't think that is a very good idea right now.' The matron was a large, powerful-looking woman and she stood squarely in front of him, backed up by the nurse. Alan knew he would have to physically move them from his path, and the outcome was by no means certain.

'I think we should go along to my office and have a talk before we do anything else, Mr Carter.'

Aware that he had no option, Alan agreed. He also realised, belatedly, it would be better if he thought matters through before confronting Dora.

In the matron's office he sat on the far side of her desk

and she sent the nurse to the kitchen to find a cup of tea. When the nurse had departed, the matron said, 'I am afraid I have very little experience of dealing with husbands and fathers, Mr Carter. Few of the girls who come here have husbands and I regret to say that a great many would find it impossible to even name the father of their child.'

'Then Dora should feel very much at home here,' Alan replied, unable to keep the bitterness he felt from his voice.

'That is possibly so,' the matron agreed, 'but when we agreed to admit her we were given to understand she was unmarried and would be unable to keep the child.'

'You mean . . . she intends to have the baby adopted?' Alan was stunned that Dora had asked him for money to keep herself and the baby when she had already made plans to give it away.

'That was the idea. She explained that the father is an American serviceman who failed to keep his promise to stay in touch with her. That part of her story, at least, may well be true.'

Alan agreed, explaining that while he was away in the Royal Navy, Dora had worked at a hospital run for, and by, the United States army.

When he had finished talking, the matron asked, 'What do you mean to do now, Mr Carter?'

'I need to think about everything that I've learned today,' Alan replied. 'Our marriage is over – Dora made that clear when I came back from the war. In truth, we never really had a marriage. We were only together for a week before I went away to sea, and less time than that when I returned. She said then she wanted nothing more to do with me. I might never have seen her again had she not written to ask me for money because she was expecting my baby. She must have known all along that it isn't mine.'

The matron inclined her head. 'I would hesitate to dispute that, but what of the baby now?'

'I can't answer that, Matron, because it isn't up to me. The baby isn't mine, so I feel no responsibility for it, but I would like to talk to Dora about that – and about a number of other things. If there is anything I can do to help, I will, but it will be a one-off payment and not an ongoing commitment.'

'That is possibly far more than Mrs Carter deserves,' the matron said, 'but it's not for me to pass judgement on her, or on anyone else, for that matter. However, I do not think it would be wise for you to speak to your wife today. By tomorrow Mrs Carter should be well enough to be brought to meet you here, in my office. Shall we say . . . two o'clock? It will be better if you can discuss the matter in private.'

Alan agreed, and once outside the hospital he found a vacant seat in a nearby park and sat there for half an hour, gathering his thoughts and assessing what this latest development would mean to him – and to Vicky. He wished more than ever that he could talk everything over with her right now.

He comforted himself with the thought that after the meeting with Dora he should have a better idea of what the future held for everyone concerned. In the meantime, he had one more call to make in the East End before returning to the Paddington boarding-house.

* * *

The cheque from the Royal Navy that had been intercepted before reaching Alan had been cashed in the pawnbroker's shop of Solomon Percival, in Hackney Road. It was a shop Alan knew well.

When he entered, he was greeted by a smell that he remembered from many years ago: the distinctive, musty aroma of close-packed second-hand clothing. Two women were in the shop before him, one trying to pledge her wedding ring for more than the pawnbroker was prepared to offer, the other redeeming a suit that had spent more time in this place than in her husband's wardrobe.

When both women had gone, one with a suit over her arm, the other with tears in her eyes and no ring on her finger, the pawnbroker turned to Alan. 'What can I do for you? If you have something to pledge that you don't want anyone to know about, you're wasting your time and mine. I don't handle stolen goods. Who are you, anyway?'

'I'm someone who has known you since the days when my dad was on a long sea voyage and his money hadn't arrived. My ma pawned a necklace that her own mother had given her. It tided us over until my dad's pay arrived.'

'So? You've come to talk to me of old times? I have work to do, and time is money.'

'It's money I want to talk about, Mr Percival. *My* money. My name is Carter, Alan Carter. A cheque made out to me was paid into your bank, but I never got the money.'

'If I accepted a cheque it would have been signed by the payee. I would have paid out every penny that was due – less a small commission, of course; I am a businessman.'

'I am not disputing that, or the amount of your

commission. All I'm saying is that the signature on the cheque wasn't mine.'

'Look,' the pawnbroker spread his hands in a gesture of resignation, 'I don't know what it is you want from me. Someone came in with a cheque, signed and endorsed to me, and I did them a favour by accepting it. I have done nothing wrong. Nothing illegal. Now, as I just told you, I am a busy man, so if there is nothing more . . .'

'Mr Percival,' Alan spoke with a patience he did not feel, 'I am trying to keep this a family matter. I think I know who cashed the cheque and I have no doubt you do too. Tell me who brought it in for you to cash and it will remain a family matter. Deny all knowledge and I will need to go back to the Royal Navy and tell them my cheque has been stolen and cashed through your bank account. The Navy will call in the police and they'll no doubt be delighted at an opportunity to take out a search warrant for your premises. I don't want a lot of fuss, and neither, I suspect, do you. The cheque was cashed by one of the Platt family, who I am sure you know very well. Tell me which one it was and we can forget we've had this conversation. If not, I have no doubt the police will be very thorough. I expect you will remain closed for a long time.'

Solomon Percival made a gesture of despair. 'The trouble that comes from helping people . . . What do you have to do with the Platt family anyway? I don't remember seeing you before.'

'I'm married to Dora, but we're not together at the moment.'

'Then you'll need to get together again if you want to

know about your money. She's the one who brought the cheque in here, so tearful and pregnant that I felt sorry for her. She had her mother with her. If she didn't give the money to you then you'll need to take it up with her. Now, if you wouldn't mind . . .'

Walking away from the pawnbroker's shop, the knowledge that Dora had been the one to steal his cheque saddened Alan. He had thought it was probably Charlie, or even Winnie. However, now he knew the truth, he would make use of it.

At first, Dora refused to go to the matron's office and talk to him, but the matron declared very firmly that she must. Dora had obtained help from the Salvation Army under false pretences. Now the truth was known it was up to her and Alan to sort matters out between them.

The meeting did not begin well. When Alan informed her that he knew she was the one who had stolen the cheque and cashed it at the pawnbroker's, she became angry.

'It was all right for you, all the years you were away. You had no idea what we had to put up with here, in London. Everything was in short supply, German Zeppelins were dropping bombs and I had no one to turn to. You owe me far more than I've taken from you.'

'It didn't take you very long to find someone else to "turn to", even though I wasn't exactly enjoying a holiday . . . but all that's in the past. What needs to be sorted out is what we are going to do now.'

'We've already done that.'

'No,' Alan said firmly. 'We agreed to an arrangement when I believed the baby to be mine. He's not, and that

270

makes a difference. A very big difference as far as the divorce court is concerned. You've had a baby that's obviously not mine – and I'll have no difficulty at all in proving that.'

'I'm not going to let you get a divorce that easily,' Dora blustered. 'You married me and you owe me something as your wife.'

Alan looked at her with incredulity. 'I don't want to punish you, Dora, but I have no intention of allowing you to hold me to ransom. The signature on the cheque that was stolen from me was forged – by you. Solomon Percival is willing to give evidence that it was you who took it into his shop. If the police become involved you will be convicted and go to prison.'

Dora paled. 'You wouldn't take it to the police.'

'I certainly don't want to, but if I have no alternative, then I will.'

Dora looked at him, and seeing he was serious she burst into tears. 'Mum threatened to throw me out on the streets unless I found money to give her for my keep. I was coming close to my time and had to do something.'

'I believe you,' Alan said, 'but I doubt if a magistrate would. Tell me, if you had money, what would you do with it?'

'I'd go to America and find the baby's father,' Dora replied without hesitation. 'He'd take care of me, I know he would, especially when he knew I'd had his baby. He'd marry me; he always said he would.'

'But you're having the baby adopted,' Alan pointed out.

Dora shook her head. 'The Salvation Army have said they won't help me do that now – thanks to you! They say I know who the father is and must get him to accept responsibility for the baby.'

After a few moments' thought, Alan asked, 'Are you really serious about going to America, Dora?'

She nodded. 'Yes.'

'All right, but you realise that if you're still married to me there's not very much that the baby's father can do, so I'll tell you what *I'm* prepared to do. You sign divorce papers admitting to what you've done and agreeing to a divorce and I'll buy a return ticket to America for you – the return half valid for a year, so that you can come back to England if things don't work out. I'll also give you a hundred pounds to keep you while you search for the baby's father.'

Dora's mind was working overtime as he was talking. 'A hundred pounds won't keep me for very long in a strange country. Make it two hundred pounds and I might do what you want.'

'I haven't got two hundred pounds, although I might be able to manage a hundred and fifty.'

It would take up almost all of his publisher's advance, but he felt it would be worthwhile. 'If you don't agree I'll get a divorce anyway. It might take longer but I'll get it in the end and you'll be left with nothing.'

Dora knew he was right. What was more, he was offering her far more than she had expected. 'All right, but I want everything in writing and done properly.'

'That's fine by me. I'll get a lawyer to come in and see you while you're still in here. Now that's decided there's nothing more to say, except to hope you treat the baby's father more honestly than you treated me. Goodbye, Dora.'

* * *

Alan went straight from the hospital to his publisher and told Julian Gimblett the whole story. When he had finished, he asked the editor if he knew of a lawyer who could act for him and set divorce proceedings in motion as quickly as possible.

'Yes, my brother-in-law,' said Julian sympathetically. 'I'll telephone him right away and arrange for you to meet him tomorrow morning. It is Saturday, but the sooner we have this settled, the sooner you can get down to some serious writing without any distractions.'

That evening Alan wrote a long letter to Vicky. He told her of all that had happened and said he hoped to return to Newlyn in the next couple of days, once the preliminary formalities for a divorce had been completed.

In the letter Alan poured out his feelings for Vicky, saying how wonderful it would be to have the spectre of Dora lifted from them once and for all and pointing out that they would now be able to plan for a future together. He added that he had never enjoyed such happiness as he had known with her and could not wait to be back in Newlyn. All he wanted was to forget all that had happened during the past few days, and to be with her for ever.

It was a Friday, so he took the letter out that same evening, hoping he would be in time to catch the last collection at a nearby post office.

He arrived at the post box with two minutes to spare and posted the letter, confident it would reach Cornwall the next day.

He could not know that the postman had made the collection three minutes earlier, in the belief that five minutes would make little difference to anyone.

273

38

For the next couple of days, Vicky was kept busy painting Desmond's portrait, but her mind was not on her sitter. Her thoughts kept returning to Alan. She had hoped he would write immediately after visiting Dora. When there was no letter from him on Friday she feared the worst.

She did not believe Alan was the father of the baby Dora was expecting, but if Dora was able to convince him that he was, there was no telling what he might do. There was a loyal trait in Alan's character that she admired – but not in the present circumstances.

Her thoughts were constantly interrupted by Fiona, who came in and out of the studio many times during the painting sessions. Vicky found her inconsequential chatter irritating but she would not have felt comfortable spending so many hours alone with Desmond, even though she had come to realise that he posed less of a real threat than some of the men she had met during her years as an ambulance driver in France. Desmond considered himself to be something of a ladies' man, but he was far less worldly than Vicky. Nevertheless, she realised that Fiona's frequent visits probably helped to prevent any possible unpleasantness, even if it was no more serious than that.

However, it was the lack of news from Alan which coloured Vicky's world during these few days, even though she told herself it was unlikely he would be able to settle things immediately. It might take a day or two.

Then, on Friday, the last day of Desmond's sitting, Fiona, Desmond and Vicky were sharing a pot of tea when Desmond said, 'I shall be passing through Oxfordshire tomorrow, Vicky. Is there any message you would like me to carry to your parents, or perhaps something you would like delivered?'

In recent letters from home it had been hinted that Vicky's mother's health was not as good as it might have been and for a moment she was tempted to send something home with him, but she said, 'No, I can't think of anything, but thank you for the offer.'

'At least Desmond will have company for most of the way,' Fiona said. 'Rupert has business to attend to in Bristol first thing on Monday morning and he will be going there with Desmond tomorrow.'

'When did you last see your parents?' Desmond asked Vicky.

'Quite a few months ago,' she admitted. 'Mother asks in every letter when I am coming home, but I always seem to have a reason for not going to see them. I suppose it is really very remiss of me, but I always seem to have so much to do here, and Burford is not the easiest of places to reach from Cornwall.'

'Surely you could spare a few days off to visit them,'

Desmond persisted. 'I have no doubt it would give them a great deal of pleasure.'

'What is it you are leading up to, Desmond?' Vicky asked suspiciously.

'I am suggesting you should come with Rupert and me tomorrow, Vicky. I could drop Rupert off in Bristol and have you home no more than two hours later. I will be returning to Newlyn in about two weeks' time, but if that did not suit, you could make your own way back here. At least you would feel you had done your duty and made your parents happy.'

At any other time Vicky would have looked for an ulterior motive in Desmond's offer, but she had become increasingly unsettled by Alan's absence and the lack of news from him. She hesitated . . . and Fiona entered the conversation.

'It is an opportunity that probably won't come up again, Vicky. You can stay with your parents for as long as you please. A whole fortnight, or no more than a weekend, if that is all the time you feel you can spare. I will keep an eye on your studio and ensure it comes to no harm.'

Vicky had not yet learned to trust Desmond, but she told herself that with Rupert accompanying them for much of the journey there would be little opportunity for him to make himself objectionable. What was more, with Alan away in London – in the company of his wife – she was finding it very difficult to concentrate on her work. A few days away might be just what was needed.

Nevertheless, she said, 'I couldn't just arrive home without any warning. There might be no one there. My parents have quite an active social life.'

'Then call them on our telephone, darling,' Fiona said. 'You are very welcome to do so, you know that. You have used it before.'

Uncertainly shifting her gaze to Desmond, who could hardly hide his delight at the possibility of having her company on the journey to Oxfordshire, Vicky asked, 'What time do you expect to reach Burford?'

'I intend leaving at about eight o'clock in the morning and will stop for lunch before reaching Bristol. I should think I will be in Burford at about eight o'clock in the evening. It will be a long day, but it is the easiest way of getting there from Cornwall, as I am quite sure you know.'

Vicky was reluctant to leave Newlyn, in case Alan returned unexpectedly, but she had heard nothing from him and she could be back in Cornwall in a couple of days. Making up her mind, she said, 'All right, but I will make a telephone call home first. If my parents are going to be there I will come with you, Desmond. Thank you.'

He was delighted, and so too was Fiona. She had been trying to pair off Desmond and Vicky for a very long time, believing she was doing Vicky a great favour by pushing her into a relationship with a man who was a potential Member of Parliament. His background was far more in keeping with Vicky's than the company she had recently been keeping.

39

The small party from Newlyn were late setting off and it was entirely Vicky's fault. She pleaded that she had not completed packing a suitcase when Desmond and Rupert arrived at the studio in Desmond's motor car, but in reality she was still hoping there might be a letter from Alan. It was not until the postman had been, with a delivery that contained only two small bills and a letter from a local gallery, that she felt able to close the suitcase and have it put in the vehicle.

For the early part of the journey Vicky had very little to say, although she was unimpressed with Desmond's driving ability. He drove particularly slowly when it began to rain and when lunchtime came they were still in Devon. They lost even more time en route to Bristol, where it was seven o'clock in the evening before they located the hotel where Rupert was to stay and saw him settled in.

When they set off again, Desmond appeared to be driving with even less skill than before. After he had made a particularly noisy gear change, Vicky asked, 'Are you all right, Desmond?'

'No. To tell you the truth, I'm finding the driving rather more difficult than I anticipated. I am not used to being on the road for such a long period of time. I usually break my journey home from Cornwall. I am beginning to feel very tired and am perhaps not functioning as well as I should.'

Looking at him in alarm, Vicky said, 'Oh, dear! You can't continue if you feel like that, and we still have a long way to go. Is there somewhere nearby where we might stop?'

'You would be happy for us to break our journey?' Desmond glanced at her, hardly able to contain his delight.

'Of course. Do you know somewhere?'

'As a matter of fact I do. The Cross Hands is an extremely good hotel not many miles along the road, at Old Sodbury.'

'Good! The sooner we reach there, the better.'

At the hotel, Desmond parked the motor car close to the front entrance and, somewhat uncertainly, asked Vicky, 'What would you like to do first?'

'I would like to eat, Desmond. I am absolutely ravenous.'

'Of course. I will have a word with the management and then we will dine.'

Settling Vicky at a corner table in the restaurant, Desmond went in search of the manager, and with the aid of a hefty tip ensured they were given adjacent rooms for the night – with a connecting door. Then he ordered the best champagne with which to wash down their meal, and was disappointed when Vicky declined to have her glass filled as often as his own.

Dinner was rounded off with a large brandy which bolstered Desmond's confidence considerably. In truth, he was slightly in awe of Vicky. Fiona had assured him that the women artists in Newlyn embraced a Bohemian lifestyle which would shock all but the most broad-minded members of society. Nevertheless, Vicky's assurance troubled him. He felt she must realise what he had planned for the night, and yet . . .

'I have had your luggage taken to your room, Vicky. I haven't actually seen what the room is like, but I am quite certain it will be suitable. However, I will inspect it with you, just in case there is anything you do not like.'

'A room, Desmond? Isn't that terribly extravagant? I only need to freshen up a little before we set off.'

For a few moments, Desmond reminded Vicky of a goldfish, mouthing against the glass of its bowl.

'I thought . . . you suggested . . . we should stop somewhere.'

'Yes, and the Cross Hands has been an excellent choice. Now I feel we should get on our way. I don't want my parents to wait up until too late for me. As you know, my mother has not been terribly well lately.'

'But . . .' Desmond was still floundering, 'I have had far too much to drink to be able to drive safely.'

'I know,' Vicky said understandingly. 'That is why I will drive.'

'You?' Desmond was startled, then he remembered Fiona telling him that Vicky had driven ambulances in both France and England. 'But you have never driven my motor car . . . It's a Rolls-Royce.'

Vicky smiled at him. 'We had a Rolls-Royce ambulance

in France. The controls were very little different from those in your motor car. Besides, it is either that, or I will have to telephone Daddy, explain what has happened and ask him to come and fetch me. I doubt if he will be terribly pleased, but he would be unhappier knowing I was stranded with a man I hardly know in an out-of-the-way country hotel. I doubt whether it would further your hopes of a parliamentary career, either . . . but, of course, you would not know. My father and the leader of the Conservative party were at school together. They still meet up when they are both in London.'

'You would not jeopardise my career in such a way, Vicky?' Desmond was aghast at the thought of what the result might be if rumours were circulated of his intentions towards Vicky, no matter how much he protested his innocence.

'Of course not,' Vicky said soothingly. 'Why should I? But Daddy is terribly protective . . .'

Vicky drove with far more assurance than had Desmond and they reached her home at Burford in good time. It had been a quiet drive with little talk between the two occupants of the vehicle. Desmond's mood had not been improved when he had been obliged to cancel the two rooms he had booked at the Cross Hands hotel.

The manager, with just the hint of a smirk on his face, had said, 'Lady changed her mind, has she, sir? Never mind, it happens far more often than you might think. Perhaps we might see you another time . . .'

When Vicky brought the vehicle to a halt in front of the large old house that was her family home, an extremely

281

subdued Desmond admitted, 'You are a better driver than I am, Vicky. Had it been left to me we would still have been miles away – even had I been sober.'

'Had it been left to you we would probably be having a rather embarrassing argument right now in the Cross Hands hotel,' Vicky retorted.

In truth, she felt more amused than angry with him. Desmond presented himself as a man of the world, but she realised that he was a man who had not yet found himself.

When Vicky's father came out to greet them, he invited Desmond to come in and have a drink, telling him he was well acquainted with his father.

Desmond declined the offer, pleading that he had probably drunk as much as was good for him when he and Vicky had stopped for dinner.

'Seems quite a pleasant young man,' said Vicky's father as he carried her suitcase into the house. 'Might be a little shy for a Member of Parliament, though. Looks as though he needs to assert himself a little more. Still, with another election not likely for a year or two, he'll have learned what Parliament is all about and no doubt be a little more confident and experienced by then.'

Vicky smiled to herself. As well as putting himself up as a candidate at a by-election, she was aware that Desmond had been hoping to extend his experience of life at the Cross Hands hotel at Old Sodbury.

He must realise how close he had come to making a disastrous error of judgement. She believed she would experience no trouble from him in the future.

40

Alan caught an early morning train from Paddington station on Tuesday, exactly six days after he had left Cornwall. A great deal had happened during that time.

Thanks to the expertise of his editor's brother-in-law, the initial stages of Alan's divorce proceedings were already under way. Statements had been taken and various documents drawn up dealing with the money Alan had promised to pay. The solicitor warned Alan that the divorce was likely to be a costly process, but the end result was not in doubt. His marriage to Dora would be brought to an end by the due process of law.

Alan was eager to tell Vicky of the progress he had made. She would have received his letter, of course, but there was so much he wanted to tell her in person. They had never actually spoken of marriage because until now it had seemed out of the question. Now he wondered, for the first time, whether it was something she had even contemplated. He had always believed that marriage was not on a suffragette's agenda, and Vicky was certainly a very independent woman ... but it was not the most important thing in their lives. They were both very happy as things were at the moment.

Alan realised he would have thought very differently about everything before meeting Vicky. Her encouragement and the way of life to which she had introduced him had changed his way of thinking.

His excitement mounted when the train arrived at Penzance and he decided to catch the motor bus that meandered westward from the station, including Newlyn on its route. It was slow, but would get him to Newlyn more quickly than if he walked.

Alighting from the bus at Newlyn, Alan hesitated for a moment, wondering whether he should call at the post office to check whether there was any mail for him. He decided against it. He had seen his publisher in London the previous day and knew all that was happening there. Anything else could take second place to his reunion with Vicky.

On his arrival at the studio he was deeply disappointed to discover there was no one at home and the door was locked. This in itself was unusual. Newlyn was a small community and doors were rarely secured in the absence of the occupants, but it posed no problem for him. He had a key to the studio flat and used it now to unlock the door and go inside, believing Vicky would soon be home and that he would be able to surprise her.

Once inside the studio he suddenly felt ill at ease. Things were not right. The first thing he noticed was that there was no fire burning in the grate. He told himself there was nothing particularly significant in this, the weather being warm enough to do without one, but the studio was also unusually tidy. There were none of the paints and brushes that Vicky was in the habit of leaving strewn about the place when she went out for a while.

Going into the kitchen, he saw there was no fire here either – and this was *most* unusual. All the cooking was carried out on the kitchen range.

Hurrying into the bedroom, Alan checked the wardrobe and could tell immediately that some clothes were missing. He wondered whether Vicky had gone to stay with friends, perhaps with Fiona. That would explain why some of her clothes had gone.

He went out into the studio once more, and saw letters piled on a table beside the door, his among them. Now he really was concerned, but was not certain what to do. While he was thinking, he decided to make himself a cup of tea, boiling the kettle on a small but efficient spirit stove kept in the kitchen. He would need to have it without milk. There was some in a jug in the kitchen, but it had turned sour, another indication that Vicky had been gone for a few days, at least.

While he waited for the kettle to come to the boil, Alan paced about the studio uncertainly. Perhaps Vicky had arranged a last-minute exhibition somewhere. He wondered who might know – and immediately thought of Fiona again. It was probably she who had been in the studio and picked up the letters.

Suddenly, Alan stopped before the easel holding the painting on which Vicky must be currently working. It was not yet completed, but he recognised the subject of the portrait immediately.

Desmond Stileman!

Surprised that she should have been painting the portrait of a man she had tried hard to avoid in the past, Alan looked at it more closely. It was good, as all Vicky's paintings were, but it lacked the indefinable something he had seen in the portrait of Paul, and in that of himself. Nevertheless, he felt disturbed by finding it here, in the studio.

A little later in the evening, at a loss about what to do next, he decided to pay a visit to the Fisherman's Arms. Perhaps someone there would know where Vicky had gone.

There were very few artists he knew in the bar this evening, but he had been in the pub for no more than ten minutes when Cecil entered the snug where he was seated on his own.

Both men were delighted to meet each other again and, after greeting Alan warmly and explaining that he had only returned from Europe late the previous night, Cecil asked, 'Where is everyone – where is Vicky?'

'I came here hoping someone would be able to tell me,' Alan replied. 'I returned to Newlyn today after a week away and discovered she has gone off somewhere.' He gave Cecil an outline of what he had been doing in London.

'She won't have gone for long,' Cecil said reassuringly. 'I spoke to someone earlier who said there was quite an important exhibition taking place in Bristol. She might have gone there. You two haven't quarrelled, or had a misunderstanding?'

'No . . . although she was very upset about me going to London, particularly in view of my reason for travelling there. I did write to tell her what was happening, but the letter is among a pile of unopened mail in her studio.'

'Hmm!' Cecil pulled a wry face. 'I know very little about the ways of women, Alan, but I can understand her feelings. She must be very unhappy, and I am given to understand that unhappy women can be somewhat irrational. I will make a few enquiries on your behalf, but it sounds very much as though Vicky might have gone off somewhere on the spur of the moment.'

Cecil's words did nothing to allay Alan's concern for Vicky. Although much of the remainder of their conversation concerned writing and poetry, he could not get her out of his thoughts and the idea of her having spent hours in the studio with Desmond increased his unease.

On his way back to the studio later that night, Alan hoped against hope that he would find Vicky had returned, but this was not a night for miraculous happenings. She was not there and he tried not to look at the portrait of Desmond.

Alan found it difficult to sleep that night in the bed he had shared with Vicky and he rose early and pottered around the studio for much of the day, not wanting to go out in case she returned. However, in the late afternoon, after brooding over a cup of milkless tea, he made his way to the shop in the village and bought some food for the remainder of the day. He enquired after Vicky here, but drew a blank. Nevertheless, he purchased sufficient groceries for two, in case she returned. He also called at the village post office to ask whether anyone there knew where she had gone. The post office was the hub of village gossip but no one knew anything about Vicky, although they were holding a number of letters for him.

Pocketing the letters, Alan made his way back to the studio. As he came closer, he could see that the door was slightly ajar. Excited at the thought that Vicky had returned, he ran up the wooden stairs and, throwing the door open, called, 'Vicky? Are you here?'

When a figure appeared in the kitchen doorway, Alan saw it was not Vicky, but Fiona.

'Oh! I saw the door open and thought Vicky must have come back.'

'I doubt if Vicky will be back for some time. She asked me to keep an eye on the studio for her – but she said nothing about *you* being here while she is away.' Fiona did nothing to hide her hostility towards him.

'Where is she?' Alan tried not to allow her attitude to upset him.

'She has gone home to Oxfordshire – with Desmond. She has been painting his portrait.'

'I've seen it,' Alan said curtly.

Fiona carried on talking as though he had not spoken. 'I have no doubt Desmond will meet with the full approval of Vicky's parents. Her father is very active politically and would be absolutely delighted to have a Conservative Member of Parliament in the family – and there is no doubt at all that Desmond will become our MP at the next election.'

Despite his alarm at Fiona's words, Alan did not – *would not* – accept what Fiona was saying. 'I hardly think Vicky would contemplate getting married to someone she hardly knows after only a week,' he said scornfully.

'Oh, there is no stopping Vicky once she makes up her mind about something.' Fiona spoke as though Alan were a stranger who knew nothing about Vicky. 'Desmond is very much the same. After a few days together, here in the studio, they were getting on wonderfully well. Vicky realised they come from very similar backgrounds and have a great deal in common. When he suggested he should drive her to Oxfordshire and meet her parents, she jumped at the opportunity to show him off to them. I would not be surprised if they announce their engagement on their return. It will be a perfect match; they are eminently suited to one another.'

Looking directly at him for the first time since he had entered the studio, she said, 'I am sure you realise that if you were to be here when they return it would prove a great embarrassment to Vicky. She is a very talented, warm-hearted and generous girl, as you must know, but she can be frightfully impulsive. She now has the most wonderful opportunity to ally her talent to a man who has a great future in politics. They can each help further the other's ambitions and I know they will lead highly successful lives together. I am certain you have no wish to deny her that, so, speaking as her devoted friend, and the person to whom she entrusted care of the studio, I would appreciate it if you would leave at the earliest opportunity. I have tidied things up this morning and will come back tomorrow and check that all is as it should be.'

41

When Fiona left the studio Alan tried to convince himself that she was wrong. Vicky would not have switched her affections so quickly – especially to a man like Desmond. But there was the half-completed portrait to give at least some credence to her story.

She had also pointed out a fact of which he was acutely aware: the vastly differing backgrounds of Vicky and himself. It was something that had always deeply concerned him, especially during the early days of their relationship. In his euphoria at having successfully persuaded Dora to agree to a divorce, he had temporarily forgotten the social differences that existed between himself and Vicky.

He was selling stories and poems regularly now, and everyone was telling him how clever he was and how the reading public was eager for his work, but in his heart he was all too aware that his use of the English language fell far short of that of many of his contemporaries. His education had been cut short by the need to go out into the world and earn money. He had not been to university, as had Cecil and most of the other writers he had met since knowing Vicky. Her own education too had been vastly superior to his own. Perhaps she had come to realise this during the many hours she must have spent chatting to Desmond while she worked on his portrait.

The longer he thought about it, the more he realised the truth of what Fiona had said and his despair increased. He felt a sudden need to get out of the studio and take a walk along the cliffs to clear his head, and try to make some sense of his confused thoughts.

It was a fine day but a stiff breeze was blowing in from the sea and Alan picked up the jacket he had worn to the shops that afternoon. He had thrown it on a chair while Fiona was talking to him. As he lifted it now a number of letters fell from the pocket where he had placed them while he was asking questions about Vicky in the post office. Picking up the envelopes, he shuffled through them.

Two were from his London publisher, their contents already discussed with Julian Gimblett. Another contained a small cheque from a magazine for a couple of poems they had accepted from him. There was also a letter from the Royal Navy in connection with his demobilisation. The final envelope bore a Gibraltar stamp and Alan remembered Mabel telling him she had forwarded it on from Quilter Street.

Shrugging on his jacket, he tore the envelope open and began to read the letter as he made his way to the door. Reaching the top of the outside stairs, he stopped, his own troubles temporarily put to one side.

The letter was from Maria. In it she complained that

Alan had not replied to previous letters written to him by herself and by his father. She also said, with considerable bitterness, how disappointed they had both been that he had not attended their wedding, or even replied to the invitation, which had included a cheque drawn on a British bank for an amount that was meant to cover the fare for Alan and his wife to travel to Gibraltar – *even though the cheque had been cashed.*

Maria went on to say that in view of this it was hardly likely he would respond to this letter, but she felt it her duty to inform him that his father's leg, badly broken in an accident she had already written to Alan about, was now improving, although it had been necessary to take him to a renowned specialist in Madrid. She pointed out that things would have been far easier for John Carter, and herself, had Alan responded to her plea for him to come to Gibraltar and help run things on his father's behalf. It would have assisted her new husband to recover more rapidly and would also have been an opportunity for them to meet Dora and give her a splendid holiday.

There was much more in a similar vein and Alan felt both anger and sadness. Sadness at the realisation that the naval cheque had not been the only one Dora had fraudulently cashed, and anger that she had forwarded none of Maria's letters to him. Had Mabel not intercepted this one on the day Dora had gone to hospital to have her baby, he would have known nothing of what had been going on in Gibraltar.

Returning to the studio, Alan sat down and wrote a hurried letter to his father and Maria. He explained that her latest letter was the only one he had received from them. Apologising for not writing before, he explained that he had not left the Royal Navy as planned on his return from Gibraltar, but had gone on to serve in the Baltic Sea where, because of the nature of his work, it had been impossible to write.

He also explained that his marriage had broken up and Dora had given birth to another man's child. No mail had been forwarded to him from the London address and, unfortunately, the cheque Maria had so kindly sent was not the only one to have been fraudulently cashed.

He said little about Vicky, but explained that although he might not be remaining in Newlyn, he would ensure that any letters addressed to him here would be forwarded to him. Alan felt certain Cecil would undertake to do this on his behalf.

Finally, Alan said that he intended travelling to Gibraltar at the earliest opportunity to see them both and would fill in all the many gaps in his narrative when he saw them.

The letter completed, Alan took it to the post office and sent it off. He was about to set off on his walk when he met up with Cecil. It was an opportunity not to be missed and when Alan said he would like to have a private talk with him, Cecil suggested they go to the snug at the Fisherman's Arms.

When Alan said he would prefer somewhere a little more private, Cecil gave him a look that took in his drawn and tired expression and invited him back to his house.

'Unfortunately, my stock of alcoholic drinks has been sadly depleted in my absence,' he complained. 'But I am sure I will be able to find a little something to brighten your day. You look as though you are in need of it.'

At the house, Cecil would not allow Alan to say anything of his troubles until he was ensconced in a comfortable chair with a very large brandy in his hand. Then, similarly fortified, Cecil declared he was ready to listen.

'I want to get to Gibraltar, leaving as soon as possible,' Alan said. After explaining his reason for wanting to make the journey, he added, 'I will need to go to London first, but how do I go about arranging a passage on one of the ships that go to the Mediterranean?'

'Southampton is the port you will need to go from. Why do you have to go to London first, and how long will you want to stay there?'

'Not very long, I hope, but I will need money for the voyage, and to live on when I reach Gibraltar. I still have money in the bank, but I am in the process of getting a divorce from Dora and the lawyers will need some to give to her. That will probably take most of what I have . . . not that there's any hurry for a divorce now, but the arrangements have already been made, so it might as well go ahead. I mean to take Vicky's portrait of me to London, find Lady Bellingham and tell her the portrait is hers, if she still wants it. She offered two hundred and fifty guineas for it at Vicky's exhibition. That will give me enough for what I need and leave me plenty to spare.'

'Are you talking of the "Hero" portrait that was the focal point of Vicky's exhibition? I thought it was your intention to keep it for yourself.' Cecil expressed his surprise.

'It was, but things have changed between Vicky, and me. I didn't tell you last night, but Vicky and I have been living together since we brought your car back from Clarice's house. Now I've found out that she's gone off with Desmond Stileman, a friend of Rupert and Fiona. He's an ex-pilot – an RFC officer, and likely to be the MP for this area before very long.'

Cecil frowned. 'This Desmond Stileman might be all you say he is, but that wouldn't necessarily impress Vicky and she is most certainly not the fickle type. How did you learn about this?'

'Fiona told me. She's looking after the studio for Vicky and had told me I'm to have my things out of there today.'

'A great deal seems to have been happening in Newlyn during my absence,' Cecil commented. 'I will no doubt catch up with it sooner or later, but right now we'll concentrate on getting you to Gibraltar. Since you are about to become homeless, we might as well get things moving right away. I have the telephone numbers of many of the shipping lines. I will begin with the most likely one . . .'

Cecil's first telephone call was the only one he needed to make. Still holding the handset, he said to Alan, 'The SS *Devinia* is sailing for the Far East from Southampton early tomorrow morning. Its first port of call will be Gibraltar, arriving early next week. It seems there is not another sailing for some ten days or so. It's most unusual for there to be such a dearth of ships heading in that direction, but the shipping agent I am talking to should know his business.'

'Tomorrow?' Alan expressed dismay. 'I can never get to Southampton in time . . . and I have to go to London first.'

Turning his attention back to the telephone, Cecil spoke into the mouthpiece. 'I would like to book a cabin for one to Gibraltar . . . for Alan Carter . . .' He continued to make all the necessary arrangements, ignoring Alan's protests that he could not possibly make it to Southampton in time.

When Cecil hung up, Alan repeated the reasons why he could not possibly take passage on the SS *Devinia*. Cecil cut his protests short.

'We'll go there in my car and I will have you there long before midnight tonight. Go off now and pack your things. I don't know what is going on between you and Vicky, but you can tell me all about it along the way. In the meantime, bring anything you don't want to take with you on the ship to me here. I will take care of it until your return.'

'But I still need to go to London to raise the money for my fare.'

'That will not be necessary. I will loan you the money and keep the portrait as surety – and you have no need to worry about it. If Lady Bellingham has changed her mind by the time you return I will buy the portrait myself. In fact, I might do that anyway. It will be a very good investment.'

When Alan began stammering his thanks, telling Cecil he was a very good friend, the other man cut him short. 'There is no time – and no need – for thanks. We still have a great deal to do. Do you wish to send a telegraph to Gibraltar to inform your father you are on your way?'

Alan thought about it for only a few moments. 'No, I would prefer it to be a surprise.'

'Very well. Now, hurry off and get your things together while I prepare the Hotchkiss. I have been longing to get behind the wheel again. This will be just the sort of journey I need.'

At the studio Alan packed clothes for the voyage, then borrowed one of Vicky's suitcases in which to put the things he would be leaving at Cecil's house. He would ask Cecil to return the suitcase to her discreetly when, or if, she returned to Newlyn.

As an afterthought, Alan wrote a brief note to Vicky. It said merely, *Dear Vicky, I am very, very sad that things have ended for us this way, but thank you for everything. I hope you and Desmond will know much happiness together. Alan.*

Finding an envelope in Vicky's desk, Alan put the note inside, together with his key to the studio. Then he placed the envelope among the pile of letters awaiting her on the small side table by the door. As he did so he found the letter he had written to her from London.

After only a moment's hesitation, he tore the letter in half without opening it and dropped the two halves into a waste bin beneath the table.

With a feeling of great sadness, he removed his portrait from its place in the alcove and left the studio, closing the door firmly behind him.

42

'I *do* feel you could at least stay at home until after the weekend, dear. The Granthams are coming for dinner on Saturday and bringing Jennifer with them especially to meet you again. You two were such close friends at boarding school and she was *so* looking forward to a reunion with you.'

Miriam Hazelton appealed to her daughter. It was Friday and Vicky had been in Burford since the previous Saturday. It was the longest period she had spent at home for some years, and the reason for the infrequency of her visits had become increasingly apparent to her.

Her mother, in particular, still treated her as though she was a schoolgirl, and was determined to order her daughter's life. It was for this reason she had invited the Granthams to dinner with their daughter Jennifer, a young woman whom Vicky had heartily disliked when they were both attending the same boarding school.

'Mother, I have my own life to lead and a living to earn. I need to get back to Newlyn and my painting.'

'I really don't think a few more days would make all that difference, dear. After all, that very handsome young man who brought you here has offered to drive you back to Cornwall next weekend – and there is no reason for you to look at me in that way. Desmond Stileman *is* good-looking. What is more, he comes from a very good family. Any girl with a thought for the future would be highly delighted to have him taking an interest in her . . . and you are not getting any younger, you know.'

'Thank you, Mother, but I intend to choose my own husband. You will be among the first to know when we are ready to name our wedding day. Are you ready, Daddy? We should leave right away if I am to catch my train. I have telephoned Fiona and she will be waiting for me at Penzance railway station.'

The reason Vicky had accepted Desmond's offer to bring her home was partly concern for her mother's health. However, Miriam was far better than Vicky had been led to believe from her letters, and now Vicky felt an over-whelming urge to return to the studio flat, in the hope that Alan had either returned, or written to say he would soon be home. Leaving Newlyn had been very much a spur-of-the-moment decision and it was one she had realised was a mistake almost immediately. She would not be happy now until she was back in Cornwall.

There was no railway station at Burford and Vicky's father had agreed to drive her to Cheltenham. Along the way, after chatting about nothing of particular importance, he suddenly said, 'You seem most eager to get back to Newlyn, Vicky. Is there someone waiting for you? Someone that your mother and I should know about?'

Vicky hesitated for only a moment before replying. 'There *is* someone, but I don't want to say anything more at the moment. When I feel the time is right I will tell you all about him.'

After mulling over what she had said, her father asked, 'Is he someone of whom I would approve?'

'I think you might, once you have got to know him. I am certain Mother would not.'

Ralph Hazelton's glance flicked briefly to his daughter. 'Is there any particular reason why Mother wouldn't approve? Is this young man a bad character, or something?'

Vicky laughed. 'No, nothing like that . . . in fact he is a highly decorated war hero. But although he is beginning to make a name for himself in the literary field, he does not belong to the world of Desmond Stileman, nor would I wish him to.'

'You don't like young Stileman, do you? Is there something I should know about him? I am not asking the question as your father now, but as a loyal Conservative with the interests of the party at heart.'

Vicky was well aware that, had she wished, this would have been her opportunity to nip Desmond's political career in the bud, but she said only, 'No. In fact I have told him I feel he will be as fine an MP as his father, but Desmond is not my type. Now, would you mind if we changed the subject? It has been delightful to be home with you both for a few days, but I do have my own life to lead.'

Ralph Hazelton knew Vicky well enough not to probe into her private life any further. They spent the remainder of the journey to Cheltenham talking of her painting.

Vicky had far less success in preventing Fiona from singing the praises of Desmond when she and Rupert met her at Penzance railway station, late that afternoon. When Vicky asked about Alan, Fiona replied curtly that she knew nothing of his whereabouts, then demanded to be told every detail of the journey Vicky and the prospective candidate had shared between Bristol and Burford. But she found Vicky frustratingly reticent. All she would say was that she and Desmond had shared the driving and that she enjoyed being at the wheel of his Rolls-Royce. Vicky really wanted to ask more about Alan, but knew she would learn nothing from Fiona in her present mood.

When they reached the studio, Vicky was first up the outside stairs and was deeply disappointed to find the door locked. It was evident that Alan was not here. Behind her, Rupert struggled up the steps with her suitcase, with Fiona close behind him, trying to hurry him along. He put the suitcase down in the bedroom with a sigh of relief, then said he needed to go home and telephone a business associate about a deal they were putting together. He suggested that he and Fiona should buy Vicky a meal in the Fisherman's Arms later on.

After thanking Fiona for lighting the kitchen fire and getting in groceries, Vicky said that what she wanted more than anything else was an opportunity to sit quietly on her own for an hour or two and enjoy the luxury of being in her own home again. Aggrieved, Fiona was obliged to accept the strong hint. After telling Vicky that if she changed her mind and felt more sociably inclined they would be in the snug, the couple left.

Throwing open the windows to the small balcony, Vicky

looked across Mount's Bay to the fairytale castle on St Michael's Mount, but noticed little of its unique beauty this evening. She was concerned about Alan. She had been certain he would have returned by now. She wondered what could have happened in London to keep him there.

Vicky sat on the balcony for a long time before the thought came to her that Alan might have written to her. She had not thought to ask Fiona whether there had been any mail delivered while she was away.

Stepping back into the studio she saw the letters piled on the small table beside the door. There were so many that Vicky was surprised she had not noticed them before. Picking them up she sifted through them quickly, until she came to one that was not stamped but was addressed simply to *Vicky*.

Recognising Alan's handwriting, Vicky frowned. The letter had obviously not been sent through the post. That meant it must have been delivered by hand . . . which indicated that Alan *had* returned to the studio during her absence. If so, why was he not here now?'

She hurriedly tore open the envelope, and as she did so a key fell from it to the floor. Without picking it up, Vicky could see it was a key to the studio. Alan's key! Opening out the folded piece of paper that had been in the envelope, she read the brief message with utter astonishment. *I am very, very sad that things have ended for us this way . . . I hope you and Desmond will know much happiness together.*

So Alan *had* been back to the studio, but what could he possibly mean? She glanced towards the easel and the unfinished portrait which stood upon it. Surely he could not have drawn some ridiculous conclusion just from seeing the painting?

There had to be another, much more serious reason for him to believe there was something between her and Desmond – and that could have come from only one source.

Fiona!

When she stooped to recover the key, Vicky's head was level with the waste-paper basket and she saw the torn letter it contained. Reaching inside, she retrieved the envelope. Removing the letter, she pieced it together on the small table and read what Alan had written to her from London.

The letter was that of a happy man. Alan had discovered that Dora's baby was not his and she had agreed to a divorce. He returned time and time again to what this would mean to him and Vicky.

By the time she finished reading, Vicky felt choked up, her eyes burning. She wondered what could have been said to hurt him so much that he had abandoned all his plans and hopes for the future and gone away believing she had turned to Desmond Stileman.

There was only one way to learn the truth and that was to find Fiona and learn what she had said to Alan.

43

The Fisherman's Arms was fairly quiet when Vicky burst in through the door. Most fishermen were either still at sea, or at the dock, unloading their catches. Many artists too were taking advantage of the remaining summer light to work late in their studios. Nevertheless, a number of people were drinking in the snug, and it was here that Vicky found Fiona and Rupert.

Vicky's anger had been fuelled by the discovery, before leaving the studio, that Alan had taken his portrait with him. It somehow gave his leaving a frightening air of finality.

'Hello, darling. Have you changed your mind . . . What is it? What is the matter?' Fiona's greeting faltered and died when she saw Vicky's expression.

'I am the one who is here to ask questions. You are the one who will answer them,' Vicky declared fiercely. 'Why did you not tell me Alan had returned to Newlyn while I was away?'

'Did I not? It must have slipped my mind,' Fiona lied.

'In the circumstances I probably felt it wouldn't be terribly important to you, either.'

'I will be the judge of what is important when it involves the things that go on in my life,' Vicky retorted. 'Where is Alan now?'

'I have no idea.' Fiona shrugged, believing herself to be on safer ground now. 'Besides, I thought Desmond might be returning with you and knew you would want to be spared the embarrassment of having him walk into your studio and find Alan ensconced there.'

'Are you telling me you told Alan to leave *my* home?' Vicky's voice rose to such a pitch that all talk in the snug ceased. 'How *dare* you? How dare you interfere in my life in such a way? What exactly did you tell him?'

'Only that Desmond had taken you home to Oxford-shire . . . I did what I believed to be in your best interests, darling . . . as a friend.'

'You are no longer a friend of mine, Fiona Graham. You are an interfering and insufferable snob.'

The colour drained from Fiona's face and someone in the snug gave Vicky a brief handclap and a muted 'Hear, hear!' Looking about her, Fiona realised that the occupants of the snug, together with the landlord and his wife behind the bar, had been listening to every word of the brief but bitter altercation with apparent enjoyment.

Putting down her glass and mustering as much dignity as she could, Fiona said to her husband, 'Shall we leave, Rupert? I am unaccustomed to such scenes, especially when they occur in a public house. They are no doubt the result of mixing with the wrong sort of people.'

As Rupert closed the door of the snug behind him and

Fiona, those inside raised a cheer and urged drinks upon Vicky. Refusing them all, Vicky asked whether anyone present knew Alan's whereabouts. A couple of the artists had seen him around a few days ago, but no one had any idea where he was now. Thoroughly despondent, Vicky left and made her way slowly back to the studio.

A very unhappy Vicky was sitting in her studio later that evening, the room lit only by the moon which had laid down a silver pathway across the waters of the bay. It was what she and Alan had often referred to as a 'smugglers moon', but all such romantic reminiscences were lost on her tonight.

Her confrontation with Fiona had been upsetting, but the reason for her angry outburst upset her even more. The letter she had retrieved from the waste-paper basket was filled with optimism. Somehow, Fiona had succeeded in killing that and convincing Alan that he and Vicky had no chance of a future together.

Vicky was aroused from her mood of despair by the sound of someone knocking at the door of the studio. It took a few moments before the sound penetrated her gloomy thoughts and she called out a cautious 'The door isn't locked', thinking it possible it was Fiona, calling to apologise.

It was not. The visitor was Cecil, and seeing him was a great surprise. She had not been aware of his return to Newlyn.

'Cecil, what are you doing here? I didn't know you were back in England.'

'And I wasn't aware you had returned to Newlyn until

I went for a drink in the snug,' Cecil replied. 'Everyone is talking of your little spat with dear Fiona.'

'It was not so little, Cecil,' Vicky replied unhappily. 'And had I given myself more time to consider what Fiona had done, it would have been far worse.'

'Tell me more,' Cecil said. 'But first, what is going on between you and Desmond Stileman?'

'Absolutely *nothing*,' Vicky declared angrily. 'To be perfectly honest, I don't even like the man – and if he ever found out that his father was responsible for having me sent to prison for pelting him with eggs, Desmond would avoid *me* like the plague!'

Cecil appeared mildly bewildered and Vicky explained the circumstances of the suffragette demonstration which had resulted in her spending a month in Holloway prison.

Suddenly chuckling, Cecil commented, 'It sounds like the sort of situation that might have inspired an Oscar Wilde play . . . but Fiona obviously knows nothing about it or she would not have been so anxious to pair you off with Desmond and drive a wedge between you and Alan.'

'If that *is* what she did,' Vicky said, having a sudden, unexpected moment of self-doubt. 'I just cannot believe someone would really behave in such a way. Not even a dreadful snob like Fiona.'

'Oh, she did it all right,' Cecil declared. 'She was guilty of all the things you accused her of – and probably one or two others. She was able to convince Alan that she was telling the truth – and he certainly did not want to believe it.'

'You have spoken to Alan? When? Where is he now?' Vicky's unhappiness changed momentarily to eagerness.

Cecil's reply was not what she had hoped for. 'We spoke a couple of days ago. As to where he is at this very moment . . . he is on the high seas en route to Gibraltar.'

Vicky looked at Cecil in dismay and disbelief. 'Gibraltar? Why?'

Cecil said, 'Shall we have some light in here, Vicky? Then we can perhaps have a cup of tea together while I tell you the full story. Then we will decide what might be done to rectify a very unhappy situation . . .'

By the time Cecil had told her all that had occurred when Alan had returned to Newlyn from London, Vicky realised she had let Fiona off very lightly indeed. But, deeply concerned for Alan, she put Fiona out of her mind . . . for now.

'Poor Alan!' she said for the third time since hearing what Cecil had to say. 'When, precisely, will he arrive in Gibraltar?'

'Early next week,' Cecil replied. 'Why do you ask?'

'I'd like to go out there to him,' Vicky replied. 'What would be the quickest way to get there?'

'A ship is as fast as any other means of travel,' Cecil replied, 'but I seem to remember that when I telephoned about a passage for Alan there was a dearth of fast ships travelling in that direction in the immediate future . . . and I think we should try to learn more about the situation there before you do anything precipitous.'

'But . . . what *can* I do?' Vicky asked in some distress. 'He will be in Gibraltar believing I no longer care for him, while I am here, in Newlyn, feeling equally unhappy. It is all my fault. I should never have left when I did.'

'We can change nothing in the past,' Cecil pointed out, 'but we should be able to put things right very quickly, if we go about it sensibly.'

'How?' Vicky was not convinced.

'Why don't I telephone to the shipping company and see if we can't send a wireless message to reach him before the ship docks at Gibraltar? We can tell him that everything Fiona told him was lies and that you are very unhappy at learning what she said. Alan will certainly believe it if the message comes from both of us – and will no doubt reply right away.'

'Cecil, you are an absolute darling. I would never have thought of sending a wireless message. Thank you. Thank you very much.' She kissed him warmly.

Embarrassed, he said, 'You had better save that sort of thing for Alan! If we are agreed I will go home now and send a message to the ship first thing in the morning. Hopefully we will have a reply some time tomorrow. Now, I don't suppose I can persuade you to come to the Fisherman's Arms with me for something to eat, so I suggest you cook yourself something, then go to bed. You will need to be at your very best if we are to undo all the harm Fiona has done . . .'

44

Vicky was trying without a great deal of success to settle down to work the next morning when Cecil paid her another visit. Eagerly, she said, 'Have you sent the wireless message to Alan?'

He shook his head solemnly, but when he saw her dismay he smiled. 'But I *have* had a telephone call from him.'

Startled, Vicky said, 'But he's at sea! How—'

'I was wrong. He's *not* at sea. The ship should have sailed on Thursday, but the crews' union called one of these strikes that have been disrupting the country this year. It seems the shipping company thought it would be settled yesterday, but the talks collapsed. Last night the passengers were told the ship would not now be sailing and the company offered to refund fares to those passengers who wished to cancel their passages. It proved fortuitous for Alan because when I explained about the lies Fiona told him he said he intends to return to Newlyn right away. He should be home with you late this evening. Oh, and I have brought this back to where it belongs . . .'

He was carrying a large bag, from which he proceeded to draw Vicky's portrait of Alan. 'Now Alan is returning to Newlyn and the shipping company is to refund his fare, he will not need to sell it after all. I know he will be delighted.'

'Cecil, as I have told you before, you are an absolute darling of a man, and a wonderful friend. Bless you!' Delighted with his news, she gave him a hug and a kiss.

Beaming with red-cheeked pleasure, Cecil said, 'This is becoming something of a habit. It's one you must break, before I find myself enjoying it rather more than I should.'

Happily ignoring his protest, Vicky said, 'What time do you think Alan will arrive home? I would like to plan a little celebration for him.'

'I think that merely being here with you will be celebration enough for him,' Cecil declared, 'but I suppose he will be hungry after such a long journey. Even if he catches each connection fairly promptly I doubt whether he will be home before dark. However, he sounded so happy when I assured him there was not even a grain of truth in anything Fiona had told him that I have no doubt he will be with you as early as possible, even if he has to run for much of the way.'

'Poor Alan,' Vicky said feelingly. 'He has had a horrible time.'

'True,' Cecil agreed. 'He is also very aware that *he* was thoughtless in his behaviour towards you. But I think the occasion of your reunion calls for celebration and not recrimination.'

* * *

Alan reached Newlyn shortly after ten o'clock that evening and hurried to the studio, hesitating momentarily only when he reached the door.

He had already accepted that the haste with which he had rushed off to London in the belief that Dora was carrying his baby must have hurt Vicky very deeply. When Fiona told him that Vicky had gone off with Desmond Stileman, he believed this to be the main reason – and felt she had every right to do so. He wondered whether Dora might still be capable of coming between them.

While he was hesitating, the door opened and Vicky was standing before him. From the studio window she had seen him hurrying towards the house and was standing behind the door when he came up the stairs and stopped. When he did not immediately turn the handle and come in, she had felt a brief moment of panic.

Now, looking at each other, the fears and doubts of both of them disappeared and there was not even a need for words. He held her and she clung to him for a long time. When the embrace ended he looked at her. For the first time ever, he saw tears in her eyes – and it really hurt him.

Among her very many other attributes, he believed Vicky to be the most courageous woman he had ever known and felt ashamed that he had hurt her so much. 'I'm sorry, Vicky . . .'

Her finger came up to his lips and she cut short his apology. 'Don't say it, Alan. We have both done unthinking things to hurt the other. It's enough that we care about it. Cecil – who is probably the best friend you and I will ever have – came to tell me you were on your way home nd he left saying tonight is for celebration, not recrimination. I was so impressed with his words that I walked into Penzance this afternoon and bought two bottles of the finest champagne I could find. As an afterthought I added a bottle of brandy. I seem to remember it is a winning formula for us.'

Alan's face broke into a delighted smile. 'I have the same memories. That's why *I* called in at a Southampton off-licence and added champagne and brandy to my luggage. It made my suitcase very heavy, but I think it is going to be worthwhile, and quite a night. If we find we have an unopened bottle left in the morning we'll take it along to Cecil.'

The following morning, it was as though Alan and Vicky had never been parted. Both were suffering hangovers, but they were very happy. They had succeeded in resolving the misunderstandings between them, in the way that only lovers can.

Walking to Cecil's house to take him not one but two bottles left over from their celebrations of the night before, they did not even notice Fiona and Rupert negotiate the road junction some distance ahead of them in their motor car, heading for Penzance. But Fiona saw them and her lips tightened in a thin, angry line of disapproval.

Cecil gave Vicky and Alan a delighted welcome and insisted they open one of the champagne bottles immediately, to celebrate their return to Newlyn – and to each other.

'Perhaps you will both settle down now and produce the wonderful work we are all expecting from you,' Cecil said as he was pouring the lively contents of the champagne bottle into three glasses. 'But what about your father, Alan? What will you do about him?'

'I wrote a reply to Maria's letter,' Alan explained. 'I'll wait until I hear from them again, then Vicky and I will discuss it.'

'That's probably the best course of action,' Cecil agreed. 'In the meantime, I suggest we have a party to celebrate the return of all three of us to the Newlyn fold. We'll make it Newlyn's party of the year. We will have it here, in the house and garden. Whom should we invite?'

Alan and Vicky agreed it was an excellent idea and after a brief discussion it was decided the party would be held the following Saturday. Instead of sending out individual invitations, Cecil suggested they should post notices in the various artists' haunts, inviting everyone to attend.

In the days that followed, it became apparent that Cecil's party would fulfil his prophecy that it would be the artistic community's occasion of the year. In spite of the need for Alan to catch up on his writing, and Vicky her painting, both found that helping to plan for it was a very pleasurable distraction.

45

When Saturday arrived, Cecil's house was a hive of activity. Alan worked hard shifting and rearranging furniture, while Vicky helped prepare the large quantities of food and drink that would be needed.

All the indications were that the party would outstrip all expectations and include not only Cecil's friends, but many of the young artists who had found their way to Newlyn in recent months. These newcomers, existing on minuscule or non-existent incomes, were as eager to take advantage of the offer of free food and drink as they were to seize an opportunity to mix with their more successful colleagues who were able to earn a comfortable living from their art.

'Do you think Fiona will put in an appearance?' Alan put the question to Cecil as they were clearing furniture from the large drawing room where dancing would take place.

'She wouldn't miss it for worlds,' Cecil replied. 'Besides, I believe she has managed to find some particularly obscure Russian princess to bring along with her. They will be like Siamese twins for the whole evening – and both equally boring, I have no doubt.

The party got off to a promising start. There was a wide variety of talent within the artists' community and before long background music was being provided by a talented pianist, playing Cecil's Steinway grand, and a violinist who had brought her instrument to the party with her.

An early arrival was Stanhope Forbes, who, like Cecil, had recently returned from a visit to Europe. Greeting Vicky, he congratulated her on the success of her London exhibition but hoped she would continue to help, even if only in a part-time capacity, in his long-established school of painting in the village.

It was an offer no ambitious artist could possibly turn down and Vicky promised she would carry on as before. She chatted with Forbes for some time as he described what he had seen in Europe, and told her of the plans he had for the future of his school of painting.

A great many guests had arrived and were spreading across the lawns when Cecil said, 'Oh dear, here is Fiona with her princess – but I must say she is far more attractive than I imagined she would be.'

Alan looked round to follow Cecil's glance, but the 'princess' had moved away and was now surrounded by a party of senior artists, some of whom had been in Newlyn for more than twenty-five years. He turned back to speak to Ella who, at the party with her companion Frieda, was behaving in her usual flirtatious manner.

Suddenly, from behind him, he heard Fiona's voice say,

'And now, dear, this is someone who has been absolutely dying to meet you, the Honourable Cecil Gormley. His father is Viscount Rockingham, the *twelfth* Viscount. It is a very ancient peerage.'

Alan turned his head to see Cecil solemnly shaking hands with the Russian 'princess' – and almost dropped the glass he was holding. The 'princess' saw him at the same time and let go of Cecil's hand so suddenly he was startled, wondering whether he might have somehow offended her.

'Alan! It *is* you. It is wonderful to meet with you again – and such a surprise!' The 'princess' was Anoushka Romanov!

Rushing to Alan, she flung her arms around him and he just had time to register Fiona's expression of utter disbelief before Anoushka was kissing him warmly.

'Anoushka . . . what are you doing here, in Newlyn?'

'I am here because you told me it is a place for artists – and you were right. I have met so many today, but I did not know you would be here too. It makes me so happy to see you again.'

Alan saw Vicky and Cecil exchanging bewildered glances, and taking Anoushka's hand he led her up to them, saying, 'Anoushka, I want you to meet someone who is probably the finest of the new generation of Newlyn artists. This is Vicky . . . Vicky, meet Anoushka.'

'But, of course, she is the one you told me about, when we were in Russia together.' Anoushka expressed delight at the meeting.

Vicky looked from one to the other in some astonishment. Cecil too showed considerable interest. Alan had never explained exactly what he was doing in the Baltic. After giving Anoushka a somewhat less than enthusiastic greeting, Vicky said, 'You did not tell me you had been to Russia, Alan – and certainly nothing about meeting such a beautiful young woman there.'

'You do not know?' Moving closer to Alan, Anoushka gave his arm an affectionate hug. 'Alan and Commander Buchanan saved my life – and the lives of my father, mother and three sisters. Then, when we were safely on our way to the torpedo boat, Alan went back to kill many Bolsheviks and rescue Commander Buchanan.' Turning to look up at Alan, she said indignantly, 'Did they not tell anyone what you did, and give you a medal? When we visited Commander Buchanan in hospital in Copenhagen he told us they would.'

'They certainly gave him a medal,' Vicky said, in friendlier tones than before, 'but no one, certainly not Alan, has ever said what it was for. However, now you are in Newlyn we will meet up at a quieter time and you can tell us all about it. Do you intend remaining here for long?'

'I would very much like to,' Anoushka said, adding somewhat less enthusiastically, 'I have come here from Paris to learn as much as I can about painting, but I am staying in a house with many students. They seem to think that drinking and having parties is more important than art.'

'Then we must see what can be done about that,' Vicky said firmly. 'But you were with Fiona, and she seems to have disappeared. Do you want to go off and find her?'

Looking about her to check that Fiona had really gone and was not likely to come upon them unexpectedly,

Anoushka said, 'I would rather remain with you and Alan. Fiona is being very kind to me, but she is far more interested in my family than my painting.' Turning to Cecil, she smiled at him and said, 'I believe this lovely house is yours? On the way through I saw many paintings I liked very much. Fiona said some were your own. Perhaps you could show them to me and we could all talk about them – and about the artists who painted them. I would like that . . .'

Cecil's party went on until after breakfast time on Sunday, but no one saw anything of Fiona and Rupert after Anoushka's demonstration of affection for Alan. Anoushka remained close to the trio whose party it was for much of the night. She was still at the house when the last of the guests had left, showing no signs of wanting to leave, and Cecil seemed disinclined to send her on her way. In fact, he suggested she should stay and have breakfast with them.

Anoushka agreed readily, but insisted that she help to prepare the meal. Commenting that four people in the kitchen would be too many, Cecil asked Alan and Vicky to set out the breakfast things on a table on a part of the lawn that had an uninterrupted view of the sea, while he and Anoushka prepared the meal.

As they worked, Vicky said to Alan, 'I don't suppose you saw Fiona's face when Anoushka greeted you like a long-lost lover. She was absolutely mortified.'

'I'm sure she was very surprised.' Alan grinned. 'Come to that, so was I.'

'Did you and Anoushka spend much time together in

319

Russia?' Vicky asked, trying not to allow her deep interest to show.

'I spent almost a week hidden in an attic flat with her and her mother in a Bolshevik-controlled part of the country,' Alan replied. 'Sometimes, when it was possible, we would come down into the main house and Anoushka would sketch from a window. She is a very competent artist, Vicky. You must get her to show you her work sometime. I think you might be impressed.'

'She is also a very beautiful girl,' Vicky commented.

'She has three equally beautiful sisters,' Alan replied, 'and before I met any of the family, Commander Buchanan told me that their mother was the most beautiful woman he had ever seen.'

'And she is a Romanov – Fiona was introducing her to everyone as Princess Anoushka. *Is* she a princess?'

'I don't think so. The family is certainly related to the murdered Tsar, but I have no idea how closely. You'll have to ask her.'

'It was close enough for Fiona.' Vicky chuckled. 'I could almost feel sorry for her. Do you know, that's the second time you have pulled the social ladder from beneath her when she believed she had moved up a rung or two?'

'It's certainly nothing I have tried to do,' Alan protested.

'Of course it isn't,' Vicky said, 'and if she wasn't such an awful snob it would never have happened.'

There was the sound of happy laughter from the direction of the kitchen and Alan said, 'Cecil and Anoushka seem to be getting along very well.'

'Very well indeed,' Vicky agreed. 'I am absolutely delighted. I realised as soon as they were introduced – by oor Fiona – that Cecil found her very attractive. He would be a very strange male had it been otherwise, but I think he is truly smitten with her.'

'Well, unlike yours and mine, it is a match that would not be frowned upon by either set of parents,' Alan commented.

It was something that still seriously troubled him, as Vicky was aware, but at that moment Anoushka emerged from the house, closely followed by Cecil. Both were bearing the results of their labours on silver trays and the subject of conversation shifted to food.

46

Two days after the party, Alan and Vicky returned to the studio after spending a large part of the day away. Vicky had been teaching at Stanhope Forbes's school of painting, while Alan had been researching details for his book in the Penzance library, leaving in time to meet Vicky and walk home with her.

There were a number of letters on the mat inside the studio door. Picking them up, Vicky frowned. 'This is unusual, a letter with a Newlyn postmark. Why should anyone waste money buying a stamp when it is quicker and easier to come and put the envelope through the door?'

Tearing open the envelope, Vicky read with increasing astonishment and Alan asked, 'What is it, Vicky?'

'It's a letter from Fiona – you know she owns the studio? She has given me a month's notice to leave!' Vicky found it difficult to hide her dismay.

'Given you notice? Can she do that?' There was no need for Alan to ask why. Fiona was getting revenge on Vicky for her outburst in the Fisherman's Arms, and on both of

322

them for the humiliation she felt she had suffered at their hands at Cecil's party.

'I only rent the studio, Alan. As the owner, she can do whatever she wishes.'

'I am at the heart of the problem, Vicky. Perhaps I should go and speak to her.'

'No, Alan.' Vicky shook her head vigorously. 'She would take great delight in humiliating you. This is quite a shock, but I really should have seen it coming. Don't worry about it. We will find somewhere else.'

'But you're happy here, Vicky. This wouldn't have happened had I not moved in with you.'

'I am happy here because you are with me. Without you I would be very *un*happy. But Fiona is certainly beginning to show her true colours.'

In spite of Vicky's attempts to play down the importance of Fiona's letter, he could tell she was very upset. The studio had been her home for a long time, but he knew she was right about Fiona's reaction, should he try to plead with her to allow Vicky to remain.

He was equally aware it would serve no useful purpose.

That evening Vicky and Alan had an invitation to dinner at Cecil's house, with Anoushka. In fact, the gathering was at her suggestion. She wanted to cook them a Russian meal to celebrate her enrolment at Stanhope Forbes's painting school.

Vicky had succeeded in persuading Forbes to accept Anoushka as one of his pupils, under her supervision. The arrangement almost came to grief even before it began, when she took with her the sketch book that had so impressed Alan to show to the acclaimed artist.

While Stanhope Forbes agreed that Anoushka had talent, he also said she still had much to learn. Anoushka was deeply disappointed, having already studied at art schools in Russia. However, Vicky said *she* thought her drawings were good and persuaded her that Forbes had, in fact, been highly encouraging. She pointed out that had he not thought she showed definite promise he would have refused to accept her as a pupil.

'He is very much the English gentleman,' Vicky added, 'but he is no sycophant. Had he thought you had no talent he would have found a polite but firm way of telling you so and declined to accept you as a pupil in his school. After all, he has to consider his own reputation.'

They were all sitting on the patio of Cecil's house at the time, and, after thinking over Vicky's encouraging words, Anoushka said gratefully, 'Thank you, Vicky, you are very kind. It is just . . . I was very tired when I went to the school for the first time today, and I so wanted to be at my very best. But some of the students where I am staying were very noisy until early this morning. I think it was someone's birthday. If I am to be a good student and a famous artist I must find somewhere to live that is more quiet.'

Suddenly thoughtful, Vicky said, 'You have not yet visited my studio, have you? It could possibly suit you.'

'You mean . . . stay there with you and Alan?' Anoushka asked eagerly.

Vicky smiled. 'No. The studio is owned by Fiona. I am leaving – but I am quite certain she would rent it to you.'

'You are leaving the studio? Why?' Cecil demanded. 'Everyone thinks of you and the studio as belonging together. Most people have forgotten it belongs to someone else. Why are you leaving? Does it have to do with the argument you and Fiona had?'

'Probably,' Vicky replied. 'She has given me a month's notice to get out. It came today – by post.'

'Why did you and Fiona have an argument? Was it over me?' Anoushka looked concerned.

'No,' Vicky said. 'Fiona told lies in a bid to part Alan and me. I became very angry and said many things that might have been better left unsaid.'

'I do not think I would be happy living in a studio that is owned by Fiona. I think she would want to become my friend and if I let her she would interfere in my life too much. I like to choose my own friends, people like you, Alan and Cecil. No, I would not want to live there . . . but I must find somewhere if I am to become a famous artist like you.'

Vicky felt a deep sympathy and, suddenly turning to Cecil, she said, 'What about your old studio – the one you once thought you might turn into a garage for your Hotchkiss?'

'To be perfectly honest, I was thinking of offering it to you and Alan,' Cecil said.

Vicky shook her head. 'It is a very kind thought, Cecil, but it would be too small. Even our present studio is not really large enough for the two of us. Alan needs a separate study for his work. But your old studio would be ideal for one person. For Anoushka.'

Cecil seemed suddenly ill at ease. 'I have no objection to Anoushka's taking it as a studio – or a home – but it could prove embarrassing for her. After all, I am a single man and the studio is connected to the house. People might jump to wrong conclusions.'

'There are those who will always jump to wrong

conclusions,' Vicky retorted. 'Especially where artists are concerned. But the studio has its own outside door. You could always have a lock fitted on the door that connects to the rest of the house and give the keys to Anoushka.'

Before Cecil could reply, Anoushka said, 'May I please look at the studio, Cecil?'

He nodded. 'Of course, but I have a lot of old suitcases and similar items in there at the moment.'

'I will show it to you, Anoushka, while the men check on the kitchen fire.' Vicky gave Alan instructions on how the fire should be prepared in readiness for Anoushka's cooking, before leading the suddenly excited Russian girl into the house.

Alan had been watching Cecil, and when the others had left them he said, 'You don't seem very keen to have Anoushka stay in the old studio, Cecil. Is there anything more than what people might say about the arrangement?'

'No ... well, yes.' Cecil's reply was contradictory and he seemed to be struggling to find the right words for what he wanted to say. Eventually, looking at Alan apologetically, he said, 'The truth is ... I have fallen very heavily for Anoushka – although I haven't told her, of course. I would love to have her living in the studio and to know she was so close. The trouble is ... I would be impossibly jealous if she occasionally brought men friends back – and she undoubtedly would because she is so damned attractive.'

'You say you haven't told her "of course". Why not, Cecil? What's stopping you?'

'The difference in our ages, for one thing. There must be ten years' difference between us.'

'I would put it closer to eight,' Alan said, 'and that's nothing. You have only to look at some of the most successful marriages in the village. In fact, it's probably an advantage. Any other reasons?'

'Yes. If she were living in my house I could hardly make my feelings known to her. I would feel I was taking advantage of the situation. Unless she felt the same way it would be most embarrassing for both of us – but especially for Anoushka.'

'I really don't think you need worry about that, Cecil. Anoushka is a very positive young woman and also very sensible. She would not allow any situation to arise that might embarrass either of you in any way and I believe you would both come to enjoy each other's company more and more with the passing of time.'

Cecil made no reply for some time, and then he said, 'Well, it might prove an entirely hypothetical problem. Anoushka might not like the studio.'

'Vicky, this is exactly what I want! It could be an absolutely wonderful studio. That room is large enough to be both bedroom and living-room . . .' she indicated a large room which currently held boxes and a couple of suitcases, '. . . and this is a studio that would satisfy any artist. It is light, airy – and with a magnificent view across the garden to the sea. It is perfect!'

Vicky had to agree. It would have suited *her* had Alan not become part of her life.

'Do you think Cecil will allow me to live here, Vicky? I will be so disappointed if he says no.'

'I think Cecil would find it very difficult to say no to anything you really wanted,' Vicky replied, 'and that could be at the heart of the problem.'

'I am sorry, I do not understand?' Anoushka's expression reflected her puzzlement.

'Cecil is the kindest and most considerate man I have ever met,' Vicky said. 'He is also probably the most honourable. He is concerned there might be scandal if you are both living beneath the same roof. Of course, the woman who comes to the house to clean each day would soon put the villagers to rights, but he would not like there to be any unpleasantness for you.'

'Scandal has been a constant companion for the Romanovs,' Anoushka said. 'Besides, who knows? One day those who lie about us might find they are telling the truth. I like Cecil very much and I agree with you, he is very kind. He would be a very good man to take as my first lover.'

It came out so naturally that it was a moment before Vicky realised what Anoushka had said. When she did, she said, 'I think you might find Cecil has more in mind than just being a lover, Anoushka. He would be very cross if he knew I was telling you this, but he is so shy with women that it might take a very long time for him to tell you himself and I would hate to see him hurt because of that. He absolutely adores you.'

Anoushka was thoughtful for a long time. Then she said, 'I will not do anything to hurt him, Vicky. If we are sharing the same house he might one day feel able to tell me the things you have told me. If he does, I think I will be able to make him very happy.'

47

Anoushka moved into the old studio in Cecil's house five days after first viewing it, and found it had been made a great deal more comfortable than on her first viewing. The room that would be her bedroom had been decorated, and furniture gathered from other rooms in the house. There was even a collection of Cecil's own paintings adorning the walls.

In the studio, all had been cleaned and tidied and, in addition to a number of pieces of useful and comfortable furniture, Cecil had provided an easel and other items she would need for her work.

Vicky and Alan helped with the move and it proved unexpectedly enjoyable. Anoushka's genuine delight with everything was contagious. When all was completed, Cecil produced the obligatory champagne, and as they seated themselves on the lawn outside the French windows of Anoushka's new home Cecil suddenly said, 'Oh, I almost forgot . . . Have you and Alan found a new home yet, Vicky?'

Vicky shook her head. 'I haven't really had time to look. I must, I suppose. Time is slipping by.'

'Well, before you do anything, go up and see old Colonel Trecarrow. I met up with him this morning, in the village, and he asked after you. When I told him you were having to move from your studio and were looking for somewhere in the area, he said you were to go and speak to him. He believes he might have just the place for you.'

'Is that the old war-horse I met at Ella and Frieda's party?' Alan asked. 'Where is the place he might rent out to Vicky?'

'Who knows?' Cecil replied. 'It could be anywhere in Cornwall – or beyond. I sometimes think the old colonel must have more houses and land than the Duchy of Cornwall. He owns at least a dozen in Newlyn, to my knowledge.'

Anoushka had been following the conversation closely. Now she said, 'In all the excitement of moving I forgot to tell you something, too. When I was taken to your party by Fiona I mentioned that I was not happy in the place where I was living. Yesterday, as I returned from the painting school, I met her. She pretended to be surprised that we should meet, but I believe she had been waiting for me. She said if I was still looking for somewhere to live she could offer me a studio which would be available at the end of this month. I think she was talking of your studio, Vicky.'

'I am quite sure she was,' Vicky said. 'I wonder if that was partly the reason she gave me notice to quit? It would have suited her very well to have me out of the studio and you there as a tenant.'

'What did you say to her, Anoushka?' Cecil asked the question.

'I told her you had invited me to move into your house.' Anoushka spoke in all innocence, but her reply caused Cecil to choke on his drink.

'What did she say to that?' asked an amused Vicky.

'Had she been drinking I think she too would have choked, just like Cecil.'

When the laughter subsided, Cecil said, 'Anoushka, you realise you have probably ruined your reputation – and greatly enhanced my own?'

'I do not mind, if you do not mind,' Anoushka said, 'but I think it is sad that Fiona can find pleasure only in what others are doing, and not in the things she does herself.'

After a discussion, it was decided Vicky should call on Colonel Trecarrow by herself, as he had a particular penchant for attractive young women artists. Accordingly, she called on him the following day.

Colonel Trecarrow was a man in his late seventies, with a bristling, waxed moustache and a military bearing that lacked only the waistline of his younger years. He lived with a small army of servants for company in a large and impressive old country house, a short distance inland from Newlyn.

Vicky was shown into the large hall, and while the servant who had let her in went to find the Colonel, she looked at the pictures on the walls. They provided a record of many of the artists who had lived or worked in Newlyn.

'Vicky, my dear, I am delighted to see you – and I really

must have more of your own paintings adorning my walls. But to what do I owe the honour of your presence here?' Colonel Trecarrow greeted her as he descended the stairs somewhat stiffly.

'Good morning, Colonel,' Vicky replied. 'Cecil said you and he had discussed my need to find somewhere else to live and you said you might be able to help.'

'Did I? Yes . . . yes, of course I did. Come into my study and we will talk about it.'

The Colonel led the way to a high-ceilinged, book-lined room in which there was a strong aroma of stale cigar smoke. Pointing to one of the comfortably sagging leather armchairs, he said, 'Sit yourself down, my dear. It's a little early in the day for a whisky, so you will have to make do with a sherry. Now, what's this I hear about you being thrown out of your studio? Been making a bit of a nuisance of yourself, have you?'

'I have certainly fallen out with Fiona Graham, who owns the studio, but I was sorely provoked,' Vicky replied.

'I am quite sure you must have been, my dear. I have never heard you utter a cross word to anyone in all the years I have known you, while Fiona has tried the patience of a great many people – myself included.'

Handing Vicky a large glass of sherry, he took a second glass to another armchair across the room from hers. 'Now, what sort of place are you looking for, eh? Somewhere to paint, of course, but do you want it large enough to entertain friends, or somewhere to shut yourself away from 'em?'

'Cecil said you had somewhere in mind,' Vicky prompted him.

'That's right, and so I had, but I am not certain it isn't just a little too remote for a young girl living on her own.'

Realising that Colonel Trecarrow knew nothing of her relationship with Alan, her spirits sank. The old colonel was very tolerant and encouraging towards those in the artists' colony, but she was uncertain whether such tolerence extended to his tenants. However, it would be impossible to keep Alan secret from him, even had she wanted to.

'I would not be alone, Colonel. Alan Carter would be with me. He is a very promising writer and poet. You met him once, at a party given by Ella and Frieda.'

'Did I? I can't say I remember. A poet, you say?' Colonel Trecarrow's manner had undergone a subtle change, his cordial manner suddenly less in evidence. 'Was he one of those conscientious objectors, or whatever they called themselves, during the war?'

'No, Colonel – far from it. He was a Navy man who won a DSM for rescuing Tom Penhaligon's trawler, just off the coast here – and he won a Conspicuous Gallantry Medal in the Baltic earlier this year.'

'Ah yes! I remember him now. A very pleasant young man. Modest, too. We spoke of my experiences in the Zulu Wars. He was very interested.' Fixing Vicky with an only mildly disapproving look, he said, 'Do you plan to marry him?'

'That is very much in the future. We need to wait until his divorce comes through. His wife let him down very badly while he was away in the Navy.' Vicky did not go into details. Colonel Trecarrow was a notorious gossip, and Alan would not want Newlyn's artist colony discussing his private life.

'There are some women who don't deserve to have a husband who serves his country with distinction,' snorted the indignant colonel. 'Did I ever tell you that I too had an understanding with a girl when I went off to Africa? She married a parson instead. True, I was away for more than four years, but to choose a parson when she could have had a soldier . . . !'

'You were talking of a house you might be able to rent to me, Colonel,' Vicky reminded him gently. She knew that once he started talking of his life in the army he would forget all else.

'Ah yes! Stream Cottage. It's in the Lamorna valley, close to the cove. Not too big. Two or three bedrooms and a large outside studio with magnificent views. I believe the light is particularly good there, too. I let it to a Canadian painter a couple of years ago. Never made anything of himself, though. Had the talent, but not the will to work. Seems he left about three months ago, but forgot to tell me. Forgot the rent too for a few months before he went. How does it sound to you?'

Vicky did not like to tell him she was disappointed. She had been hoping the cottage would be in Newlyn, where she felt settled. 'It sounds idyllic – but it is a little way from Newlyn, and I am teaching in Stanhope Forbes's school.'

'That should be no problem, my dear. Buy yourself a bicycle. I am told they are becoming extremely popular. Can't ever see myself riding one, of course. Much as I can do to climb on a horse these days, but the world and its new-fangled gadgets are for the young, not for old fogeys like me. Tell you what, I'll give you the keys. Go up there and have a look at it. Take this sailor of yours with you. Let him look at it with a poet's eye. If you like it come back and see me and we'll discuss rent. No doubt an occasional painting would suit both of us.'

48

'It *is* a little way from Newlyn, Alan, and perhaps difficult to reach, but Newlyn is not the centre of the universe! As Colonel Trecarrow says, with a bicycle we could be in Newlyn, or even Penzance, in no time at all.'

Vicky was trying to persuade Alan that a move to Lamorna Cove was not out of the question. He had expressed doubts about moving away from Newlyn, where she was established. She secretly held similar doubts, but was trying to keep an open mind on the subject.

'At least let us go and see it. After all, we have to move from the studio by the end of the month and two weeks have gone by already.'

'All right.' Alan was still not convinced, but Vicky was right: time was not on their side. 'I suppose there's no time like the present. Let's go now and get it over with.'

They walked, mostly hand-in-hand, westward along the edge of the coastal cliff, stopping frequently to admire the view, or to watch a sailing ship or steamer carving its own path through the choppy waters of the English Channel. In due course they arrived at their destination and were looking down into the depths of the Lamorna valley, where the Lamorna stream bustled its way to the sea.

'It's certainly a very beautiful place,' Alan conceded, 'but it's still a fair distance from Newlyn and your work with Stanhope Forbes.'

'True,' Vicky agreed, 'but let's find Stream Cottage and see what that's like before we make up our minds about anything. It would certainly be cheap living for us, with Colonel Trecarrow wanting nothing more than an occasional painting to keep him happy.'

Following a zig-zag path that led to the valley, they turned towards the sea before climbing a steep slope, heading towards the source of a smaller stream that tumbled towards Lamorna. Here, half hidden by a small copse of trees and bushes, was Stream Cottage.

The land levelled out in front of the cottage. While not isolated, it was secluded, and it had breathtaking views to the cove and the sea beyond. Neither Vicky nor Alan said a word as they walked along the path to the cottage door, but when they spoke about it later they discovered that each had been reluctant to say how taken they were with the place, for fear that the interior would not come up to their expectations.

Opening the door with one of the keys that had been given to her by Colonel Trecarrow, Vicky entered the cottage first. The previous occupant might have left without giving the owner either notice or the rent he owed, but he had been a very neat tenant. The cottage was fully furnished in a simple but comfortable manner and was both clean and tidy.

Vicky and Alan went from kitchen to dining room and lounge, then upstairs to the three bedrooms. From the window of the main bedroom there was a stunning view of the cove and the sea beyond. They ended their inspection having commented only on things of minor importance, such as the neat kitchen range, the attractive oil lamps and the colour of the curtains.

Then Alan said, 'Let's have a look at the studio. It's probably the most important place of all.'

The studio was detached and to one side of the cottage, in what appeared to have once been a combined stable and barn. It had been converted many years before, glass taking the place of tiles over a third of the roof and two windows being enlarged to make French windows. There were slate shelves and built-in niches in the walls for lamps, and the whole had a smooth grey slate floor. There was even an expensive artist's easel and stool taking pride of place in the centre of the studio.

Their inspection at an end, Alan said hesitantly, 'Well . . . what do you think of it?'

Vicky countered with her own question. 'No, what do *you* think of it?'

'I think . . . I think it's rather a special place, Vicky.' It was all Alan would trust himself to say.

'*Rather* special? Alan, it is absolutely *wonderful*! It is a dream home!'

'I wouldn't argue with that,' he said. 'In fact . . . I think we could be very, very happy here, Vicky.'

'Oh, Alan, I am *so* relieved. I love Stream Cottage so

much already. I love you . . . and I even love Colonel Trecarrow too for offering us all this . . . and for virtually nothing! I will never ever say anything against him again.'

They embraced happily before Vicky suddenly drew back. 'There's just one thing . . . we will need bicycles, and I have never learned to ride one.'

'Neither have I,' Alan admitted, 'but I'm sure we'll soon get the hang of them. We'll just need to stay away from cliff-edge paths until we've learned, that's all.'

Alan and Vicky moved into Stream Cottage on a Sunday, just over a week later, Cecil transporting their belongings and paintings in the Hotchkiss. He needed to make a number of journeys and Anoushka helped in the move, remaining in the cottage with Vicky while the two men went back and forth to Newlyn.

Anoushka had fallen in love with the cottage and its surroundings immediately and had brought her sketch pad with her in the hope that there might be an opportunity to make a couple of sketches while she was there.

'You will be able to produce some wonderful paintings here,' she said to Vicky as they wielded duster and broom in the downstairs rooms. 'I must come and visit you often. I will learn much from you.'

As Anoushka was speaking, Vicky glanced out of a window. A man of about forty years of age with a neatly trimmed beard and wearing a tweed suit with knickerbocker trousers and an old, somewhat battered tweed hat was walking along the path towards the cottage. He was accompanied by two attractive girls, one in her teens, the other aged about ten.

'We have our first visitor,' Vicky cried, 'and it is someone who could teach us both a great deal about painting.'

Hurrying to the door, she greeted the visitor warmly. As Anoushka appeared in the doorway behind her, she said, 'John, this is a friend, Anoushka. Anoushka, meet John. You will have heard of him as Lamorna Birch, one of our greatest painters – and these are his daughters, Mornie and Joan, the most painted girls in the whole of Cornwall.'

Anoushka was looking at the man in awe. When she finally found her voice, she said, 'You are *the* Lamorna Birch? The artist whose paintings I have so much admired in the Royal Academy, in London?'

He smiled at her. 'What a delightful accent – and the only other Lamorna Birch I know is Mornie. Can I presume that you too are an artist?'

'A student,' Anoushka replied. 'I have studied in Russia and Paris and now Vicky is helping to teach me at the Stanhope Forbes school, in Newlyn.'

Assuming an enigmatic expression, Lamorna Birch said to Vicky, 'I heard you were helping old Stanny. Shame on you, Vicky. I would have hoped you might have offered *me* your services.'

'I would be delighted to help out with any of your pupils,' Vicky replied eagerly. 'I work with Stanhope for only two days a week. I would even bring Anoushka with me as a pupil. I think she would benefit greatly from your teaching. Anoushka . . . run inside the cottage and fetch your sketch pad.'

Anoushka had turned away when Lamorna Birch called after her, 'Just a minute, young lady. Mornie has something

340

ou can take with you and put in the kitchen.' To Vicky, he said, 'We heard from the Colonel that you'd be moving in today. Mouse thought it would be neighbourly to cook a casserole for you. It only needs heating up.'

Mouse was Lamorna's pet name for his wife, Houghton. A talented artist herself, Houghton had been taught by her husband and they were an exceptionally close couple.

When Anoushka entered the cottage clutching the casserole, Lamorna said, 'She's a very pretty girl, but does she have any artistic talent?'

Vicky nodded vigorously. 'She is very good indeed. She is benefiting from her tuition at Newlyn, but I feel she needs a more stimulating environment in which to open out and realise her full potential. Perhaps more encouragement and less criticism – but here she comes with her sketch pad. Have a look through it and tell her what you think.'

Anoushka handed the pad to Lamorna somewhat apprehensively. She became increasingly nervous as the distinguished artist turned the pages slowly, occasionally lingering over a particular sketch.

He said nothing until he came to the last few drawings. 'These later works . . . have they been done since you joined Stanny's . . . Stanhope Forbes's school?'

Anoushka nodded. 'Yes.'

'They are good . . . very good. Stanny has sharpened your attention to detail. Now I think you need to get out and about and capture the mood of your subject, whether it be a tree, a rock, or a landscape. Watch how it changes with light and weather. Learn to love your subject, whatever it is.' Handing back the sketch pad, he went on, 'I would like you to become one of my pupils, Anoushka You are a fine artist now. One day you will be a *great* artist. I would like to feel I had helped in some small way.'

Anoushka was delighted with such a positive assessment of her talent from an artist of the stature of the visitor to Stream Cottage. When Cecil came into view, carefully nursing the Hotchkiss along the rough track, she hurried to meet him and tell him what Lamorna Birch had said, Mornie and Joan running happily beside her.

'What an utterly charming young girl,' Lamorna said, when she was out of earshot. 'Where did you find her?'

Vicky described briefly the party where Fiona had introduced her 'princess', and the reunion between Anoushka and Alan.

'Ah yes, your sailor-boy,' Lamorna said. 'I read one of his poems in a magazine when I was last in London. It was extremely good. He seems to be causing something of a stir in London literary circles – as you are in the art world. It's splendid that we are attracting such talent to Lamorna. You and he must pop up to Flagstaff Cottage one evening this week and have dinner with Mouse and me. No need to let us know in advance, just drop in when it's convenient. Now, let's go and meet Alan and Cecil. It looks as though they have brought some of your paintings. I am interested to see what you've been up to since we last met.'

49

Alan and Vicky settled into Stream Cottage quickly and easily, and, although it was now quite late in the year, Alan found himself gardening for the first time in his life. As he explained to Vicky, the houses in which he had lived in London had possessed only yards at the back of them. They were so small and cut off from the sun by surrounding houses that even the most ardent gardener would have had difficulty in persuading anything to flourish there. The closest he had come to gardening before coming to Lamorna was watering his aunt's aspidistra, which grew in a pot on a table in the passageway, reviled by all who needed to sidle past its drooping leaves.

More difficult than settling into their new surroundings was mastering the transport which would enable them to venture out from the valley whenever it became necessary. Neither had ever ridden a bicycle before and they soon discovered that maintaining one's balance on two narrow, in-line wheels was not a skill that came naturally.

Vicky was the first to try out one of the new machines

which they had bought in Penzance and carried to Lamorna in the ever-helpful Cecil's Hotchkiss. After the saddle had been adjusted to suit her height and with Alan walking beside machine and rider, supporting both, she wobbled her way along the path from the cottage.

Unfortunately, the path went downhill and it was not long before Alan found it difficult to maintain the increasing speed. He was eventually forced to release his hold on the bicycle – and on Vicky.

It was a moment or two before she realised she was on her own, and then, suddenly losing confidence, she immediately tried to slow the machine. She partially succeeded, but in so doing found herself pulling the handlebars first one way and then the other. The bicycle wobbled even more violently than before as Alan chased after it, calling out impossible instructions which Vicky could not have obeyed, even had they been audible above her screams in which mild terror rapidly gave way to a growing hilarity.

Eventually, the inevitable happened. Vicky twisted the handlebars too violently and the rear wheel of the machine left the ground, causing bicycle and rider to fall into the ferns at the side of the pathway.

'Are you all right?' Concerned that she might be hurt, Alan reached Vicky and lifted her to her feet. He was relieved to realise she was laughing.

'That was really quite fun,' she said unexpectedly. 'But watching you is going to be even more so. Come along. We'll go back to the cottage and you can try *your* bicycle.'

Alan protested in vain that they should leave it for another day. Vicky insisted that he try now. He was initially no more successful than Vicky had been and it helped neither his pride nor his dignity when Mornie Birch, brought to the scene by Vicky's shrieks and laughter, mounted one of the bicycles and rode it confidently back to Stream Cottage ahead of them.

However, within a couple of days the eccentricities of bicycle-riding had been mastered and Vicky made her first ride to Newlyn, to teach at Stanhope Forbes's painting school. Here, an eager Anoushka wanted to know when she might come to Lamorna to attend a class with the man who had taken his name from the valley.

Vicky had to confess that she did not know when would be the best time – or even the most suitable day. Unlike Forbes, Lamorna ran painting classes with an informality that the Newlyn painter would have found infuriating.

Aware of Anoushka's deep disappointment, Vicky said, 'I suggest you come there whenever you have a free day. You'll be welcomed whenever it is and allowed to join his class. Let us say tomorrow. Come to Stream Cottage and we'll go along to Flagstaff together.'

Anoushka arrived at Stream Cottage at 9 a.m. the next day, driven to Lamorna by Cecil. After sharing the couple's breakfast tea, Anoushka accompanied Vicky to Flagstaff Cottage, arriving just as Lamorna was about to take half a dozen pupils to the cove for a painting session in one of his favourite spots. He insisted they should both join him.

Meanwhile, in Stream Cottage, Cecil was talking to Alan. They had been speaking about nothing in particular when Cecil suddenly blurted out, 'What is Anoushka's father like? I mean . . . what sort of man is he?'

'I can't say I got to know him terribly well,' Alan admitted. 'We were together for a very short time. No more than a matter of hours, really. He is certainly a family man. He succeeded in keeping his wife and daughters safe and bringing them out of Russia against all the odds. I came to know Anoushka's mother better. She, Anoushka and I were closeted together in the attic of a remote country house for some days. She is a woman very like Anoushka. Beautiful and charming – but quite positive. I would say she is the one who is used to making all the major decisions for the family. Why do you ask?'

Cecil hesitated uncertainly for a few moments before saying, 'I have thought for some time of taking Anoushka to Paris to see her family. She said she would like to visit them and let them know she is settled and happy in Newlyn. I have offered to accompany her.'

Observing Alan's quizzical expression, Cecil added hurriedly, 'I am always happy to have an excuse to visit Paris. It is my favourite city. Anoushka has suggested I stay at her parents' home. I thought I would ask your opinion of them.'

'I have no doubt at all that they'll make you feel very welcome,' Alan said, 'just as you have helped Anoushka to settle into Newlyn. Not only that, you'll be surrounded by beautiful women. As well as her mother, Anoushka has three sisters, each quite as lovely as she is.'

'I find that difficult to believe,' Cecil said. 'Anoushka is the most beautiful woman I have ever met.'

Cecil was not a man who would normally share such feelings with others and Alan realised how much

346

Anoushka must mean to him. 'Have you told her yet how you feel about her?' he asked.

'Of course not!' Cecil was shocked. 'It would place her in an impossible situation. I am her landlord. To all intents and purposes she is living beneath my roof. She would compromise herself whatever she replied. I can't do that to her.'

'That's very noble of you, Cecil,' Alan replied seriously, 'but I think you should try to let her know your feelings. If you don't, she could feel you are completely indifferent to her and, as you say, she is a very beautiful woman. Others will be just as aware of that as you and I.'

Cecil's concern was apparent as he said unhappily, 'Yes, I can quite see that, but it does put me in a very difficult situation – and I desperately want to do the right thing.'

On the way to Lamorna Cove, Vicky said, 'It was very kind of Cecil to drive you here this early in the day, Anoushka.'

'He is very kind, but I do not think it is only for me. Cecil is kind to everyone he knows.'

Something in Anoushka's voice made Vicky ask, 'Are you getting along all right with him, Anoushka?'

'*Very* well,' the other girl replied emphatically. 'Cecil is teaching me some very good things about painting too, but . . .'

Vicky prompted her. 'But . . . ?'

'I do not think he sees me as a woman,' Anoushka blurted out.

'What on earth makes you say that?' Vicky demanded.

'I am with him often, and we are alone in the house

347

most of the time, but sometimes I think he is not happy to have me there. That perhaps he wishes I was somewhere else.'

Vicky came to a sudden halt and, surprised, Anoushka followed suit.

'You could not be further from the truth, Anoushka. I know Cecil and he talks to me as he would to a sister. He is absolutely *besotted* with you. I have never known him to be like this with any other girl. Unfortunately, he is painfully shy with women and lives by a code of honour that went out with the Victorian age. I think it might be something to do with the school he attended, and his own interpretation of right and wrong. If he believed that he might be considered to be taking advantage of you, he would back off.' She grimaced. 'I know that can be very frustrating for a woman, but that is the way he has been brought up to think. That is the way he is – but please don't make the mistake of thinking he doesn't care about you. If it is possible, he cares too much.'

Anoushka was very thoughtful as they continued on their way. Eventually, she said, 'Thank you for what you have told me, Vicky. If you are right about the way Cecil thinks of me it will make me very happy – and I think I can make Cecil happy too.'

With this, she gave Vicky a smile that would have sent Cecil's senses reeling.

The first few weeks in Stream Cottage passed swiftly for Alan and Vicky. Cecil and Anoushka were both frequent visitors and it was evident they were increasingly happy in each other's company.

One evening, when Alan and Vicky had cycled to Newlyn to meet Cecil and Anoushka for a meal, Cecil said, 'I heard today that Fiona has let your old studio, Vicky.'

'Oh? Is it to anyone I know?' Vicky was thinking of the many artists who had visited her there and who had expressed an interest in its favourable position in the village.

'Yes, but it's not to an artist. It has been taken by Desmond Stileman, your political friend. It seems the date of the by-election is due to be announced at any time. Desmond feels it will help his cause if he is able to give a local address for his nomination.'

Vicky was unreasonably indignant. 'Of all the people I know, he is the one I would least want to be living in the studio. The occupant should be an artist. Its uniqueness is wasted on him.'

'Nevertheless, that is who has taken it. What is more, Desmond will be living there when he holds a meeting to speak to his future constituents on the fifteenth of next month in the Masonic Hall, in Penzance.'

'Do you think there is any likelihood that he will win the seat, Cecil?' Vicky asked.

'Yes, I do,' Cecil replied seriously. 'No one seems to have met his opponent and Desmond is relying very heavily upon his war service.'

Vicky was indignant. 'I doubt if he ever flew in combat. Desmond Stileman is a fraud.'

'He was a Royal Flying Corps pilot,' Cecil pointed out, 'and they had an appalling casualty rate. They are all looked upon as heroes.'

'He flew an aeroplane,' Vicky retorted. 'No more than

that. After all, a great many men carried rifles during the war, but not all of them used them against the enemy.'

Vicky would have been even more unhappy had she known of the conversation that took place between Desmond and Fiona when she was showing him over the studio, prior to Desmond's agreeing to rent it from her.

He had been in the studio before, but not as a prospective tenant. He would not be living here permanently, of course, but it would be a useful place to stay during his election campaign, and also on the occasions when he needed to visit his constituency once his anticipated election to the House of Commons had been achieved.

'Yes, Fiona, this is a splendid little flat. I will certainly rent it from you,' Desmond said, as he closed the French windows after standing out on the small balcony to take in the view of Mount's Bay. 'The only drawback from my point of view is that I will never be able to enjoy the place without expecting to look up and see Vicky at work on my portrait.'

'You were very fond of her, Desmond, I know. I realised it at the time and did my very best to bring you together.'

'I certainly found her more attractive than most other young women I have met,' Desmond agreed.

'She was attracted to you too,' Fiona lied. 'It is most unfortunate that she allowed herself to be influenced by that . . . ex-sailor. He has not only spoiled Vicky's chance of meeting a man of her own class, but succeeded in putting an end to my friendship with her. I sometimes feel I failed in my friendship by not writing to her family and informing them of Vicky's unsuitable association with him. Unfortunately, I have never met her parents. While I am convinced they would not approve of this Alan, I do not know how they would react to a letter from a complete stranger telling them about him, however well intentioned it might be.'

'They would most probably be very grateful to you,' Desmond said sympathetically, 'but I have a better idea. Vicky's father has recently retired as the Conservative agent for his constituency and a knighthood is in the offing for him. He will be anxious to keep his name to the fore. Why don't I write to him, suggesting he comes to Cornwall to advise me on my campaign, at the same time taking the opportunity to bring his wife with him to visit Vicky? Between them they should be able to sort out the situation. I have met him only briefly, but he impressed me as quite a positive man.'

'What a splendid idea!' Fiona said gleefully. 'It would be doing both Vicky and her parents a great favour. One day, I am convinced, Vicky will be extremely grateful to you.'

50

Towards the end of October 1919, when the weather at Lamorna was undergoing a noticeable change and grey, white-capped waves agitating the sea beyond the cove made Alan thankful he was no longer a sailor, a letter arrived at Stream Cottage that cast a shadow over the happiness of its occupants.

It was from the solicitor handling Alan's divorce from Dora. He said he had been awaiting her return from America in order to serve certain papers on her. She was now back in London, but had refused to come to his office and sign the documents that would allow the divorce to pass through the courts uncontested.

The solicitor felt it was a ploy to obtain more money from Alan, but he warned that proceedings would undoubtedly be held up as a consequence. Alan was despondent, but after her initial dismay Vicky was philosophical about the apparent setback.

'It doesn't really matter, Alan. It is not going to alter our life together and it will not affect the ultimate outcome of the divorce. Whatever she does or doesn't do, she is still the guilty party. To be perfectly honest, I feel sorry for her. You and I have so much and she has so little, even though it is entirely her own fault.'

'That's a very generous way of looking at it,' Alan said, 'and, yes, you and I do have so much that she will never have. I wonder what went wrong for her in America? To be perfectly honest, I'm surprised she went there. I thought the money I gave her would be squandered here.'

'Perhaps she thought more of the father of her baby than any of us realised,' Vicky replied. 'If so, that's even more reason to be sorry for her.'

'What do you think I should do?' Alan asked, still disturbed by the solicitor's letter, in spite of Vicky's philosophical acceptance of the situation.

'You'll acknowledge the solicitor's letter, then we'll continue with life in Stream Cottage. You writing your book and me painting – and we'll both be deliriously happy.'

Vicky and Alan were not the only ones having a bad week. Cecil was too – although his problem would eventually result in considerable gain for Alan.

It was early evening on the day the solicitor's letter arrived at Stream Cottage. Alan was writing in the house, while Vicky was framing pictures in the studio workshop, when they both heard the sound of a motor car coming along the track towards the cottage. Going to the window of his study, Alan saw it was the Hotchkiss, with Cecil and Anoushka inside. By the time he had put aside his writing and reached the front door of the cottage, Vicky was already outside greeting their visitors.

'This is an unexpected surprise,' Alan said to Cecil. 'I thought you were in London.'

Cecil had gone to London a few days earlier, leaving Anoushka to cycle to the valley for her lessons with Lamorna.

'I *was* in London,' Cecil replied, 'and just as well, too. It seems the press has just learned about the part the Royal Navy played in rescuing Anoushka and the Romanov family from Russia. It was reported in one of the London evening newspapers the day before yesterday, together with a scurrilous report that Anoushka is now living with the son of a peer of the realm in a Cornish village. Living *with* me! I was so furious I telephoned my solicitor yesterday morning to institute an action for libel on behalf of Anoushka and myself unless the newspaper prints a full and unequivocal apology immediately.'

'Cecil is very upset,' Anoushka said nonchalantly. 'I think it is simply . . . amusing.' Glancing at Cecil, she added mischievously, 'Of course, if my father hears of it he will demand that Cecil marries me. I think that is what is upsetting Cecil most of all.'

'That is *not* what is upsetting me, Anoushka.'

Feigning delight, Anoushka cried, 'So you *do* want to marry me!'

'No! I mean, yes . . . you *know* what I mean, and it really is not a joke. The newspaper has attacked your honour. It must not be allowed to go unchallenged.'

'I appreciate your concern for me, Cecil, I really do, but it is a very unimportant matter. The report was in a London newspaper, where I am not known, and I doubt if anyone here will ever hear about it.'

'That is not the point . . .' Cecil was reluctant to allow the matter to drop, but Anoushka interrupted him.

'I think you have something of far more importance to tell Alan.'

'Oh, yes . . . of course. Thank you.' Turning to Alan, Cecil said, 'The night the report was in the newspaper I was taken to a literary event by Julian Gimblett and there we met a naval acquaintance of yours – Lieutenant Donald Ferris, who was there with his father. We discussed the newspaper report about the Baltic and Donald revealed that he was commanding the boat that carried Anoushka and her family to safety. Julian was terribly excited and suggested that Donald should write a book about the rescue. Donald replied that he could not because he is a serving naval officer, with an assured future ahead of him. He then suggested that *you* could write a far more exciting account of what happened because he only picked the Romanovs up at the end of the rescue, while you were ashore in Russia and in constant danger from the Bolsheviks.'

'That is true,' Anoushka said. 'Alan was very brave. He and Commander Buchanan.' Smiling at Alan, she said to Cecil, 'Alan and I were sharing an attic for many days. Your London newspaper would have said *we* were living together, just as I am supposed to be living with you.'

Clearing his throat quickly in an expression of embarrassment, Cecil said, 'Yes . . . well . . . as I said, Julian was very excited at the prospect of a book about the whole operation. He said I was to tell you to put torpedo boats on hold and write about the rescue of Anoushka and her family instead. He said he will forward a contract in the next day or two – but you are to start work on the book right away.' Smiling for the first time since he had arrived, he went on, 'It will be a good contract, Alan. I even managed to persuade Julian to offer you an advance four times as high as the one he gave you for your present book.'

'That is *wonderful* news, Cecil.' Vicky could not contain her delight, kissing first Cecil and then, with more passion, Alan. 'I suggest that we forget all about rumours started by London newspapers and go to the Wink to celebrate the *good* news.'

The Wink was Lamorna's public house, popular with the artists of the valley. When Cecil agreed, Anoushka slipped her arm through his and squeezed it affectionately, saying, 'There, I told you we must come to see Alan and Vicky because they would be able to cheer you up.'

The celebrations at the Wink certainly helped Cecil to forget the story printed in the London newspaper. In fact, after telling everyone in the pub that they were celebrating Alan's good fortune, he ordered the landlord to bring out his entire stock of champagne – which, fortunately, amounted to only fourteen bottles – and insisted that everyone in the Wink drink a toast to Alan's success.

He succeeded in becoming more intoxicated than anyone had ever seen him, forgetting his shyness to such an extent that he protested everlasting love for Anoushka more than once on the way back to Stream Cottage, assuring her that if her reputation was sullied in any way he would 'do the gentlemanly thing' and marry her.

Cecil was so drunk that there was no question of allowing him to drive back to Newlyn, and Alan put him to bed in one of the spare rooms. While he was doing this, Anoushka, who had drunk far less, said mischievously, 'Perhaps I should go to bed in the same room and when Cecil wakes tell him it is all right because he has promised to marry me. Do you think that would frighten him?'

'Yes,' Vicky replied honestly, adding, 'but it would delight him. He would probably rush off and arrange a wedding before you had time to change your mind.'

'Then why does he not behave in a romantic way towards me when he is sober? He has not even kissed me . . . well, not a *proper* kiss.'

'Do you want him to, Anoushka?'

Suddenly very serious, Anoushka said, 'Yes . . . yes, I do. I want him to very much, but in Russia it is not for the woman to make the first move, and I think it is the same here.'

'Yes, it is,' Vicky agreed. 'Although that isn't the way it was for me with Alan, but Cecil is terribly old-fashioned when it comes to women. He would expect to have to make the first move, but would never do anything that might be construed as taking advantage of you – he has said so, on more than one occasion. But don't despair, Anoushka. True love will win in the end, I am convinced of it – even though it might need a little help from your friends.'

51

There was a great stir in the Lamorna post office when a telegram was received, addressed to Alan at Stream Cottage. The postmaster's son arrived at the cottage breathing heavily from the exertion of riding at speed on his bicycle in order to waste no time in delivering the urgent missive.

When Alan took delivery of the telegram, the messenger waited expectantly. Alan was momentarily puzzled. Then, when enlightenment dawned, he fished in a pocket and produced a threepenny piece which he gave to the young man. However, although he touched his cap in a gesture of acknowledgment, the delivery boy showed no sign of leaving.

'Is there something else?' Alan asked, expecting the telegram to have something to do with the book he had agreed to write for Julian Gimblett.

'Post Office regulations, Mr Carter. I have to wait, just in case you want to send an immediate reply. The Post Office prides itself on getting an answer back to the sender as quick as possible, even when it's from somewhere as far away as Gibraltar.'

'Gibraltar . . . ?' Alan tore open the envelope and read the contents with dismay. It read, *Father suffered serious heart attack. Asking for you.* It was signed, simply, *Maria*.

'Is there any reply?' the messenger asked.

'I don't know. Wait here a few minutes.' Clutching the telegram, Alan hurried off to the studio where Vicky was working. Thrusting the telegram at her, he said, 'This has just come, Vicky. What do I do?'

Quickly reading the brief message, Vicky said, 'You don't need me to tell you, Alan. You must go to Gibraltar – and as quickly as you can. We'll go to Cecil and see what he can help to arrange.' Through the open door she saw the postmaster's son waiting patiently outside the cottage. 'Is he waiting for a reply?'

'Yes.'

'Then write a telegram to be sent to Gibraltar, saying you will be there on the first available ship. I'll clean my brushes and we'll go and see Cecil.'

Twenty-four hours later Alan reached Southampton and boarded a passenger liner that sailed on the afternoon tide the following day. On Sunday, at dawn, it berthed at Gibraltar.

Taking a taxi across the border, Alan discovered that the mention of Maria's name was sufficient to reduce the fare considerably and it was not long before he was knocking on the door of her house.

She opened the door to him, and when she saw who it was she burst into tears. Recovering, she told him there

359

had been no improvement in his father's condition, adding, 'The doctors say a recovery is unlikely. It is only a matter of time before his heart gives up.'

'Might seeing me prove too much of an excitement for him?' Alan asked anxiously.

Maria shook her head. 'No. He knows you are coming. He also knows he is dying. His greatest concern has been that he might not live until you arrived. Now you are here – but you will have had nothing to eat or drink . . .'

'That can wait, Maria. Let's go and see him right away.'

The hospital where John Carter was being cared for was within walking distance of Maria's home, and on the way, Maria asked questions about Dora and what had happened when Alan went home to her.

Maria was very much a woman of the world, but she was scathing about Dora's behaviour. Angry that she had stolen the money she sent to pay for Alan and Dora to come to the wedding, she was even more indignant about the way Alan had been treated by his wife.

'There are those who point to my bar-girls as not behaving as women should,' she said. 'Yet there is not one of them – not a single one – who would treat a good man in such a way. It is good that you have left her and London behind and are now living in Cornwall. I know where that is because your father has showed it to me on a map, but what do you do there to earn a living?'

Alan told her about his poetry and the books he was writing, and at first Maria seemed concerned. 'Can you earn a living in such a way?'

Her doubts vanished when Alan told her the amount of the advance he was to receive for his book on the Baltic.

'.hat is very impressive,' she said. 'Your father will be so proud of you . . . I am proud of you.' Suddenly showing unexpected perception, she added, 'But life is not all about money. Have you found anyone else to share your life?'

'Yes . . .'

Alan told Maria about Vicky, of how they had first met, and of Vicky's talent as a painter. When he stopped talking, Maria said, 'This Vicky sounds much more the sort of girl a mother would wish her son to have. She makes you happy?'

'Yes, very.'

'That is good. You must bring her to Algeciras. There is much to paint here and she would be made to feel very welcome – but here we are at the hospital.'

John Carter was in a clean and bright private room off a corridor that led to one of the wards. When Maria and Alan entered the room he was lying back on a sloping mound of pillows. Turning his head wearily towards the door he saw Alan, and the weariness vanished.

'Alan! Maria told me you were coming, but I never expected to see you so soon.' Holding out his arms, he embraced Alan, then treated Maria in the same way. 'When did you arrive?'

He put the question to Alan, but it was Maria who replied. 'He came to the house no more than half an hour ago and would not wait for breakfast, or even for a drink. He insisted we should come straight to the hospital.'

'You should have let Maria cook something for you,' John Carter said. 'She's a superb cook, son . . . but it's good to see you. Although you needn't have felt you had to come all this way to see me. You have your own life to lead.'

'And he is making a very good job of it,' Maria said, telling him about Alan's writing career.

When she ended, John Carter looked at his son with great pride. 'Well! Had anyone told me I would one day have a son who earned a living writing books I would have thought they had taken leave of their senses. You've done well, son. I'm proud of you.'

'Thank you,' Alan said, more moved than he wanted his father to know. 'But if anyone had told me my dad would one day be managing the finest bar in Gibraltar and that it belonged to his wife, I would have thought them just as mad. We've both done well, Dad, and for the same reason. We have very special women in our lives. I have Vicky and you have Maria. We are incredibly lucky men.'

It was then Maria's turn to tell her husband what had been happening in Alan's life. When she came to an end, John Carter lay back on his pillows and closed his eyes for so long that Alan thought he had gone to sleep, but then his eyelids flickered open.

Reaching out for Alan's hand, he took it and said, 'You're right. We have both been very lucky, son. Life had us on our knees, but instead of delivering the final blow it reached out and lifted us back on our feet. I found Maria and now you've found your Vicky. I reckon luck must run in the family.'

Maria and Alan stayed with John Carter until 11 o'clock that morning and left promising to return that afternoon.

At 12.30 a messenger from the hospital arrived at Maria's door. John Carter had died peacefully half an hour before.

52

On the day Alan left for Gibraltar, Vicky was tidying his study when she came across the letter from his solicitor telling of Dora's change of heart about the divorce.

She and Alan had discussed the letter and what they would do about it, but had arrived at no firm decision before the telegram from Maria arrived and took precedence over all else. Now Vicky sat down at Alan's desk and read the letter once again.

Knowing what she did of Dora, it angered her. Alan had been more than generous to his unfaithful wife, and had been given nothing in return. Vicky sat thinking for a long time before reaching a decision. Abandoning her cleaning, she changed into outdoor clothes and a few minutes later was on her bicycle, heading for Newlyn.

Cecil was writing when Vicky called on him. It was one of the days when Anoushka was attending the Stanhope Forbes school of painting and he was alone in the house. Surprised at seeing Vicky, his immediate thought was that something might have gone wrong with Alan, or his father.

'No, Cecil,' Vicky said. 'There has been no more news from Gibraltar and Alan should be with them in a couple of days. I have come to ask if I might use your telephone. I am going to London and I want Sylvia Pankhurst to arrange something for me . . .'

Vicky caught a train to London the following morning. Much to her delight, when she arrived at Paddington station she was met by Molly Shields, the suffragette who had spent so many years working among the poor in the Hackney and Bethnal Green districts. Vicky had told Sylvia on the telephone that she would like to speak to Molly as a matter of urgency, but had not expected to meet up with her so soon.

On the way across London on an underground train, Vicky told Molly all that had happened between Dora and Alan since they had last met. When Vicky came to the end of her story, Molly asked, 'Are you and Alan together now?' Vicky admitted they were. 'Will you marry when he is divorced from Dora?'

'I would like to think so,' Vicky replied, 'but marriage is not important. We are together and will be whether we are married or not. What I want is for him to be free to make a choice.'

Thoughtful for a while, Molly asked, 'How do you need me to help you?'

'You know details of how Dora behaved during the first year or two of their marriage. I am going to call on her and threaten to tell the police about the cheques she stole unless she keeps her promise in respect of the divorce. I will tell her I am aware of the previous baby she was expecting and would like you to be there to back me up when I meet her.'

364

'I am quite happy to do that,' Molly said. 'When are you thinking of calling on her?'

'Why not right now?' The reply took Molly by surprise, but Vicky explained, 'I have been thinking about it on the train all the way from Penzance. I would like to get it over with, then take you and Sylvia out for a celebratory meal. If all goes the way I hope, it will be something worth celebrating.'

Although Molly had been taken aback by Vicky's determination to have things settled as quickly as possibly, she was quite willing to go along with her. 'Why not? It's high time Dora Carter got her just deserts. She is a thoroughly nasty piece of work.'

Vicky deposited her luggage at Molly's flat, which was above her Bethnal Green office, and after a quick cup of tea the two women set off for Quilter Street.

They arrived at the Platt house at just before six-thirty in the evening and Vicky's knock brought a young woman to the door. Guessing who she was, Vicky said, 'Hello. You must be Mabel. Is Dora in, please? I would like to speak to her.'

Nonplussed that the caller should know her name, Mabel replied cautiously, 'She's only just come in from work. Is she expecting you?'

'No,' Vicky said, 'but I am a friend of Alan and have something I wish to discuss with her.'

Mabel's face lit up immediately. 'You know Alan? How is he?'

'He is out of the country at the moment, but he is keeping well. Now . . . Dora?'

'I'm not sure she'll want to speak to you,' Mabel said uncertainly. 'Are you from Alan's solicitor?'

'No,' Vicky replied firmly. 'We are here to discuss a matter that is in Dora's interests.'

'Wait here,' Mabel said. 'I'll see if she wants to speak to you.'

In the kitchen, Dora had just finished eating her supper and was talking to her mother when Mabel hurried in. 'There are two women to see you, Dora. They know Alan and say they have something to talk to you about that's to your advantage. I think they might be from his solicitor, though they say they aren't.'

'Then tell them to write to me,' Dora said. 'I don't want anything to do with any solicitors.'

'You heard what our Mabel said.' Winnie spoke sharply to her eldest daughter. 'They have something to say that's to your advantage. In lawyers' jargon that means they're going to offer you money. You refuse to talk to them and they're likely to go off in a huff and you'll be the loser. If you want more money out of 'em then you'll see them, my girl.'

For a few moments it seemed Dora might stand her ground. Then, shrugging, she said to Mabel, 'All right, show 'em into the front room and I'll come and speak, when I'm good and ready.'

Vicky and Molly were kept waiting for ten minutes before Dora put in an appearance, followed by her tight-lipped mother. Arrogantly, Dora said, 'I believe you're from Alan's solicitors and have come to offer me more money to sign the divorce papers. It had better be a lot more than he's given me so far. If it's not, then you're wasting your time.'

366

Vicky took an instant, albeit a not altogether surprising, dislike to Dora. 'I don't think I have mentioned anything about money,' she said, 'and I am not from the solicitors.'

Taken aback, Dora said, 'Then . . . who are you and why are you here?'

'I told your sister that it would be in your interest to speak to us, and that is so. Either we reach agreement here and now, or I go to the police.'

'What have the police got to do with anything?' Dora demanded. 'They don't get involved with divorces.'

'That is perfectly true,' Vicky agreed, 'but they *are* interested in people who steal cheques, namely one from the Royal Navy and another from Gibraltar. They are also very interested in women who have abortions and try to obtain money by false pretences. Just in case you don't understand, I am talking about an attempt to obtain money from Alan by pretending that he was the father of your baby . . . and while we are on the subject, where is the baby now, Dora? I didn't see a perambulator in the passageway, or any other sign that there is a baby in the house. Where is he?'

'That's none of your business.' Dora was more frightened than angry, but she tried to brazen it out. 'I don't have to tell you nothing.'

'That is quite true,' Vicky agreed. 'In fact, if I am perfectly honest I would much rather that Molly and I told everything we know to the police and let them deal with you. It would help Alan too, I have no doubt. If you were unable to appear in the divorce court because you were in prison, his divorce would be granted with no more fuss.

Yes, you are quite right. That is what I should have done in the first place. I believe you know many of the policemen in the area, Molly. We'll go and see them now.'

Winnie had been following the conversation closely and now she said belligerently, 'Don't let the likes of these two put the wind up you, Dora. If the court hears they've been trying to put the frighteners on you they'll be on your side.'

'I doubt it.' Molly entered the conversation. 'Not once they've heard how she carried on while her husband was off fighting for his country. That reminds me, you're Winnie Platt, I believe? I go to Scawfell Street regularly and hear your name mentioned there quite often. Next time I visit them I'll tell them I've spoken to you. I am sure some of them would like to meet up with you again. But we don't want to take up any more of your time. Shall we go, Vicky? We can call in at Old Street police station. It's on our way, and I know the inspector there.'

'Just a minute,' Winnie called to them as they turned to leave the room. 'Who's been asking about me in Scawfell Street?'

'I really can't remember,' Molly said. 'I talk to so many people. It might have been Mother Hennessey, or Mary Powell. On the other hand it could have been . . .' Molly went on to name half a dozen women who lived in Scawfell Street, adding, 'It might even have been Mr Barnet, the rent collector, or Mrs Harrison at the corner shop. I meet up with both of them most weeks.'

'There's no need for anyone in Scawfell Street to know you've seen me.' Winnie was no longer belligerent and her tone was almost conciliatory. 'I wasn't getting on very well with most of 'em there; that's why I left Scawfell Street and brought the family here, so we could make a fresh start. It hasn't been easy, what with one thing and another, and it wasn't made any easier when our Charlie went to prison. Now I've only got Dora's and Mabel's money coming into the house – and Mabel's talking of going off to live with her friend Rene. I don't know how we're going to manage. That's why Dora's asked Alan to let her have a bit more money. I mean, he's fallen on his feet, ain't he, whereas we're on our uppers.'

'Alan has done far more for Dora than might have been expected of him in the circumstances. What happened to the money he gave her to take her to America?'

'You seem to know a great deal about Alan,' Dora said. 'Are you the one our Charlie saw him with in the car?'

'Who I am doesn't matter,' Vicky said. 'I also know a great deal about you. Far more than I've mentioned so far. More, even, than Alan knows. Come along, Molly, we have wasted enough time. The police can take it from here.'

'Now . . . let's not do anything hasty,' Winnie said, deeply concerned. 'I'm sure—'

She was interrupted by Dora. 'All right, I'll sign the papers.'

Vicky and Molly stopped and turned back to her.

'When?' Vicky demanded.

Trying to retain a vestige of defiance, Dora shrugged. 'When I have time . . .'

'No,' Vicky said firmly. 'You'll go to the solicitor first thing in the morning. I will give you until noon. If you have not been to see him by then I go straight to the police.'

'I can't go tomorrow,' Dora protested. 'You heard what

Ma said about us being short of money. If I don't go in to work tomorrow I'll lose a day's pay. Besides, tomorrow's pay day. I can't afford to take it off.'

Producing a purse, Vicky took out a folded five pound note. Handing it to Dora, she said, 'This will more than cover your pay and you can pick up what's owed to you on Monday. It also means you have no excuse for not going to the solicitor – by taxi, if need be. Remember, I will telephone him at twelve noon. If you have not been to see him and signed the papers I will not come calling on you for excuses. I will put down the telephone and go straight to the police and let them deal with you. Is that fully understood?'

Dora merely nodded, but Vicky refused to accept the gesture. 'I asked you a question. I want to hear your reply.'

'I'll be there.'

'Good,' Vicky said brusquely. 'Shall we go now, Molly?'

'Yes . . . but I have a question to ask first. Where is your baby, Dora? The one born in the Salvation Army hospital?'

Quite unexpectedly, Dora's eyes filled with tears. 'He's in America, with his father. Delroy is married, and was when he came to England, but his wife has said she'll bring up the baby as her own. He'll have a far better life there than I could ever give him.'

Outside the house, Vicky said to Molly, 'You know, I believe that giving up her baby is probably the first unselfish thing Dora has ever done. I think she really cared for it.'

'Perhaps.' Molly was more cynical. 'I think it was more likely to be a bid to gain your sympathy. She went to

America intending to use the baby to persuade this Delroy to marry her. When she learned he was already married she didn't want to be lumbered with the baby and was probably quite willing to give it up. She might even have made money out of it. Believe me, Vicky, I have more sympathy than most with East End girls who genuinely try to lift themselves out of their environment. Dora isn't one of them.'

Inside the Quilter Street house, the five pound note Vicky had handed over was already causing dissent. When Dora went to leave the room, Winnie stood in her path. 'Before you go anywhere you can hand half the money you were given over to me. We're in this together, my girl. If the police get involved we'll both go down. If they don't . . . well, we'll each be a couple of pounds better off than we were before they came.'

53

At three minutes past noon the following day, Vicky replaced the handset on Sylvia Pankhurst's telephone and, turning to Sylvia and Molly, said, 'Dora has kept her word. She has been in to see the solicitor and signed everything that required her signature. Alan's divorce will go through uncontested. Thank you, Molly – and thank you too, Sylvia. Now I think we should plan a celebration for tonight. Where would you like to go?'

The three women settled for a West End restaurant, and although Sylvia was critical of its ostentation, she approved of the quality of its food. But during the course of the evening a deep difference of opinion threatened a long-standing friendship when Sylvia learned that Alan had been decorated for his part in the war against the Bolsheviks. It seemed that Sylvia was a staunch supporter of the new Russian order, although she expressed concern at their ruthlessness in killing off those who had been in authority during the Tsar's rule – and the slaughter of the Tsar himself, together with his family.

Fortunately, Vicky was able to switch the conversation to a discussion about the unsatisfactory nature of the Representation of the People Act, which offered only partial emancipation to women by giving the vote to those over the age of thirty years – but only if they were occupiers or wives of occupiers of property which had an annual rateable value of more than five pounds, or held degrees from recognised universities. It was agreed that this was a step in the right direction, but it still left women in the position of second-class citizens.

'The fly in this particular ointment is Sir Randolph Stileman,' declared Sylvia. 'He is still implacably opposed to giving women the vote and has whipped up support for his stand in every debate that has been held on the subject in the House of Commons. If it had not been for him we might have achieved full suffrage.'

'His son is tarred with the same brush,' Vicky said, 'and he is standing for election in our constituency's by-election. I have met him and neither like nor trust him.'

'Is he likely to be elected?' Sylvia asked.

'Almost certainly,' Vicky said. 'I don't even know the name of his opponent. Desmond Stileman is putting himself forward as an ex-wartime pilot who served his country well. I know he is a fraud. He spent his time in France delivering reconditioned aeroplanes to front-line squadrons.'

'I have never met the younger Stileman,' Molly said, 'but he has shared the platform with his father on at least two occasions when Stileman senior was campaigning for his party in west London. Whatever he has to say about women's suffrage during his election campaign in

Cornwall, he is as opposed as is his father to women being given the vote.'

'The frustrating thing is that there is nothing we can do about it,' Vicky said.

'Don't be too sure of that,' Sylvia replied. 'Annie Kenney will be in London next week. We don't see eye to eye on everything, but she has always been dedicated to the cause and she was the organiser of the west country suffragette movement. I'll speak to her and see if we can't persuade some of the old stalwarts to take their banners out of the closet and attend one or two of young Stileman's meetings. It might liven things up a little.'

Vicky returned from London well pleased with all that had been achieved during her time there. Alan's divorce should now go through without a hitch and it was possible that she had breathed a little fire into Desmond Stileman's proposed election campaign.

She was met at Penzance railway station by Cecil and Anoushka, having telephoned details of her arrival time from London. From them she received news that made her wish she had done even more to oppose Desmond's election to Parliament.

As he was carrying her suitcase to the Hotchkiss, Cecil said, 'I have some news that might make a difference to any plans you have made for the next few days, Vicky.'

'What is it?' Vicky was immediately worried that something might have gone wrong with Alan's visit to Gibraltar. 'Have you heard from Alan? Has something happened?'

'It's nothing to do with Alan – although the fact that he is not here at the moment probably means that a great deal of unpleasantness has been avoided. Your parents are here, Vicky.'

Startled, Vicky asked, 'Here . . . ? You mean in Newlyn?'

'They were in Lamorna this afternoon, at Stream Cottage. Anoushka was in your studio putting the finishing touches to one of her paintings when they arrived. They were with a man who, from Anoushka's description, was probably Desmond Stileman.'

'What on earth were they doing with Desmond? Unless . . . My father only recently retired as the Conservative agent for his constituency in Oxfordshire. Desmond met him once, but only briefly, as far as I know. He might have asked for his help in his election campaign. Yet Desmond must have his own team in Cornwall, so why ask my father here – unless he is trying to cause mischief because my parents are not aware that Alan and I are living together. If that is his intention then I sense Fiona's involvement.'

'Surely not,' Cecil said sceptically. 'Fiona can be malicious, but what has she to gain from making life difficult for you?'

'She was spiteful enough to put me out of my Newlyn studio, Cecil, and she is deeply resentful of Anoushka's friendship with Alan and me. Did my parents say where they were staying, Anoushka?'

'No. I told them you would be back some time this evening. I did not know what time then. They said they would call to see you again tomorrow. I am sorry, Vicky. I should have asked more questions.'

'You have nothing to apologise for, Anoushka. I am very relieved that you were at the studio when they called, otherwise their presence in Cornwall would have come as an even greater shock to me. At least I will now be prepared for them – and for their enquiries.'

'That's what I thought,' Cecil said. 'Now, you are coming to our house before you return to Lamorna. Anoushka has cooked a meal for you and you can tell us all about what happened in London while we eat. Afterwards I will take you home to Stream Cottage.'

The following day was Sunday, and Ralph and Miriam Hazelton arrived at Stream Cottage in the late morning, when Vicky had completed her household chores and was in the studio framing some of her more recently completed paintings.

After a warm exchange of greetings, Vicky's father said, 'What a delightful little cottage you have here, Vicky. It must be the most perfect spot along the whole coast for an artist. You have all the inspiration you will ever need, all around you.'

'It is very lovely,' Vicky agreed, 'but I think Lamorna Birch would dispute the fact that Stream Cottage has a superior situation to his own home.'

'You know Lamorna Birch?' Her father sounded impressed. 'I saw some of his paintings in the Academy when I was last in London. He is very highly regarded.'

'He is my closest neighbour,' Vicky replied. 'No doubt we will have a visit from one or both of his young daughters while you are here.'

'I am relieved to know you have friendly neighbours, dear. It must get very lonely for you here.'

The comment came from Miriam Hazelton and Vicky

caught the warning glance that her father threw at his wife. Aware that there was a hidden question implicit in the statement, she was more convinced than ever that Fiona had been instrumental in bringing her parents to Cornwall.

'Why should the Lamorna valley be any lonelier than anywhere else? I have my work and my friends – I believe you met one of them yesterday.'

'That's right, the foreign girl,' her mother said dismissively. 'I don't think she told us her name.'

'It is Anoushka . . . Anoushka Romanov. Needless to say, she is Russian.'

'Anoushka Romanov? Would that be the princess Fiona was telling us about at dinner last night? How very exciting.' Miriam could not hide her delight, but it was not this that surprised Vicky.

'You had dinner with Fiona last night? Fiona Graham?'

'That's right, dear . . . but of course, you would not know. The very clever young man who brought you home on your last visit is standing for Parliament. You were aware of that, I have no doubt? Well, he heard that Daddy had retired as Conservative agent for our constituency and, having met him, and in view of his many years of experience, he invited Daddy to come to Cornwall and offer an opinion on how his election campaign might be improved. It offered such a wonderful opportunity to visit you that Daddy just could not refuse. We are even staying in your old studio, which I understood is being rented from Fiona by Desmond. I really cannot understand why you ever left it, dear. It has the most wonderful views, and you should have felt far more secure in your tenancy, knowing it was owned by a friend.'

'Fiona is no friend of mine,' Vicky said firmly. 'She is a scheming, interfering busybody – and I did not leave the studio by choice. Fiona and I had a disagreement about her interference and I was given notice to quit. Not that I am unhappy about it now. This is a much nicer house and I give the owner an occasional painting in lieu of rent, so it is also much cheaper. Even more important to me is that I am now able to live my life without being constantly reminded that I am obliged to Fiona Graham. Incidentally, she is the only one to give Anoushka the title of "Princess". It sounded more important when she latched on to her and began introducing her to people. Anoushka *is* distantly related to the late Tsar of Russia, and to our own royal family, but she insists she has no claim to any title.'

Undismayed by Vicky's words, Miriam said, 'I have no doubt Fiona was doing her best to ensure Anoushka would be accepted into society at a level to which she had been accustomed in Russia. The poor girl's life must have been turned upside down by the murder of the Tsar and his family, and the dreadful events in her homeland.'

'It has certainly not been easy for her,' Vicky agreed, 'but she is among friends here and is very happy to be improving her artistic talents.'

'Of course, dear, and I am quite certain you have been a great help to her. But we have not come to Lamorna to talk about Russian exiles, however important they might be. I am far more interested in your life here. May we have a look round your delightful cottage?'

'Of course. You and Daddy go now. I will not be very long. I just want to finish this frame, and then I will join you and make us all a cup of tea.'

378

Before Miriam could express agreement to the arrangement, her husband said, 'You go on to the cottage, Miriam. I will have a look round the studio and come to the cottage with Vicky. It's a long time since I had an opportunity to study her work.'

Miriam hesitated, but only for a few moments. Vicky and her father had always been very close. In Miriam's absence they were quite likely to discuss matters she would not learn about until much later. She would have preferred to persuade Ralph to come with her, but decided not to argue with him. It would give her an opportunity to look round the cottage on her own.

When his wife had left the studio and could be seen making her way to the cottage, Ralph Hazelton said, 'It was very brave of you to give your mother carte blanche to snoop round the cottage without you present, Vicky.'

'Why, Daddy?' Vicky asked, as she adjusted a painting in its prospective frame. 'I have no doubt at all that Fiona gave you both all the details of my personal life. If Mummy wishes for confirmation she has only to ask me. After all, I am twenty-seven years of age and leading a very comfortable, contented and independent life.'

'Fiona and her husband said nothing specific about you,' Ralph Hazelton said, 'but Fiona did hint that you were involved with a man she felt to be totally unsuitable . . . a married man.'

'Fiona is a spiteful and vindictive bitch – and I make no apologies for using such a word to you. I have no doubt at all that she is behind Desmond's invitation to you to come and "offer an opinion on his election campaign". He

379

is a despicable man whom I intend to oppose tooth and nail in his bid for election. As for Alan, my unsuitable man, come and see my portrait of him.'

Taking her father's hand, Vicky led him to a corner of the studio where she had gathered together the paintings that would not be offered for sale. Stopping before Alan's portrait, she said, 'This is Alan, the man Fiona feels is "NOCD".'

Pointing to his double row of medal ribbons, she said, 'And those are the Conspicuous Gallantry Medal, the Distinguished Service Medal, a Mention in Dispatches – and the last two are Russian medals, awarded to him for his part in rescuing Anoushka and her family.'

'He would appear to be a very pleasant as well as an extremely brave young man,' Ralph Hazelton commented. 'Are we likely to meet him while we are in Cornwall?'

Vicky shook her head. 'He sailed for Gibraltar earlier in the week. His father lives in Spain and has suffered a serious heart attack. He will have arrived there only this morning and has not yet been able to tell me what is happening.'

'You are very fond of him, aren't you?'

'I love him very, very much, Daddy – and he feels the same about me.'

'But I understand he is a married man. What of his wife?'

Vicky gave her father an outline of what had happened between Alan and Dora, adding, 'Only this week his wife signed a statement for Alan's solicitors, admitting her guilt. They should be divorced very soon now.'

'And what will you do then? Does he have work?'

'He is an extremely talented writer and poet, Daddy. I can show you copies of his published work and he has recently been commissioned to write two books, one about his part in the escape of Anoushka and her family from Russia. Apparently he went back to rescue a wounded naval officer who was surrounded by Bolsheviks – and it was Anoushka who told me about it, not Alan.'

'He would appear to be a most interesting young man, Vicky. I am sorry he is not here so that I might meet him. As you say, you are twenty-seven years of age now, and your wartime experiences mean you have seen more of life than either your mother or I. Your mother will need to be convinced that you are doing the right thing by standing by Alan, but you have my blessing and I will do what I can to bring Miriam round to my way of thinking.'

Giving her father a warm hug, Vicky said, 'I knew you would see things from my point of view, Daddy. Thank you.'

'It is what fathers are for,' Ralph Hazelton said, trying not to allow his pleasure at her gesture of affection to show. 'Now, tell me your thoughts on Desmond Stileman before your mother comes back to question you about what she has discovered in your cottage . . .'

54

Miriam Hazelton had wasted no time in seeking out evidence that Vicky was sharing Stream Cottage with a man. She stood, hands on hips, in the centre of the cottage lounge, radiating silent fury as she awaited the arrival of her husband and daughter.

Choosing to ignore her mother's almost palpable anger, Vicky said cheerfully, 'Well, what do you think of Stream Cottage? Is it not absolutely delightful?'

'Never mind the cottage . . . I had a look in the wardrobes in your bedroom. One is a *man's* wardrobe, containing a man's clothing.'

'That would be Alan's wardrobe. It is private, of course, but I doubt whether he will mind you looking in it.' Vicky spoke openly and dispassionately, making no attempt to evade the issue. Her attitude did nothing to calm her mother.

'Don't try to be flippant with me, young lady. Who is this Alan – and where is he? Skulking away somewhere until we have gone away, hoping we will not learn about him?'

'I have a feeling he is not the sort of young man to "skulk" anywhere, dear. He is certainly not lacking in courage.'

Ralph Hazelton's mild observation only added to his wife's fury. Rounding on him, she said, 'Are you telling me that Victoria has discussed this . . . this *relationship* with you and you have not told me? Why did you say nothing last evening, when our hosts dropped very strong hints about what was going on? Am I the only one in the whole world who does not know that my daughter is living with a married man . . . and a married man from a dubious background, at that?' Miriam was probably the only person in the world who still used Vicky's full name.

Vicky's resolution to keep her temper no matter what was said suddenly deserted her. 'You sound just like Fiona – who has proved herself to be a vindictive and narrow-minded snob. Alan does not come from a "dubious" background, but a working-class one – and it has not been particularly happy. Nevertheless, he has proved his courage and trustworthiness and is more of a gentleman than someone like Desmond Stileman will ever be. He includes among his friends men and women who might look down their noses at *us*, were they so inclined. He also possesses a talent that is recognised by those who measure men and women by ability and not by accident of birth. Yes, we live together, and what is more we love each other very much. Now, is there anything more you would like to know from me, or would you prefer to go back to Fiona and hear her version of the life Alan and I are leading? I have no doubt she can concoct an account tailored to your expectations.'

'Well! I never expected to hear my own daughter speak to me in such a manner.' Miriam Hazelton bristled with indignation. 'And in defence of a way of life that disregards everything she has been brought up to believe is good and decent.'

'I have never abandoned any of the principles in which I believe. What is more, Alan embodies a great many of them without having had the benefit of parents like you and Daddy to teach him. To pass judgement without even meeting him is totally opposed to another principle I was always taught to look upon as being important. That of tolerance.'

'I am not prepared to stay here and be given a lecture on principles by you, my girl. One day, when you have come to your senses, I hope we may talk together as mother and daughter once more. Until then I doubt whether we will meet again. Come along, Ralph. You may take me back to Newlyn.'

Turning away, Miriam Hazelton walked stiffly down the path, away from the cottage and her daughter.

Aware that Vicky was very upset, her father stepped forward and gave her a warm hug. 'Don't take anything she has said too much to heart, Vicky. You know what your mother is like when she gets angry. *I* am on your side. I hope you will stay in touch and contact me right away should you need me. In the meantime I will try to talk your mother round. Tell that young man of yours to take care of you and say I am sorry not to have met him while I was here. I hope he has found his own father in better health than expected. Thank you too for giving me your opinion of young Stileman. I don't think I shall remain in Cornwall to help further his ambitions.'

Vicky was left feeling far more upset than had been apparent, even to her father. For as long as she could remember, she and her mother had argued, and some of the arguments had been particularly heated, but she could not recall ever having had a difference of opinion which threatened their whole relationship in such a way as this.

Ralph Hazelton drove his wife away from Newlyn that same afternoon, after telling a bewildered Desmond Stileman that he did not feel able to advise his electoral team, or support his bid for a seat in the House of Commons.

Realising that, despite the rigid stance she had taken over Vicky's relationship with Alan, his wife was also deeply distressed by her altercation with Vicky, Ralph said nothing about what had gone on. He would leave it to Miriam to broach the subject when she was ready.

They drove in silence for much of the way and it was not until darkness had fallen and her husband was unable to see her expression that Miriam said, 'I found the visit to Victoria extremely upsetting. I was also very hurt that you felt unable to give me your support on such an important issue. I never expected you to condone our daughter's immorality.'

'I neither condoned nor condemned what she is doing,' Ralph said without taking his eyes from the road ahead. 'I tried only to understand the situation from both points of view.'

'What is there to understand?' Miriam demanded. 'Victoria is living with a man, which is bad enough in itself, but when that man is married to another woman it is quite disgraceful. Even the most besotted father should consider such behaviour to be quite unacceptable.'

'I don't pretend to be overjoyed with the situation,' Ralph admitted, 'but I believe the young man involved really is rather exceptional. He is certainly a war hero and seems to have a promising future as a writer.'

'He also has a wife,' Miriam reminded him tartly.

'I understand that Alan is the innocent party, and a divorce is imminent.'

'No doubt that is what Victoria has chosen to believe,' Miriam snapped, determined not to admit any mitigating circumstances in the situation. 'She has always been inclined to allow her emotions to overrule common sense. Had it not been so she might have become the wife of a Member of Parliament.'

Casting a quick glance in her direction in the darkness, her husband said, 'If you are suggesting it might have been Desmond Stileman, then I am happy she is not involved with him in any way. I was not particularly taken with him when we first met and nothing he has said or done since has given me cause to change my mind about him. I do not think he is an honourable man. Anyway, it was hardly likely to come to anything between them. It was Desmond's father who had Vicky sent to prison, for throwing an egg at him when he was giving a talk opposed to women's suffrage. I believe Desmond has similar diehard convictions.'

'I don't think you can blame Desmond for an incident involving his father,' Miriam said, slightly less vehemently. 'It was Victoria's fault for throwing the egg in the first place, and it must have been a policeman who arrested her, not Desmond's father. Thank goodness she has got over *those* years, at least. I really do not know how we managed to hold our heads high among our friends – and now her behaviour is giving us even more cause for concern. Why could we not have had the sort of daughter all of our friends seem to have?'

Ralph smiled to himself in the darkness. He had always been secretly proud of Vicky's independent spirit. He also had a suspicion that Vicky had not left the militant years behind her. However, reverting to their earlier discussion, he said, 'I think we have to accept that you and I were brought up in the Victorian age, Miriam. Vicky is the new generation who has fought for the emancipation of women and braved the dangers of war close to the battlefront to prove her case. She is twenty-seven years of age and no longer a little girl who needs to be told what she should or should not do. But whatever she does, she is still our daughter. I am quite certain you love her every bit as much as I do, so why don't we think of ways to build bridges between us, and not means of knocking them down?'

55

The week following the visit from her parents was an eventful one for Vicky. It began with a telegram from Alan on Monday, informing her of the death of his father and telling her he would be remaining in Algeciras until after the funeral. He promised that a letter would follow.

On Tuesday Cecil called to say he had heard from his solicitor that the London evening newspaper had agreed to retract their story that Anoushka was living with him and would be printing an apology that very evening. They had also agreed to pay damages to both Cecil and Anoushka.

Cecil was particularly pleased with the result because details of the libellous article had reached Anoushka's parents in Paris. Although they had decided not to make it into a major family scandal, they had written to Anoushka and asked her what it was all about.

Now, with the matter resolved, Cecil intended to sit down and write to Anoushka's father, telling him of the proposed apology from the newspaper and adding that he would be soon visiting Paris and would like to call upon the Romanov family.

Meanwhile, word reached Vicky that Sylvia Pankhurst and her friends had wasted no time in contacting west country suffragettes who had been active in the years before the Great War. They had already made their presence felt at one of Desmond Stileman's political meetings and planned even greater disruption at Penzance, when Sir Randolph Stileman, MP, would be on the platform in support of his son.

Unfortunately, the Penzance meeting fell on a day when Stanhope Forbes had to be away from Cornwall and Vicky was teaching in his place at the artists' school in Newlyn, and she was unable to attend. However, Desmond was giving another electioneering speech in Newlyn on the Friday and Vicky was determined she would be there. A great many fishermen also meant to attend, in the hope of discovering just how much this particular parliamentary candidate understood about the fluctuating fortunes of their industry. A number of artists would undoubtedly also turn up, if only out of curiosity.

Vicky went to the electioneering meeting with Prue Penhaligon. Prue had been too young to be a member of the suffragette movement before the war, but had always taken a great interest in women's suffrage and would question Vicky about the movement whenever they spent any time in each other's company. She was also indignant that she would not be entitled to vote in an election for another ten years.

The hall was surprisingly crowded but, ominously,

there were a number of muscular men who did not sit among those attending the meeting. Instead, they stood against the side walls scanning those who entered. The men were strangers to Newlyn and there was a great deal of muttering, among the fishermen in particular, when word went round that they had been employed by the Conservative candidate to ensure that the disruptions of his earlier meetings were not repeated in Newlyn.

Most of those attending the meeting were known to others in their particular section of the community and they used the occasion to chat and gossip among themselves. However, there were a number of women present who were not known, but, because they entered the meeting hall separately, and not in a single group, were not immediately identified as suffragettes. Only a couple of them were recognised by Vicky, but she felt a thrill of excitement when she saw them. She realised that the next few hours were likely to be as lively as any she had known in London before the late war.

The meeting began with a speech by Desmond in which he set out the aims of his party, reminding his audience that the furtherance of such policies would only be possible when the present coalition, led by the Liberal David Lloyd George, gave way to a Conservative government.

This statement won a few handclaps, but they were quickly drowned out by a louder chorus of jeers which made his security men noticeably nervous and gave Desmond Stileman a clear indication that he lacked support from the majority of those present at this meeting.

Desmond's policy on fishing was extremely vague, and when he finally decided to throw the meeting open to questions there was a whole barrage of demands for him to clarify his views on the subject. Eventually, he was forced to admit that he knew very little about the problems of Cornish fishermen, but he assured his sceptical listeners that he was anxious to learn, and hoped that all those present would vote him in and then meet with him to discuss their problems.

It was apparent that those who had posed the questions were less than satisfied with his replies, and when their scepticism was at its noisy height one of the suffragettes who had infiltrated the meeting rose to her feet and asked Desmond to tell the audience where he stood on the emancipation of women. Desmond's reply was that he did not believe it was an issue that should have any bearing on the present by-election, as Parliament had already granted considerable concessions to women.

It was at this stage that Vicky rose to her feet and challenged him. 'It has a direct and very important bearing on your election,' she shouted. 'What is more, women are not asking for "concessions". We are demanding that we be given what is our entitlement. Equal rights to those enjoyed by men. Rights that would have been granted by Parliament had your father not consistently blocked them. Thanks to him, I, and many other women in this hall tonight, am not able to vote for or against you. Where do you stand on this issue?'

Recognising Vicky as his questioner, Desmond smiled at her in what he hoped was a disarming manner and said, 'I am very happy that the Representation of the People Act granted certain voting rights to women, but such radical changes cannot be hurried . . .'

'I suggest that a great many young women earned their right to be treated as equals by virtue of their war service. I and a number of others saw far more active service than you,' Vicky retorted. 'Are you saying that, despite this, we should still be regarded as less important than a man who did nothing to help his country during the war?'

A good proportion of those in the hall knew Vicky and were aware of her outstanding war service. They set up such a chorus of demands for Desmond to give a suitable reply to her question that the men employed by him to keep the peace became even more nervous. At a signal from their leader, a number of them began to push their way through the seated audience, heading for Vicky, their intention clearly being to evict her from the hall.

On the way they met the suffragettes and were immediately subjected to physical attack. The men retaliated, chairs were knocked over and some of the fishermen, realising that Vicky was the intended target of Desmond's bodyguards, leapt to her defence.

Within minutes, the hall erupted in a state of uproar. Brawls broke out in half a dozen different places, chairs were utilised as weapons and one would occasionally be hurled through the air towards the speaker on the platform, who soon sought refuge in the nearby cloakroom.

A few policemen had been detailed for duty outside the hall and they now joined in the fray, arresting a number of those involved in the fracas inside the hall, including Vicky and Prue Penhaligon.

They were conveyed with the others to the police station in Penzance and had resigned themselves to spending the night in the cells when Desmond Stileman put in a brief appearance to inform the inspector in charge that he would not be pressing charges against any of the men and women involved in the Newlyn hall disturbance.

The police inspector was relieved. The fishermen of Newlyn, Mousehole and Penzance had begun to gather in large numbers outside the police station and there was a strong suspicion that they were about to make a determined attempt to release the prisoners held in custody.

Unfortunately for Desmond Stileman, reporters from the local newspapers had been among those who attended his electoral meeting and they were not inclined to allow the issues raised in the hall to go unanswered. They demanded, through the columns of their newspapers, that Desmond reply to the questions posed by Vicky and her suffragette friends. Somehow, they had also obtained details of the would-be MP's wartime service and compared it, unfavourably, to hers.

For the man who hoped to be elected to Parliament, the meeting had been an utter disaster.

56

The funeral of John Carter took place on a day that was as dismal as the occasion. The ceremony was conducted in Spanish and attended by Maria's relatives and many friends, very few of whom spoke any English. After the ceremony the mourners adjourned to the house where John Carter had lived with Maria and it was not until evening that the last of them departed, solemnly shaking Alan's hand and offering him genuine but incomprehensible condolences.

When they had gone, Maria went to a cabinet and brought out a bottle of malt whisky, saying, 'This was your father's favourite drink. Every evening he would enjoy sitting here, or outside in fine weather, drinking his whisky. Occasionally he would look through his telescope at the ships going in or out of Gibraltar and tell me where they were bound, or where they had come from. John and I had a very contented life together, but he never lost his love of the sea.' Pouring Alan a generous measure of whisky, she handed it to him and said, unhappily, 'I am ng to be lonely without him. We had such a short time gether.'

'But it was a very happy time, for both of you. I hope you will remember that, Maria. I will. Look . . . why don't you come back to England with me for a few weeks? Vicky and I live in a delightful little cottage and she would make you extremely welcome, I know she would. We have often spoken of you and would both enjoy having you to stay with us.'

'That is very kind of you,' Maria replied, deeply moved by his offer, 'but you have many problems of your own. When they are no more and you are able to be married to your Vicky, perhaps you will invite me to your wedding.'

'Of course!' Alan said. 'We wouldn't dream of not inviting you.'

'Then I accept in advance,' Maria said. 'Now, if you do not mind, I feel I would like to go to my room and be alone. It has been a long and difficult day for me.'

'Of course, if that's what you want to do. If you decide you want company, I will be here for a while, thinking my own thoughts.'

'I will see you in the morning,' Maria said. 'You will want to find out about returning to England. Hopefully, I will be able to forget much of my grief in my work and I have many friends in Algeciras and Gibraltar. But before you leave I have something I wish to show you. We will go to look at it tomorrow morning.'

The next morning another of Maria's taxi-owning relatives arrived to take them on a short journey along the coast. This one did not speak English, but he drove just as

furiously as the kinsman who had first brought Alan
Maria's home, when he was still in the Royal Navy.

They eventually arrived at what was evidently a small
fishing village tucked away in a small, sheltered cove. Here
the driver brought his vehicle to a halt outside a small but
picturesque house on the edge of the village, with a view
southwards to the sea.

'What a delightful spot,' Alan said admiringly. 'Is this
another of your properties, Maria?'

'It was,' she replied.

When Alan looked puzzled, she explained, 'As I think
I told you when you first came to Algeciras with me, my
first husband left me with many properties, but this is not
one of them. This one was bought by me shortly before I
married your father, and it was bought for a purpose. We
hoped that you and your wife would be coming to our
wedding and knew you had never enjoyed a proper
honeymoon together. We agreed that this was an ideal
place for a young couple to spend their honeymoon. Sadly,
the plan never worked out for any of us – but now you
have found Vicky and you hope one day to be married.
When you do, this house will be waiting for you both.'

'That is incredibly kind of you, Maria. I am sure Vicky
would be delighted to come here for her honeymoon. It
is the sort of place she adores. The only problem is . . . she
would probably spend the whole of the honeymoon painting, it is so picturesque. But you said you are no longer
the owner.'

'That is so, but Vicky will still have many opportunities
to paint here, when the honeymoon is over. You see, this
will be my wedding gift to you. In fact, it already belongs

you. I had it put in your name when we expected to welcome you to the wedding.'

'But . . . I can't accept something like this, Maria! It is far too generous.' Alan could not hide his astonishment.

'Is it wrong to be generous to family? No, of course it is not. I am a rich woman, Alan – far richer than your father ever knew. I have bought homes for my two sisters, and taxicabs for the men in the family. Your father would never allow me to put any of my property or money into his name, but he did agree that I could buy this small house for you. It gave us great pleasure to think you would one day spend time here, with your wife.' Making a brave attempt at a smile, she added, 'I would like to think that he and I will still share happiness in having you here. It is what he wished and it is my gift – to our son.'

Almost as close to tears as was Maria, Alan did not trust himself to speak and chose to hug her close to him instead.

She clung to him for a few minutes. Then, kissing him quickly on the cheek, she pulled away and said, 'Thank you, Alan. That is a moment I will always treasure. Now, come inside and let me show you your house.'

That afternoon, a Friday, Alan was able to book a passage on a ship sailing from Gibraltar to Southampton on Monday evening. It would have him back in England on Thursday, only a little over a fortnight after leaving Lamorna.

He sent a telegram to Vicky giving his travel details and saying he had much to tell her. It made no sense writing to her about the funeral and the unexpected and

generous gift of the Spanish cottage. He would be back i.
Lamorna before the letter arrived.

Maria bade Alan a tearful farewell on the jetty in
Gibraltar. Some of the girls from the Trocadero were there
too, ostensibly to bid Alan farewell, but he realised they
had come to keep Maria company and ensure she did not
become too upset. Alan was glad a number of newly
arrived merchant seamen were also on the dockside. The
Trocadero girls were known to them and their rowdiness
prevented the parting from becoming too emotional.

He and Maria had promised to remain in close touch
with each other over the coming months, during which
he hoped he might resolve the situation with Dora, and
be able to issue an invitation for Maria to come to Cornwall
on the occasion of his marriage to Vicky.

He remained on deck waving to Maria until the ship
passed out of Gibraltar harbour. Then he went to his cabin,
where he would spend the next couple of days working
on the manuscript of his book, thinking of how much he
had to tell Vicky, and hoping that life had not been too
boring for her during his absence.

57

The P & O liner bringing Alan back to England on a dull November day was gently nudged into a berth at Southampton docks at just after 4 p.m., two days and twenty hours after leaving Gibraltar.

Ready to go ashore, Alan had decided he would catch the first available train bound for London. There he would book into a hotel and telephone to Cecil, asking him to tell Vicky of his safe arrival in the country and inform her he would be catching the first available train to Penzance the following day.

His plans underwent a dramatic change when he heard his name being shouted as he disembarked from the ship. Looking down from the gangway, he was astonished to see a figure in the waiting crowd leaping up and down and waving frantically as she called his name. It was Vicky!

Almost falling in his haste to reach the quayside, Alan met Vicky at the foot of the gangway and embraced her in a hug that lifted her from the ground. When he eventually put her down, he said, 'What a wonderful

surprise! I was completely wrapped up in my own littl
world, warmed by the thought that I would be with you
by this time tomorrow . . . and, suddenly, here you are!
How did you manage it?'

After commiserating with him on the death of his father,
she replied to his question. 'I came by motor car . . . *our*
motor car. It's a Sunbeam – and it's a beauty, Alan. You'll
find it a perfect vehicle in which to learn to drive.'

'Me . . . learn to drive? But never mind that – can we
afford a motor car right now, Vicky? I mean . . . there's
been the expense of my trip to Gibraltar, the things we
need at Stream Cottage . . . and Dora. Perhaps Dora most
of all. I've thought about it a lot while I've been away and
have decided that however much she wants from me I'll
raise the money somehow, so that we can put her behind
us once and for all and look forward to an uncomplicated
future together . . . just you and me.'

Kissing him again, she said, 'That makes me very
happy, Alan, but . . . no! I am absolutely bursting to tell
you all my news and to hear about your time in Gibraltar,
but I just want to enjoy being with you again for a while.
I have booked us into a hotel outside Southampton – as
Mr and Mrs Alan Carter – and, should anyone ask, I have
come to Southampton to welcome you home from abroad.
We will check in, arrange to have dinner, and *then* catch
up on all that has been happening during the last couple
of weeks.'

They arrived at the hotel with a couple of hours to spare
before dinner, and spent the time in bed. It was there,
snuggled up to him after they had made love, that she

of all explained her purchase of the Sunbeam motor
in which she had come to Southampton.

'It was a wonderful stroke of luck,' she said happily,
'and thanks entirely to dear old Colonel Trecarrow. He has
a friend – an old army colleague – who is almost as old
as himself, but decided he wanted to keep up with the
trends of the modern world, so he bought the Sunbeam.
He had driven no more than twenty miles before he
decided he was too old after all to master the technical-
ities of such a new-fangled machine. When he said he was
going to sell it, Colonel Trecarrow thought of me. He said
he knew I had been an ambulance driver, and, with the
winter coming on and us living in such an out-of-the-way
place, it was just what we needed. I spoke to his friend –
and he sold it to me at half the price he paid for it! It is a
new motor car, Alan, and an absolute bargain!'

Pulling her to him, Alan said, 'You are a very clever
woman, Vicky Hazelton, and I love you very much.'

'Yes, and I love you too . . . but not again just yet, Alan.
I have much more to tell you.'

When Alan still pursued his amorous advances, Vicky
said hastily, 'My parents came to Stream Cottage. They
expected to find you there . . . at least, my mother certainly
did.'

Startled, Alan pulled away and looked down at her.
'What were they doing in Lamorna . . . and how did they
learn about me?'

Vicky told him of Desmond's invitation and her
suspicion that Fiona had somehow been involved, adding
that their scheme had backfired on Desmond, because her
father had withdrawn his support for the prospective MP's

campaign and he would doubtless air his views ab
Desmond among his influential Conservative friends.

Then Vicky disclosed the part the suffragette movemen
had played in Desmond's meetings, and broke the news
of her arrest. She told him about spending some hours in
the cells of Penzance police station.

'It was quite exciting while it lasted,' she added, 'but I
must admit to a feeling of relief when we were told that
Desmond was not pressing charges and were all released
from custody. I think he realised that pressing charges
would have cost him the election – and he was correct in
his assumption. The local newspapers were scathing about
his failure to give a straight answer to any of the ques
tions that were thrown at him. His opponent was quick
to seize his opportunity and express his sympathy with
the cause of women's suffrage. He has gained a great deal
of support as a result, and has the added advantage of
being a Cornishman, born and bred, both his father and
grandfather having been fishermen in their time. He
understands their needs far better than Desmond does.'

'If your suspicions are right, then Desmond will get no
more than he deserves, but how was it that the suffra
gettes decided to target him? I thought the movemen
virtually disbanded when the war began.'

'There are still a great many who will not cease their
activities until we gain full suffrage,' Vicky explained. 'A
for their involvement . . . I had a word with Sylvi
Pankhurst about it when I was in London . . . while yo
were in Gibraltar.'

'You've been to London?' Alan shook his head in dis
belief. 'And there was I thinking about you leading

402

eaceful and uneventful life in Stream Cottage while I was
way! Why did you go to London?'

'I went to Quilter Street to see Dora, and took one of
my friends – another ex-suffragette – with me. She knew
of the Platt family when she was working in a welfare
office in Hackney and Bethnal Green.'

'You saw Dora? Why, Vicky? You could have got into
serious trouble with that family, especially if Charlie had
been there with a few drinks inside him.'

'Charlie is in prison,' Vicky replied. 'Although no one
explained why. As for my reason for going there . . . I too
decided it was time Dora no longer had the power to
disrupt our lives – but I had no intention of letting her
extort any more of your money. Had we done so she would
have come back for more every time she found herself in
debt, and it would not have mattered whether you were
divorced or not. As it is, she has signed all the documents
put in front of her by your solicitor and the divorce will
go through without any further trouble. I hope that is what
you really want, Alan.'

'What I really want . . . ? Vicky, you are a miracle-
worker, as well as being both beautiful and clever . . . but
I think you had better tell me everything that went on at
Quilter Street, and then you can explain why you delayed
telling me such an important piece of news until now.'

'Do I really need to explain that? If I do, then perhaps
I should show you, once again . . .'

58

In Newlyn, Cecil knocked at the front door of Anoushka's studio flat and, when she answered his knock, told her he had written a letter to her father. It was largely in response to his request for her to explain the article in the London newspaper stating that she was living with the son of a peer of the realm. Cecil said he would like her to read the letter before it was posted. Enclosed in the envelope to accompany Cecil's explanation was the retraction and apology published by the newspaper.

Amused that Cecil had chosen to call at the front door and not knock at the interior door which connected the studio to the house, Anoushka invited him in and he sat in her small but comfortable lounge while she read what he had written.

In his letter, Cecil first apologised to Anoushka's father for any embarrassment that might have been caused to her family by the newspaper article, but hoped the official retraction would make it clear there was no truth in what had been published.

He went into details of their arrangements, even enclosing a plan showing that her part of the house was fully self-contained and assuring Alexander that they were living as neighbours, with Anoushka leading her own life – although he was happy to be near at hand should she need help of any kind.

Then he pointed out that Anoushka had some very good friends in the community, including Alan, whom they knew, and who was making his way as a successful author; Vicky, one of the most exciting new painters in the country; and Lamorna Birch and Stanhope Forbes, two internationally respected artists.

Cecil also felt obliged to point out that he was the second son of Viscount Rockingham and prided himself upon being an honourable man who had the highest regard for Anoushka – so high that he would do nothing to put his hopes for the future in jeopardy.

He ended by requesting that Alexander would allow him an opportunity in the not too distant future to explain himself more fully.

When she had finished reading the letter, Anoushka gave Cecil a quizzical look as she handed it back to him. 'I do hope your letter doesn't give my father the wrong impression. He could be forgiven for thinking you are hinting you wish to meet him in order to ask for my hand in marriage.'

'Perhaps it would not be a wrong impression, Anoushka.'

Anoushka's eyes opened wide at his unexpected reply. 'But . . . how can it be anything else? You have said nothing to me. Have never even hinted at it.'

'How could I, Anoushka? You are renting your home from me – and although I would never dream of using that to influence you in any way, you might feel you needed to at least humour me to a certain extent because of it. On the other hand, you might feel unable to remain in the studio knowing how I felt. Either way, I would be dreadfully unhappy, whereas now it gives me very real pleasure to know you and I are living beneath the same roof – even though you have your full independence, of course.'

'Why should I want to make you unhappy? Have you ever thought that I might return your feelings?'

'Do you?' Cecil asked eagerly, scarcely able to believe what she was saying. 'Do you feel the same way?'

'How can I know? You have never put your feelings for me into words. Until you do, it would be quite improper for me to tell you how I feel about you.'

Anoushka was playing Cecil at his own game, but she had said enough to enable him to overcome his acute shyness. 'I . . . I think I have loved you from the very first time I saw you, Anoushka. I thought you were the most beautiful woman I had ever seen. I still do, and now I know your beauty goes deeper than your looks. I . . . I really do want you to marry me, Anoushka. Having come to know you as well as I do I just can't imagine you not always being a part of my life.'

Having said far more than he had intended, he waited apprehensively for her reply. When she said nothing, he became increasingly dismayed. Surely she had not been leading him on for the sake of it . . .

'Do you . . . ? Don't you . . . ?' He was floundering.

'How will I know until you have kissed me, Cecil? Is that not what should accompany a declaration of love? It is usual in Russia; I thought it would be the same in England.'

When Cecil kissed Anoushka, all the pent-up passion he felt for her took over. She returned the kiss with equal passion, but suddenly pulled her head back and looked up at him.

'Cecil?'

'Yes?'

'I think you should go out and post the letter to my father right away. What you have told him is the truth – today. If you wait until tomorrow you might find it difficult to write such a letter. When it has gone I will tell you how I feel about you and we can talk about the future together. I would like that. I think I will like it very much . . .'

Vicky and Alan were the first to learn of the new relationship between Cecil and Anoushka, and both were delighted. They agreed, at the insistence of the happy couple, that they would say nothing to anyone else until a reply to Cecil's letter was received from Alexander Romanov. As a consequence, it was a private party that was held at Stream Cottage, but, as Vicky said to Alan later, it was doubtful whether it would be a secret for very long. Cecil and Anoushka were far too happy in each other's company.

However, the local community had other things to think about. The by-election would soon be upon them and the two candidates were campaigning feverishly.

No one worked harder in support of Desmond than Fiona. She was with him at all his public meetings, attended the daily conferences held by his support team and, if there was ever a spare moment, was out, whatever the weather, delivering election material to houses throughout the constituency.

Yet, despite all the efforts of his supporters, Desmond did not have the local press on his side. It seemed to have made up its mind that Desmond was not the man who should represent this particular corner of Cornwall in the House of Commons.

When polling day came round, Vicky and Alan found themselves in demand to ferry Lamorna voters to the polling booth, which was in a nearby village. Although Alan's driving skills were not yet up to the standard of Vicky's, he was now a competent, albeit over-careful, driver and he enjoyed the additional practice afforded by the occasion.

It was apparent from the conversations of those being driven to the polling booth to cast their votes that Desmond had very little support in Lamorna, and this seemed to reflect opinion in the Fisherman's Arms, where Vicky and Alan met Cecil and Anoushka when the polling booths closed, later that night.

Somehow, the election seemed very personal to the four of them, but it was evident by the time the pub closed its doors that there would be no results that night, so everyone went home to await the results that would be made public the next day.

59

Late the following morning, Vicky was painting in the studio in Stream Cottage and Alan was writing in his study when they both heard Cecil's Hotchkiss coming along the track to the cottage.

Cecil and Anoushka were inside the vehicle and highly excited, waving gaily long before they arrived. As soon as the motor car came to a halt, Anoushka jumped out. Running towards Vicky and Alan, she shouted excitedly, 'Desmond has lost the election by more than a thousand votes. He will not be a Member of Parliament!'

'But that's not all,' Cecil said, stepping down from the driving seat. 'You'll never guess what has happened. Fiona and Desmond have run off together!'

'Fiona and Desmond! Surely not?' said an astonished Vicky.

'It's true,' Cecil assured her. 'The Grahams' house-keeper was talking in the post office this morning, which, as you know, is the fountain of all knowledge. It seems Fiona did not return home last night. That was not entirely surprising, in view of all that was happening, but Fiona' absence from home had nothing to do with the by-election. She and Desmond were seen entering your old studio together in the early hours. Then, immediately after the results were announced, Fiona returned home and gathered some belongings together, then she and Desmond were seen heading east, out of Newlyn. The housekeeper says Rupert is closing down the house indefinitely and moving to a flat he owns in London.'

Cecil quite obviously relished passing on the gossip, but Vicky expressed sympathy for the deserted husband. 'Poor Rupert! He will no doubt be better off without Fiona, but he thought the world of her. He will be absolutely devastated.'

'I wonder what Desmond will do for a living now he's failed to get elected?' Alan queried. 'Does he have money of his own? I doubt if his father will want to be seen to support him. Running off with Fiona is a scandal that could affect the Conservative Party.'

'Desmond has some money of his own,' Cecil said, 'but he cannot match the wealth of Rupert. Fiona will need to curtail her notorious spending habits, and I doubt very much whether that will please her for very long.'

'While we are on the subject of being pleased . . .' Anoushka said. 'Tell them about the letter from my father.'

'Of course!' With only the slightest hint of embarrassment, Cecil said, 'Anoushka's father has fully accepted my explanation of the newspaper item and, what is more, has expressed a wish to meet me.'

'He has invited us both to Paris, to spend Christmas

with the family,' Anoushka said, unable to remain silent any longer. 'Cecil has said we can go, but first we are to spend a weekend with *his* family. I think he wants to be quite certain they will approve of me as a member.'

'They will be delighted to welcome you,' Vicky assured her. 'But it will be a disappointment for Alan and me not to have your company over the Christmas period.'

'Then why not come with us to Paris?' Anoushka suggested instantly. 'My family would wish you to be there – you know that, Alan. Without you there would have been no Christmas for any of us.'

'It's very kind of you to offer, Anoushka, and I look forward to meeting your family again in more relaxed circumstances, but it will be a very important occasion for you and Cecil. Besides, I really am looking forward to spending Christmas with Vicky, here in Lamorna.'

He did not add that taking Vicky to Paris would undoubtedly be an embarrassment for the Romanov family, however keen Anoushka was on the idea.

When the Newlyn couple had left Stream Cottage, Alan spoke wistfully. 'It seems likely that Cecil and Anoushka will make it to the altar before us, Vicky. It's something I never dreamed would happen.'

'I am very pleased for both of them,' Vicky replied. 'They are a charming couple and perfect for each other. I have no doubt Anoushka's parents will be able to see that right away.' Aware of what had prompted his comment, she added, 'I am perfectly content with our way of life here, Alan. I know you would like us to be married, and for that reason so would I, but it really is not important

411

to me. I would live as we are for the whole of our lives, if things had to be that way.'

'So would I, Vicky, but seeing Anoushka so happy at the thought of being with her parents at Christmas reminded me of the rift I have caused between you and yours. I would give a great deal to put that right.'

'The rift is not of your making, Alan, and there would be no problem winning over my father. My mother is the one who refuses to bend.'

'Do you think it would help if I followed the course taken by Cecil and wrote a letter to your parents explaining what was happening?'

'No!' Vicky said positively. 'And, as I said, it doesn't matter. Now, why don't we get back to work? I am behind with my painting, and your publisher has said he wants the first draft of your book as quickly as you can produce it.'

Julian Gimblett had written to Alan some time before, asking him to send him the first three chapters of the Baltic book when they were ready. At the time Alan received the letter he had completed twelve chapters, and he sent them all by return of post.

The publisher's response had been ecstatic. He was convinced they had a best-seller on their hands; so convinced that he planned a nationwide promotion campaign and advance details were already going out to the bookshops.

After telling Vicky she was the most beautiful boss he had ever slaved for, Alan went to his study and settled back to work. He had set himself the end of the year as a target for completing the book and was working to meet his own deadline.

With the Christmas period soon upon them, he had reluctantly accepted that he might take a week or two longer than he would have liked. However, now that Cecil and Anoushka were going to Paris, there would be a lot less socialising than he had anticipated, and the book might be back on schedule.

On the day before Christmas Eve, when Lamorna had woken up to an unexpected sprinkling of snow covering the slopes of the valley, the village postmaster's son laboured up to Stream Cottage with the second telegram he had delivered to Alan at that address. Once more it was from abroad, but on this occasion it was Paris and not Gibraltar.

The telegram was from Cecil and he asked that Alan and Vicky go to his house, for which they had been given a key, and take a telephone message from him that evening at six o'clock.

Wondering what could have happened, Vicky drove them to Newlyn, relieved that the snow had melted during the daylight hours, and they entered the house to await the telephone call. It did not come until twenty minutes past six, by which time Alan was beginning to think there might have been some misunderstanding, but then the telephone bell rang, startling them both.

Snatching up the earpiece, Alan said, 'Hello,' and was relieved to hear Cecil's slightly distorted voice at the other end of the line.

Fearing the worst, Alan said, 'I received your telegram, and Vicky and I wondered what was happening. Is everything all right with you and Anoushka?'

'It couldn't be better, old boy,' Cecil said jubilantly 'Anoushka's whole family are absolutely charming. I have fallen in love with her mother and every one of her sisters . . .'

The sounds at the other end of the line told Alan that Anoushka was not very far from Cecil.

'. . . In fact, they are all so wonderful that I have decided to join the family. Anoushka's father has agreed that we can marry, but he would like it to be a low-key wedding. Intelligence sources have told him that the Romanovs are still a target for the Bolsheviks. If the wedding were to be a high-profile affair, it could attract their attention. We don't want that, so the British ambassador, here in Paris, has agreed to conduct the ceremony in the embassy on New Year's Eve. My father and brother are coming over, but I, Anoushka and her family would like you and Vicky to be here too. After all, you are our closest friends, and had it not been for you we might never have spoken again after Fiona introduced us. I would like to add that Anoushka's mother was particularly keen that I should invite you.'

As Cecil was speaking, Alan was relaying his words to Vicky, and she was nodding vigorously.

'Well, first of all, Vicky and I are absolutely delighted that you and Anoushka are to be married – Vicky is with me and signalling that we accept your invitation. She speaks for both of us, Cecil. I never doubted for one minute that Anoushka's family would welcome you with open arms, and, yes, we will certainly be there for the wedding. Now, becoming practical, where exactly are you, and when would you like us to be there?'

Minutes later Alan replaced the earpiece and looked at the piece of paper on which he had written the details given to him by Cecil.

'Well, that's another happy ending, Vicky, and it couldn't happen to a nicer couple. Now, all I need to do is complete my book and perhaps we could drop it in to Julian on our way back from Paris.'

60

Christmas at Stream Cottage was a memorable occasion for Alan and Vicky. On Christmas Eve a choir from a neighbouring village gathered outside the cottage and sang a number of carols. Invited inside for a drink and something to eat, they went on their way with a generous donation to their church funds.

On Christmas morning, Mornie and Joan Birch arrived with presents from the family. Fortunately, Vicky had anticipated the event and there were gifts at hand to exchange with them.

Christmas lunch was enjoyed, as they wished, on their own, and afterwards they exchanged presents. Then, in the evening, they were invited to join Lamorna Birch, Mouse and some of their friends at a party at their cottage.

It was exactly the sort of Christmas Alan and Vicky had hoped for and one they would remember for ever.

Then, the day after Boxing Day, they set off for Paris and the wedding of Cecil and Anoushka. They took the Sunbeam to France, and as they drove through the northern plain,

ky would occasionally point out places that had a
poignancy for her because of their association with the
war years.

Alan's reunion with the Romanov family was far more
emotional than he had anticipated. Alexander and Alyona
Romanov made it perfectly clear that they believed they
owed their lives to Alan and Commander Buchanan and
it was in this capacity that he was introduced to their
friends.

As the family had wished, the wedding of Cecil and
Anoushka was a quiet affair, but the presence of a viscount
and his heir meant that the British ambassador was fully
aware of the importance of the occasion.

The festivities celebrating the marriage continued for a
full three days, even though the newly-weds departed for
a Swiss honeymoon on the evening of their wedding day.
When the parties came to an end, Alan and Vicky returned
to England, planning to deliver the completed manuscript
of Alan's book to his publisher on the way home.

They had booked into a London hotel for two nights before
returning to Cornwall and Vicky stayed in the hotel while
Alan took his now completed manuscript to his publisher.

Julian Gimblett met him in the reception area and
greeted him warmly, but on the way to his office he said,
'Before I tell you how thrilled I am with the first part of
your manuscript, I would like to say how sorry I am about
your wife, Alan. I know you were on the point of divorcing her, but you must be upset at the manner of her death.'

Coming to a sudden halt, an astonished Alan said, 'Dora
is dead? When . . . ? How did it happen?'

'You don't know? My dear boy, I am so sorry. I f⋯ certain the police would have told you . . . and my brother in-law told me he had written to say that her death had brought the divorce proceedings to an end.'

'I have been in Paris,' Alan said. 'Cecil was married to Anoushka Romanov. But you still haven't explained . . .'

They had moved on, and now reached Julian's office. Holding open the door, he said, 'Come in and sit down. I will tell you all I know, and then you may use my telephone to call my brother-in-law. He will be able to explain anything that may not be clear.'

When Alan was sitting, Julian took his place behind his desk and said, 'It was in all the London papers, but, perhaps fortunately, your name was never mentioned. It seems your wife had a particularly violent brother, with a fondness for drink.'

'Yes, that would be Charlie. I thought he was in prison.'

'I believe he was . . . and is once again. He came home after a heavy night's drinking and demanded that his mother cook him a meal. She refused and told him there would be no more food for him until he put some money into the housekeeping. There was a blazing row and when he became violent his mother ran upstairs to escape from him. He followed her and began kicking down the door of the bedroom in which she had taken refuge. Your wife remonstrated with him and he either hit or pushed her, depending upon whose version you care to believe, causing her to fall down the stairs and break her neck. The coroner's court recorded a verdict of unlawful killing and her brother has been committed for trial on a manslaughter charge.'

In a state of near-shock, Alan sat saying nothing for a

while. Despite all she had done, he felt desperately sorry for Dora. Hers had been a sad life, even though much of the unhappiness had been of her own making. Charlie's part in her death did not surprise him. He had always been prone to violence, especially towards those who were weaker than himself, and those closest to him had always been in the most danger.

'Are you all right, Alan? Can I offer you a drink?' Julian was concerned by his continued silence.

Alan shook his head. 'No, I'm all right. I was just feeling sorry for Dora, that's all. She never had any of the good things of life, and with her family background just never had a chance.'

Julian thought that if Dora had remained faithful to her husband she would have been enjoying the good things of life at this moment. He knew enough about books to realise that the manuscript that lay on the desk in front of him would shortly enable anyone so closely associated with Alan to enjoy a very good standard of life indeed.

'May I make that call to your brother-in-law?' Alan asked. 'I would like to know what my legal situation is now.'

'Of course.' Julian opened a book on the desk and pushed it across to Alan. 'There is his number, the telephone is all yours. I will be in my secretary's office when you need me. I am sorry to have been the bearer of such news. This should have been a day of celebration for all of us, but we will have plenty of time ahead for that. When I return you can tell me all about Cecil's marriage. I knew nothing about it. Indeed, I was beginning to despair that he ever *would* marry. I am very pleased for him.'

* * *

419

The solicitor had acted with considerable efficien. Unable to contact Alan, he had acted on his own initia tive to obtain a copy of Dora's death certificate and forward it to Stream Cottage.

He was able to tell Alan that with this document in his possession he could carry on with whatever plans he had intended making when the divorce came through, but instead of being a 'divorcee', Alan was now a 'widower'.

Furthermore, the solicitor said he would make quite certain that Alan's name never came up at the trial. As far as the court was concerned, Dora would be described as a woman 'with a failed marriage behind her'. No further details would be necessary and the case was not unusual enough in that part of London to make national headlines. It would be of merely local interest. Just another crime of violence.

It was not until Alan was walking from the publishing house to the hotel that the solicitor's words really began to sink in. He was no longer a married man. What was more, he would not carry the stigma that society attached to a divorcee, whether innocent party or not.

He was a widower, free to marry in church if he so wished.

Free to marry Vicky.

61

When they returned home to Stream Cottage, Alan and Vicky had a serious talk about their situation now there was no longer the complication of Dora to consider.

Alan felt they should marry right away, but to his surprise Vicky did not agree. Despite the long estrangement between him and Dora, she did not feel it was right to marry so soon after her death, adding that they were both happily living together without the blessing of the church, so she could think of no immediate reason for changing their way of life.

The discussion lasted well into the night, but Vicky remained adamant. She saw no reason for them to get married. Although he was disappointed, Alan decided he would not argue further with her on the subject.

They *were* very happy together and the next few months were especially so. It was a quiet period in the Lamorna valley and neighbouring Newlyn, with few distractions for the artists in the adjacent communities. When Cecil and Anoushka returned from their honeymoon the two

couples resumed their socialising together, spending man，
evenings in each other's company, but neither Vicky nor
Alan allowed it to affect their work too much. They had
a lot to do.

Most artists took the opportunity of the quieter months
to produce works for the forthcoming summer season, the
younger, less established ones in particular hoping that
this would be the year in which they would make their
mark upon the wider world.

Vicky was working hard, producing paintings for her
forthcoming exhibition in London, while Alan continued
with his book on the activities of the wartime torpedo
boats. He wanted to complete as much as possible before
Vicky's exhibition, which coincided with the launch of his
Baltic book and would cause a considerable disruption of
their present strict routine.

The fact that the book launch and the exhibition were
both taking place at the same time was fortuitous. It meant
that Alan and Vicky would be in London together, even
though both would undoubtedly be kept busy promoting
their own work.

Julian Gimblett had kept his promise about arranging
publicity for Alan's book. As publication date drew near,
advance copies went out to reviewers and, as a result,
letters began to arrive at Stream Cottage requesting interviews with Alan, and asking questions about the book and
the years he had spent serving in the Royal Navy.

There was to be a well-publicised launch party at the
Garrick Club. In the week or so that followed, Alan would
be signing his books at many major bookshops in London
and the home counties.

Advance copies of the book were delivered to Stream Cottage ahead of the publication date and Alan's pleasure at having a book in print was more than matched by Vicky's pride in his achievement and in the highly favourable publicity the book was already beginning to receive.

Copies of the book were immediately given to Cecil and Anoushka, Colonel Trecarrow and Tom Penhaligon. Alan had maintained his friendship with the fisherman, who was currently housebound, nursing an injured knee hurt in recent rough weather at sea.

After dedicating a book to Vicky, and setting another aside for the Romanovs in Paris, there were still seven copies of the book piled on a small table in his study and Vicky said hesitantly, 'Would you mind if I sent a copy to my parents, Alan? I know my father would enjoy reading it.'

'Of course we'll send them one. I'll dedicate it to them now and we can drop it in at the post office this afternoon. I'll send one to Maria at the same time. She'll be thrilled.'

Alan was pleased that Vicky wanted to send his book to her parents. He hoped it might help in some small way to heal the rift between them, but he was not unduly optimistic.

Vicky had received a Christmas card in which was written, simply, *Love from Mummy and Daddy*, and a card for her February birthday, but in a departure from the usual pattern of Hazelton card-writing, both were in her father's handwriting.

Although Vicky commented only briefly about this,

423

Alan was aware she found it hurtful and he wished he might find some means of effecting a reconciliation between them.

A little more than two weeks before they went to London, Alan and Vicky were snuggled up together in bed at the cottage when for no apparent reason Vicky asked, 'Do you really enjoy the life we have here, Alan?'

Hugging her to him, he replied, 'Of course. In fact, I can think of only one thing that could possibly make me happier – and that would be for you to agree to marry me.'

It was something he had said to her on a number of occasions in recent weeks and the answer had always been the same. Everything was perfect as things were now. Why change them?

Tonight, she made no reply. Concerned that he might have offended her by bringing up the subject yet again, he said hastily, 'It's all right, Vicky. I am very, very happy as we are. As long as you feel the same and we are together, I really don't care whether we are married or not.'

'Have you ever thought how embarrassing it might prove if we wanted to marry here, Alan? We would have to be married in Paul church and the vicar there preaches most Sundays about the "wicked ways" of couples like us who are living together without being married. He might even refuse to marry us.'

'It wouldn't need to be in a church. We could have a civil service. Come to that, we could be married in a register office when we are in London. Do you remember the wedding we saw at Caxton Hall?'

Marrying in London would certainly save a lot of embarrassment for us, but you have to be resident in a place for some time before you are able to be married there.'

Turning towards her in sudden excitement, Alan said, 'This is the first time you have even wanted to talk about getting married, Vicky. Are you finally having a change of heart about it?'

Ignoring his question for the moment, Vicky mused, 'Mind you, being married in London would be the answer if it were at all possible. Cecil and Anoushka are always going there and they could act as our witnesses. I think only two are needed in a register office wedding. And Caxton Hall would be a venue that meant something – to me, at least. It was a favourite suffragette meeting place, being close enough to Parliament for us to set off from there when we were marching to make many of our protests. I also went to a wedding there when one of the ambulance drivers married an army officer.'

'You haven't answered me, Vicky. Are you seriously considering marrying me, at last?' Alan could hardly contain the delight he felt at Vicky's unexpected willingness to talk about marriage.

'I think the time has come when I must, Alan. It's still very early days, but I think I might be pregnant . . .'

62

Once he had recovered from the shock of Vicky's announcement, Alan began to panic about the problems they might meet having a baby and bringing it up in such an isolated place as Stream Cottage.

He had got as far as the difficulties they would encounter in taking it to school when Vicky brought his train of thought firmly to a halt. Theirs would not be the only baby to have been born and brought up in the Lamorna valley and she could think of no more idyllic place for a child to live. Besides, it had not yet been confirmed that she *was* having a baby. However, she promised that if Alan would try to go to sleep and not keep her awake for the remainder of the night, they would speak to Cecil the next day about the possibility of arranging a wedding at Caxton Hall when they were in London in a couple of weeks' time.

They both travelled to Newlyn the next morning to pay Cecil and Anoushka a visit, having already agreed to tell the newly-wed couple the reason why they wanted to

…arry, and why they felt it would be a good idea to have the wedding away from Cornwall.

Anoushka was very excited about the prospect of their wedding – and the thought that Vicky might be expecting a baby – and after Cecil had made a brief telephone call to his sister Clarice, he said there should be no problem about using her address in order to be married at Caxton Hall.

'Where are you both staying while you are in London?' he asked.

'Vicky was going to stay in Sylvia Pankhurst's flat and I was going to book a room in a hotel,' Alan replied, 'but Sylvia will be abroad and has said we might both use her flat, if we wish.'

'Clarice rather thought Vicky would be staying with Sylvia,' Cecil said, 'but to avoid any unlikely residential problems, she suggests you stay at her house in Knightsbridge during the promotion of your book. Actually, there should be no problem. Clarice says that two of her friends have used the address in the past so they might marry at Caxton Hall, but in order to obtain the necessary licence you will need to go to London as soon as possible and apply in person.'

Vicky travelled to London by train with Alan two days later when he went to Caxton Hall to apply for a marriage licence. It was all comparatively straightforward and, after dining with Clarice, they spent the night in St Ermin's Hotel, alongside the building where they were to be married.

It was a brief but enjoyable excursion and they set off

on the return journey to Cornwall having accepted Clarice's invitation to hold what would be a small wedding reception at her home.

Thinking of the reception, Alan broached the subject of informing Vicky's parents of their plans. It was a suggestion she rejected immediately.

'No, Alan. We have managed to live our lives very happily without them, even though I often wish it had been otherwise. I do not want my mother to be there only because she felt it her duty to attend her daughter's wedding.'

Alan had his own ideas about the matter, but he was not going to say anything to Vicky about them just yet.

At Truro, Vicky saw Colonel Trecarrow on the platform, about to board their train. She immediately invited him to join them in their compartment and the old landowner accepted with pleasure.

As garrulous as ever, Colonel Trecarrow first of all congratulated Alan on what he described as an 'excellent book', saying how fortunate Vicky was to have found 'a man of initiative and action' – someone who was just the way he had been himself as a young man.

After praising various incidents in the book, Colonel Trecarrow said, 'Actually, meeting you on the train today has saved me making a visit to you at Stream Cottage – and my old bones no longer enjoy travelling so far on a horse. I have just been to Truro to see my solicitor. You see, although I hate to admit it, even to myself, I am no longer a young man and have no sons or daughters to inherit from me. When I go, everything I own will be divided between a great many avaricious and quarrelsome nephews, nieces and cousins.'

When Vicky protested that she hoped he would have a great many years yet to enjoy what he had, he waved her to silence.

'It's very kind of you to say so, young lady, but I decided to face facts and it will be much simpler for everyone if there is just money and not land and property to be divided. So, after discussing it with my solicitor today, I have decided to sell everything except the house I am living in. That will go to the National Trust when I die.'

Vicky looked at him in dismay. 'Does that mean . . . you will be selling Stream Cottage?'

'Everything, my dear . . . but don't be dismayed. You, and all my other tenants, will be given the opportunity to buy the properties you occupy. I shall not be asking the earth, and you will be given time to pay if the purchase price is not readily available.'

'How much will you be asking for Stream Cottage?' Alan asked apprehensively.

'My solicitor will be sending out the letters and he has the figures but, as far as I remember, I decided on a price of two hundred and fifty pounds.'

This was much lower than either Alan or Vicky had expected and they exchanged relieved glances. It was a sum they could easily raise, and, with her forthcoming exhibition and the publication of his book, Stream Cottage should be theirs.

'If it presents any problems, there will be no need to discuss it with my solicitor. Pop along to see me and we'll talk about it. But let's not discuss money matters any more.

I have had enough of that for one day. Tell me about your next exhibition, Vicky. It must be very nearly time for it. Is that why you have been to London?'

The official launch of Alan's book took place three days after Vicky's exhibition opened, and she was able to be at the Garrick Club with him. Her presence added to the occasion and Julian Gimblett declared himself delighted with the evening and charmed by Vicky.

For the next few days they compared reviews each morning on the telephone and snatched whatever time they could with each other in what proved to be an extremely hectic schedule, for Alan in particular. He was kept busy with interviews and signing sessions, and Julian even slipped in a couple of talks on the subject of his books.

The thought of these terrified Alan, but the first was well received and the next came more easily.

When he had signed books at most of the large London bookshops, Alan was taken farther afield, to Cambridge, Leicester, Nottingham, Bristol – and Oxford.

In Oxford, as Alan was busy scribbling his signature, he noticed a man who stayed close to the table where he was signing and once or twice appeared to be about to come and speak to him, only to be thwarted by the book-buyers who came to have a book dedicated to a brother, or an aunt, or themselves.

The man was tall and rather distinguished and Alan thought he was not the type to allow himself to be put off speaking to him, had that really been his intention. However, the man was still nearby when the signing

ssion came to an end, and as Alan put his pen away and
ose to his feet he did come across to speak to him.

'Alan . . . Alan Carter?'

'Yes. I noticed you nearby while I was signing. Are you
wanting to buy one of my books?'

'No. I have already read it . . . and found it wonderfully
thrilling. In fact, you sent it to me. I am Ralph Hazelton,
Vicky's father.'

Alan was taken aback, but Ralph Hazelton was holding out his hand. 'I am very pleased to meet you, Alan. It
is a meeting that should have taken place a long time ago.
I am sorry it did not.'

Recovering his composure as best he could, Alan said,
'I am sorry too. It would have made Vicky very happy.'

'Yes, I have always been aware of that. Unfortunately,
when Vicky's mother and I came to Cornwall, things were
said that should not have been, and time has not proved
to be the healer it is supposed to be.'

At that moment Julian, who had been speaking to the
shop's proprietor, came across to them and said, 'We need
to leave now if we are to be back in London before dark,
Alan.'

Dismayed, Ralph Hazelton said, 'I had been hoping we
might have a chat . . . somewhere more private, perhaps?'

To Julian, Alan said, 'Could you give us half an hour,
Julian? This is Vicky's father and it's the first time we've
met.'

Aware of Alan and Vicky's situation, Julian said, 'Of
course. We have a couple of interviews scheduled for later
this evening, but it will not matter if we are a little late. I
will see you back here in half an hour or so.'

There was a coffee shop with only a few customers short distance from the bookshop, and Vicky's father and Alan found a corner table that was reasonably secluded. After ordering coffee, Ralph Hazelton asked, 'How is Vicky? Is she keeping well?'

Feeling only slightly uncomfortable at not being able to disclose Vicky's condition, Alan replied, 'Yes, she is very well – and very happy. You know she has an exhibition on in London at the moment?'

'Yes. I was hoping I might be able to go to see it . . . but I fear it might prove difficult.'

'That's a pity,' Alan said. 'I know she would wish you to be there. You and Mrs Hazelton.'

'And I would dearly love to see her and the exhibition,' Ralph Hazelton confessed. 'The problem is that Miriam and I have ideas that are hopelessly out-dated. We were brought up in a different age from the one in which you and Vicky live. I have been involved in politics for a long time and have watched things develop over the years. Miriam has not. She finds it difficult to accept the changes. She had a very sheltered upbringing and thought, when Vicky was born, that she would grow up as Miriam herself had, accepting the authority of her parents without question and with little interest in anything beyond the fashion of the moment and making a good marriage. That is the way girls were brought up in Victorian times. It was not easy for her to discover that Vicky had a mind of her own and a will that more than matched her mother's – or, indeed, mine, come to that. Vicky took up art, became a suffragette and, when war came, went off and saw and did things that Miriam believed no well-bred girl should even know about!'

Alan gave the older man a wry smile. 'And then she met me.'

'Well . . . yes, and then she met you. I hope you are honest enough to admit it is not the situation any parent would want their daughter to be in. To be living with a married man – whatever the circumstances. Surprisingly, perhaps, as the father of a daughter, I find it easier to accept than Vicky's mother, but that is because I have learned to trust Vicky's judgement. And to be quite honest with you, after reading your book, I am inclined to admire her choice of a man. I only wish there was not the complication of your wife and the stigma – however unjustified it may be – that attaches itself to all involved in a divorce.'

In a gesture that was intended to be apologetic, Ralph Hazelton continued, 'I have been very frank with you, Alan, more frank than I intended. I hope you will accept that as a compliment. I have nothing against you personally. Indeed, I am filled with admiration for what you have done, and what you are achieving now. Your book will be a best-seller, and I have read some of your poetry. No, my misgivings are purely for Vicky and her future.'

'Vicky is always foremost in my thoughts too, Mr Hazelton, and I think I can put your mind at rest about a number of things that are of concern to you. First, there will be no stigma of divorce hanging over our relationship. My wife's death brought my divorce proceedings to an end. She was killed . . . in an accident.' He thought it neither wise nor necessary to go into detail.

'You mean . . . you are no longer married? You are free to marry Vicky?'

'I have been free for a couple of months, Mr Hazelton,

but Vicky would not marry me right away, even thou
I asked her on more than one occasion. Her argument wa
that we are content as we are, so why change? And, as
you have admitted, she is very strong-willed.'

Ralph Hazelton nodded in agreement and Alan continued, 'However, she has finally said yes, and we are to be
married at three p.m. on Friday of next week, in Caxton
Hall, in London.'

Once again, Alan was aware he was leaving much
unsaid, but he added, 'It will be only a small private service, with no invitations going out. The difficulty has been
not *whether* we should tell you, but *how*. Vicky was very
hurt by the attitude of you and her mother – her mother
in particular. She did not want to be upset on her wedding
day if you both refused to attend. I think she felt it would
be better not to say anything rather than have that happen.
I agree with her. However, you have come here today to
see me and tell me how you feel about Vicky and me, and
I have done my best to do the same. It would make both
Vicky and me very happy indeed if you and her mother
wanted to come to the wedding, but it might be better,
perhaps, if there could be a reconciliation *before* the
wedding.'

'Yes, I can see that.' The news of Vicky's imminent
marriage had left Ralph Hazelton stunned. Gathering his
thoughts, he said now, 'I can quite see Vicky's dilemma –
and yours, of course – over informing us of the wedding.
After all, it is your day, and a most important one. But
Vicky's mother will be extremely distressed to think that
the rift she has caused – and I know that in her heart she
is aware she is to blame – that the rift is so serious that

r only daughter would have married in secret. I will go home and have a very serious talk with her.'

'Thank you, Mr Hazelton. I will say nothing to Vicky of our meeting unless you let me know you will be at the wedding.'

'Of course. That is very sensible. But how may I contact you?'

'I am staying in Knightsbridge, at the home of Clarice Hammond-Hardy – the Honourable Clarice Hammond-Hardy. I will write down her telephone number for you.'

As he wrote the number on a paper napkin, Alan explained, 'Cecil Gormley, Clarice's brother, is a very good friend of Vicky and myself. He is married to Anoushka, the Romanov girl you and Mrs Hazelton met when you called at Stream Cottage while I was in Gibraltar. They are to be our witnesses at the wedding.' Handing the napkin to Ralph Hazelton, he went on, 'I really do hope that you and Mrs Hazelton will feel able to come to the wedding. It would be the finest possible present anyone could give to Vicky.'

'I will do my utmost to persuade her mother.' Extending his hand, Ralph Hazelton said, 'I am glad I came to Oxford to meet you today, Alan – very glad. I look forward to speaking to you again.'

63

Alan returned to Clarice's house alone that night. For the next two evenings Vicky would be attending functions with the gallery owner and his wife. Alan had been invited to go with them, but the events clashed with his own publishing commitments. The most he could hope for would be a telephone conversation late at night.

Clarice met him in the hallway with the news that Cecil had telephoned with details of a telegram that had been received at Lamorna for Alan. Thanks to a previous arrangement with the village postmaster, it had been passed on to Cecil.

The telegram was from Maria and contained the disappointing news that her elderly father was seriously ill and she would be unable to attend the wedding. However, she said that a pair of open return tickets for the voyage to Gibraltar were on their way, and Alan's cottage would be ready for him and his bride upon their arrival.

It was a typically generous gesture from his stepmother and Alan wrote a thank you letter that same night.

The next evening, after another long day spent in the company of Julian, Alan returned to Knightsbridge to learn that there had been a telephone call for him from Ralph Hazelton.

He had said he would call again later, but Clarice, well aware of the problems between Vicky and her parents, asked, 'Is he Vicky's father?'

'Yes.' Feeling he owed her an explanation, Alan told her of the Oxford meeting.

'Then I think it might be as well if you called him back right away,' Clarice said. 'I have the number here, some-where. Vicky gave it to me when she was staying with me once, a long time ago.'

Waiting for the operator to connect him, Alan had an attack of nerves. He wondered what would happen if Vicky's mother had refused to meet her daughter, and planned something calculated to upset Vicky . . . or the wedding.

'Hello?'

A woman's voice coming through the earpiece startled him.

'Hello,' he replied. 'Could I speak to Mr Hazelton, please?'

'Who shall I say is calling?' asked the voice in his ear.

'It's Alan,' he replied.

'Oh!' There was a pause at the other end of the line and for a moment he feared the woman had hung up. Then, in a rather hesitant voice, she said, 'It is Miriam Hazelton here. I would just like to say . . . I am sorry . . . and thank you. But here is my husband . . .'

A few moments later the voice of Ralph Hazelton crackled through the earpiece, saying, 'I overheard that,

Alan. I trust it will remove any doubts you might have about the sincerity of Vicky's mother's wish to bring about a reconciliation.'

When Alan agreed it had, Ralph Hazelton said, 'Before the wedding we would both like to come to London to see the exhibition, and take you and Vicky for a meal. When would you be free?'

'I have only a few more signings now,' Alan replied, 'and none at all on Monday.'

'Monday would fit in very well,' Ralph Hazelton said. 'We will come up to London by train in the morning, take you to lunch, and return home in the evening. We should be at the gallery at about twelve noon. Would that suit you?'

'Yes. I will tell Vicky. Perhaps it would also be better if I arranged for you, Mrs Hazelton and Vicky to meet in the gallery owner's office first of all.'

'That is very thoughtful, Alan,' Ralph Hazelton agreed 'I look forward to seeing you there.'

Clarice studied Alan's face anxiously when he returned to the sitting room after making the telephone call. 'Is everything all right?'

'I think so. We are all meeting at the gallery on Monday and then going for lunch. I believe they will come to the wedding.'

'I am so glad. Had they not been there it would always have been a cause for resentment in the family.'

Vicky listened in silence as Alan told her of the meeting with her father and the subsequent telephone call. It was Saturday, the day after the call. The gallery was closed for the day and Alan had no commitments.

They had met at Knightsbridge Underground station and were walking in the spring sunshine in Hyde Park.

'Did you tell my father that I was pregnant?' Vicky demanded.

'No.'

'That's just as well. It has turned out to be a false alarm. I am not expecting a baby after all.'

Alan could not hide his deep disappointment and Vicky said, 'It means you don't have to marry me if you don't want to.'

'What sort of thing is that to say?' Alan asked indignantly. 'We have lots of time in the future to think about children, and having them will be far easier than persuading you to marry me. We are getting married next Friday, as arranged.'

'I am glad, Alan – but what exactly did my father say? Will he be coming to the wedding?'

'I am convinced both your parents will be there, but I felt it might be best if we all met up before the wedding, so there would be no misunderstandings on the day. They are coming to the gallery on Monday and taking you and me to lunch. I suggested it might be best if we met first of all in the owner's office.'

'Thank you, Alan, but do you think my father will be able to persuade my mother to actually come to the wedding?'

'I believe she has already decided to be there.' Alan told Vicky about the few words spoken to him by her mother.

Vicky could not quite hide the emotion she felt when he said, 'If you knew my mother, you would realise just how difficult it must have been for her to tell you she was

439

sorry. I don't know what it was you said to Daddy in Oxford, but it must have been very effective.'

'It was he who took the initiative by coming to see me. I believe he is a very loving father, Vicky, and I like him.'

'I am so glad, Alan.' Squeezing his arm hard, she declared, 'You know, I am really looking forward to my wedding day now.'

He hoped Vicky's anticipation would not be misplaced. The meeting with her mother at the gallery had yet to take place.

Alan need not have worried. He remained in the background when Ralph and Miriam Hazelton were shown into the gallery and led straight to the office where Vicky was waiting.

Fifteen minutes later, Vicky's father came out of the office and shook Alan warmly by the hand. 'Everything is fine, Alan. Come into the office; Miriam is anxious to meet you.'

Inside the office it was immediately apparent to Alan that both Vicky and her mother had been crying, but as soon as he entered the room Vicky reached for his hand and said, 'Mummy, I want you to meet my wonderful man. This is Alan, your future son-in-law.'

To everyone's surprise, Miriam not only took his hand but also kissed him warmly. 'I am delighted to meet you – although after reading your book I feel I already know far more about you than do most prospective mothers-in law at a first meeting. I can only apologise that we have not met before.'

It seemed she might become emotional and Alan said

hastily, 'Why don't we all go out and look at Vicky's paintings? Then we can talk over lunch.'

For a while it might have been possible to detect the faintest hint of unease between them, but it disappeared over lunch and by the time Vicky and Alan went to Paddington station to see Vicky's parents off on the train, Alan felt that Miriam had genuinely warmed to him.

It was an elated couple who returned to Clarice's house that evening, to tell Cecil's sister about the meeting and inform her that Vicky's parents should be added to the list of wedding guests.

The wedding day produced a number of surprises for both the bride and the groom and careful planning had gone into ensuring they were not revealed until the very last minute.

Two days before the wedding Alan had booked into St Ermin's, the hotel adjacent to Caxton Hall, while Vicky had moved from Old Ford Road to Clarice's Knightsbridge house. This made it easier for Cecil, Clarice, Vicky and Anoushka to keep the presence of some unexpected guests from the groom.

Molly and a number of Vicky's fellow suffragettes who had been active in pre-war days were able to travel to Caxton Hall on the day for the ceremony, as did Ralph and Miriam Hazelton. Meanwhile, Clarice's house held a great many guests whose presence was kept a close secret until they arrived at Caxton Hall.

Alan was flabbergasted to see seats in the room where the ceremony was to take place occupied by the whole of the Romanov family from Paris. With them was Captain

– ex-Commander – Marcus Buchanan, now head of Naval Intelligence. Also present for the ceremony were Lieutenant Donald Ferris and his publisher father; Julian Gimblett, Tom and Prue Penhaligon, and the suffragettes.

Afterwards, Alan remembered little of the service, but the press had got wind of the gathering and were outside the hall to take photographs of the newly-weds and their guests, causing Julian Gimblett to rub his hands in glee, declaring it was worth even more than the thousands he had already spent to promote Alan's book.

The reception was held in Clarice's spacious dining room, and during the many speeches Alexander Romanov made much of the fact that Alan had been the means of saving the lives of him and his family.

When he replied to the speeches, Alan pointed out that Vicky had done the same for him, ensuring he reached hospital swiftly after the duel between his torpedo boat and the German U-boat, then donating her own blood to him when it was urgently needed.

The celebrations went on far into the night and it was not until the following day, when Alan and Vicky sat back on the train taking them to Southampton and the liner that would carry them to Gibraltar and their Spanish honeymoon, that they were fully able to take in the fact that they were now Mr and Mrs Alan Carter.

Both had led interesting and eventful lives as individuals, but neither felt they had given up anything by marrying. Instead, they looked forward to enjoying a new and exciting future together.